HEY KIDS!

WARNING

UNCLE HENLEY HACKENSLASH SAYS THAT THIS ISN'T YOUR MUM'S BEDTIME STORY.

THIS BOOK CONTAINS GRAPHIC GORE, FOUL LANGUAGE, SHOCKING SCARES, AND ENOUGH BIG HAIR TO MAKE A GLAM ROCK BAND JEALOUS.

ONCE YOU PRESS PLAY ON THESE TALES, THERE'S NO STOPPING.

PROCEED AT YOUR OWN PERIL.

Edited by TC Phillips
Specul8 Publishing
Rockhampton, Australia
Copyright © 2026
ISBN: 978-0-9756211-7-2

TABLE OF CONTENTS

▶ PLAY

WHAT'S THE MATTER FRIEND?

Y'ALL HAVING
TROUBLE SLEEPING?

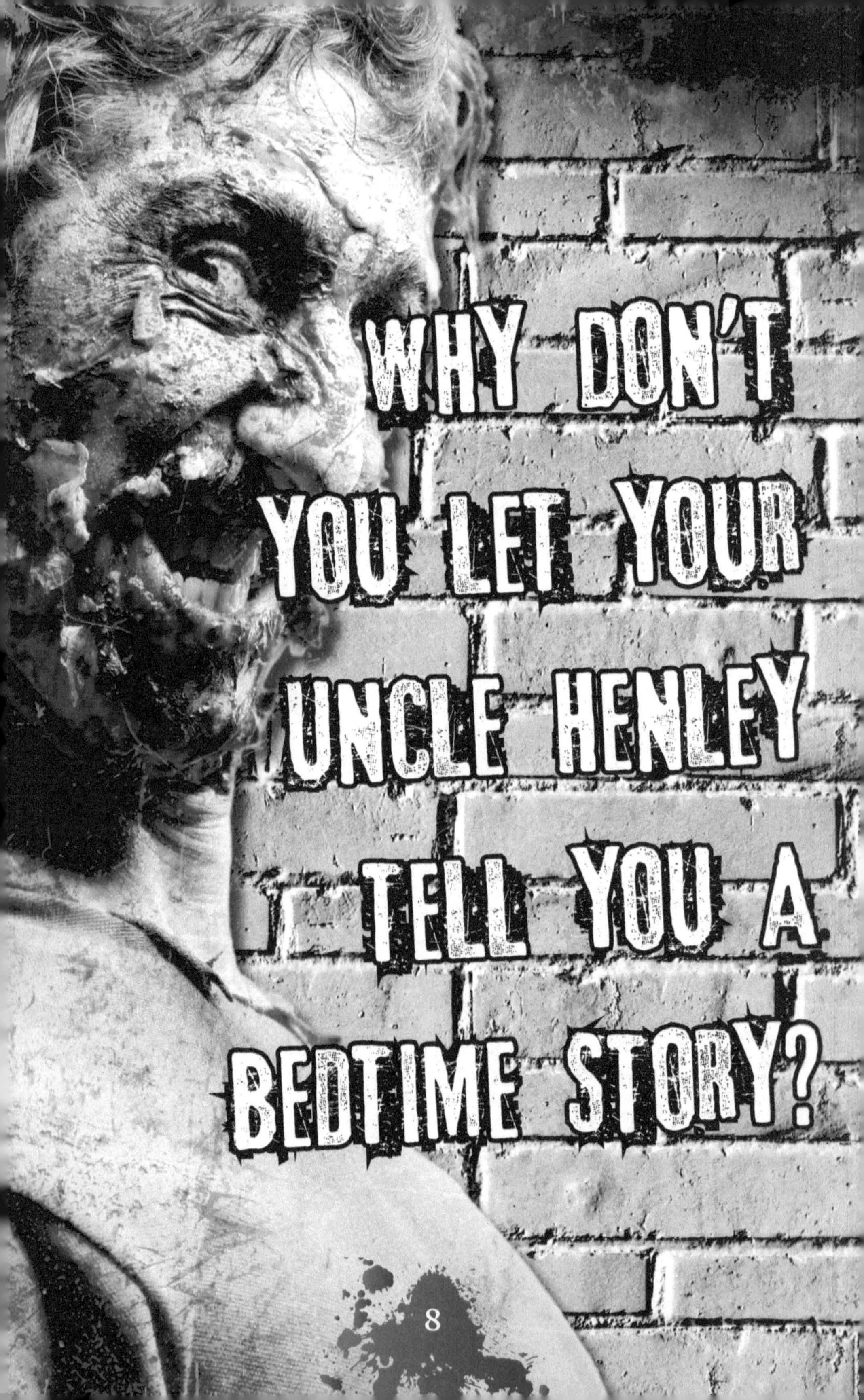

WHY DON'T YOU LET YOUR UNCLE HENLEY TELL YOU A BEDTIME STORY?

IING
Pretty, DEAD
BY HAMISH RANKINE
Music by CHARLES BERNSTEIN · Director of Photography JACQUES HAITKIN · Editor RICK SHAINE · Executive Producers STANLEY DUDELSON and JOSEPH WOLF
Co-Producer SARA RISHER · Produced by ROBERT SHAYE · Written and Directed by WES CRAVEN
R RESTRICTED

PRETTY, DEAD

BY HAMISH RANKINE

My feet burn with every lunge forward along the dry ground of the woods. Sharp rocks poking out of the dirt threaten to cut my feet open if I'm not careful. Even so, all my attention is on running as fast as I can while not sprinting directly into a tree. I'm further from any path than I've ever been.

I don't know how Todd ever convinced me to go on this trip with him, we've only been dating for a few months after all. I clutch the pink heels in my hand and hold up my skirt from the ground. The only thing worse than getting murdered would be getting such an expensive outfit dirty.

As I keep running and the woods grow quieter, I begin to feel something crawl along my spine and a voice screaming in the back of my head. Turning my head to look behind me, even if only to dampen my anxiety, I forget to slow my pace at all.

Falling after my impact with a tree, I quickly look back behind me once again, searching through the shadows created by the thick canopy of leaves above. Looking down, tears begin to run down my cheeks, absolutely ruining my makeup as I notice the tear in my skirt. If I don't die here, mother will most definitely have my head.

The snapping of a twig in the distance, echoing all the way through the woods, brings me back to my senses. Sobbing, I push myself up to my feet, grab my heels from the dirt and turn to avoid the tree I had hit.

Every joint in my body freezes up as I spin around and see a torn, blood-stained shirt. As I look up to meet the concealed face of the man in front of me, my eyes struggle to focus, instead shaking from side to side as if I were not meant to see him. The tears flow faster like a stream from the pools forming in my eyes. He leans down closer to me, letting me get a better look at his face.

But all I see is Todd's face. Despite it only being the skin, I can still see his fear stretched out over his killer's head. The blood underneath the skin is still wet, dripping down along his neck. My entire body shakes with every pulse of my heart. Despite my blurry vision, I manage to make out the lifelessness of his eyes, as if he were already a corpse. He raises up his rusty knife to my face as he clutches a hammer in his other hand. As I feel the cold steel run along my cheek, I scream as I stand frozen in place.

Just as he raises up his blade, I manage to force my legs to jump to the side, feeling the air against me as I narrowly avoid his attack. I fall against the tree next to me, bruising my porcelain skin and barely keeping myself upright.

He breathes heavily as he slowly turns to me. As he steps towards me, I push myself off from the tree and fall to the ground before crawling back to my feet and running as fast as I can. The wind streams through my hair, pushing me back, closer to him. I look over my shoulder to see him slowly continuing towards me, yet somehow, I feel he could catch up to me at any minute.

Twigs snap as I heedlessly run through the woods, ruining my hair and makeup. Despite my blurry vision, I can make out a wooden structure up ahead. I push through the burning pain in my legs and sprint to the cabin. Scrambling onto the porch, I leave scratch marks on the wood as I desperately pull myself closer to the door. The impact of the door against the wall echoes throughout the cabin. I slam it shut before stumbling through the lounge room, tears dropping onto the floorboards beneath me.

"Cody! Sammy!" I attempt to call out to my friends, but my throat is dry after screaming my heart out. My cries for help amount to nothing more than a choked-up whisper.

As I stand in place, straining my throat so much I feel blood pooling in my mouth, I begin to hear footsteps on the front porch, slowly making their way to the door. As fear wraps around my neck, I stop trying to scream altogether and, in exchange, cry a flood of tears. My legs buckle in weakness, and I almost fall over before catching myself on the wall.

I make my way into one of the bedrooms just as the door flies open. Slowly shuffling past the bed and to the wardrobe. I continue to listen to every footstep getting closer. He searches each room thoroughly before moving on to the next, giving me just enough time to take out a pile of clothes from the wardrobe and hide them under the bed. Slowly stepping back into it, I shut the doors of the wardrobe and hold my breath.

I feel comforted by my blanket of darkness in the wardrobe, save for the sliver of light projecting on my eye through the crack between the doors. Before I get a chance to calm my breathing, my hand shoots up to my mouth as I watch him slowly walk into the room. I feel a giant bug crawling around in my throat and ramming against my mouth, begging me to scream out. My hands shake profusely as I hold back every tear and cry for help, my subconscious struggling to let them out.

From across the room, I can't tell if he is staring at me or not, especially with Todd's face covering his own. He takes his time, thoroughly searching the room, clearly aware that I hadn't made it far.

My throat tightens, and my hands instinctively grip my face as he leans down and scans underneath the bed. As he slowly rises back up, as if his body were heavier than he could lift, he turns his head back to the wardrobe, back to me.

I cry and shake more with every step he takes closer. Surely someone will come to save me. Surely Cody or Sammy escaped and got help. Surely, he doesn't think I'm in here, right?

My mind goes blank as the doors fling open. He stands towering over me, staring down at me through Todd's face. I don't have enough energy left in me to scream or cry out for help. I can't imagine there would be much point now anyway. I'm sure I've been abandoned by all the others.

As he raises his hammer above his head, I close my eyes and try to wake up from the nightmare. I imagine that I'm back at the salon with mother, getting our nails done together, as Madonna and Wham! playing in the background is drowned out by our chatting and gossiping. I want that neon sign out front to be the last thing I think of before I die, but my illusion is shattered as I am struck on the side of the head.

I fall to the bottom of the wardrobe, blood spilling out of the left side of my head, spraying all over my outfit. Trying to scream, I realise that my jaw has been completely unhinged, only hanging on by a thin piece of flesh. I feel the air against the inside of my skull. He raises his hammer once again, making sure that I am looking up at him before slamming it back into my face. I hear my skull cracking as it is crushed over and over again as I am repeatedly hit in the head with the hammer. My mind fades more every time. I can barely comprehend how I am still alive.

When I finally die, when the pain stops, and his bloody hammer remains idle in his hand, I continue to stare up at him with my one remaining eye. The entire left half of my face is mashed up and strewn across my body. The blood and chunks of flesh run along my body, down to my legs and up to his already blood-stained shirt. My skull is brittle, and my brain leaks out of what remains of my left eye socket. The rest of my body lies limp and coiled up in the corner. His eyes widen as he stares at me, and his breath quickens. Todd's face stops me from being able to tell if he is angry or excited. At this point, I can't even tell if that was Todd's face to begin with; it's so torn up that it could be anyone's.

I lie calmly as he takes each heavy step toward my corpse and leans down, grabbing my leg so hard it bruises almost immediately. Not a hint of fear or panic makes itself known to me. He paints the floors with blood as my body is dragged along the ground, leaving a crimson path leading back to the place of my death. The ceiling washes over me like the rippling surface of the ocean, as the wounds on the back of my head are stretched out and torn open.

As I am gradually pulled out of the room and closer to the cabin door, I take notice of the vintage imperfections of the ceiling. The planks push against each other and flow like waves in a rainbow of brown shades. I begin to notice the dimly lit lamps complementing the rest of the room.

Thinking back to when I first arrived at the cabin with Todd, I was disgusted with how little notice I had taken of each room. He didn't seem to care too much, though, since he was more excited to spend this holiday with us. I don't know how I didn't notice his smile as we stepped inside.

My thought process is interrupted by my head slamming against the door frame as my body is dragged out onto the porch. A circular blood spatter stains the door, dripping down and connecting with the rest of the trail left behind by my remains. I begin to wonder how my makeup looks now; the dead don't need to be pretty.

For a moment, I am blinded as I am taken outside. My right ear is filled with the sounds of the leaves rustling in the forest as my other remains completely silent, giving room for my thoughts. As my eyes adjust, I finally see the rolling clouds flowing above me, like curtains for the sun. Feeling the breeze against my skin, I don't mind the air flowing through my eye socket and around the inside of my head before making way for more. The wind finally makes my mind feel clear and clean, as if everything that made me unique had been washed away as soon as that hammer hit my head.

My head bounces up and down repeatedly as my body is dragged down the short flight of wooden stairs. Each step is coated in a crater of blood with every impact. The blood quickly dries in the harsh sunlight, as I feel the same being done to the inside of my head. Dust is kicked up into my skull as I am dragged along the barren dirt path leading to the cabin. As my head rolls over to the side, the lake by the side of the cabin comes into view. The first thing I notice is the sunset reflecting off the shimmering water, like hundreds of stars dancing along an ice rink. My blurry vision brightens it further, highlighting its majestic patterns as if I were looking at it through a glass pane. I never even considered going in the water at first; I just assumed it would be rancid and dirty. I think I regret that now that I see it.

Further down, closer to the edge of the lake, I see a corpse staring back at me with cold, glazed-over eyes. My reflection would have made me scream in the past, not that I physically can now anyway, but I don't want to either. I can't bring myself to feel much for my reflection one way or another, just as the rest of my body feels numb. As parts of my brain spill out of my head, I feel those parts of me being left behind and replaced with the terrifying calmness that comes with death. My emotions are dampened, and my thoughts are less coherent and logical than they would have been, but I can't miss how I was, no matter how hard I try. My reflection continues to dispassionately stare at me before the final strand of skin attaching my jaw to the rest of my face finally snaps off, leaving the bottom half of my mouth behind me in a pool of blood.

My leg suddenly falls to the ground, rolling my body over onto my back as it does. Watching my killer walk past me, I barely see the bottom half of his mouth beneath the skin stapled onto his face. He frowns as he walks past my head and leans down to my jaw, as if he were disappointed that I couldn't stop myself from falling apart. He dusts off my jaw, being careful not to flick off too much skin or flesh. Delicately wrapping his hands around it, he wanders back over to my legs and grabs my ankle once again, continuing to drag me further along. No matter what explanation I think of, nothing about this man makes sense to me. There surely can't be any logic to what he is doing, but he isn't an animal.

He tightens his grip on my leg as the ground begins to elevate, and we make our way up a hill. The grass begins to grow onto the path and cover it as he takes us deeper into the woods. As we plunge deeper into the labyrinth, my vision fades further as the sun is blocked by a blanket of leaves far above me, only a few beams of light pushing through. My blood seeps into the dirt, feeding the greenery and sending me back into the ground. Flies begin to swarm around my corpse, crawling around the inside of my skull and underneath my skin, birthing their young in their new home. I am now a breeding ground for the vile filth of the earth.

Despite the centipede crawling around under my eyelid blocking my vision, I still manage to make out the shape of a cabin sitting in the middle of a small clearing. As he takes us closer, the insect falls out of my eye, and a fluttering butterfly leads my eyes to the trails of dry blood leading up to the door, which become more visible in the single exposed patch of sunlight. I become a part of them, my blood painting the grass red as I am taken closer to the door. My killer aggressively shoves the door open as if it had hurt him, and pulls me inside, my head knocking against the single step leading into the cabin.

I can barely see a thing as we enter, my vision becoming dark. I only manage to see his silhouette moving around in the darkness. I can only tell that I am staring directly up at the ceiling, given that I'm not lying on my face. The curtains are opened, revealing the corpses of Todd and Cody, each hanging on a meat hook on the wall. Soon, I, too, am lifted, and my corpse joins the other two. The hook plunges into my back, piercing my skin and latching onto my spine. My neck stays completely limp, hanging my head all the way over, facing the other two. I barely recognise them anymore.

Todd's completely blank eyes stare at the skin of his face hanging off his killer's like a cheap mask. I only know he would've been insulted; he took pride in his looks. Luckily, though, he didn't let it consume him. His exposed teeth create a wide smile on what remains of his face. The rest of his body is covered in cuts and bruises. He must have tried his best to fight the killer off. If he couldn't do it, I have no idea why I thought I had a chance of surviving, but I guess I didn't have much time to think. His bottom half is completely covered in his own blood, some still dripping down to join a slowly growing puddle of crimson. It's hard to even tell how he died, only what happened to his corpse afterwards.

Even though Cody still has his face, he is missing a lot more. His entire torso is sliced open, giving his organs room to fall out onto the ground beneath him and mix with Todd's blood. As I look back through my memories, I come to realise that the last thing I said to Cody was "ew". I can't help but regret that now. Cody was the first one of us to go.

He was probably high and wandering around the woods when he died. I think that's the only reason he wanted to come anyway. He was never the type I would have spent any time with, but he was Todd's friend, so I couldn't help it. I like to think that if I had a second chance at life, I would be a bit nicer to him, but I know that wouldn't happen. I lived my life too quickly to worry about that.

My train of thought is interrupted by a deep wailing, as if a cow were being slaughtered. Our killer drops to his knees in front of us, his hands on his head, crying out in pain. Picking up his knife, he stabs Todd several times in the chest, spilling blood all over him. He carves and tears at every one of us as he screams in pain. The hooks creak as our corpses are battered against the wall. Throwing the knife into my chest, he runs off into the corner of the cabin and snatches a Walkman from the windowsill and slides the headphones over his ears. He rocks back and forth with his arms wrapped around his knees as he groans in pain and listens to whatever is playing through his headphones. He seems to calm down as he sits alone in the darkness. Through the skin stapled to his face, I see his eyes wide in terror as he stares at our corpses. Is he scared because he thinks we're alive or that we're dead?

For a few moments, the cabin is completely silent save for the creaking of the meat hook, which resonates throughout my body. As time passes, my joints begin to stiffen, and my corpse grows cold as my blood dries, attaching me solidly to my hook. After having been knocked around, I get a good view outside of the singular window across from where I hang. A spider crawls along the dirty glass, returning to its delicate home in the top corner of the ceiling. It continues to crawl unfazed as a crow arrives and begins to tap at the window, failing to understand why it can't eat the arachnid. It tries for several minutes before finally leaving as the spider crawls back up to its webs. I used to hate spiders. I also used to hate birds.

A muffled motorised noise slowly approaches from outside the cabin door, cutting through the silence and disturbing the peace. Just as the killer takes off the headphones and raises himself from the floor, Sammy bursts through the door, chainsaw in hand. The motor hums as the blades spin violently away from her, as if it had its own grudge against the killer. Sammy yells profanities at him as she charges forward, immediately plunging the chainsaw into his chest, spraying blood across the room as his chest is churned up into chunks of meat and bone, adding to our rotting corpses. The two both yell out in pain and in anger, echoing throughout the room, before the killer's screams slowly fade. Even after his body goes limp, Sammy keeps chopping away at him, as if she can't control herself.

As she stands over what is left of his corpse, Sammy clenches the chainsaw with trembling hands as if he could get back up at any moment, despite his body being barely recognisable as human anymore. Finally, her legs give in, and she drops to the floor, sitting down in a nest of gore, clinging to her weapon as if it were a blanket. Her tears fall into the puddles of blood beneath her as she looks down, trying her hardest not to look up at the three of us.

Until this point, I had forgotten that Sammy had even come with us, or at least until I was in danger. She never stood out unless she was being such a goody two-shoes that it stopped us from having fun. She always blended into the background, the same colour as the paint on the walls.

Now, though, even if I may not owe her my life, I owe her an apology.

DO Y'ALL WANNA MEET THE ABOMINABLE AUTHOR RESPONSIBLE FOR THIS DELICIOUSLY DARK DELIGHT?

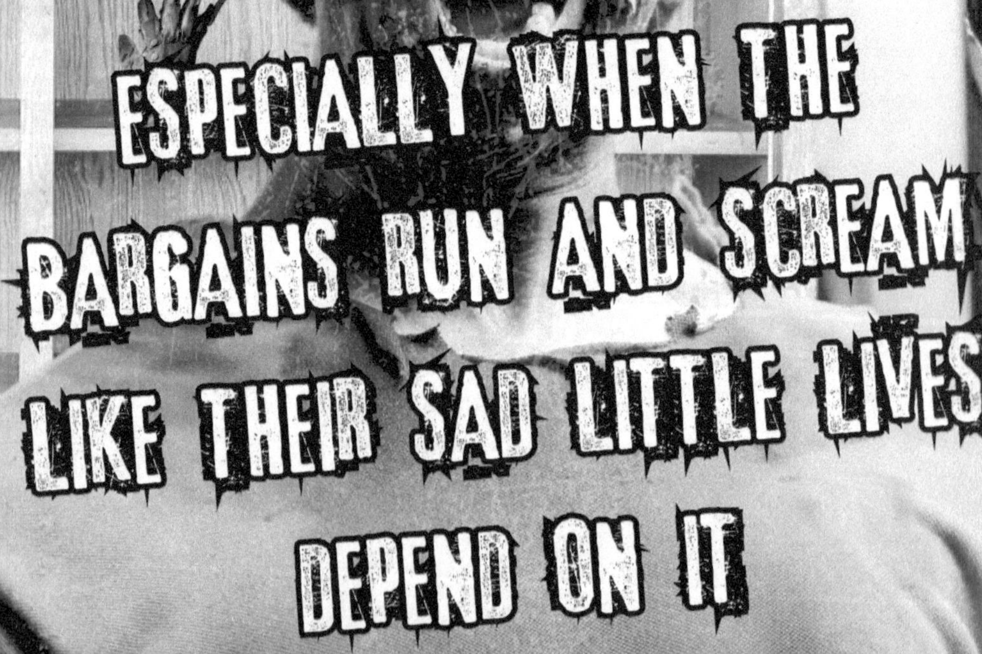

I DO SO ENJOY A LITTLE
BARGAIN HUNTING
ESPECIALLY WHEN THE
BARGAINS RUN AND SCREAM
LIKE THEIR SAD LITTLE LIVES
DEPEND ON IT

THE MAN THE MYTH THE JACKET

BY IAN GIELEN

THE MAN, THE MYTH, THE JACKET

BY IAN GIELEN

"**B**loody hell, that flick was a shocker," Brandon declared loudly as the group emerged from the exit of the movie theatre. His exclamation caused scowls from the other moviegoers around him, who evidently thought the opposite. Brandon didn't notice. Or didn't care.

"Oi, keep it down, ya galah," Crystal said, giving him a playful nudge.

"Well, I thought it was scary," Heather said, winding a strand of her perm around one finger while she blew a fat bubble with her Hubba Bubba. It popped with a sharp smack, making an old couple jump as they shuffled past in matching beige windbreakers. They gave her a filthy look as she rolled her eyes and stuck out her tongue. She stared after them like a hawk as they huffed off down the footpath, muttering as if they'd just seen a punk rocker in church.

Amber, Crystal and Heather all cracked up laughing. Brandon, Jason and Ryan pulled up a short distance away and stopped to grab a cigarette from Jason and passed around a lighter to spark up. The air turned thick with the sharp, burnt stink of Winfield Blues. They leaned back against the wall of the cinema, watching the girls whip out their compacts and touch up their makeup. The whole scene looked like something out of one of those music videos that were all the rage at the moment.

"Well, boys, I reckon it's been a top night," Jason said, puffing out a near-perfect smoke ring. Brandon gave it a crack himself, only managing a wobbly-looking one that fell apart like a frozen meat pie in a servo microwave.

"How the hell d'ya get it so spot-on?" Brandon asked with a frown, trying again but failing miserably.

"It's all in the tongue, mate," Jason replied with a wink at Heather, who went beetroot red. Amber and Crystal rolled their eyes and kept dabbing at their makeup.

"Get a room, why don't ya," Brandon said, giving Jason a shove.

"Aww, look at that. Someone's jealous," Jason said, shoving him right back. Soon Jason had Brandon in a headlock, knuckling his perfectly blow-waved blonde mop as Brandon squawked and wriggled.

Ryan looked on, feeling that familiar gut-twist of envy, and not only because of the girls. He was always the odd one out, the third wheel of the group, looking in from a distance. He was flying solo while the other blokes were living it up with their missus. His eyes drifted toward Amber, knowing he was punching above his weight even dreaming about her. If he had the power to change that, he would, but no amount of mooning and bending over backwards for her had worked. She had never bit. He knew it was hopeless to try, but try he did anyway. She was the sort of girl who turned heads without even trying—long brown hair, eyes like melted chocolate, and a kind of old-school glamour that made her stand out. Plus, she had a body that'd stop traffic, and she liked to flirt. Ryan was pretty sure most of the blokes who were in the same lectures at Uni liked her, but she never got with any of them. She loved the attention, sure, but never let anyone get close. He sighed, stubbing out his spent cigarette on the ground, and scanned the street, trying to shake the feeling that he'd always be stuck on the sidelines.

It still spun him out seeing so many shops open this late. Just last year, you'd be lucky to find a servo still running after dark on a Friday. The old trading laws from way back in '46 had finally been binned, and life was far better for it.

These days, Friday and Saturday nights were buzzing, and tonight was no different. Teenagers in ripped denim and leather jackets loitered around lampposts, ciggies dangling from their lips as clouds of smoke curled into the air like ghostly graffiti. Laughter echoed down the street, mixing with the thump of boombox beats. Girls were dolled up to the nines, wearing fur coats with shoulder pads so wide they could take flight and leopard-print tights clinging to their legs, their stilettos clicking on the pavement. It was pure Countdown energy, like the whole street was ready to crash a Chisel gig.

A shop across the road caught his eye as a light flickered in its window before it finally caught, revealing a brightly lit glass case. His eyes widened when he saw what was in it. A leather jacket, looking in deadset mint condition, slick as anything. At least it looked that way from where he was. It looked like the one the lead bloke wore in the flick they'd just seen, the kind that screamed rockstar or rebel. The boys had been whispering about it during the movie, all wide eyes and quiet "bloody hells," until some old ducks shushed them. Jason, being a proper smartarse, flipped them the bird without missing a beat. Ryan was pretty sure it was the same couple Heather had startled with her gum popping earlier.

"Oi, fellas," he said, but his voice was lost in the ongoing playful scrap between Jason and Brandon.

"Oi!" he said louder, enough to put a pause on the wet willy Jason was giving Brandon.

"What's the go? Can't ya see I'm bloody busy?" Jason said, giving one last twist of his moist finger in the ear of Brandon before releasing him.

"Cop a look at that," Ryan said, pointing across the street at the lit-up display.

"Strewth!" Jason exclaimed, walking up to join him and staring in wonder at the jacket.

Ryan could just about see the movie reel spinning behind Jason's eyes. The way he was staring at that jacket was as if it were pure gold. You could tell he was already picturing himself strutting down Chapel Street, thinking he was the next Jimmy Barnes.

"Forget it, mate. No way you've got the coin for that," Brandon said, lifting the bottom of his shirt and dabbing it in his ear with visible disgust.

"We'll see about that, won't we?" Jason said with a grin as he started forward and darted across the road, dodging the traffic to the sound of angry car horns as they hit the brakes, the drivers swearing at him as he passed.

Brandon looked at Ryan and shrugged as he followed Jason across the road, doing the same thing.

Ryan sighed and shook his head before he followed, but unlike the others, he stopped until there was enough of a gap to be safe.

"Oi, wait up!" Ryan could barely hear Heather's voice over the sound of the boombox coming from a mob of teens loitering near the corner of a shop.

Ryan came to a halt and waved at the trio of girls who had started to follow, pointing toward the shop with the leather jacket. They gave him a thumbs up, and he legged it to catch up to Brandon and Jason, who were already glued to the glass like kids at a lolly shop.

By the time he reached them, Jason was pushing open the door to the shop, Brandon on his heels. He followed them inside and found them waiting for the shopkeeper to unlock the display case. Jason and Brandon exchanged grins, their eyes shining with excitement as the shopkeeper opened the display case and reached in. He presented Jason with the jacket, his overly accommodating smile screaming of a snake oil salesman. Ryan took a closer look at the man. He looked dodgy as, a sweaty, twitchy unit with a hook nose and darting eyes. He frowned and gave a nudge to Jason, trying to get his attention so he could talk to him in private. Jason just gave him a look of annoyance before returning his attention to the jacket, his eyes gleaming as if he'd just found buried treasure.

"Mind if I give it a whirl?" Jason asked the shopkeeper, who had a blocky name tag proclaiming him as *Silas Montgomery* pinned to his sweat-stained dress shirt.

Silas hesitated, his eyes gliding between the jacket and Jason before he gave him a wide smile.

"Of course, sir," he said in a reedy, thin voice. Brandon sniggered, plainly amused by the man before he clammed up at the strangely empty glance Silas gave him. Silas returned his attention to Jason, the wide smile once more in place.

Jason removed his denim jacket and chucked it at Brandon, copping him fair in the face. Brandon let out a grunt, rubbing his nose as Jason took the leather jacket off its hanger and threw it over his shoulders. He slipped his arms through as if he'd done it a hundred times and shrugged it into place. The jacket settled on him just right, as though it were made for him. He zipped it up and checked himself out in the mirror that Silas guided him towards, changing positions to check himself out from every angle.

"This is bloody ace," Jason exclaimed as an overly wide smile came over his face, which was all teeth. His eyes were lit up like a pokie machine, a desire that spoke of how much he was frothing for the jacket.

Ryan watched the scene, a prickling sense of unease running through him. A strange sort of dread was settling in the pit of his stomach. Something about that jacket gave him the creeps. He couldn't say why, but deep down he knew it was trouble. He had to talk Jason out of buying it somehow before things went pear-shaped.

"Looks mint, mate," Ryan said carefully, "but reckon it's gonna cost ya a bomb, yeah?"

Silas snapped his head toward Ryan, sharp as a whip-crack. His smile twitched.

"Well, actually, I just happen to be running a sale at the moment. Fifty percent off. But just for you," Silas said, giving Jason a clap on the shoulder, "just for you, I'll make it sixty percent. How's that sound?" He placed his hands on his hips proudly, the sweat that had previously been beading on his forehead now freely dripping down his face. Sweat stains were now plainly visible under his armpits. Neither Jason nor Brandon seemed to notice. Either that or they just didn't care.

"I dunno..." Ryan said, but was cut off by a gasp at the shop entrance as Heather and the girls stepped inside, their eyes firmly on Jason.

"Baby, you look so gooooood," Heather said, approaching Jason and hooking an arm around his waist over the leather jacket.

"Oi, hands off!" Jason snarled, shrugging her off hard as he spun around, his eyes blazing with anger, his face twisted in fury.

"Mate, chill out," Ryan said, stepping between Jason and Heather.

Jason's eyes shifted to him, something unreadable sparking for a second before his face eased up. He took a step back, raising his hands up, grin on full display.

"Yeah, nah, you're right. Sorry, love," he said, looking over Ryan's shoulder at Heather.

He turned back to Silas, who stood there watching the exchange silently, his face frozen with a smile that didn't reach his eyes.

"I'll take it." Jason grabbed his wallet, pulling out a handful of notes and counting them. His excited smile turned to a frown as he counted the last note.

"Bugger. I'm twenty short," he muttered, his eyes flickering to the pouty expression of Heather as she huddled together with the girls before settling on Brandon, who was oblivious to the whole exchange and was busy adjusting his hair in the mirror.

"Oi, mate—lend us a twenty? You know I'm good for it," Jason said.

"Huh? What?" Brandon said distractedly, running his hand through his hair one more time.

"A twenty?" Jason repeated, his voice a little harder in tone.

"Oh, yeah, sweet as," Brandon said, as he reached into his pocket and flicked open his wallet, pulling out a scruffy-looking note and handing it to Jason.

"Legend," Jason said with a toothy grin. He added the note to the ones already in the palm of his hand and handed them over to Silas, who nodded in thanks, a visible look of relief in his eyes that no one but Ryan seemed to recognise.

"You have a great night now, won't you?" Silas said as he gestured toward the door.

"Now, if you'll excuse me, I'm going to close up for the night. My wife, you see, she's not used to me working at night. Always worrying that one," he continued as he guided them toward the door.

As Ryan took his last step out the door, it slammed shut unceremoniously behind him, as if Silas couldn't wait to get them out of there. The click of a lock and the blinds drawing were followed a few seconds later by the light switching off, leaving the group in darkness, lit only by the passing glow of car headlights.

"Bloody rude," Amber muttered, flipping the bird at the shuttered shop window.

"Deadly jacket, mate. You just need the curls and a mullet, and you'd be on Countdown next to Molly Meldrum," Brandon said with a laugh.

Everyone else was silent, still shocked by Jason's cold behaviour in the shop.

"Reckon I'm ready to bail," Heather muttered, turning away from Jason and Brandon with a huff, the girls following behind, casting deadly glares over their shoulders. Though there was something more in Amber's gaze as it fell upon Jason. A spark of something—was it desire?

Ryan's gut dropped like a lead balloon. Amber was out

of his league—he'd accepted that, but that look she gave Jason? It stung more than he cared to admit. It felt like something had shifted, like he'd missed his shot without even knowing it. The weekend away at the lake next week was looking dodgier by the minute.

"Heather, c'mon, don't be like that," Jason called out as he jogged toward her and the girls, Brandon as usual on his heels.

Ryan rubbed his temple, the night weighing on him like a hangover. It had almost reached the point where it wasn't worth the hassle of hanging out with this lot anymore. He figured he'd give it one more crack. If next weekend turned to shit, he was out.

One week later

Ryan rattled his old Datsun down the gravel driveway, his nerves kicking in as the suspension groaned like a pensioner's knees. Trees zipped past on either side, and with the shocks shot to hell, every pothole felt like a punch to the guts, no matter how carefully he tried to avoid them.

At least he didn't have to worry about being stranded with the group if things went wrong this way. The plan was to split the group into two cars, but Ryan had made up a yarn about helping his folks so he could take his own wheels. It gave him an out if things went sideways.

He couldn't shake the feeling that something was off about Jason ever since he'd bought that jacket. He'd been wearing it every single day, to university, and after it, as far as Ryan could tell. And he wasn't the same bloke anymore either. He was cold. Quick to snap. Acted like he was too good for the rest of them. If anyone got within an arm's length of him, they copped a filthy look or a snarl until they backed off. His usual larrikin charm was gone, swapped out for a cocky, unapproachable strut that didn't sit right. Brandon was still hanging out with him, but Heather looked like she'd had a gutful and could split at any moment. The pair of them had barely hung out all week. Ryan, too, had kept his distance. He was worried about Jason, but what could he do about it, really?

Now here he was, pulling up to Jason's old man's lodge beside Lake Eildon. The lake was normally a hot spot in summer but a ghost town in winter, it turns out. According to Jason, the fireplace would keep the place warm, but Ryan wasn't so sure it would be enough to thaw the chill that had grown between the group.

He would soon find out, he thought as the trees parted as if magically before him, and he emerged into a clearing, a large and clearly old lodge appearing through a few trees, the crystal-clear shoreline of the lake visible just beyond it. Smoke rose from the lodge's chimney, dissolving into the air, lost amongst the backdrop of grey, rain-laden clouds.

He pulled up next to Jason's gleaming Holden Monaro GTS and Amber's far less showy but well-kept Ford Escort. Bloody typical of Jason to have a car like that. Image was important to him, and he was lucky enough to have rich parents. He had it all, really: rich folks, movie-star looks, muscles and the charm to match. Well, not so much of the charm lately. Still, Ryan couldn't help but feel a flicker of envy as he climbed out of his own rust bucket, which groaned in protest. He patted it with affection all the same. It might be beat up, and its paint might be peeling off, but it got him where he needed to go.

He circled around to the back and opened the boot, grabbing his duffle bag, before slamming the boot shut behind him. He had to give it a couple of solid whacks before the lock finally clunked shut.

"Fair go," Brandon laughed from the direction of the lodge. "You need a new set of wheels, mate."

Ryan looked up to see the grinning Brandon with Crystal and Amber, all three of them staring at him as if the scene was the funniest thing in the world.

His face flushed red in embarrassment. He nodded in agreement, looking anywhere but at Amber as he walked past after getting a slap on the back from Brandon. The girls cracked up laughing.

The first thing he saw when he walked into the cabin was the welcoming orange glow of the fireplace and the crackle of the wood burning within. The flickering firelight cast shadows that danced like ghosts on the walls and the gleaming wooden floor. It would've made for a peaceful scene if it weren't for Jason and Heather going at it somewhere down the hallway.

He set his duffle bag on the ground just in time to see Heather stomp down the hallway, wiping angry tears away from the corners of her eyes as they rose to meet him.

She struggled to mask the anger she was clearly feeling as she smiled and came over to greet him with a hug. Behind her, Jason showed up, his leather jacket slung on like he was born in it. He stopped dead, glaring at Ryan, his fists clenched and jaw tight, his eyes tinged with a hint of jealousy.

"Hey," she said, releasing him after a few awkward moments. "C'mon, I'll give ya the grand tour." She reached for his hand and pulled him past a twitching Jason toward the kitchen. "This here's the kitchen," she said, gesturing with her hand toward the obvious, ignoring Jason as he stepped forward toward them.

Ryan took a quick glance, feeling the edge in the air between them like static off a dodgy TV. It was enough to see the laminate bench tops, the chipped enamel sink, and a battered-looking Kelvinator fridge standing sentinel in the corner, cluttered with pictures of Jason and his family held up by magnets shaped like footy boots and brewery logos. A stovetop stood opposite, an electric coil model by the looks of it, with a range hood above it that looked like it'd seen one too many burnt chops. Fluorescent lights buzzed overhead like a mozzie zapper, letting out the occasional *tink* sound as the glass adjusted to the heat. Resting on the bench overlooking the living room was a phone, its plastic cracked, and buttons worn like it had seen more than its fair share of rows between family members.

"You saw the lounge when you came in, so next up, the bedrooms. Down this way." She started walking toward the hall as Ryan followed.

"I'll take it from here," Jason said, stepping in front of Ryan to cut off Heather.

He smiled at Ryan coldly, his eyes catching the mix of firelight and flickering fluoro like something out of a horror flick.

"Fine," Heather snapped, spinning on her heel and brushing Jason's shoulder as she passed, making him inhale sharply and his expression darken with fury.

Jason stood there for a moment, staring after Heather, his eyes wild like a kicked dog ready to bite, before he turned and led the way down the hall.

The pair passed a few doors without any explanation until they reached one at the far end. Jason opened it without a word and walked in, clearly expecting Ryan to follow him.

Ryan gulped nervously before entering. Jason was standing in the centre of the room, staring out the window facing the bush with his back to Ryan. Other than a couple of beds on either side of the room with a few ancient-looking cedar nightstands next to them, there was only a wardrobe present, in an alcove near the door.

"This is yours and Amber's room," Jason said, turning to face him. He was stiff as a board, his face as blank as a brickie's lunchbox.

"Mine and Amber's...?" Ryan stumbled in shock. He wasn't sure what the sleeping setup was going to be, and he didn't ask, but bunking in with Amber was not something he had on his bingo card.

"Yeah. Got a problem with that?" Jason asked, his voice low and sharp like a flick knife, his eyes narrowing as he took a step toward Ryan.

"N–nah, course not. I just didn't think..." Ryan stuttered, instinctively taking a step back from Jason, who looked more and more like he was ready to throw down.

"Didn't think what?" Jason said, taking another step toward him and crowding his space as though he owned it. "Lemme guess, you were hoping to shack up with Heather, yeah?"

"What? No! Heather's your missus, I'd never—"

"I saw the way she smiled at ya. That hug. You reckon I'm blind?" he said, a cold, unsettling smile extending across his face as he kept closing the gap to Ryan.

"No, Jason, mate, there's nothing going on, I swear!"

Ryan matched each forward step with one of his own backwards until his back hit the wall. Jason stepped up to him and pressed his forehead against Ryan's, pressing him into the wall, pinning him like a bloke squaring up outside the pub.

"Don't lie to me, Ryan. Don't make me belt the truth outta ya."

"Jason, I didn't... I'm not... wait!" Ryan yelled as Jason grabbed a handful of his shirt and swung his other arm back, his eyes wide and wild like he'd snapped.

"Jason! Pull ya head in. What the hell are ya doing?" Brandon's voice came from the doorway before he rushed toward the pair and grabbed hold of Jason's arm that was poised to swing.

"Get off me!" Jason snarled at Brandon, throwing an elbow back and hitting him in the side of the head with a dull thud.

With a cry, Brandon stumbled backwards, clutching his head.

"Jason, what the bloody hell's wrong with ya? Cut it out!" Heather yelled as she burst into the room with Amber and Crystal close behind. She tugged at Jason, who still had Ryan's shirt in his hand, and then he finally let go.

"You can have the moll," Jason spat, shooting Heather a look full of venom before storming out. His boots thudded down the hallway, then the front door opened and slammed shut like a shotgun blast.

The room fell into stunned silence. Crystal rushed to Brandon, checking him over before wrapping her arms around him, holding him tight.

Heather shook her head and left the room, tears falling silently down her cheeks, leaving Amber to stare in shock at Ryan, who shrugged at her sadly, smoothing down his shirt.

"So... looks like we're bunking in together, hey?" he said lamely, giving Amber a weak smile, who remained staring at him for a few moments longer before she turned to follow Heather.

"Cheers, mate. For stepping in. Dunno what's crawled up Jason's arse lately," Ryan said.

"No problem," Brandon muttered with a wince as Crystal walked with him out the door and headed to the bathroom. Or what he assumed was the bathroom, given how little he could see of it from where he was.

"Well, this'll be a bloody ripper of a weekend," he whispered to himself. He sighed and walked back to the living room, where he had left his duffle bag, already wishing the weekend was over.

The rest of the day cruised by peacefully after that. With Jason gone on a walk to cool his jets, or so the crew thought, the rest of them decided to do what they came there for: kick back and chill. After unpacking a few things, Ryan joined the group who had decided to go sunbathing after the sun had poked its head back out, with a book in hand.

He settled down on the warm wooden dock where the group had left their things. The girls and Brandon, who was now sporting a large egg on the corner of his forehead, were in and out of the water for the next few hours like a backyard pool party until Heather decided to pull the plug and return to the cabin to see if Jason had shown his mug again. The rest of them stayed behind, the sound of giggling, splashing water and chatter like background music for Ryan's reading between bouts of dipping in and out of the water himself.

Before long, the sun was sinking behind the trees, painting everything in a classic orange glow, the temperature dropping alongside it.

"Heather not back yet?" Crystal asked Ryan as she, Amber and Brandon pulled themselves up onto the dock where Ryan was finishing off a chapter of the latest Stephen

King novel.

"Nah," Ryan said with a frown. Now that he thought about it, it had been at least a few hours since she'd been gone.

"Maybe they're busy patchin' things up in the bedroom, hey?" Brandon joked, giving Crystal a wink and a nudge like he was in some dodgy sitcom.

"Gross, thanks for putting that picture in my head," Crystal laughed, giving him a shove in the shoulder that nearly sent him back into the drink.

"Best way to make up after bein' a dickhead, right Ryan?" Brandon said, flashing a grin.

"Wouldn't know," Ryan said with a chuckle, no longer reading but keeping his eyes fixed firmly on his book and away from Amber, whose bikini was doing absolutely nothing to help his crush on her.

"Well, never say never. You and Amber are sharin' a room, yeah?" he said, tossing a theatrical wink Amber's way, who snorted at him in disgust.

The group, having slipped on their discarded shorts and shirts, started the walk back to the cabin, the surrounding forest echoing with their footsteps and chatter. The shadows of the trees seemed to grow and stretch, the group's earlier lightheartedness fading the closer they got to the cabin.

Brandon opened the door to silence, and the group walked in, exchanging grins when they saw the closed door to Jason and Heather's room.

"Least they could've done is light the bloody fire before gettin' down to business," Brandon said with a grin, shaking his head. He headed toward it and stacked some kindling inside that had already been left beside the fireplace in preparation and soon had it going, the first wave of warmth taking the edge off the chill as it hit the group.

"They're probably out cold," Crystal said, hunching down and hovering her hands near the flames.

"Worn themselves out, more like," Brandon said with a laugh. "How 'bout we do the same?" he said to Crystal, who rolled her eyes and wandered off toward the kitchen.

"Righto then, while we wait for the lovebirds, who's keen for a drink?" she said.

It didn't take long before they were all parked around the fire, drinks in hand, swapping stories from the week and tossing around gossip like footy scores. The mood was easy and familiar, the kind that only comes with old mates and a few cold ones. Ryan joined in, but something wasn't sitting right. That niggling feeling in his gut kept growing, like a mozzie you couldn't swat. Finally, he couldn't take it any longer, and he stood up, setting his drink down on the table and heading toward the closed door of Jason and Heather's room.

"Oi, what're ya doin', mate?" Brandon called out. "Leave 'em be. They'll come out when they're good and ready."

"I just wanna check they're alright," Ryan said, glancing back. "None of us has seen Jason since brekkie, and Heather's been MIA for hours. Doesn't it strike you as a bit off? We've been back for what, two hours now?"

A look at the ancient plastic clock on the wall confirmed he was correct. It was now just after 8 pm. The group had walked in just before 6 pm.

"Your funeral," Brandon called out, raising his drink in salute. The girls burst out laughing behind him.

He lifted his hand to knock, but before his knuckles could make contact, the lights flickered and died.

"Oh, you've gotta be kiddin' me," Brandon cried in disgust before he cupped his hands around his mouth and shouted out toward the closed door of Jason and Heather's bedroom. "Oi, Jason! You forget to pay the bloody power bill, ya muppet?"

Ryan headed toward the light switch in the hallway and

flicked it a couple of times with no response. Brandon was doing the same at the front entrance, jabbing at the light switch for the living room as if it owed him money. Only the flickering flames of the fire illuminated the darkness. They still had that at least.

"This joint got a fuse box or somethin'?" Amber asked.

"Or a backup genny?" Crystal added, looking at Brandon questioningly.

"How the hell would I know? I don't own the bloody place," he answered with a shrug. His shoulders slumped as he sighed. "Guess I'm gonna have to go out there and check, aren't I?" he muttered to the answering nods of Crystal and Amber. "But I'm not goin' out there solo. Let's go, Ryan."

Ryan gave him a nod, and the pair headed toward the door before Crystal's voice came from behind them.

"Forgettin' somethin', boys?" The two of them turned around to see her holding two flashlights, a look of playful scolding on her face.

"Bloody legend," Brandon said with a grin as he accepted the flashlights, handing one to Ryan. "Righto. Let's get this over with." Brandon opened the door, and a wave of cold air rushed in, as if it had been biding its time to enter.

Ryan followed Brandon out the door into near utter

darkness. Not even the moon was visible, which was likely a sign that the cloud cover had once again thickened above them.

"Alright, let's split up. See if we can find the bloody fuse box," Brandon said, already heading down the side of the cabin.

"Guess I'll take the other side," Ryan muttered. He rounded the corner of the log cabin, sweeping his torch beam over the wall as he walked. He was nearing the halfway point of the cabin when he heard Ryan call out. "Found it!"

The side of the cabin he was on was on the same side as Heather and Jason's room. Just ahead of him, he could see the outline of their window overlooking the thick scrub that was a few paces away from the cabin.

He paused for a moment, deciding whether or not to sneak a peek in to make sure the couple were okay. The feeling that something was off about the day's events had been hard to shake, especially after experiencing Jason's strange behaviour firsthand. *Stuff it*, he thought. Even if the couple got angry at him, it was worth the risk. Better safe than sorry. Careful to avoid any sticks and dry leaves like he was sneaking past a sleeping dog, he stopped just beside the frame of the window. Taking a deep breath, he leaned to the side and shone his light up toward the room to illuminate it.

He didn't even have time to see inside before a loud, bloodcurdling scream startled him, causing him to drop the torch, the glass shattering on the ground with a resounding crack.

"Shit!" he said with a gasp. The scream wasn't coming from the room; it was coming from the other side of the cabin where Brandon had gone.

Picking up the busted torch, he tried flicking it on and off as he bolted around the side of the cabin, but it was cactus. Brandon's scream had stopped, but was now replaced by the dual banshee-like screams of the girls.

Ryan tore around the last corner of the cabin and saw the girls ahead, clutching each other like leaves in a storm, shaking and crying as they stared at something on the ground. No, not something. Brandon.

He skidded to a stop and stared down at the body of his friend, the pool of blood he lay in lit up with his abandoned torch. His tattered shirt was stained with multiple bloody patches, the ragged flesh beneath showing clear signs of stabbing and cutting, both violent and forceful. If that wasn't enough, his throat was slashed open and leaking fluid, adding to the spreading crimson pool beneath him.

"What the... What the bloody hell happened?" Ryan whispered. His mind was numb with shock. He couldn't make sense of what he was seeing in front of him. It was the cries of the two girls that eventually snapped him back to his senses.

"Inside. Now. Whoever did this could still be hangin' around." He guided the shivering forms of the girls back to the door, which had been left open. Probably by the girls when they bolted out to see what was happening.

He closed and locked the door behind him and sat the girls down on the couch. He crouched down before them, his breath still ragged from the shock, his heart beating like a jackhammer. The light from the fire cast long shadows across the girls' faces, which were pale and streaked with tears.

"What happened?" he asked, his voice low but urgent. "Did you see anything?"

Amber shook her head, her whole body trembling. "No. We heard Brandon outside opening the fuse box, and then, a few seconds later, his voice. Like he was talkin' to someone. Then, there was a heavy thump against the side of the cabin. Then... Then the scream."

Crystal sobbed uncontrollably beside her, her shoulders shaking as Amber laid a hand on her back and rubbed slowly, wiping her own tears away with her other hand.

"It... It wasn't just a scream," she whispered. "It was like he was being tortured. Torn apart."

Ryan's stomach turned. He'd seen the body. The torn shirt and the wounds beneath. The throat, slashed clean through. And the blood. Way too much blood.

He stood and paced to the window, peering out into the dark. The torch Brandon had dropped was still out there, its beam angled into the dirt, illuminating his ruined body like some grim spotlight.

He turned away, feeling a sudden rush of dizziness and nausea. "No one ran past?" he asked, taking breaths to try to soothe his roiling stomach.

"Nah," Amber said. "We bolted out when we heard him scream. It was already done."

Ryan's mind was spinning. "So, whoever did it... they were bloody quick. Or they're still out there."

Amber looked up sharply. "Don't say that."

"I'm not tryin' to scare ya," Ryan said, grabbing the fireplace poker and checking the lock on the door again.

"But we need to be smart and think about what to do. We need help."

"Oh God, Heather and Jason," Amber cried, standing bolt upright from the couch.

Amber and Ryan looked toward their closed bedroom, and Ryan gulped nervously. He never did get a look to make sure the couple were okay. Was it possible they were already dead? Taken out by whoever killed Brandon?

"Shit," Ryan muttered again, tightening his grip around the poker. He glanced toward the kitchen, his eyes resting on the battered-looking phone sceptically.

"Amber, can you give the cops a ring? I'm gonna check on Heather and Jason."

Amber nodded and started to move away from the couch before Crystal grabbed her hand and brought her to a halt.

"Don't leave me," she muttered between desperate, ragged breaths.

"I won't, love. I just need to call the cops, alright? I'll be back in a tick."

Ryan left Amber to it and headed toward Heather and Jason's room slowly, raising the poker to his shoulder. The cold steel gave him a sliver of reassurance, not much but enough to keep his legs moving.

He stopped at the door and reached for the handle, twisting it slowly as he heard Amber walk toward the kitchen and pick up the phone. He gave the door a nudge, stepped in and immediately froze. His grip on the poker faltered, his arms shaking as his eyes locked onto the horror sprawled across the bed.

Heather was there wearing only her underwear, all four limbs splayed and tied to the bedposts. Blood soaked the mattress beneath her in dark, sticky pools. Her pale skin was a canvas of jagged wounds. Her eyes were permanently wide with shock, her face twisted in agony, a bloody handprint left on one cheek like a final insult.

"Holy shit," Ryan gasped, stumbling back until he hit the hallway wall with a thud.

"The bloody phone's dead! It's not workin'!" Amber yelled in frustration, the sound of the plastic receiver slamming down following soon after.

"Yeah... probably 'cause I cut the line," said a familiar voice from the front entrance with a low chuckle.

Ryan snapped his head toward the door to see Jason, grinning as though he'd just won a meat tray from the pub. In one hand, he held a bloodstained carving knife, the other twirling a set of keys like he was about to head off for a Sunday drive.

"G'day," he said, eyes flicking between Ryan, Amber, and Crystal. "You lot havin' a good time?"

"What did... What did you do?" Amber cried, taking a step back further into the kitchen, her face ashen.

"You mean why did I off Brandon and Heather?" he replied, his voice as smooth as a servo milkshake. Then, without warning, he moved with impossible speed toward the couch where Crystal sat huddled.

As she scrambled toward the back of the couch to escape, Jason slashed at her, the knife descending in a blur, piercing her eye and pinning her head to the couch in a torrent of blood.

Amber screamed and bolted for the door. Ryan stumbled toward her with a cry of his own as Jason looked down at Crystal with a satisfied smile on his face, like he'd just nailed a perfect shot at the pub pool table.

"Don't bail just yet. Party's just gettin' started," Jason said as he pulled the knife free from Crystal's head with a sickening squelch and wiped it on his already blood-spattered jacket.

Amber tugged at the door before realising Jason had

locked it behind him. She reached for the deadbolt as Ryan watched Jason warily, his eyes widening in disbelief when he saw the blood vanish into the jacket, leaving its surface completely clean once more.

"Amber, we need to go. Now." Ryan muttered, watching Jason, who was now brushing down his jacket like he'd just stepped out of a dry cleaner's. He glanced over at Jason, grinning widely.

"Ahh, so you've clocked how special the jacket is," Jason said, his voice full of pride.

"I can't get the bloody door open!" Amber cried, her voice cracking as she rattled the knob and yanked and twisted at the deadlock with frantic desperation. The old metal groaned but held fast, sealed by something unseen.

Jason's grin widened as he watched her struggle.

A chilling dread settled into Ryan's stomach, as if ice had been dropped there.

This was all wrong. So very wrong.

Jason stood in the centre of the cabin, silhouetted by the flickering firelight. His shoulders were hunched, his head tilted slightly, like he was listening to something only he could hear. Crystal lay limp on the couch behind him, her head lolled to one side, eyes glassy and vacant. Blood had soaked deep into the cushions, spreading like oil on bitumen.

Ryan stared, his heart thudding. How could Jason, the same bloke he'd sunk beers with at the footy, the one who always had a smartarse comeback, be behind this? Sure, he was full of himself. Bit of a knob to be honest. But not a psycho. It had to be that bloody jacket.

"You can stop now. That door's not gonna open. Not for you. Not for anyone." Jason let out a strange, low chuckle. Almost too low for a human throat to make.

He turned slightly, revealing a yellowish gleam in his eyes and a twisted grin that stretched wide like his mouth didn't know where to stop.

"Why don't you just make it easy, eh? Step away from the door. Come sit by Crystal. Take a load off."

Amber glanced at him and backed against the door, trembling, her hand still on the knob.

"The jacket's hungry. It tells me things, y'know. Like how Heather was a lying, cheating moll. Like how Brandon was just a leech. Using me to climb the social ladder."

"What about Crystal?" Ryan asked casually, realising he still had the poker in his hand and taking a step toward Jason as he talked, hoping he didn't notice. Jason's eyes were glazed over, lost in thought.

"I actually liked her. She didn't do anything wrong, just picked the wrong bloke. Wrong place, wrong time and all that. That's why I made it quick."

Ryan moved again, closing in slowly.

Jason didn't notice. He had turned back and was staring at Crystal's body, lips twitching like he was having a private chat with something no one else could hear.

Then, without warning, he turned toward Amber. Fast. Too Fast.

Amber screamed as he lunged, and Ryan didn't hesitate. He swung the poker hard, catching Jason across the back. Jason staggered, snarling like a feral dog, then turned on Ryan with a guttural growl that didn't sound human.

Ryan leapt at Jason and connected with his chest, sending them both crashing onto the coffee table, splinters flying like shrapnel. Jason's strength was monstrous. He rolled on top of Ryan like it was nothing, his hands clawing at Ryan's throat, his breath hot and sour, his eyes blazing like headlights in the dark.

"It needs to feed!" he roared.

Ryan twisted, grabbed a broken table leg and jammed

it into Jason's side. Jason howled as blood spurted from the wound, but still managed to wrap his hands around Ryan's throat and squeeze as if he wanted to pop his head clean off.

As his vision filled with black spots, Ryan reached for the poker just outside of his grasp, his fingers scrabbling uselessly to bridge the gap they couldn't make. Then Amber was there, wrenching at Jason's jacket, trying to drag him off. It was enough to give Ryan the room he needed. Just enough. He grabbed the poker and brought it down on Jason's head. Once. Twice. Three times.

Jason collapsed, his body twitching as Ryan rolled out from beneath him, panting on all fours, his face red and lungs burning as he sucked in breaths.

Beside him, Jason's eyes fluttered open one last time. The strange yellow glow was now gone.

"I... I didn't mean to," he whispered. "Heather begged me to stop. I thought she was lying. The jacket said she was lying." His voice broke. "I killed them. All of 'em."

His chest rose once more, then fell for the last time. Silence filled the room before Amber's sobs broke it, tears streaming down her face, her body trembling as she collapsed to her knees beside Ryan.

Ryan embraced her gently before he felt a sudden onset

of dizziness hit him like a punch. It wasn't until he fell to the floor, seeing Amber's pale, fear-filled face hovering over him, that he realised something was wrong. Then his vision folded in on itself, like the edges of a photo curling in the heat, and the darkness swallowed him whole.

Ryan's eyes fluttered open to the blur of white light and the pungent smell of antiseptic. It took a few moments before his vision cleared enough to see an unfamiliar ceiling accompanied by the buzz of fluorescent lights. His body felt like it'd been run over by a ute. Heavy, aching and wrapped in stiffness.

He shifted uncomfortably and winced at the twinge of pain shooting down his side like someone had jabbed him with a screwdriver. He turned his head slowly to see Amber sitting there on the seat beside the bed. She looked wrecked. Her face was drawn, and her eyes were ringed with dark circles, like she hadn't slept in days. She leaned in and grabbed his hand, giving it a squeeze.

"Ryan," she whispered softly as if she were afraid

the simple act of speaking would send him under again. "Bloody glad you're awake. Things were gettin' real dicey there for a bit."

"Where?" he said, his voice too raspy to make sense. He licked his dry lips and tried again. "Where am I?"

Amber handed him a glass of water from the bedside table and spoke while he drank like he'd been lost in the desert.

"Hospital. You copped a nasty hit from that busted coffee table. Bit of wood went right into your side."

Before he could ask more, a nurse stepped in bearing a clipboard. "Ryan! Good to see you back with us," she said, smiling. "Just gonna check your monitors, alright?" She circled the bed and checked his readings, scribbling on the clipboard like she'd done it a thousand times.

"You gave us a scare," she said. "Vitals are lookin' better now. Just take it easy. We'll keep ya in for observation tonight. I'll get the doctor to check on ya in a little while, okay?"

Ryan nodded weakly.

Then the nurse paused, glancing toward the doorway.

A figure stood there. An old lady, whom Ryan didn't recognise, smiled warmly at him. She was wrapped in layers of faded wool and lace like she'd stepped out of a country op-shop catalogue. A long silver braid hung down her shoulder, and her eyes were sharp as broken glass. There was something about her, like she knew things she shouldn't. Things no one should.

"I'll leave you to it," the nurse said, brushing past the woman. "But don't go overdoing it, alright? Rest up." She disappeared down the hall.

"I heard about the killings," the old lady said, stepping inside without invitation. "And the jacket."

Amber stiffened. "Who are you?"

The woman ignored the question, her gaze fixed on Ryan. "You saw it, didn't you? The way it fed."

Ryan swallowed. "I... I dunno what I saw. Jason went off the rails, but it wasn't just him. It couldn't have been."

"No," she said. "It was the jacket. That thing was never meant to be worn."

She sat at the foot of the bed, her voice low and steady, like she was telling a ghost story around a campfire.

"I'll keep this short as time is getting away from us. Years ago, out west in the hills, a mob of demon-worshipping cultists performed a ritual. A cow was sacrificed. Not for blood, but for passage. A door was opened. And something came through. Something they didn't plan for."

Amber leant forward. "A demon?"

The woman shook her head. "Not a demon. A parasite. It needed flesh. It found the cow first. Burrowed deep. When the hide was tanned and stitched into that jacket, it carried the parasite with it. And it waited."

Ryan's skin crawled.

"It feeds on resentment," the woman continued. "On betrayal. On blood. It whispers. It twists. And once it's worn, it begins to influence its host."

Amber's voice trembled. "So, it made Jason do those things?"

"It made him want to," the woman said. "And that's worse."

Ryan sat up slowly, the IV tugging at his arm. "What do we do?"

"You must destroy it," she said. "Before it latches onto someone else."

Amber's eyes widened. "Where is it now?"

The woman stood. "Still with the body. Downstairs. In the morgue."

The room went dead silent. Ryan looked at Amber,

then at the old woman. Then toward the hallway beyond the door.

The hospital suddenly felt much colder.

A few minutes later, Amber and Ryan were moving through the dim hospital corridors, avoiding doctors and nurses and using the hum of vending machines and announcements to mask their footsteps. Soon, the pair were standing in the morgue. The air was as cold as a fridge. Still as a grave. A dead silence wrapped in stainless steel and chemicals.

The coroner led them to Jason's body, which lay there, pale and slack, but without the jacket.

"That's him," Ryan confirmed, to the coroner's nod as he jotted down the confirmation in his notes like he was ticking off a grocery list.

"But where's his jacket?"

"His jacket?" the coroner asked with a frown. "Oh, my assistant took it. Said it was needed for evidence. Left with it about twenty minutes ago."

Ryan and Amber exchanged glances, both pale as ghosts.

Outside, thunder cracked, and lightning split the sky as a figure bolted from the back entrance of the hospital, the leather jacket clinging to him like a second skin. Its whispers were the only thing the figure heard amidst the gathering storm.

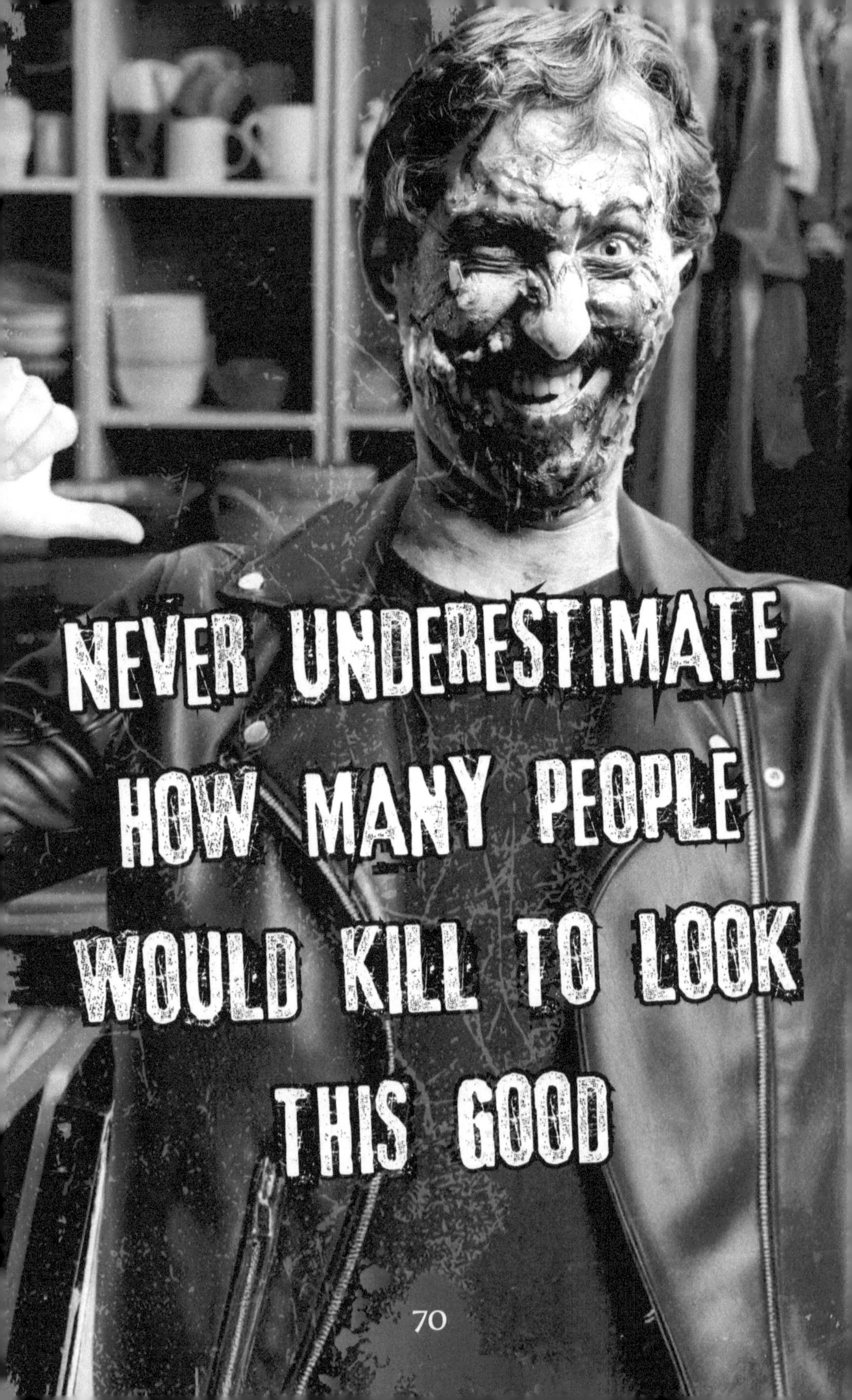

NEVER UNDERESTIMATE
HOW MANY PEOPLE
WOULD KILL TO LOOK
THIS GOOD

WANT SOME FASHION ADVICE FROM THE COLD-BLOODED COOL CAT WHO CONJURED THIS CRUEL CALAMITY?

NEED A BATHROOM BREAK THERE KIDDIES?

YOU WOULDN'T WANNA SOIL THEM DRAWERS NOW

RED
BLUE
GREEN
BY HARRISON SMITH

RED, BLUE, GREEN

BY HARRISON SMITH

The grimy toilet cubicle transformed into a paradise. Every touch, every vicious kiss, every time he spun her around, and around again, were consecutive moments of unbridled ecstasy. Pure, sinful euphoria. Her unblemished skin was purer and far softer than the freshest snowfall. A perfect foreign delight. Her porcelain face, exotic. Her flesh, a gift. Both a trick and a treat. Different to anyone, anything he could have back home.

The lowly nightclub bathroom acted as a purgatory from the Halloween party beyond the walls. A quiet, still place some would deem hell. But for those who already believe their life is damnation, the privacy of powder rooms offers spoiled souls a place to glimpse into heaven. A refuge for their vice. Either way—Black Sabbath's imagining of 'Heaven or Hell'—the synchronous tiled sanctuary was illuminated by the same gentle neon rays that hummed through all Tokyo. Pouring in through two slim awning windows nearly touching the ceiling, the light alternated between red, blue, green. Red, blue, green.

When he turned her around and took her from behind, the woman stared stone-faced down into the putrid toilet bowl. Though this was no strategy to detach herself. Below the foul water, looking back up at her, was Sakura. Ruby red eyes glowed from under the obsidian water. Unperturbed, the woman grinned. October was harvest time. When the veil between the natural and the supernatural is at its thinnest. When spirits stir. When beings from arcane worlds wake, breathe and walk in the mortal realm. A time when the ethereal turns flesh. Weeks where spectres may lurk in the shadows of their former lives. A month for demons and damsels to find common ground. A toilet ghost named Sakura and a maiden dressed in scarlet. This was their plan. This was always their plan.

Shortly, the man noticed rust-coloured streaks smeared across the mucky cubicle wall. The hue of old blood, a warped oxidised brown. At first, he noticed one, then two, then more. Right next to his face. All around him. Next, he beheld the smell. Some metallic, corrosive miasma yawning through the air. A foul stench that was undeniable. A malodorous tang that crawled down his gullet and burrowed in his gut.

Upon realising how utterly encircled he was in mire, the man became startled. Too startled to finish. He immediately released his firm grip from the woman's waist and pulled away sheepishly. She stood straight. He collected his wallet from the pants caught around his ankles and began to count a fistful of notes. She shifted her red mini dress back down into place and tucked her hair behind her ears. Whether the gown of carmine sequins was some costume or her regular attire mattered not to him. He paid her. She left. His wife was in Sydney with their children—a continent away—she would never know.

The man departed the partition and sauntered towards the basin to fix himself in the mirror. Little effort was required to restore the quality of his caveman outfit. The fuzzy yellow and hazel ensemble now appeared to match the state of his ruffled hair. Vibrant electronic melodies that threw revellers on the dance floor into a hypnosis swirled through the walls, as if the music permeated every gap in the mortar of the brickwork. A lambent yellow bulb fixed above the mirror buzzed periodically, jolting itself back to life before instantly dying. In the reflection of the mirror above the sink, the man glanced over his shoulder at the open cubicle. The stall had silently degenerated to its natural state. Nirvana no more. Only filth.

After running his fingers through his matted locks and returning his cheap, polyester leopard-pattern toga over his shoulder, the caveman took out his wallet. The next most jarring fallacy of his costume was the bulky Rolex bound to his wrist. A gift from his wife. A gift bought using his own money. A gift nonetheless. The obnoxious trinket rattled up and down his forearm as he placed the wallet on the basin. Kim Wilde's 'Kids of America' came on.

The caveman thought of his daughters. By now, they would be trick-or-treating around Vaucluse. His eldest would be dressed as Kylie Minogue. His youngest, a Ghostbuster. He imagined them clinging to the black plastic handles of their jack-o'-lantern buckets as tightly as their taut smiles. The orange containers brimmed with Freddo Frogs and Caramello Koalas. He saw their stained-glass grins, meaning his girls were satisfied with their haul, and the fact that they were completely oblivious to the man their father truly was.

With that, his thoughts returned to the freedom of his

overseas business trip. The kind of jaunts rich men take in the name of banking as an excuse to feel alive again. Their companies pay the bill, as do their wives. The caveman's children had candy on Halloween. So did he.

The caveman retrieved a small, sealable bag of powder from a pouch in his wallet. Instantly, he realised that if he acted swiftly enough, he could snort the powder off the basin instead of within the confines of a rancid cubicle. Though the caveman was unaware of the luxury of time he truly possessed. There was no rush, for his mistress in the scarlet dress was on the other side of the door, guarding the entrance, making sure no one else could come inside.

From the same wallet, the caveman withdrew his credit card, which became the tool. Rising and falling, the numbers on the plastic card bounced frantically in the incandescent neon light as the caveman chopped up his powder, making full use of his opposable thumbs. As a series of thin rows began to take shape, a furious gargle erupted from the cubicle. Abruptly, the toilet rumbled—more of a low growl than a splutter—as if a lion was drowning in the porcelain bowl.

The quick roar made the caveman cease. Again, he glanced up at the reflection of the cubicle in the mirror. But the gurgle had stopped. Nothing. Just an empty, open stall. He paused and frowned at the occurrence of the strange noise. Yet soon, the caveman returned to his task.

Meanwhile, Sakura rose slowly out of the toilet bowl to study her prey. The ghost trapped within the toilet appeared similar to that of a little girl. Fittingly, she acted in such a manner pertaining to her appearance. Sakura tilted her head and observed the caveman with the same naive curiosity as a child. Sable water droplets fell from her hair onto the round resin seat surrounding her—making a brief spattering noise—similar to a small trickle of rain. The momentary patter wrought the caveman's attention once more. As soon as he spun around, Sakura sank down into her toilet.

On this occasion, the man stared into the mirror for what seemed like a small eon. Moments moved like minutes. That fear of the unknown. That fear of waiting to witness what lies behind the dark. That fear of what goes bump in the night. His diaphragm heaved from the chilling nothingness, causing his bated breath to fog the glass before him. The neon rays from the digital billboards beyond the club beamed through the pair of windows and bounced off the condensation: red, blue, green. Red, blue, green. Like flickering bursts of lacklustre lightning, the yellow bulb above the glass blinked. Flick, flick, flick.

Despite the eerie clamours, the reflection of the partition before the man seemed to remain still, as if the mirror was now as permanent and unchanging as an artwork. So the caveman decided to complete his endeavour with utmost haste. Sakura waited.

The man busied himself with his work once more. Two delicate lines of powder soon formed on the basin. Little rows of white escape. A brand of sugar that packs more punch than any packet of Wizz Fizz ever could. As the caveman lifted his frame and tensed his nostrils to sniff his treat away, Sakura rose out of her toilet. This time, the caveman saw her all too clearly in the reflection of the mirror. Her sudden, heinous presence now vandalised the picture within the mirror. He froze.

There, sticking halfway out of the toilet, was the torso of a girl. When the yellow light above the mirror flashed on, the caveman could discern each one of her ghoulish features. Sakura's necrotic skin flaked from her muscles, revealing glimpses of her rotten, ashen arteries. When the light blinked off, he could scarcely distinguish the outline of her ghastly silhouette and the shape of her wet hair sticking to her carrion cheeks that streaked down her shoulders. All the while—between the flashes—her ominous red eyes glowed like satanic jewels. Orbs meant for some resurrection or conjuring, as if they were part of a demonic ritual, the man assumed he was now part of.

Then, Sakura smiled the most wicked smile. The ends of her grotesque lips diverged and curved up her face to unnatural proportions—impossible for any living creature to achieve—mimicking the shape of a pointed crescent moon. Sakura's impish grin revealed her virulent grey teeth. Each prong, a gnarled razor. A litany of lethal knives. Unable to move or scream—the man became entirely confined—suffocating in a cage of terror, looking upon an apparition that could not be real. A phantom that smiled like his daughters. All he could muster was a single desperate question.

"Who are you?" murmured the caveman. His palms clung to the cold basin. The yellow light above the mirror flickered. Sakura kept still, just smiling and staring. Flick, flick, flick.

"I am Sakura," she whispered. Her voice was crocodile skin and shrapnel. "Killed by my father. My despair made me this way. Now I stay. I stay forever. They call me Sakura-san of the Toilet. What are you?"

"This is just an outfit," stuttered the man. "I'm dressed as a caveman. My name is Michael. I'm a banker." Beads of sweat trembled on his quivering brow. Sakura leant forward in her bowl.

"You are Michael the Banker," she hissed. "Your despair made you this way. Now you will stay. Stay forever. Stay with me."

Michael slowly turned toward the door and casually made to leave, like his departure was somehow preordained. "What do you mean?"

As if Sakura possessed the mandible of a python, she arched her jaws open wide, seizing Michael's attention completely. Rows of jagged teeth flared across the insides of her mouth, cupping around her green tendril of a tongue.

Synthetic beats from the nightclub thumped louder and faster now. Masked revellers on the dance floor exulted. The air churned with the intensity of the quickening beat, matching the berserk palpitations of Michael's overloaded heart. Blood rushed uncontrollably through his veins, seemingly spurred on by the hectic rhythms and the vision of the wretched revenant before him. Michael felt every sinew—every fibre in his body—writhe in trepidation and twist with dread.

"I have never tasted a banker before," growled Sakura.

Michael made to run. The DJ played Eurythmics' 'Sweet Dreams'. As the first beat thumped through the air, Sakura lunged at Michael like a serpent made of shadow. Her elongated torso stretched out from the toilet bowl and lashed across the room. Instantly, her sawtooth gums clamped around Michael's ankle like the iron spikes of a bear trap. Her acid saliva burned the surface of his flesh while her fangs drilled into his skin. When he collapsed onto the floor and groaned from the wraith's blazing inflictions, Sakura began to pull him backwards towards the cubicle. Michael bucked and screamed as Sakura dragged him towards his doom, towards her stall. All the while, her caustic maw remained fastened around the base of Michael's leg, corroding and slicing the tissue surrounding his shin as lyrics about travelling the world and the seven seas played overhead. Sakura snarled quietly, constantly. Though her sputterings were no mark of fury, but rather excitement, as if she were a ravenous dog about to have her fill.

Constant drumming blared through the club. Rapturous howls from the costumed patrons on the dance floor overpowered Michael's desperate shrieks and pleas for help. The sound of his flailing limbs slapped violently against the ground. His one free leg kicked the floor in retaliation, fracturing his toes with every strike. In vain, Michael's fingers clung to the glossy tiles and the slippery edges of the cubicle. His wrists bashed against the mucky laminate dividers, making white streaks on the walls of the unkempt stall. Records of another struggle. Records of another victim.

Sakura pulled the caveman into the toilet and beneath the murky liquid, bending and snapping his entire skeleton as she lugged him down into her world. Her supernatural ferocity stripped Michael's muscle from his tendons like he was a tender hunk of lamb, his soft meat falling easily from the bone. Barbarous cracks echoed around the bathroom. His pelvis split to pieces. His ribcage shattered. Every vertebra in his spinal column crunched and burst like popping candy. Marrow spewed forth from Michael's broken bones and curdled with the frenzied toilet water, as did his final wail that comprised the entirety of his last breath.

Blood poured from out of the bowl, oozing down onto the tiles, flooding the bathroom floor with vermillion sludge. Michael's Rolex soon emerged from the cardinal torrent. An expanding garnet-coloured pool caught the dim rays of the neon rays that cycled: red, blue, green. Red, blue, green. The yellow bulb above the mirror buzzed intermittently, lighting up the scene and irradiating the red. Flick, flick, flick.

The woman in the scarlet dress returned to the bathroom. She gathered Michael's credit card from the basin and collected his blood-soaked wallet from the puddles of crimson gore that began to spill through the drains spotted around the floor. The knock of her high heels reverberated loudly around the now quiet room. Seeing her reflection in the mirror, she paused to reapply her lipstick, restoring her guise. Then, the woman strode into the cubicle and stood over the ruddy toilet. The place where Michael had glimpsed into the essence of heaven only minutes ago. The place that soon became his hell. The place where the only remnants of Michael were globules of his entrails and a watch.

A deep voice echoed through the bathroom.

"More," grumbled Sakura. Her sanguineous eyes glowed from under the toilet water, as if she were one with the onyx substance. Like she was made from it. Both her home and form.

A wedding ring flung up from the base of the bowl. Sakura's accomplice caught the gold band in the air. The ring lay exposed—meek—in the middle of her palm. She looked down at Michael's round token of baseless commitment, now tainted with blood.

"There's always more," said the woman in the scarlet dress.

She vacated the nightclub bathroom to fetch another. Another victim for her. More prey for Sakura. More appetite for their mutual profit. Perhaps a vampire from *The Lost Boys* group. Perhaps two at once. Maybe the drunken ET attempting to phone home with a witch who's clearly not interested. Or even one of the lecherous 'Thriller' zombies standing in the corner, ogling at those more confident than they to partake in the mosh pit. Though it mattered not. October was harvest time. There were always enough men too ripe for the picking. Crops of willingness. Fields of carnal desire. The motivation in man that is all too easily manipulated. Rows of insatiable exhilaration, like Michael's powdery rows still stranded on the basin. The neon lights changed their colour. Red, blue, green. Red, blue, green.

DON'T FLUSH YOUR CHANCE TO MEET THE MISCHIEVOUS MIND BEHIND THIS MARVELLOUS MONSTROSITY

WE ALL GOT OUR SECRETS

BUT IT AIN'T THE SKELETONS HIDING IN YOUR CLOSET THAT YOU SHOULD BE AFRAID OF

HOLLYWOOD
Velvet
BY ALEXANDER MICHAEL

VELVET

BY ALEXANDER MICHAEL

Sirens in Los Angeles were more common than birdsong. Tonight was no different.

They announced their righteousness to the world. Criminals fell under their batons. Deviants were caught red-handed and red-cocked. Everywhere, the law stalked its prey.

He laughed at their naivete; no one could put the Fear of Good into him. He was invisible. Unknown. Powerful. And so, he played his games and lived his bliss.

The sirens wailed. He dismissed them as feeble. While he waited, he dwelled on his Desire.

He'd first seen her from across the street. Through windows. Between slips in the curtains.

Sometimes she'd dance.

Sometimes she'd read by the window.

Some afternoons would see her succumbing to a warm doze.

What dreams spun behind her sleeping eyes? Bougainvillaea and bird of paradise swayed by her door. The setting sun always disappeared just as the streetlamps ignited. She would forget to close the curtains completely. So would he. Her curled form on the sofa was a question mark, a street and a million miles away.

She was always alone, except for the night of the party. The night they met, two weeks ago.

Did she ever think of him? All these questions and more ran through his mind. The answers would come tonight.

So, he sat in his Void and waited. What a place it was, this nothingness that could be filled with whatever his mind perceived. He did so now, pulling images from within and slipping them onto the projector screen that was the darkness around him. The images he chose concerned that special night.

There she was. Her smile was radiant. The sparkle of her immaculate teeth matched that of her eyes. She greeted him at the front door as she greeted all the other guests, and he noted the crystalline depths of her eyes.

Now, two weeks later, he could not even say how he'd gained access to the party; which one of his acquaintances had invited him into the halls of Shangri-La? It didn't matter. He was less himself now. His memories—even of his own identity—were out the window. This was a fortnight of obsession. Now, in his little silent Void, images from that night of commencement ran riot.

Her name was Matilda. So perfect. She had worn a slip of a dress, black as sin, save for tiny jewels that glittered in the downlights. Her high heels ascended her a foot to goddess-hood, though she didn't need them. She towered over all her guests with energy alone. Her hair was a shade lighter than her dress, cascading over her shoulders. Her forehead boasted a central part that put him in mind of a crown. She was pale statuary, boiled pink by pumping arteries; avenues much kinder than those of LA.

That night passed into memory. Members of the Who's Who were in attendance, actors and actresses, producers and the like. Some with names still known, though their star had dimmed of late. Others were budding flowers all set to bloom.

A sure-fire sign that he was losing his mind: he was a screenwriter, yet he spent the night ogling the hostess rather than engaging in creative networking.

It had been easy to find the spare key. It was taped to the inside of her medicine cabinet.

Two weeks down the line, here he was in the Void he often visited. It truly was a magic place—a No Place, as he sometimes liked to call it. This Void could have been anywhere, any nation, and at any time of the day or night. It was always the same place, yet the entrances to this black colossus were various.

He could be in Los Angeles, as he was now, in Matilda's apartment off Sunset. In the suburbs of San Bernardino. Up in the Hollywood Hills. Hell, anywhere. At any of these places, he could enter the Void. Tonight's entrance was, of course, Matilda's closet.

He sat on the floor. Her clothes hung around him like rent skins. They stared down at him in a cluster, forbidding and impartial in turns. Her scent filled him up, as he longed to fill her. Of course, he wouldn't. It was not his MO. All he did was watch. They never knew, these beauties he chose. They never knew someone lingered in their closet, watching and watching and watching. Some would call him stalker, had they only known who he really was. Others, a monster. He disagreed wholeheartedly with these terms. He was simply "voyeur". In a city subsisting on voyeurism, he couldn't see the problem.

Life was a movie, after all. Especially here. Watch and enjoy!

It had been a movie that had given him this idea: to sneak in, to wait in her closet, and discover the undiscovered. The 80s were good for so much, most of all, giving the misunderstood dark vistas to call home; shadowed boudoirs; down-on-their-luck and high-on-desire bedfellows lit by neon.

There she was again. Matilda. Her hair was obsidian fire. So strong was his imagination that he could believe she was in the closet with him, reaching for his leg with those painted nails.

They were scarlet, as glimmering as a slit throat; a gash in a bloated stomach; as beautiful as the gristle behind the eyes. He'd seen this redness, this shocking brightness, countless times in his favourite movies. It spurted, usually followed by over-exaggerated gasps and cries. Aliens burst forth from split torsos. Unlucky bastards fell into meat grinders and went from Average Joe to Sloppy Joe. Pumping synth ruled the speakers. Life was a dark dream.

But to inflict damage in the world outside the projector

screen was a notion that sent his system into somersaults of revulsion.

Who the hell would ever want to tear down the beauties of the world? They were goddesses. Their skin was too precious to maul. In truth, they were Art, and he would do all he could to protect them. That included watching them. In their homes. At their offices. Strolling down Hollywood Boulevard on the weekends. The wind in their hair at the Santa Monica Pier was kin to him.

Hands were taboo. Eyes were like the wind.

The jangling of keys!

His body tensed. He sat up. The clothing behind him whispered its excitement. The light in the entry came on. He frowned. There was more than one shadow. This was rare, but not necessarily a bad thing. This way, there was more chance of a show.

Only the front hall was illuminated. He never imagined this place could look so stark. The abundance of shadow still cloaking most of the apartment drabbed it in loneliness. He himself felt lonely as he looked out the little slits in the wooden door of the closet. Never again would he experience this place as he had that very first night, all the downlights sparkling, the rooms filled to bursting with The Beautiful

People. It was a night to believe in things, to think that maybe the future was to be bright: that goals and dreams could come true.

But without the glistening bodies drinking champagne, this place roared in its empty spaces. How could one woman stand it?

There were sounds in the hall. Wet, smacking sounds.

Discoveries of this nature always reared their head on nights like this, peering out of the Void onto real stories.

Sights and sounds made him *feel*, and what a blessed condition. Even seeing an empty room, its curtains drab, the carpet stained, could get him dreaming awake. He'd seen such a place not two months ago, having chosen a heroin addict to binge. She'd crept into her place, a two-room hovel behind a wrecker's and stripped off all her clothes. She collapsed into the dark and immediately fell asleep. There was no lamp. No bed. Nothing but the sound of deep breathing.

He had found himself seeing her dreams.

They played for him on either side of his vision, the Void all too happy to entertain itself. He found the strength of her yearning far stronger than any of his other chosen women. Her dreams had as much piquancy as reality.

Was he nothing but a character in her night visions? This thought sent him running.

Why he did what he did was simple enough: to discover whether or not love was merely a storytelling device. He would search for that answer again tonight.

The voyeur stood up slowly, doing his best not to jangle any coat hangers. Now at his full height, he took in Matilda's apartment in all its lonely glory, waiting to be filled by light and by her beautiful presence. He wondered what she was wearing tonight. Oh, he was excited. His skin was bristling. His eyes peered out of the little slits onto the Great Drama.

A man stepped into view.

The voyeur frowned. He had shoulder-length hair. There was a piercing in his right eyebrow. The blue jeans he wore clearly hugged him far too tightly. The bulge at his crotch put the voyeur's to shame. What's more, he wore a black leather vest. He nodded, taking in the sight of the apartment. "Not bad," he said.

The voyeur hated him on sight. The eyebrow ring sparkled as it transitioned from the lit front hall into dimness.

Matilda followed him in after the sound of the door locking. Fabio was clearly intoxicated. He could smell it from within the closet. Matilda looked her best. The darkest of dark hair. A smile to match. He watched as she pulled the fool into her embrace. How he wished to be enfolded in those arms. To feel that soft skin wrap around him, hands caressing his body and his hair.

The fool kissed her. Matilda kissed him back. Hard. The monster in the closet felt a stirring in his pants.

This scene of heavy breathing and wet lips was definitely not Oscar-worthy. The fool's clumsy hands snatched at her breasts.

The voyeur could have done a much better job.

His hands then went to her rear.

The monster in the closet could not see it, but he could see the shadow her ass cast, and boy, it looked just fine. Matilda pulled away from the drunk. He came at her again. Her perfectly manicured hands—those jagged nails as scarlet as they had been two weeks ago—stopped him in his tracks with a finger to her lips. "Wait, love," she said.

"Wait for what?" he sighed. The voyeur smelled a fresh wave of beer. "I want you so bad."

"I want you too." Matilda calmed him with a kiss on the lips. One hand went to Mount Kilimanjaro. "I want this in me."

The voyeur swallowed. To see this all in a mess of shadow was too beautiful to describe. There was *mood* here. There was *contrast*. A lot of work for Fabio to do to pick it up, but Matilda was carrying the day. What a *bingeworthy scene!* Bravo!

She took her hand away from his crotch. "Wait here on the sofa. I'll be back."

The fool let her go. The clothing behind the voyeur whispered its complaint. Two sets of male eyes watched the woman in the dark dress, the strappy shoes, disappear into a far hall.

Time passed in the darkness. The fool spotted some unlit candles on the coffee table. He set them burning with a match he had in his pocket. With the job done, he crashed onto the couch. The room now appeared as a cave, the golden hue from the candles presenting an almost curved formation of light.

Matilda stepped from her bedroom into the hall. Gone went the dress she had been wearing. She now appeared before the fool resplendent in a scarlet night gown, all velvet, all shimmering. The voyeur's skin tingled again. He wanted to touch, though he knew that was against the rules. The Void spoke up behind him. *Just a little caress. Where's the* harm?

No, he answered the whispers. *Break a rule, and what has it all been for?*

Fun?

This isn't fun. It's a masterpiece. Now be quiet.

She was short without her heels. The fact of her power was all the more marvellous for that. He noticed it before the fool did: she wasn't wearing a top beneath the gown. It hung open, presenting him with tantalising hints.

Cream globes. Heavy. Their own marvellous weight bore them down. Their whiteness glowed in the pale light from the hall. All the darkness did was personify her corpse-like pallor. This coldness aroused the voyeur to no end. How could starkness and sensualism marry this way?

The fool stood from the couch. He looked her up and down. Her bare feet. Her bellybutton curtained by the red velvet. Her perfect breasts, nipples hidden. The sleekness of her neck. The candlelight failed to penetrate the bowl between her throat and shoulder. She smiled at him, holding out her hands. He collapsed into her. The voyeur could hear the sucking sounds. He was kissing her neck while she began undressing him.

The Void ached. The voyeur trembled. The moment

was near.

She pulled his jeans down, and he bounced to attention. The voyeur could make out its impressive size even in the dimness. She was so petite. Could she take it all?

She stood. Her hand wrapped itself around the jutting member. The gaps in the closet allowed him to see her squeezing the fool. He was hers completely. The fool slipped her nightgown off her shoulders. Her nakedness hit the voyeur like a punch. Matilda was illumination at one instant and darkness the next. Every little move she made as she guided the fool by his dowsing rod over to the couch changed her form completely.

The fool pinned her to the couch, his ass infuriatingly aimed right at the closet. Precious little of the voyeur's infatuation could be seen, save the smoothness of one of her legs. It was a stream of silk. The fool ran his stinking, drunken hands up and down it. It surely felt like sandpaper to the poor woman. Her moans seemed to disagree with the voyeur's hypothesis. They were full and throaty, coming from deep within her. How could she feel pleasure at this poor display?

Just when the fool began grinding on her skin to skin, Matilda slipped one hand down to this eager gentleman's ass. At first, she clasped his cheeks, spreading them wide.

The voyeur cringed.

Then she slipped her thumb into that little brown bud.

The fool let out a cry and pulled himself off her. "What's wrong?" Matilda asked. "You don't like that?"

"Give me some warning, at least," her suitor mumbled into her neck. "Or let me do that to you."

"Soon. And warning is for the wary. You're not wary, are you?"

"Hell no."

"You want me, don't you?"

"Mhmm."

"You want to fuck me, right? Hard?"

"Yes."

"Tell me how deep."

"So fucking deep. I want to feel you."

"You fucking better."

She thrust one leg around the fool. Before the voyeur could discern motion, she swung around and perched on the naked man's back.

The fool was as shocked as the man in the closet. Was she some kind of athlete? With that body, he wouldn't be surprised. Beneath her, the fool turned himself over. Now he faced her, and that face of his was in her breasts. He nodded his head up and down, smiling at the light tickle of her nipples on his nose.

"Mama," he moaned.

Jesus Christ, the monster in the closet despaired.

"Shhh..."

Thank you.

Matilda hushed him with a long, slow kiss.

The man spoke again. "I'm your fuck pig tonight."

Oh, you are kidding me...

"Yes. Yes!" He squeezed her ass.

The voyeur finally saw her: the roundness of her; the cleft between her cheeks; a holy serving of its raptures. To be drawn into warm velvet. To be sodden. To be ridden. To fuck her hard and hear her cries. If only...

She ground on him, her hands on his chest, their bodies still unconsumed. His face was all idiot delight, him and his eight-inch clanger. His stomach glimmered from her silken leavings.

The clothing in the closet behind chittered away in amusement. He couldn't see what for... This display was puerile. How could these godly attires bear to see their mistress in congress with this imbecile?

"What do pigs do?" she asked the man lost in bliss.

She began to make her way down his body, kissing every inch of him.

"Tell me, darling. Pigs. What do they do?"

If he says it...

"Oink! Oink!"

She laughed. Matilda grasped his thickness in both hands. The purring woman was studying its length. Would she impale herself on it?

One hand left his cock and sought something beneath the couch.

What's this?

The fool had no clue. His eyes were open, but he was too drunk to see. He offered a final pig squeal.

"No, darling," she said.

Matilda brought something into the golden glow. The voyeur frowned. It was hard to discern in the murk. A nail file? Strange time for maintenance.

"Pigs bleed."

And he was opened like a present.

Crimson lace and tissue padding erupted from the widening slit of the wrapping paper. His eyes shot open in horror at this unexpected gifting. His head rolled back onto the cushion. Shock assailed him. He was useless.

The voyeur was frozen in something he had never experienced before.

Fear.

At its purest.

Another cut. Two more, running off from the initial gash.

What business did this sacred liquid have in running from the man's body in a river? This night was meant to be about watching. No flesh was to be rent asunder, no life ended. There were rules, for God's sake!

But what was this spasming thing on the sofa but a reminder that rules were broken every day? The blood ran in rivulets over her hands, soaking the cushions, drowning his flailing rod. It had impossibly shrunk on the instant. It was a flapping balloon now, and Matilda smiled as it struck her hand.

The voyeur slammed a fist over his mouth to keep the scream in.

No 80s film ever mentioned what violence smelled like. It was in the air like its own monster. No VFX. No CGI. This view from the closet did not match the view from the film that sent him here.

Only when the victim stopped struggling did Matilda snatch two of his fingers between her teeth and rip them clean off.

The Void blared its confusion. The voyeur slid to the bottom of the closet.

Matilda faltered.

She turned. Fingernails jutted from her mouth. Blood and bone were a mashed cocktail between her lips. She pulled one of the fingers out while crunching the other like a dog to a bone. The forgotten digit fell to the carpet. The fool made no complaint. He had died sometime in the last several seconds. His body was wet with sweat and blood, bodily fluids he would have been certain had no business mingling tonight. Matilda sat up, perched on the edge of the couch. She kept chewing. Those painted nails of hers scratched an itch at her stomach indifferently. Her swallow was audible.

The voyeur's gorge rose, and he planted the fist firmly on his mouth. It didn't work. Up it came, splattering on the door. He turned, projecting the chunky stream onto her clothes at the back of the closet. When the spasm ended, the voyeur opened his eyes.

He stared. The Void was gone. His beloved place of

sanctuary.

The back of the closet had opened at some point in the last few minutes. The voyeur was staring at the highest rung of a ladder.

This couldn't be real.

This didn't happen during his binges.

He was in control. Was this a trick of the Void?

He crept over to the ladder and peered down into the hole. The diminishing rungs were claimed by murk. A sound behind him made him turn. Through the holes in the closet, he could see Matilda standing up. Candlelight painted her torso in gore. "You cannot run..."

He screamed and dove into the hole headfirst.

Gravity snatched at him.

Screaming all the way, a frightened child, he reached out to break the fall. His right hand caught on one of the final rungs and snapped.

He collided with earth. Pain made a lunatic of him. Numb. Nerve endings screamed in anger. The damn thing was, he knew that his broken hand saved his life.

The voyeur sat up. Blood oozed from his nose. The back of his head was wet. He couldn't yet muster the courage to look at his hand. He instead turned upward, and there she was. What a sight: still naked, still dripping, advancing down the ladder like a giant pussy on legs.

Up he stood, surveying the tunnel. There was nothing to see, no break in the nullity. A concrete passage stretched ahead. He caught a glimpse of the maimed mess that was his right hand, and another wave of stomach gore pushed its way out of his mouth.

The voyeur ran. His bleeding head threw the world before him into a crazy whirl of disconnected images. His pace was slow. His bruised body an insult to its past form. He slammed into a wall. From that moment on, he used it to push himself forward. The voyeur knew she had reached the bottom. She must have! His pace was that of a bloodied snail. She was a hunter, powerful and brimming with bloodlust.

Doors passed him by. All of them were shut and bolted. He even knocked on the doors. He no longer cared if he was discovered to be a deviant who watched women in the back of their closets. Hell, he was still technically in the back of someone's closet.

Police! Where were the sirens?!

The voyeur was no longer invisible, no longer a force to be reckoned with.

He remembered his name was Lance Lazenby, and he sold tyres at Bob's Big Rig.

The young man made his way through this fucked up *The Lion, the Witch, and the Wardrobe.* He was dead meat, his brain soggy, his body mangled. Finally, he reached a door that opened to his touch. In he went, slamming it behind him. He might have seen a shadowy form in the distance of the concrete passage, yet he might not have. Reality was a mystery now. There were no answers. Just plot twists.

He froze once more. What a night for discoveries.

Before him stretched a bank of television screens, showing black and white scenes. From this distance, it was impossible to discern the activity. He stepped closer.

A flurry of movement coalesced into a threesome in a dark room. Two women lay on a bed, on their backs. Both of them were screaming uncontrollably as they stared at the ceiling. He moved to the next screen. A bundle under a blanket lay sleeping and alone. Moving on, one man sat perched on the end of the bed, talking to someone who wasn't there. On and on and on.

A murder. Two lovers whispering sweet nothings. A suicide. An impromptu jam session with guitars. The sniffing of cocaine. The injecting of heroin. A mother speaking softly to her child. Someone suffering a nightmare. The dildo, the ass, and the contortionist. Syringes. Knives. Cheese graters. Endless screams. Pleasure and pain were indivisible here.

Los Angeles post-midnight.

The voyeur's eyes went to the next row. He cried out. Every single screen depicted men, and some women, sitting or standing in closets. Voyeurs, the lot of them. Their eyes were peeled, leering on the activity in the bedrooms—the activity being broadcast on the other screens.

"What the hell is this?" No one answered.

The activity went on and on. The sexual liaisons. The violence. The arguments. The few quiet scenes of sleep. The insane speaking to phantoms. The people in the closets binged these scenes on and on. His brothers and sisters, story addicts all.

Then he saw it. Some of the faces on the screens were familiar. Some of the voyeurs were partygoers from that precious night two weeks ago. Others participating in the orgies or the illicit dealings were familiar too.

It was the Who's Who once more, and some of them had been in attendance the same night. What the hell was this? Had that been a party for deviants, invited into the midst of the Hollywood elite on purpose? What purpose?

This purpose. To be watched. Someone was watching the watchers.

Why why why???

The door opened. He spun around. Matilda stood before him, resplendent in her own flesh and the fool's blood.

In full light, he saw the tattoo above her pubic bone: a solitary eye below a bloated sun, its lids open, its gaze piercing.

Two men stood behind her, fully dressed. The voyeur's face went slack. One man was a world-famous actor, his star rising and rising. The other was a musician, sought after by all.

"What the hell is this?" he asked.

Matilda smiled.

"What's going on here? Answer me!"

The two men stepped forward.

"Fucking tell me! Why do you watch? Why do you watch?? *Why do you watch?!*"

It was almost as though he were asking the question of himself.

Bafflement entered Matilda's cheeks, as though he

should have known the answer. She shrugged. "Welcome to Hollywood."

They rushed him. The voyeur closed his eyes, hoping his loving Void would snatch him quickly.

It did not.

She tore his eyelids from his head before passing him to the men. No one heard his screams. No sirens came to save him. No Academy judged his howls bingeworthy.

They carried him from the room and into the halls. As limp as a shocked ragdoll, he heard her whisper, "Take him to the mansion off Mulholland. He can watch. Loss of eyelids won't kill a man. This is the night of her Return! The horned mistress! He'll be a gift. I'm certain she's hungry."

The sirens wailed. The night went on. He watched and watched and watched.

WANT TO TAKE A PEEK
AT THE TORTURED TELLER
OF TALES BEHIND THIS
TROUBLING TRAGEDY?

I DO LIKE IT WHEN
THEY FLASH THEM
PRETTY LIGHTS ATOP
THEM FANCY CARS

IT MEANS THEY WANNA PLAY

REDNECK HICK
BY SAMUEL LANDY

REDNECK RICK

BY SAMUEL LANDY

Deputy Donaldson sat in the passenger side of the idling police cruiser, snoring. Chief Saxon smoked in the driver's seat as he watched Donaldson sleep. He couldn't blame him. Prom night was usually slow, until the after-party started anyway. Even then, it was more of a stern warning to some drunk teenagers after dropping them back to their parents. But this wasn't a regular prom night.

Saxon blared the siren for a second, making Donaldson jump out of his skin. "Wha—" the deputy started as he pushed open the passenger side door.

Saxon grabbed his shoulder, keeping him in his seat. "It's alright, Baz, wipe the drool off your chin, doesn't look good to be sleeping on the job tonight."

"Ah, come on, Chief, you don't think that nutbar is going to make it all the way here? Especially considering you were the one who put him in Clearview," said Donaldson. The deputy used the sleeve of his uniform to wipe the spittle from around his mouth. A newspaper sat on the dashboard between them. The title page read, *REDNECK RICK ESCAPES CLEARVIEW INSTITUTION*, in bold letters.

"Well, I didn't take prom duty just to watch my daughter make more poor life choices," Saxon said. He flicked his cigarette into a nearby garden and put his window up.

"She's still with the scumbag then?"

"Unfortunately. I mean, how do you and Linda do it, Barry? You got five of them. I can barely keep one in line," Saxon said.

Donaldson paused for a moment and looked out at the car park of Chapel Hill High. They had parked outside the entrance of the school's gymnasium. From inside, they could hear the distorted sound of the prom band, with lots of bass and a heavy emphasis on the synthesiser. "It doesn't matter what you do; they're going to be who they are. We're just here to guide our kids."

"Yeah, well, let me know how that goes when one of your daughters takes up with a known drug dealer."

"Fair point," Donaldson said as Saxon got out of the car

and stretched his legs.

"I might do a round, Barry. See if I can spot Jenny."

"Sounds good, Chief, can you bring us back a cup of punch?"

Saxon gave Donaldson a thumbs-up as he made his way into the gymnasium. Above the door hung a banner saying, *Chapel Hill High, Prom, 1987.*

He scanned the dance floor, a sea of over-teased hair and mullets. The girls wore pastel-coloured polyester and sequins, while the boys wore formal suits, some even opting for a tuxedo. A few of the teachers greeted him, but most of the students averted their eyes.

He saw Jenny sitting at a table with her friends. She was smiling and laughing, and Saxon smiled at the sight of her happiness. He made his way to the refreshments table, scanning the crowd of teenagers, looking for his daughter's dipshit boyfriend.

The refreshments table was unmanned, which Saxon thought strange. There was an assortment of finger food arranged around a bowl of red punch. A student stood at the punch bowl, so Saxon waited. The student looked familiar even though he couldn't see his face. *It's a cop thing, everyone looks familiar,* Saxon thought to himself. But he had learned enough in his time to trust his hunches. The student turned without looking and ran straight into him. In an instant, Saxon realised it was Wade Waterman.

"Hey, watch it," Waterman said, stepping back and looking up from something in his jacket. His face dropped at the sight of Saxon, then regained composure. "Jeeze, sorry, Chief. I didn't hear you sneak up behind me."

"Having a good night?" Saxon said. "Glad to see you and Jennifer made it here safe and sound."

"Of course, you only get one magical night like this, right?" said Waterman. He held up his hands to show all the magic, a mix of dim lights and streamers. "You have a good night, Chief, don't work too hard," Waterman winked and went to walk away. As Waterman walked past the Chief, Saxon realised he didn't have any cups in his hands.

"Hey, Waterman, forgot something?" Saxon said. He grabbed a plastic cup, ladled some red liquid into it and held it out to the teenager.

"I guess the surprise of seeing you made me forget why I came up here." Waterman smiled and went to take the cup, but Saxon snatched it away before he could. The Chief held the cup under his nose and took a deep breath. Waterman's stomach dropped. His knees went weak, and when the Chief looked up from the cup and winked, he knew he was fucked.

Wade Waterman couldn't believe it. He was getting arrested to Culture Club. Chief Saxon pushed Wade's face against the wall of the gymnasium as the prom night band started their cover of 'Do You Really Want to Hurt Me'.

"Hands on the wall, now," said Chief Saxon, his voice clear as steel over the music. Wade knew the drill; he and the Chief had a long history.

He raised his arms as far as the shoulder pads in his sequined blazer would let him. Chief Saxon patted Wade down as the singer of the band did his best to hit those high notes, but he was no Boy George. The sound made Wade laugh as the Chief found the half-empty bottle of Vodka. There was a hole cut in the lining of Wade's blazer for such precious cargo.

"You think it's funny spiking the punch, Waterman?" said Chief Saxon into Wade's ear.

In this proximity to the Chief, Wade got a whiff of Marlboro Reds and Old Spice.

"Dad, stop, people are starting to watch," Jenny said from somewhere behind both of them.

"Let them watch," said Chief Saxon. "Let it be a lesson to both of you." He ripped Wade's arms from the wall and twisted his wrists into a set of cuffs. Wade started to say something, but it came out strangled as the Chief pulled him from the wall by his shirt collar. They spun together, and the Chief guided Wade forward toward the gymnasium entrance.

"Stop," said Jenny, keeping pace beside them. She got in front and blocked their way, stopping them near the dance floor. Wade looked around, seeing a few teachers watching, shaking their heads. Only a couple of students had noticed, but already a small crowd was gathering. They stared while others pretended to dance. "What are you arresting him for?" she asked, pointing a lace-gloved hand at her father.

"Public intoxication," Chief Saxon replied, and pushed Wade forward. Jenny moved so they wouldn't run into each other as Wade sucked a swollen lip and tasted blood.

Chief Saxon turned and said to Jenny, "Stay here, dance with your friends and enjoy prom. But your boyfriend is done tonight. We'll discuss your relationship's future later. And if I find out you have anything to do with what this idiot was doing, well, like I said, enjoy tonight."

Wade and Chief Saxon passed through the gym doors into the car park. They made their way straight to the police cruiser, which was idling near the entrance. Wade saw his own rusted-out pick-up truck at the back of the relatively full car park.

"Jenny didn't have anything to do with it, Chief," Wade said.

"Shut up," the Chief tightened his grip on Wade's collar.

"It's the truth!" said Wade, the pressure on his throat so tight it made him sound like Donald Duck. They got to the police car, and Chief Saxon threw him onto the hood. "What's your deal, Waterman? Why Jenny? I'm sure there are plenty of dimwits that would settle for a piece of shit like you, but why my daughter? What does she see in you?"

"Honestly, Chief, I've been asking myself that same question." Wade turned to face Chief Saxon. The older man's face was tomato red, his hand resting on the butt of his holstered revolver. "But spiking the punch. That was all me. She didn't know. No one knew. I thought it'd be fun."

The Chief stood for a moment, watching Wade without blinking. Wade broke under the man's gaze and looked away. His stomach churned, and a burning feeling spread from his guts.

The Chief pulled his radio from his belt. "Donaldson, location?" Inside, the band started playing 'White Wedding'. There was no response from Donaldson. "Donaldson, you copy?"

"Maybe he's gone for a piss?" suggested Wade. The Chief told him to shut it as he made his way to the passenger side of the cruiser. Wade turned and watched him freeze as the Chief looked through the window.

Movement caught Wade's eye from the trees that lined the car park. "Dispatch, I'm going to need back up at the high school, ASAP," Saxon said to his radio. Dispatch copied, and he put his radio back on his belt. He grabbed Wade, pulling him to the passenger side of the car. "Okay," Chief Saxon said. "Here's what's going to happen."

Wade could hear the Chief speaking, but didn't catch anything. He watched the figure walking towards them, weaving its way through the car park. As it got closer, Wade made out that it was wearing a trucker hat, pulled low across its face, and some dirty coveralls. The figure walked with purpose, beelining straight for them.

"Do you understand me?" Chief Saxon said. The figure stepped into a car park light, and Wade saw that their worn and ripped clothes were covered in dirt and muck. The cap was missing a chunk on the scalp through which straw-like hair frazzled out.

"Hey," Chief Saxon said, clicking his fingers to get Wade's attention. "You got me, kid?"

Wade tried to speak but couldn't as the dishevelled figure walked up behind the Chief. The Chief turned in time to get smacked in the face with the butt of an axe. Chief Saxon dropped to the ground as if his bones had turned to rubber. The stranger took two more steps and raised the axe. Wade tried to put his hands up to defend himself, forgetting they were cuffed behind him. "Wait, wait, please."

The axe came down like a guillotine, splitting Wade's face in two with a meaty crunch. Wade's mouth opened and closed like a fish drowning from oxygen while his eyes turned in to look at the blade. His legs went out from under him.

The stranger pinned Wade to the cruiser with a crusty, booted foot to the midsection. He ripped the axe from Wade's skull, bringing with it a trail of blood and viscera.

Chief Saxon could taste blood. The back of his head throbbed where it had hit the pavement, and his broken nose made his eyes blurry. "Wait, wait, please," Wade said, then crunch. Between his teary eyes and the dim light of the car park, Saxon watched the shadow play that was Wade Waterman's death. Saxon tried to get up, tried to move, but his limbs floundered like a newborn.

"Billy, Billy boy. Is that you?" The man said with a thick southern accent. Footsteps scuffed their way toward Saxon, and he tried to sit up again. He was kicked back to the pavement as the figure leaned over him. "Billy Saxon, that is you. A bit older, a bit greyer, a lot fatter, I see. My, my. It's a shame, I already done killed a few piggies on my way here. Would have loved for you to pop my cherry." A dry, barking laugh followed.

From the voice alone, the lazy drawl that made the words all run together, Saxon knew exactly who had hit him. Despite Deputy Donaldson's hopes, Rick Scule had returned to the town of Chapel Hill.

Saxon blinked tears away, and the man became clear. Time in a cell had not been kind to Redneck Rick. Past the frayed and torn clothes, the patchy beard and the splattered, dried blood, Saxon could see the murdering son of a bitch that had caused his town so much pain.

He drew his pistol with shaking hands. Before he could level it at his attacker, Redneck Rick kicked it away. "Now, is that any way to greet your old pal Rick? Well, I can't blame you, I suppose. I did fuck up your face." Rick laughed again.

Saxon mumbled something, trying to speak, trying to get up again. Rick stomped on Saxon's chest, and the Chief coughed, rolling side to side. "Speak up, boy. Enunciate!"

"Redneck Rick," Saxon said around bouts of coughing, trying to catch his breath. For all that trouble, Saxon copped a boot to his broken nose.

"You say it like being a redneck is a bad thing, Billy boy. Well, my neck is red, and I don't mind it one bit." He pointed to a faded, jailhouse tattoo of the Confederate flag on the side of his neck and giggled.

"Only a stupid fucking redneck would escape prison, just to come back to the town he got arrested in."

"And I told you," Rick said as he placed the top of the axe blade across Saxon's throat, "you ain't see the last of me." Rick pressed down on the axe handle, driving the blunt part of the axe blade into Saxon's throat. Saxon tried to hit the axe away, but Rick just pushed down harder. Someone was screaming as Saxon drifted into nothingness.

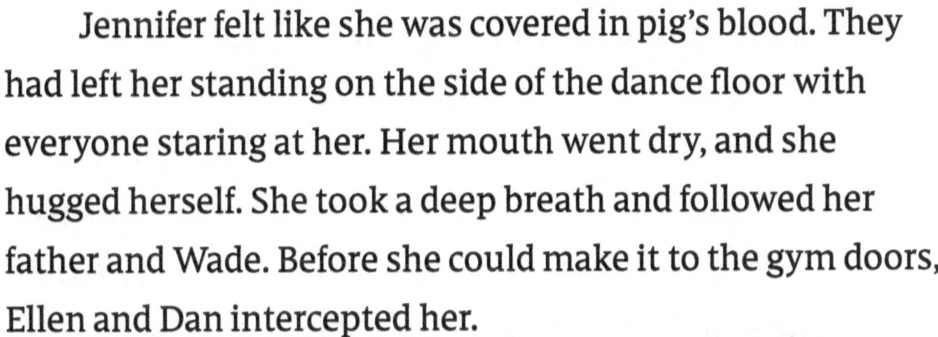

Jennifer felt like she was covered in pig's blood. They had left her standing on the side of the dance floor with everyone staring at her. Her mouth went dry, and she hugged herself. She took a deep breath and followed her father and Wade. Before she could make it to the gym doors, Ellen and Dan intercepted her.

"Are you alright?" Ellen asked as she rubbed Jenny's arm. "What happened with Wade and your dad?" Ellen was wearing Dan's pastel blue jacket over her black dress. Dan's pink bow-tie lay undone around his neck with his shirt collar open.

"I don't know, looks like Wade got caught spiking the punch."

"Really?" Dan asked, a stupid smile spreading across his face. "I hope he didn't use the rest of the Vodka."

Ellen poked Dan in the gut, which made him drop the smile.

"I have to try and talk some sense into dad," Jenny said as she kept walking.

"So, he's arresting Wade then?" Ellen asked as she and Dan followed.

"He cuffed him," Jenny said over her shoulder, walking through the doors to the car park. Wade sat on the pavement, propped up against the car, bleeding from a cavern in his face. A few feet away, her father was pinned to the ground with a man standing over him, leaning on the handle of an axe. The top flat part of the axe's blade pushed into Chief Saxon's throat, choking him. Chief Saxon tried to fight as the man leaned hard on the axe. His arms started to go limp, then fell to the ground.

Ellen's high-pitched screams ripped through the silence of the car park. The man looked up from Chief Saxon's body and hefted the axe into both hands. Jenny recognised him. Redneck Rick, the psycho who had been all over the news for the past two days. He walked towards them, blood coating the axe. Jenny froze. Her mind went blank.

Ellen's hands scrambled to grab Jenny's arm as Rick lifted the axe over his head. He was still well out of reach, and it took her too long to realise what was happening. He swung the axe down and released his grip. Jenny heard the axe chopping through the air like a helicopter blade as it spun toward her. Dan pushed her out of the way. She tripped and fell into the doorway of the gym.

The axe thudded deep into Dan's chest. The impact pushed him back two steps before he fell to his knees. His hands gripped the handle, trying to pull the axe from his chest, then he fell. Ellen watched the life leave his eyes while she screamed his name.

Jenny sat up in time to see Redneck Rick tackle Ellen to the pavement. He straddled her back and grabbed a fistful of hair, pulling her head back with a sharp yank. "What's a guy gotta do," Rick rasped with a distinct southern lean, "to hear that pretty scream again?" He produced a knife and flashed it in front of her face. Even though her lungs were empty, she screamed.

The knife disappeared under Ellen's chin, and Redneck Rick sliced through her throat. Her scream died with her. Rick held Ellen's head while the blood flowed from the smile across her throat. Redneck Rick stared at Jenny as Ellen drained of blood, his blank, shark-like eyes fixed on her.

Somewhere, deep inside, a part of her was screaming. It got louder as Rick dropped Ellen's head like a child dropping a broken toy. The screaming grew as he pulled the axe from Dan's chest. Then it was all around her as arms slid under her own and lifted her to her feet.

They pulled her further into the gym, which had turned into a stampede. "Everyone to the fire escape. Get to the fire escape now!" Principal Hode screamed into the microphone. He stood alone on the stage surrounded by abandoned instruments. His comb-over was blown everywhere, revealing a bald pate in the spotlight.

Jenny looked around and saw her history teacher, Mr Hanson, was guiding her to the fire escape. He kept asking if she was alright, but she couldn't answer him. They were halfway across the dance floor when Mr Hanson got an axe to the back of the head. Jenny looked back and saw a trail of bodies behind her. Redneck Rick was only a few feet away, gutting the captain of the football team. She watched Wilson Garris' intestines fall to the floor, then ran.

Saxon woke coughing. It felt like an overweight cat was sitting on his chest. The same cat must have reached in and used his oesophagus as a scratching post. He sat up, let the coughing fit pass, and spat a phlegmy red glob. He took a few more deep breaths, trying to ignore Wade's corpse and stood.

His head became light, and he staggered the few steps to the cruiser. He leaned against it till the dizziness had passed. The cool metal of the car helped to ground him. A dull throb was building in the back of his skull. Saxon touched where the pain was, his fingers coming away red. He opened the driver's side door and saw the pool of blood staining the passenger seat. Saxon grabbed the shotgun, trying not to think about Donaldson.

The car radio broke into static. A voice cut over the white noise, saying, "We need paramedics at the mall ASAP, it's a fucking massacre. Where are the paramedics?"

"Ambulances en route to your location, car thirty-one," the dispatch operator said.

Saxon grabbed the transmitter from the cradle. "Maple, it's Saxon. Where is my backup at the school?"

"They needed to get here yesterday," said the officer from car thirty-one.

"Hey," said Saxon, "hello, anyone copy?" The officer and dispatch continued as if they hadn't heard Saxon. Reaching in, he pulled on the transmitter cord and found it was cut from the radio. He dropped the transmitter back into the car and closed the door.

Saxon racked the shotgun and made his way into the gymnasium. He passed the two corpses at the door. Recognition flashed through the pain in his head, but he pushed it away. Inside the gymnasium was an abattoir. Colourful lights danced on the walls while bodies lay strewn across the floor. Limbs and organs swam in a river of blood leading to the fire escape.

Through the fire escape, Saxon followed the carnage to the oval. He passed through a break in the stands into the open air of the football field. A single figure limped to the other side. Even from this distance, Saxon knew it was Jenny. He called out to her as he ran, dropping the shotgun to the ground.

Saxon closed the distance, still calling Jenny's name. She didn't respond until he was behind her. Jenny spun, slashing a knife through the air. Saxon stepped back, putting his hands up, but he was too slow. Jenny slashed through her father's shoulder and stepped forward, stabbing at him. Saxon took the cut to the shoulder, side-stepped Jenny's thrust and grabbed her wrist.

She struggled in his arms while he tried to hug her. "It's me," Saxon kept saying until he felt her melt. Jenny dropped the knife, and Saxon guided her to the ground. "Are you okay? Are you hurt?" Saxon said, trying to assess her without letting go. Jenny burst into tears and buried her father's chest.

Jenny tried to speak, but it came out as a blubbered mess. Blood trickled down his arm as his shoulder burned.

"Well, ain't I a lucky duck," a voice came from behind them. "I get to kill you and this bitch, together. Two birds for the price of one."

Saxon stood and spun in the direction of the voice. He went to grab his pistol, but instead slapped at the empty leather holster on his belt. Redneck Rick stumbled toward them through the football field, axe in hand. He adjusted his cap with a bloodied hand and bared the few rotten teeth he had. "Billy, Billy boy. This bitch someone special to you?"

They charged at the same time. As Redneck Rick raised the axe, Saxon went low and tackled him to the ground. He got on top of Redneck Rick and started throwing heavy punches. By the third punch, Rick's jaw broke.

Rick screamed with pain. He started bucking and shaking, and Saxon had to put his hands out to stop him from falling off. Rick grabbed an arm and twisted his body, throwing Saxon onto his back. Rick picked up his axe from where it had fallen nearby and stood.

As Rick advanced on Saxon, Jenny grabbed the knife. Rick didn't hear her bare feet as she ran at his back. Jenny drove the knife into his left kidney and kept going. Rick went to his knees and tried turning to face her. Jenny ripped the knife from his back and brought it down again. Her arm became a piston. The knife shredded Redneck Rick's flesh until he fell on his stomach and stopped moving. The field was silent. The blood pooled around the twitching body of Redneck Rick.

She left the knife in Rick's back as she and her father stood. A gentle breeze ran through the stands as they walked away, tickling the sweat on their skin. Saxon stopped at the shotgun. He bent over and grabbed the gun despite the throbbing pain in his head.

Saxon looked at his daughter; her makeup was a mess, her dress was ruined, and her friends were dead. He put a hand on her shoulder and tried to think of something to say.

"Billy boy!" Redneck Rick yelled as he stumbled to his feet. He spat a tooth and ran at them, his face a mask of hatred. As Saxon pulled Jenny back, a gunshot rang through the football field. Redneck Rick's head snapped back, his skull exploding. Saxon held the shotgun ready as he turned and saw Deputy Donaldson limping toward them. He was holding a wad of cloth to a large wound across his stomach. "Hey, Chief, you guys alright?" Donaldson said as he lowered his pistol, "I'm feeling a little woozy."

Sirens grew in the distance. They sat in the stands, tending to their wounds as they waited.

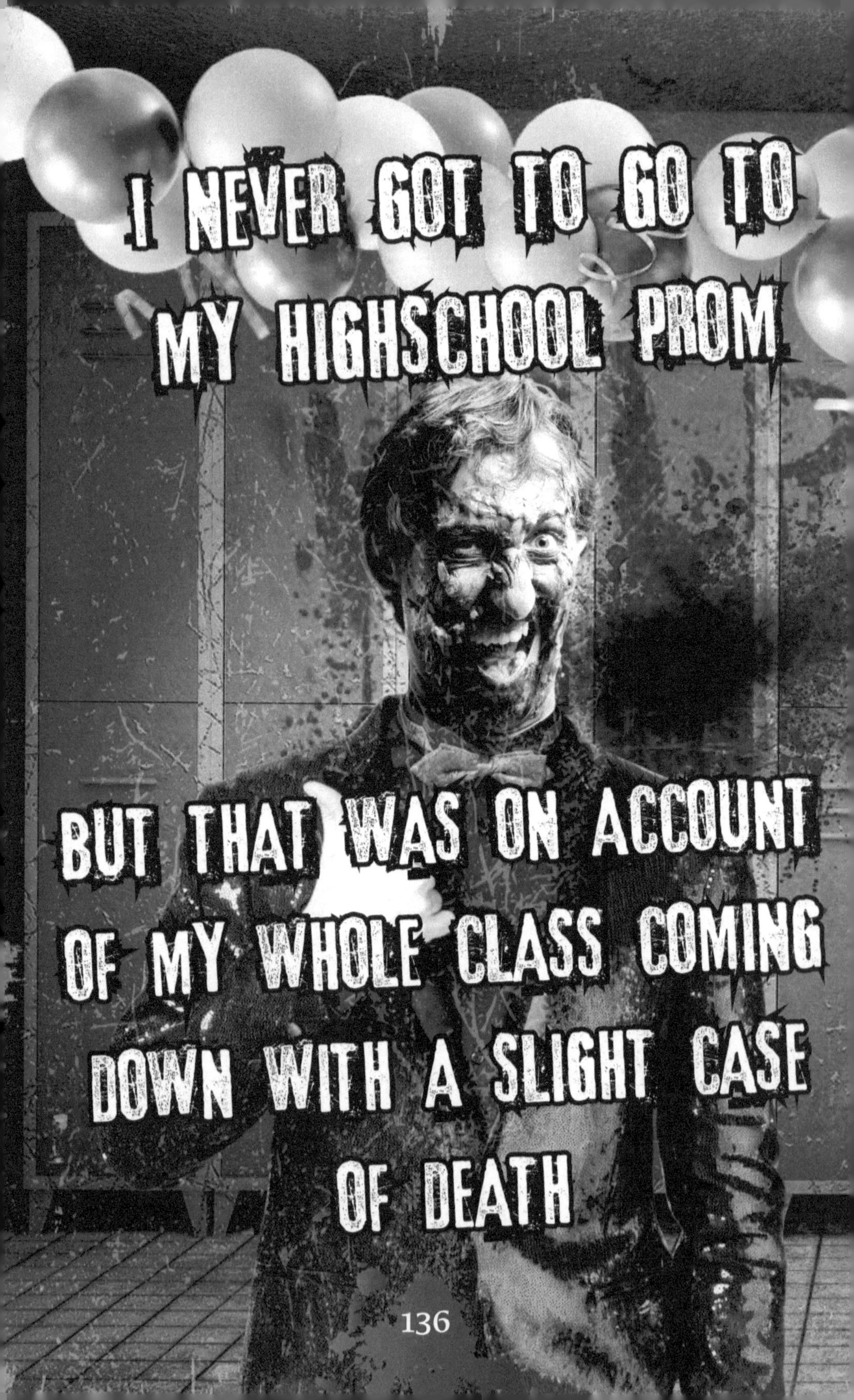

I NEVER GOT TO GO TO MY HIGHSCHOOL PROM

BUT THAT WAS ON ACCOUNT OF MY WHOLE CLASS COMING DOWN WITH A SLIGHT CASE OF DEATH

WANNA MEET THE
ROCKING PARTY ANIMAL
RESPONSIBLE FOR THIS
ROLLICKING REVELRY?

THERE'S NOTHING QUITE LIKE A SCARY MOVIE NIGHT WITH THE GIRLS
JUST BE CAREFUL ABOUT WHO YOU GO AND INVITE

THICKER
THAN
WATER
BY TC PHILLIPS

THICKER THAN WATER

BY TC PHILLIPS

"**R**un!" The sudden scream erupted from the loungeroom, prompting an outpouring of similar warnings.

"Not in there!"

"Are you stupid?!"

"He's behind you!"

Just when it seemed that the panic-stricken chorus had finally reached a crescendo, the simultaneous cry of half a dozen teenage girls watching Jason Voorhees unleash bloody havoc on VHS tore through the air.

In the kitchen, however, a frustrated Mrs Denley rolled her eyes and covered the phone's handset with her free hand. "Girls!" she yelled back. "If you want pizza, I need to order. Keep it down!"

"Sorry," she said, returning her attention to the voice

on the other end of the phone. "Are you still there?"

The response came in the form of a deep, slowly exhaled breath.

"Are you..." Mrs Denley stumbled. "Sorry, I'm trying to order. Are you there?"

Another breath, and this time, she swore she could almost feel the heat of it emanating through the receiver.

"Is this some kind of joke?" she demanded. "I'll happily take my business elsewhere."

This time, a breathy chuckle, followed by a coarse whisper, "Do it!"

"Do what exactly?" Mrs Denley asked, hovering somewhere between annoyance and unease.

"This," another whisper answered, but this time it came from directly behind her.

She would have screamed, were it not for the eight-inch blade that had been thrust straight through her larynx from the back of her neck, instantly severing her spinal column in the process.

As the blade was pulled back out, Mrs Denley collapsed under the weight of limbs she was no longer able to feel or control. Trying desperately to speak, to warn the girls squealing in the room next door, all she could manage was a faint gurgle followed by the bursting of the blood bubbles seeping from the wound in her throat.

She watched helplessly as the killer's bare feet walked into her darkening field of vision. While she could not lift her head to see the face staring back down at her, a flood of recognition raced through her already panicked mind.

Hot tears filled her eyes, and she managed another gurgle before the blade was embedded in her temple.

Earlier that day, Danica had pleaded with her mother to let her stay home. Despite being only a few months older than her, the Denley twins had never ranked high on her list of favourite relatives. Even after years' worth of shared Christmas celebrations and increasingly awkward childhood birthday parties, she had often done her utmost to avoid crossing paths with her cousins wherever possible.

Primped, styled and manicured within an inch of their lives, Madeline and Melanie were, on the surface at least, the personification of a particular brand of teen suburban glamour that Danica found increasingly distasteful. With their blonde locks, flawless complexions, and seemingly unlimited access to Uncle Jeff's credit card, the twins had launched into their adolescent years with the voracity of two young girls desperate to discard any last vestige of their childhood selves behind.

The Denley twins were envied by every girl in their grade and the not-so-secret objects of desire of practically every boy. Even the senior boys, who two years earlier would have barely given either of them a sideways glance, now ogled the pair with hungry eyes and regaled their friends with an array of off-colour jokes and anatomically dubious boasts about what they would do if given the opportunity to romance both twins at the same time.

It was sickening, really. But Danica was not concerned with Mady's and Mel's tireless attempts to present themselves as young women, despite having barely left their dollhouses behind. Nor was it their vaunted position in their high school's social hierarchy that Danica found so troubling.

Instead, it was the pair's wanton cruelty that was so easily hidden from anyone it was not directed toward. Beneath all their battered eyelashes and disarming smiles, Mady and Mel could be as callous as they could be superficially charming.

Danica still could remember the carnage they had left six years earlier, when she discovered what they had done to her beloved Mr Cuddles. Her mother was allergic to cats and had spent many tear-filled nights explaining why she could never have one to call her own. But when Mr Cuddles had wandered into their yard, half-starved and nearly frozen to death, Danica took it upon herself to nurse the poor creature back to health in secret.

However, it was a secret that would not remain hidden for long.

"J-j- ju-just leave him alone!" Danica had pleaded one late afternoon, attempting to block their way into the garden shed that Mr Cuddles called home.

"J-j- ju-just make us," Mady laughed, mocking the stutter that often announced the onset of an oncoming seizure.

"You c-c-ca-can't stop us," Mel chimed in, roughly pushing her to the side.

She wanted to fight back, but it was too late. The ringing in her ears grew louder, and her vision began to blur. It had been that way ever since the accident, when the blood and twisted metal had taken her father and, in exchange, had left her with post-traumatic epilepsy and a lifetime of nightmares.

When she awoke, the sun had already set, and the twins were gone. Noticing the door to the shed had been left open, she climbed her way back onto unsteady feet.

"Mr Cuddles?" she asked hesitantly.

While fumbling for the cord that turned on the shed's light, something unseemly squelched beneath her toes.

"Mr Cuddles?" she asked again, finally locating the cord and snapping the light on.

At first, it was hard to understand exactly what the crimson mess she was standing in was. But as her eyes took in the bloodied claw hammer, still covered in clumps of wet fur, it soon became apparent what had happened to her precious little kitty cat.

"A stray dog," her mother had offered by way of an explanation at the time, and no one would believe that the twins had done it.

"They saw you start to seize," she continued, "and ran to find help."

Bullshit.

It was bullshit then, and it was bullshit now that the twins had invited her to their little movie night.

"You don't need to stay overnight, sweetheart," her mother offered. "My shift ends at eleven thirty, and I'll head straight over to your Uncle Jeff's pick you up. I just don't like having you home alone."

She couldn't have felt any more out of place. While Mady, Mel and the rest of their mindless peons were all bedecked in their satin pyjamas, Danica still wore her usual denim shorts and favourite hand-me-down t-shirt.

"Black Sabbath, kiddo?" her Uncle Jeff pointed at her shirt as he greeted her at the door, his smile almost a perfect reflection of the one her father used to wear whenever she entered the room. "Did you know that your dad and I saw them live back in '77, before they went and gave Ozzy the flick. You were barely out of nappies at the time, and your mother was ropable."

Danica offered an awkward smile and nodded. A bootleg copy of one of their concerts had been playing in the tape deck of her father's car on the night of the accident.

"Anyway, hope you like scary movies," he offered. "Your cousins picked some doozies."

"Ah, sure," she answered, not willing to admit that she hated horror movies almost as much as her cousins.

At first, the night had been tolerable. Mady, Mel

and the rest of their friends were content to ignore her completely, and Danica took the opportunity to bury her nose in the pages of her latest library find.

But once the manicures and make-up gave way to their collection of rented slasher films, the lights in the loungeroom went out, putting a swift end to her only means of escape.

Danica had tried moving into the kitchen, where she could at least continue reading and avoid the barrage of gore and naked flesh playing out on her uncle's TV, but Aunt Jackie quickly put a stop to that.

"You should be in there having fun with your cousins," she admonished, as if such a thing were possible.

It was pointless to complain. No one ever listened anyway, least of all Aunt Jackie, who swore her demonic spawn could do no wrong. Instead, she merely nodded, replaced her bookmark and headed back toward the loungeroom.

"Psst," a whisper caught her attention as she made her reluctant way back.

Danica turned and sighed when she saw the twins waiting to ambush her in the adjacent hallway.

"What'd you have to come for, freak?" Mady hissed

through clenched teeth, quietly enough not to be overheard by her mother, given the noise echoing from the TV in the next room.

"Not my choice," she shrugged, looking to push past them.

"She can be our first," Mel cooed, putting her arm up to block Danica's escape.

"She's not part of the plan," Mady shot back.

This time, it was Mel who shrugged nonchalantly. "Plans change."

The twins exchanged a glance that caused a trickle of iced water to inch its way down her spine. As they turned their attention back to her, the rising panic caused a familiar ring to sound in her ears.

"P—p—p—please, just let me…"

Danica never had the chance to finish her plea, as Mady gripped her arms from behind, while Mel stifled her cries with her hand.

Struggling to free herself, Danica could feel the blood rushing through her veins as her vision began to blur. It had been almost two years since her last seizure, and for a moment, she had thought the new medication her mother had been foisting upon her each morning had all but rendered them impotent.

"...into the garage... "

"...Dad's in there..."

Fragments of the twins' voices swirled, and while she could hear the words, they no longer held any meaning. Opening her mouth, she tried to call out, to somehow get her aunt's or uncle's attention, but her brain had already betrayed her.

As they shoved her through the doorway into her uncle's garage, the darkness took her.

When she finally woke, face down on the concrete floor, Danica tried to roll onto her back and quickly discovered that her left arm had been broken. Attempting to stifle the scream, lest the noise bring her cousins back, she bit her tongue hard enough to feel her mouth filling with blood.

Sitting up and trying to get her bearings, it took her a moment to realise that the thick pool of liquid seeping out from underneath her uncle's car was not motor oil.

Swallowing hard, she lifted her fingers to her eyes, taking a moment to focus on the crimson gore covering her fingers.

"Uncle Jeff?" she asked hesitantly, rising to her feet.

The only answer was silence, and the pounding drum of her own heartbeat in her ears.

At first, she saw the hammer, covered in chunks of skin and bone like the one the twins had used six years earlier. Except this time, it was not cat fur that was clumped beneath the tool's metal claw.

His smile, so much like her own father's, was gone. So too was the rest of his face.

Meanwhile, the neck of a broken beer bottle remained embedded in his throat. Stepping back in horror, Danica's right foot found the remnants of the very same bottle.

Grunting in pain, she leaned against the car and attempted to pull the inch-long glass shard from her heel. It would have been much simpler if her left arm had been able to be moved. Instead, it hung uselessly by her side.

With no small amount of effort, Danica had finally managed to wrangle the glass free from her foot and considered her next move. The twins, it would seem, had long since graduated from helpless kittens, and Danica was not going to offer them another easy kill.

Placing her weight carefully on the ball of her right foot, so as not to antagonise the wound further, she hobbled over to the nearby workbench. Always one to insist on the finest of toys, Uncle Jeff's garage was filled with all manner of tools, each of which was a potential weapon.

Initially grabbing hold of a hefty adjustable wrench, Danica's eyes instead settled on a small hatchet that hung upon the pegboard next to an assortment of saws, chisels, and other woodworking tools.

Discarding the wrench for the hatchet, she gave her new weapon a test swing before limping her way back into the house. It was time to show the twins what she really thought of them.

Danica did not remember all of the details about the car crash that had taken her father, but she definitely remembered the blood. At first, she had thought it was her own, but then she saw the metal pole that had been driven all the way through his chest and out the back of the driver's seat.

She never thought there could ever be as much blood in one place as there had been that night.

She was wrong.

The loungeroom, still lit by the flickering glow of television static, was soaked in crimson. Between the upended chairs and spatter painting the walls, it was clear that some of Mady's and Mel's friends had attempted to fight back.

One of them, the petite redhead whose name Danica could never quite recall, and never really felt compelled to learn, still had an iron fire poker clutched in her hand. Not that it seemed to do much good, the wounds to her neck were so deep that her head now lay at an impossible angle compared to the rest of her body.

The rest of her friends did not fare much better, and Aunt Jackie's beloved shag carpet had been transformed into a swamp of blood and viscera.

One thing that the carnage in the loungeroom was missing, however, was Mady and Mel. Wondering if the two had already made their escape, Danica thought about doing the same. If she could just make it to a neighbour's house, perhaps flag down a passing car, she could be done with this nightmare.

But what if that's what they were expecting? The thought echoed in her mind, putting a swift end to her plans of escape.

No, if the twins had already engineered this much wanton slaughter, there was no doubt that they could plan an ambush.

Phone for help.

She remembered that Uncle Jeff's house had two phone lines, one in the kitchen and another upstairs. The twins were forever boasting about listening in on their parents' phone calls, discovering secrets that neither would wish to become juicy fodder for schoolyard gossip.

Between their father's business connections and their mother's endless supply of drunk neighbourhood rumourmongers, Mady and Mel possessed access to all the sordid details of the town's shadier business dealings, rampant infidelity and questionable sexual proclivities. Whether it be their chequebooks, their sullied marital beds, or in the backseat of their babysitter's car, in these suburbs, it seemed that someone was always getting screwed.

And the twins were more than happy to use the information they gleaned from that upstairs phone line to solidify their teenage reign of terror. By spilling the tawdry details of a local swingers gathering, one hosted by the school's otherwise prudish vice principal no less, they had not only quickly cemented their status as high school legends, but were also directly responsible for the resignation of one of their school's most reviled faculty members.

Not that Danica had much sympathy for their school's now former vice principal, but her cousins would just as easily take joy in seeing the marriages and reputations of far less objectionable townsfolk ruined thanks to little more than a carefully placed whisper.

Making her way into the kitchen, where the nearest phone resided, Danica nearly tripped over the body of her Aunt Jackie in the process. But it was the corpse that lay next to her that really gave her pause.

While she was missing her head, there was no mistaking the matching satin pyjamas and pink slippers that belonged to one of the twins. Whether it was Mady or Mel, she could not tell, but from the sheer savagery that would have been needed to decapitate their sibling, it was clear that not even their shared sororal bond was immune to their unique brand of psychopathy.

It was when Danica limped over to the phone that she

finally discovered where the missing head had gotten to. Staring up in horror from the kitchen sink, with empty eye sockets that appear to have been plucked clean, the final insult was a dirty dishcloth that had been shoved into her cousin's open mouth.

A mouth with a small beauty spot that hovered delicately above her upper lip.

It was Mady then, surprising given that Danica had always considered her to be the more dangerous of the two. If such a thing were actually possible.

She idly wondered what Mel had done with her sister's eyes, but pushed the thought aside, given the urgency of her current predicament. Turning back to the phone, Danica considered the handset that had been left hanging by the cord. Unable to lift it with her injured arm, she looked around for a place to put her hatchet down and, instead, settled on embedding it into Mady's face with a satisfying *thunk*.

It's not like she'll feel it anyway. She thought wryly.

Picking up the handset, she was surprised to hear voices on the other end.

"Police are already en route," a woman's voice echoed through the phone. "Are you in a safe location?"

"I'm.. I'm upstairs," Mel's voice answered through a flood of crocodile tears. "She's killed them all, my cousin's gone psycho."

That fucking bitch! Danica's face flushed red. *She's trying to put the blame on me.*

Not this time.

Slamming the phone down on its hook, she pulled the hatchet out of Mady's head and made her way upstairs. It was time to finally set things straight.

Mel heard the phone in the kitchen slam down, and the line went dead.

Oh fuck, she thought. *She's coming for me.*

Danica was never even invited; it was supposed to be a night for her sister and their friends. No one wanted that freak there, least of all her and Mady.

"Be nice," her mother had admonished them at the time. "It's hard enough on your aunt having to work night shifts and raise Danica by herself."

Thanks, mum. That worked out real well. Now you're dead.

They're all fucking dead.

It was just supposed to be a prank, just like all the others they had planned for that evening. Locking Danica in the garage was just the first, just a harmless prank like the rubber cockroaches they'd hidden in their friends' popcorn, or hijacking mum's phone call to the pizza place from the upstairs phone.

Besides, Dad was in there, tinkering on his car as usual, and he would have let her out anyway. Instead, she smashed his face in, just like she could have sworn she had done with that mange-ridden stray that she had once tried to blame her and Mady for.

Even when Cara had broken the bitch's arm with the fire poker, it still hadn't stopped her. Instead, she just continued her rampage unfazed, wearing that expressionless gaze as she nearly took Cara's head off with mum's favourite butcher's knife.

The heavy sound of footsteps coming up the stairs brought Mel back to the present.

Clutching her craft knife like some kind of holy talisman, she slowly backed into the shadows of her parents' darkened bedroom, never once taking her eyes from the open door. If she was going to die, she was sure as hell wasn't going to be taken by surprise.

A silhouette mounted the stairs and slowly made its way toward her hiding place.

Mel could feel her heartbeat in her throat, and she prepared herself to strike out with her craft knife as soon as her cousin came within arm's reach.

"Danica?" the silhouette asked, its voice drenched with worry. "Girls?"

Aunt Jo!

Mel let out a breath she didn't know that she was holding and burst into tears. Running to her aunt, she buried her face into her chest and began to sob.

"Danica.." she tried to explain between gasps. "Danica... she lost it... She killed them. She killed all of them."

"LIAR!"

Mel clung to her aunt, even as she spun to face her demonic spawn. Drenched in blood and with a hatchet raised and ready to strike, Danica looked like she had stepped straight out of one of their horror movies.

"Danica?" Aunt Jo asked.

"Get away from her mum," Danica screamed. "They planned the whole thing!"

Mel felt her aunt's hand gently take hold of her own as

she slowly pulled the craft knife out of her grip.

"Oh, sweetheart," she said. "It's happened again, hasn't it?"

Before she knew what was happening, Mel felt her throat sliced open with the razor-sharp blade of her own weapon. Clutching her neck as she dropped to her knees, the last thing she saw was the flashing red and blue of police lights shining through the windows.

"Don't worry, darling," Aunt Jo said as she dropped the blade and moved to embrace her daughter. "I won't let them take you away. It's not going to be like last time."

MOMMA HACKENSLASH ALWAYS SAID, "THERE AIN'T NO SUBSTITUTE FOR A MOTHER'S LOVE."

DID Y'ALL WANNA MEET THE MENACING MOMMA'S BOY RESPONSIBLE FOR THIS FREAKY FANTASY?

GETTING A LITTLE STUFFY IN THAT BEDROOM OF YOURS?

MAYBE YOU SHOULD TAKE A WALK IN THE WOODS AND GET A LITTLE FRESH AIR

CLAWS
BY LJ MCLEOD

CLAWS

BY LJ MCLEOD

When Chloe had invited her to the lake cabin for drinks after the game, Scarlet had thought she'd been forgiven for that whole situation with Brad. Now she was beginning to get a bad feeling. Sure, everyone was drinking and having a good time, but something felt off.

Val had told her not to go. Val always told her not to go; she just didn't understand. Being a cheerleader was everything to Scarlet. As head cheerleader, Chloe could kick her off the squad, and she was so grateful that she hadn't.

"Another beer?" Chloe pressed a red plastic cup into her hands. Obediently, Scarlet sipped the cheap alcohol.

"You know," Chloe continued, raising her voice, "I think it's time for a moonlight swim!"

Cheers filled the cabin.

"I didn't bring my swimsuit," Scarlet whispered to her.

"You won't need it," Chloe declared. She took Scarlet's hand, and then they were outside, heading into the woods, weaving between trees in the dark. Brad and his football buddies were laughing and chasing each other through the brush up ahead. Bonnie and Janet were whispering to each other behind them, but Chloe held her hand, and Scarlet felt so happy that they were friends again.

Something hooked her foot, and suddenly she was on her hands and knees in the dirt. Looking up, she saw she was in a clearing. The full moon lit up the area, illuminating her friends standing before her in a semi-circle.

"What's happening?" she said. Bonnie and Janet looked at each other and giggled.

"You tried to steal my boyfriend, you heinous skank!" Any trace of friendliness was gone from Chloe's face.

"I didn't! He kissed me!" Scarlet tried to stand, and one of the football jocks pushed her back down.

"Liar. You must be punished," Chloe said.

"No, wait!"

The jock grabbed one of her arms, and Brad grabbed the other. They hoisted her up between them and dragged her forward.

"Chloe, please!" Scarlet cried. Fear coursed through

her, and her heart began to race. Chloe stood with her arms crossed, while Brad pushed her against a tree and held her there. Two of his friends wrapped a rope around her and the tree, pulling it tight and knotting it repeatedly.

"Please! Chloe, don't do this," she tried again. Chloe remained impassive. Bonnie and Janet wouldn't stop giggling. Scarlet pulled at the rope, and it dug into her skin. Her cheerleading outfit didn't provide much protection from the rope's coarse fibre. Brad walked over and slung his arm around Chloe, smirking at her as he did. Scarlet looked at the pair, at Brad's three friends, at Bonnie and Janet still laughing, and fury surged through her.

"You're all going to regret this," she told them.

"Yeah, right. Let's dip," Brad said. He led Chloe back into the trees, the others following. Within moments, Scarlet was alone. She pulled at the rope until her skin burned. The bark of the tree scratched her exposed legs and lower back. A warm dampness trickled down her arm, and she realised the rope had made her bleed.

A deep roar split the night, shocking Scarlet into silence. She held her breath and listened, staring hard into the dark. Heavy panting came from off to her left. Something moved in the shadows. Something big.

A huge, shaggy head appeared as the bear stepped into the clearing. Ropes of frothy saliva dripped from its long, yellow teeth. It sniffed the air and swung its head towards her. Rising up onto its hind legs, the bear roared again. Scarlet screamed.

"Val! Get up!" Val groaned and pulled the blanket over her head.

"VAL!" Somebody banged on the door.

"What?" Val yelled back. She pushed her tangled green hair out of her face and sat up.

"Phone for you!" Message delivered, she could hear her younger brother stomping back down the hallway. Her clock read 8:03am. Who would be calling this early on a Saturday morning? She grabbed her Dead Kennedys shirt and pulled it on, opened her door and made her way to the kitchen. The phone receiver lay on the kitchen bench. She picked it up, automatically twisting her fingers into the spiral phone cord.

"Hello?"

"Val? It's Cynthia. Is my daughter there?"

"Mrs Driver? No, Scarlet's not here."

"Do you know where she is? She never came home last night."

A sick feeling rolled through Val's stomach. She had warned her!

"No, I don't. Sorry, Mrs Driver. The last time I saw her, she was with the cheer squad."

"I was afraid of that. If you see her, can you get her to call me?"

"Sure thing. Bye, Mrs Driver."

Val hung up the receiver and untwisted her fingers from the cord. What had Scarlet gotten herself into? Whatever it was, she was willing to bet it was Chloe's idea. Val was done with that bitchy poseur and her airhead followers. She wasn't going to get away with anymore of her crap if Val had anything to do with it.

Dressed in her studded leather jacket and army boots, with her green mohawk spiked up, Val looked as scary as she possibly could. She'd even taken a minute to layer on some more eyeliner to the days' worth already coating her eyes. She set her features into a scowl and knocked on the door. Chloe opened the door, then tried to slam it shut when she saw who it was. Val jammed her boot in the doorway and grabbed Chloe by the front of her blouse.

"This is silk, you freak! Let me go!" Chloe shrieked. Val hauled her forward and gave her a shake.

"Where is Scarlet?" she demanded.

"How would I kno—" Chloe cut off as Val shook her again.

"Ok, fine! I'll tell you," she said.

"No, you won't. You're going to take me to her," Val said.

"Whatever. Just let me go," Chloe said. Val did, and she tried to slam the door again, but Val's boot was still in the way. She raised her eyebrow at Chloe, and the girl sighed. She stepped outside and closed the door.

"You want me to ride in that? As if!" Chloe said when she got a look at Val's old orange Ford Pinto.

"Just get in," Val sighed. She hoped it wouldn't be a long drive.

Picking her way through the underbrush, Val was glad she wore her boots. Chloe was having more difficulty in her expensive, strappy sandals and was trying so hard to pretend she wasn't.

"It's just up here," Chloe said.

"What? She's gone!"

Val stepped around Chloe and into the clearing. Blood was everywhere. A large pool of it surrounded the base of a tree in the middle of the clearing, and the ground around the tree was torn up. Val moved closer and saw a rope lying half-hidden amongst the dead leaves. She picked it up and found one end was a frayed mess, as if it had been chewed through. Tufts of rough, brown hair were caught in the rope's fibres.

"What did you do?" Val yelled, shaking the rope at Chloe.

"Nothing! It was just a prank, we didn't mean it!" Chloe yelled back.

"You tied Scarlet up and left her out here AS A JOKE!" Val felt like her head was going to explode. This was way worse than she had feared.

"It was just a joke. I don't understand," Chloe had started to cry.

"Oh no. No, you don't. You don't just get to cry your way out of this!" Val grabbed Chloe's arm and shook the rope at her again.

"We are taking this and going to the cops. You are going to tell them what you've done."

Chloe started to sob. Val didn't care. She kept her grip on the girl's arm and dragged her back toward the car.

The police station was empty, except for one harried-looking officer with a phone in one hand and another pressed to her ear. Deeper in the building, another phone was ringing. The officer held up a finger to Val and Chloe standing at the front desk. She made a few "uh-huh" noises and scribbled something in a notepad. She hung up one phone, then swapped to the other. Several "uh-huhs" and some more scribbled notes later, she hung up and focused on the girls.

"Sorry, it's been a crazy day. There's a rabid bear on the loose, and all our officers are out chasing it. It's already mauled two people. Hang on," the officer cut off, as the phone rang again. Val's mouth fell open when she answered it and turned her back on them. Chloe huffed, leaned over the desk and pushed down the button in the phone cradle, disconnecting the call.

"Excuse me, Officer Miller?" Chloe said, staring pointedly at the cop's badge. "Our friend is missing, and we would appreciate your help."

"And you are?" Officer Miller snapped, still holding the dead phone.

"Chloe Worthington," Val watched recognition dawn on the cop's face as she realised she was dealing with the Mayor's kid.

"How can I help?" Officer Miller said, her tone considerably nicer.

Chloe explained what had happened, and it even sounded like she was mostly telling the truth. It began to occur to Val that she was genuinely worried about Scarlet. Officer Miller listened, employing her "uh-huh"/note-taking routine and when Chloe finished, she tapped her pen thoughtfully on her teeth.

"I'm not supposed to leave the station unattended, but I can put a call out to all our officers to get them to keep an eye out for your friend," Officer Miller said. Chloe protested, and the two started to bicker, while Val puzzled over something the officer had said earlier. She ran the rope through her fingers and touched the brown hair. Scarlet was blonde. Wait, hair? No, fur.

"Who did the bear maul?" she interrupted.

"Uh..." Officer Miller hedged. Chloe put her hands on her hips and stared.

"Look, I'm not supposed to say, but... it was Chet Riley's boys."

"Tad and Teddy?" Chloe gasped, "They were there last night."

Staring at the neon yellow monstrosities on Bonnie's legs, Val couldn't help but wonder what horrible thing she had done to deserve this punishment. Chloe had insisted on collecting up her cronies and bringing them to her house to plot their next nefarious move, and somehow Val had been roped into acting as chauffeur. Janet hadn't been home, but unfortunately, Brad was. He had insisted on picking up his buddy Freddy, and now Val was never going to get the smell of football bozo out of her poor Pinto. Chloe was currently trying to explain what was happening to Bonnie, but Bonnie had noticed Val's stare.

"What are you looking at, freak?" Bonnie called from the sidewalk.

"What the hell are you wearing?" Val called out the Pinto's window.

"My leg warmers? It's called fashion, loser!" Bonnie turned back to Chloe. "You can't really expect me to get in that with her!"

A hurried whisper conversation ensued, which resulted in Bonnie sulkily getting into the backseat with the boys. Chloe climbed back into the front with a heavy sigh. She opened Val's glove box and rifled through the cassettes inside. Picking one, she shoved it in the tape deck and The Ramones' 'I Wanna Be Sedated' started up. Val stared at her in shock. Chloe Worthington, the Mayor's little princess, only smirked.

The sun had only just started to set, but Val was more than done with this day. Scarlet was still missing, Mrs Driver was bordering on hysterical, Officer Miller had nothing useful to contribute, and somehow, she was stuck at the Mayor's house with the most vapid teens in town.

The Mayor and his wife weren't even home; they were out of town for the weekend. Brad had managed to pick the lock on the liquor cabinet and was busily trying to get everyone drunk. Val had declined all offers of alcohol, but she stayed just in case someone let something slip in their drunkenness that might help her find her best friend. It was infuriating—these morons had taken Scarlet into the woods, and now she was gone. And all that blood! Scarlet's mauled body could be lying in a ditch somewhere, and there was nothing she could do.

A scream filled the air, and everyone froze. Val looked at Chloe, then they were both running outside. Janet was kneeling in the front yard, clutching her stomach. Chloe ran right up to her, but Val stopped when she saw the blood.

Janet's face and chest were covered in it, and there was something crooked about her jaw.

"Janet! Oh my God, what happened?" Chloe cried. Janet opened her mouth, and her jaw flopped loosely to one side. A horrible gurgle bubbled out. Chloe tried to push Janet's jaw back into place, and blood spilled over her hands. Janet slumped forward, and her hands fell away. Her intestines slid out of the wound in her abdomen, piling onto Chloe's feet. Chloe screamed and jumped back, letting Janet's body fall to the ground.

"The bear," Val gasped. She looked around and couldn't see it. That didn't mean it wasn't here.

"Chloe, the bear!" she yelled. She grabbed the other girl's arm and dragged her back towards the house. The boys were standing just outside the front door, so she yelled at them too.

"In! Everybody get inside!"

She shoved them all into the house and slammed the door, locking it for good measure.

"What the hell was—"

"Did you say bear?"

"—happened to Janet?"

"—going on—"

Val ignored the panicked voices and tried to think. Why would a bear be attacking teenagers specifically?

"I'm going to get a beer. Brad, you want one? Ladies?"

If the bear attacked Scarlet, where was her body? Janet was still in the front yard. The other two—Tad and Teddy?—had also been found mauled. So where was Scarlet?

"What are you doing... *agh*!"

The yell came from deeper in the house. Val looked around and saw that Freddy was missing. Chloe and Bonnie were locked in some sort of catatonic, blood-covered hug.

She looked at Brad, hated her life, then said, "Come on."

The two raced down the hallway and skidded to a stop in the kitchen. Freddy lay on the floor, clutching his throat, blood gushing from between his hands. Above him loomed a nightmare.

Dressed in a red and white cheerleader uniform, complete with long blonde pigtails, stood Scarlet. But not the Scarlet that Val knew. Livid, red claw marks tore across her chest, stomach, and right leg, leaving her covered in dried blood. Her left hand was gone, replaced by a huge, brown bear paw complete with five jagged, yellow claws. The paw was tied onto Scarlet's wrist stump with a frayed length of rope—the same rope she had been tied up with!

"Scarlet," Val whispered. Her friend stared at her, and it was like looking at a stranger. Scarlet's left eye was opaque white between the bloody gouges. Blood dripped from Scarlet's new claws. Beside Val, Brad made a strange moaning sound.

She watched as Scarlet stepped carelessly over Freddy's twitching body, walked straight past Val, and sank her claws into Brad's stomach. His mouth gaped open, and he clutched at the bear paw now inching its way up towards his sternum. Scarlet took another step closer and shoved her arm elbow-deep into Brad's chest. She ripped it back out with his still beating heart impaled on her claws. Brad's body collapsed, but Val couldn't tear her eyes away from the sight of Scarlet's even, white teeth sinking into his heart. The organ squelched as she ripped a chunk out and swallowed.

Scarlet finally met Val's eyes, and a slow smile spread across her blood-smeared face. Somehow, it was the worst thing Val had seen so far. It jolted her out of her shock, making her back up until she hit the wall. Scarlet lost interest and started down the hallway towards Chloe and Bonnie.

"Chloe! Run!" Val screamed, forcing herself to follow

her mutilated best friend into the lounge room.

Chloe had taken one look at Scarlet and was trying to pull Bonnie towards the front door. Bonnie took a moment to work out what was happening until she saw Scarlet stalking towards her. Her eyes bugged out, and she screamed, an ear-splitting noise that went on, and on.

It only stopped when Scarlet shoved her bloody claws into Bonnie's mouth and up into her brain. Val's common sense finally caught up with her, and her adrenaline spiked. She lunged across the room, past Scarlet, trying to shake Bonnie off her claws, grabbed Chloe and threw them both out the front door.

She had Chloe's hand, and they were running and if they could just make it into the woods...

A horrible, broken scream split the air, and Val knew Scarlet was chasing them. She was hunting down the ones that had hurt her, and she wasn't going to stop.

How had it come to this? Chloe gasped, and her hand was tugged out of Val's. Val stopped and turned; Chloe had tripped and fallen face-first onto the ground. She cried out and curled into a ball, clutching at her ankle.

"Chloe, get up!" Val grabbed her arm and pulled, but Chloe collapsed back down.

"My ankle," she sobbed.

"Please, Chloe. You have to—"

Heavy footfalls pounded through the woods, and then Scarlet was there. Blood dripped from her pigtails, and her chest heaved, but her face was blank.

"Scarlet," Val said. She stepped forward, putting herself between her best friend and the girl who had tortured her.

"Scarlet, this isn't you. You have to stop."

Scarlet stared at her, and slowly emotion began to creep across her face. A tear welled from her one good eye and ran down her cheek. Her lips trembled. She opened her mouth to speak, and a trickle of blood escaped her mouth. Her tongue was gone, ripped completely out of her mouth.

Val felt tears in her own eyes. Her best friend in the whole world was so hurt. Her beautiful face was ruined, and Val would never again hear her voice telling her about all the things that had happened to her in a day. Her best friend.

Val reached out and wiped the tear from Scarlet's cheek. Scarlet's eyes were full of pain. And anger. So much anger.

Behind her, Chloe whimpered. Chloe was also in pain. But not nearly enough.

Val stepped aside. A beautiful smile lit up Scarlet's ruined face.

From the ground, Chloe started to scream.

AIN'T TRUE FRIENDSHIP A BEAUTIFUL THING?

EVERYONE NEEDS A BESTIE WHO'LL STEP ASIDE WHEN IT'S TIME TO DISEMBOWEL YOUR ENEMIES

WANT TO MEET THE BARBARIC BELLETRIST RESPONSIBLE FOR THIS BEARISH BLOW-BY-BLOW?

MAYBE YOU SHOULD PUT A LITTLE MUSIC ON

UNCLE HENLEY'S KILLER MIX TAPE

B

THERE'S NOTHING LIKE HAVING SOME KILLER TUNES TO SLAY BY

THE
ROLLER
DISCO
KILLER
BY M.P. NORMAN

THE ROLLER DISCO KILLER

BY M.P. NORMAN

The Jupiter Mall roller rink on a sweltering summer's evening in downtown Chicago smelled like Pepsi, popcorn, pizza, sweat, and something not quite dead, trying to stay groovy on the last-ever Saturday session of disco skating before its eventual and timely closure.

Under the twinkling disco lights, teens spun like records inside the rink, wearing neon leg warmers, neon tights, neon t-shirts, plastic neon jewelry, and statement earrings. The bolder and more colourful, the better. While all the hairspray-can girls and boys held their massively large permed heads high, even George Michael would have been intimidated by the amount of hair on show.

While the skaters flaunted their style as much as their skating skills. The rink wasn't just for skating—it was a place to showcase the latest fashion trends, dance to your favourite songs, and enjoy a collective, liberating experience. Out of the rink, people who weren't into a neon rainbow of colour wore the comfy outfits of choice—sweatsuits—or anything that Molly Ringwald and the rest of the Brat Pack would wear, and you'd be on point.

Around the rink, the speaker stacks throbbed with a mix of Depeche Mode, Cindi Lauper, Madonna, and Salt-N-Pepa.

In the elevated sound booth in the middle of the rink, DJ Rory O'Brien, sporting a voluminous, feathered hairstyle cut in layers, giving it a full and airy look, fed a fresh cassette into the state-of-the-art deck player.

"This next track's gonna blow your brains," he laughed into the mic, acting like king of the world because... he was the great pretender, always entertaining the crowd, leading dance-offs, and tossing out shoutouts to skaters over the speakers. Rory kept the energy high and ensured nobody left without hearing at least one song they'd be singing for weeks. "But don't let that stop you from grooving to my tunes."

Soon, the unmistakable lyrics of MJ's 'Thriller' thundered from the speakers, overcutting the DJ's deep radio-style voice.

Three songs in, and a blonde high school senior hit the floor... hard. Blood gushed from her headphones like they were pumping Kool-Aid instead of bass. Her legs twitched in time with the beat.

Click, clickity, click.

No one noticed at first until some Ice Cube look-alike dressed in a striped pink and white short-sleeved shirt skated into her, screaming so hard that the mirrored ceiling could have cracked as her body limped to one final beat.

Then the lights went out. The rink went dark, but the music continued. A new track kicked in—low, warbling, off-pitch like a violinist about to fall off stage. A voice rasped over the entire complex: "Skate... or die." It became unbearably louder, echoey, scratchy, as if someone was scraping their fingernails across a blackboard. Some patrons held their ears while others booed the DJ. "Time to decide, children... skate or die?"

Sparkly-clad Dina Starr was already skating as fast as possible around statues of other skaters, mesmerised by the ultimatum through the smoke from the fog machine. She had seen enough horror movies to know a blackout at a mall party meant someone was about to get slashed. And she wasn't about to be final girl fodder either—not without a fight—even though today fell on Friday the 13th.

She kicked open the gate to the DJ booth and found Rory O'Brien slumped over the controls, strangled with his own headphone cord. His eyes were blotchy-red, and his lips were swollen. But what disturbed her the most was the blood pouring from his sockets, dripping on a cassette case labeled: *SIDE A – DEATH ON THE DANCE FLOOR.*

Miriam Bradbury, with her curly ruby locks and plain porcelain complexion, wasn't a superhero like her best friend, who was now scooting toward the DJ booth. Instead, she was just a number in a crowd—a blurred digit—at best. However, she knew she couldn't just be another sheep led to the slaughter by something so despicable and evil that the hairs on her arms stood on end, like soldiers standing to attention on parade. So, she grabbed the heaviest lava lamp from the nearest table—red and yellow swirls of wax mixture sliding around inside the glass vessel—and headed for the ring's exterior. The fog machines were still going, and beyond the veil of smoke, she saw her best friend, Dina, disappearing into the booth entrance.

Miriam wanted to call over, but a creep in full Jason Voorhees mode loomed across the rink, and the fear entrenched her entirely, squashing her voice.

Dina pulled the tape inside free, but something was... was drastically wrong. It shimmered, twitched, and vibrated in her hand. As if it was breathing somehow, like life was passing through it, like the Statue of Liberty being animated with the special ectoplasm from her favorite film, *Ghostbusters II.*

Then, Dina heard screams from across the floor but turned... too late.

A warped figure stepped from the fog wearing a mirror-ball helmet and a purple and gold shredded staff jacket. Wires snaked from his wrists like puppet strings she'd once seen at a cousin's birthday party. Where his eyes should be were instead, spinning tape reels—round and round they went, whirring with hypnotic energy. Dina noticed something shimmering midriff. Squinting, she saw a serrated vinyl record like a sawblade in his left hand, and with every stomp, he swung the blade.

With the flashing strobes, pulsing neon, and swirling-coloured lights of the arena, skaters fell around the rink like a performance from *Les Misérables*. It was as if the killer moved in harmony with the beat as he slashed and cut, cut and slashed again. Amid blood and screams, finally, his taped eyes found her dead ahead.

He swung back the record and released.

Dina skated from the booth as the vinyl record came crashing over the top of her skull like a frisbee, embedding itself in the backboard. She didn't dare stop or look and reached the other side of the rink, crashing over the barrier with speed.

Within moments, she was up on wobbly, grazed legs, grabbing Miriam's hand and pulling her best friend away from the maniac through an adjacent gift shop. Past Claire's, where mannequins bled glitter from their headless torsos. Past the Slushy Juice shop, where something ungodly growled in the blender, even though it wasn't on. Around the mall, every speaker crackled with the same cursed voice, now looping:

"Rewind your soul. Fast-forward your life. Your time on earth is about to end."

A blood-slicked skater slammed into them, breaking the friend's connection. Dina shoved him off. It was Brandon, her ex. He stumbled backward with dead eyes, swaying unnaturally with other patrons, blood pooling from their eardrums.

The music had them in a psychedelic trance.

The friends needed to kill the beat, or the beat would end them.

When Miriam took the tape from her friend's hand for some unexpected reason, something clicked in her brain from watching the local news reports regarding music tracks containing subliminal messages when played backward. It was a phenomenon often referred to as Backmasking,

Knowing exactly how to end the mayhem, she tugged Dina away from her dying ex. "We gotta run, like now!

"But—"

"No buts, c'mon, because we only have one chance to stop this nightmare, D!"

They bolted into a Sam Goody megastore—the only place open with analog gear and navigated to the nearest aisle. Just as the Roller Disco Killer stepped into view with the sharpened record in hand—blood dripping from its edges, Miriam found a dusty tape deck, jammed in the cursed cassette, and hit REWIND.

Instantly, the lights flickered in the store while the music screamed in reverse: "Going to take back your life. Going to set your soul free. Let the light shine on thee." With it, a swelling vortex of energy appeared, sucking the maniac through the doors of the megastore to the middle of the roller rink.

While teens collapsed inside the rink, twitching like dying VHS tapes, the Roller Disco Killer staggered into view, clutching his helmet or head; it was hard to tell where one ended and the other started as his entire body violently shook, trapped by invisible forces.

Miriam hit EJECT and then smashed the cassette with

the lava lamp.

WHOOMMP—another burst of energy shot through the mall like a death rattle.

Above the rink, the mirrors shook and cracked, finally shattering around the remaining skaters. And the Roller Disco Killer fell into pooling smoke—spools of tape unraveling from his chest like intestines blown apart by a grenade.

Then, the complex's lights failed and were replaced with the sounds of the dying.

By morning, the police blamed faulty wiring, a gas leak, and the "group panic" that had consumed the Jupiter Mall roller rink, turning it into a chaotic mess of death and destruction.

From two eyewitness statements, they only retrieved a shredded purple and gold staff jersey from the middle of the roller rink.

But Miriam and Dina knew better—they knew the truth, even though they couldn't explain everything they had witnessed. Somewhere out there, another cassette was waiting with another mix in another mall in another roller rink in another city.

Because horror never dies.

It just flips to Side B.

FEELING A LITTLE LEFT OUT ON A SATURDAY NIGHT?
DO Y'ALL WANNA BORROW MY SKATES AND JOIN THE FUN?

WHILE YOU'RE THERE, MAYBE YOU SHOULD ASK THE DEMENTED DEVIANT BEHIND THIS DEVILISH DITTY FOR A SPIN AROUND THE DANCE FLOOR

Y'ALL HAVING A GOOD TIME YET? JUST KEEP ON PRESSING THOSE BUTTONS NOW
GAME OVER
YOU WOULDN'T WANT IT TO BE GAME OVER ALREADY

THE ARCADE MURDERS

BY JOFF LECOMTE

THE ARCADE MURDERS

BY JOFF LECOMTE

Insert Coin.

Look, I know how this sounds. I know what you're thinking before I even start telling you about what happened at Neon Dreams Arcade that summer. You're thinking I'm just another kid making excuses, trying to explain away something that can't be explained. But I'm telling you the truth, and the truth is that sometimes the games play back.

My name is Danny Reeves, and I'm seventeen, or I was seventeen when all this started. Now I feel about a hundred years old, like I've lived through every horror movie ever made, except instead of watching from the safety of my couch with a bowl of popcorn, I was right there in the middle of it all, trying not to become another casualty in what the newspapers would later call "The Arcade Murders."

But they got it wrong, see. The murders didn't happen at the arcade. The murders happened because of the arcade. Because of one game in particular, tucked away in the back corner where the carpet was worn thin, and the air conditioning barely reached. It was a game called *Slaughter House Five*—and no, not after the Vonnegut book, though I bet whoever programmed it thought they were being clever with the reference.

If you're the kind of kid to have red Air Jordans and your father wears a shiny suit in his red 3-Series BMW, then you've probably got no idea what I'm talking about. The arcade is where people like me go because of people like you.

It was Marcus who found the game first. Marcus Delacroix, my best friend since third grade, the kind of kid who could beat any video game you put in front of him. His fingers moved across those buttons like he was playing piano, like it was some kind of dance he'd been born knowing. When the rest of us were still figuring out how to do a hadouken in *Street Fighter*, Marcus was already discovering secret levels and hidden characters we didn't even know existed.

He was the jock of the arcade; his name was always first on the top scores of any cool machine. To say we were underground would go some ways to understand us, if underground was a club where we could escape above-ground life and Air-Jordan-thug-jocks.

Membership was a quarter.

"Dude, you have to see this," he called to me that Tuesday in July—the one that started everything. The arcade was mostly empty—it was barely noon, and all the normal kids were either at summer jobs or sleeping off their hangovers from the night before. But Marcus and I, we were the arcade rats, the ones who showed up when they opened and stayed until they kicked us out.

I walked over to where he was standing, my flip-flops making that annoying slapping sound against my heels. The game cabinet was different from the others—older, with that wood-grain panelling that screamed early eighties. The screen was bigger, though, and the graphics... man, the graphics were something else. They looked almost photorealistic, which should have been impossible for an arcade cabinet that looked like it belonged in a museum.

"Check out the attract mode," Marcus said, feeding

another quarter into the slot.

The screen lit up with a scene that made my stomach turn. A suburban house, viewed from outside, windows glowing yellow in the darkness. Then the perspective shifted, and we were inside, moving through darkened hallways while something that sounded like breathing filled the speakers. The graphics were so detailed that I could make out family photos on the walls, could see the texture of the wallpaper.

I could feel the bass from the speaker in my chest. Instinctively, I grabbed at it when the door slammed. *Wow, wow, freaking wow.*

A figure appeared on screen—tall, wearing what looked like mechanic's coveralls and a mask that might have been welded together from scraps of metal. In his hands was something that took me a moment to recognize: a modified nail gun, the type that construction workers use, except this one had been fitted with extra barrels and what looked like a scope. The worst parts of the best horror writers, twisted into these graphics.

"Holy shit," I whispered.

"I know, right? It's like they made a game out of every slasher movie ever." Marcus was already starting to play his character—some final girl type in a pink sweater—creeping through the house, looking pretty scared of something, judging by how she was moving. "The goal is to survive until dawn. Check this out."

He moved his prom-queen character into what looked like a bedroom, and suddenly the screen was filled with screaming. Not the tinny, electronic screaming you got from most arcade games, but something that sounded so real I looked around to make sure it wasn't coming from somewhere else in the arcade. The killer burst through the door, nail gun raised, and Marcus' character died in a spray of pixels that looked disturbingly like actual blood.

Game Over flashed on the screen, but it was written in what looked like blood—dripping red letters.

Then *well done for making it past the prologue* appeared, followed by two play mode options. Option one was called *Hunter,* and two was called *Hunted.*

"Where the hell did this thing come from?" I asked.

Marcus shrugged. "Jimmy says it just showed up one morning. No delivery truck, no installation guys. Just sitting here like it had always been there."

Jimmy Castellanos was the owner of Neon Dreams, a sixty-something guy who had been running arcades since the original *Space Invaders* craze. If Jimmy didn't know where a game came from, that was weird. Really weird.

"Next you're going to tell me it isn't even plugged in and that it's powered by some interdimensional and possibly demonic source!" I said, snickering.

"You watch way too many shitty films bro, you should look into that," Marcus said back, but looking at the screen. Even though we both watched literally every horror together and even read the parts when it got boring or Freddy was holding his own against Jason.

"Want to try?" Marcus asked, already digging in his pocket for another quarter.

It's funny how today's red flags were yesterday's green ones; I mean I ought to have done my impression of Carl Lewis and gotten all eight levels of hell out of there. I should have said no. God, I should have said no and walked away and never looked back. But I was seventeen, and the game looked cool, and Marcus was my best friend, and saying no would have made me look like a coward.

So I fed my quarter into the machine and pressed *START*.

Player Two Has Entered The Game.

The first thing I noticed was how responsive the controls were; the feedback and game physics were spot-on. Most arcade games had a little lag, a tiny delay between when you pressed a button and when your character reacted. But *Slaughter House Five* responded instantly, like the machine was reading my thoughts before I even moved my fingers.

I felt like Tony Stark after he integrated with the suit using nano-tech to make it a living, faster, smarter version of all suits past. It was the ultimate upgrade, and he paid the ultimate price for it.

I was still reeling from a smackdown I got courtesy of three members of our highly prized, highly praised football team. How these knuckle-draggers keep getting away with their bullshit has baffled kids like me for decades and will probably continue to do so. So yeah, my jaw still feels like I lost a fight with Captain America, so I chose Hunter Mode, which upon reflection, may not have been my best idea.

My character was different from Marcus'—a lanky guy in a letterman jacket who looked suspiciously like me. Not just similar, but actually like me. Same dark hair, same nose that had been broken in seventh grade when Tommy Martinez decided my face would make a good testing ground for his new class ring. Even the scar on my chin from when I'd crashed my bike trying to impress Sarah Chen was there, rendered in perfect pixelated detail.

"Dude," I said, "does my guy look like..."

"Yeah," Marcus said, and his voice was weird, tight. "Mine looked like me, too. Exactly like me."

The house my character was exploring was different from the one Marcus had been in, but just as detailed. This one looked like a split-level ranch, the kind they built in the suburbs in the seventies. Fake wood panelling in the basement, shag carpet in the living room, those brass light fixtures that were supposed to look classy but just looked cheap.

It looked exactly like the house I'd grown up in. The house where my Mom still lived, where I still technically lived when I wasn't crashing at Marcus' place or sleeping in my car after we'd stayed out too late.

"This is fucked up," I muttered, but I kept playing. Of course I kept playing.

My game character appeared faster this time, bursting through the front door while I was still trying to figure out the controls. But instead of the nail gun, he was carrying a machete, the kind they sell at army surplus stores to kids whose parents think camping builds character. The kind I'd bought the summer before, when Marcus and I had convinced ourselves we were going to hike the Appalachian Trail and live off the land like some kind of modern-day mountain men.

"Ouch, shit!" I took both hands off the controller. I felt a little zap, not enough to hurt, but I was surprised nonetheless. Then the scene changed, fading out from the house to a street, then my guy was coming up on a parked truck with music blaring out, and I could make out three of the starting line-up for our school's blue ribbon football team.

"Hey, isn't that?" Marcus said, standing over me.

"Hell yeah," I said, putting more pressure on the go-forward control.

The truck was parked on a dimly lit street occupying three parking spaces, which was in itself a metaphor for the obnoxious trio inside. I moved my guy up on the driver's side rear and bashed the rear light in with the machete and slid it back into the sheath on his back.

It was enough to get the attention of all the virtual passengers inside.

"Hang on, isn't that Martinez's truck? Those 22-inch rims are the giveaway," Marcus said, pointing at the gigantic, midnight black Ford F250 that my avatar was creeping up on. I nodded a yes.

"Yo, what the fuck bro, what the fuck son!" said James Martinez, the QB1 or first choice all-American quarterback tipped for great things by our local rag after we cleaned out Washington state last month to win regionals. Then the other two gorillas got out as if in some formation. You have to understand, in real life, these oxygen thieves did everything in a trio—winning games, intimidating people trying to occupy the same sidewalk—oh, and beating kids like me. But what the hell were they doing in my game?

"Hey Martinez, it's that skinny fuck—Reeves ain't it?" Both Young and Brady said, checking in with each other. I never got their first names on account of not wanting to. I only remember the large letters on their backs.

In the real world, they were the offensive linesmen,

both in team placement and general conduct towards everyone. But this was like a dream playing out in perfect vision, the kind of dream you have to force to play out because you know dreams rarely go your way.

"Yo, yo—yeah it's little man Reeves. What's up bro, you come back for more?" the game version of Martinez said with both arms extended wide as if his words weren't enough for my character to understand. Just like their coach's board in a time-out huddle, both of his wingmen took up positions behind me as if to execute a play. Neither of the gorillas noticed the machete case on my back.

I could feel my jaw, but not because of the bruising caused by these assholes in real life—it was clenched and tightening. "Yeah, you fuck, I came back for more," I said under my breath, but loud enough for Marcus to hear.

"Is that Brady behind you man? Watch out, he's making a move." Marcus said, glued to the screen.

"This is seriously messed up," I said, but I was already reaching for another quarter. I was again surrounded by assholes, but this time I had a machete on my side, and I was pissed.

"Tell me about it," Marcus said. He was standing next to me now, watching me play instead of playing himself.

"But it's also kind of amazing, right? I mean, the graphics alone…"

I could tell Martinez was getting nervous as my guy wasn't moved in any way by the show he was putting on, not flinching or speaking. Then, as if my avatar heard Marcus, he spun his right arm, grasped the machete with enough force for a whole 360-degree turn, which halted the two massive guys behind. I felt resistance from the controller feedback on my hands, but didn't know why as it happened so fast.

It wasn't until my guy turned back again that I saw Brady and Young on the ground, face down, trying to roll over. The shock on their faces was replaced by the agonizing realization that both of their arms were no longer attached to their bodies.

Marcus took one half step back. "Dude, what the…"

My guy stomped their heads before they could let out screams to pierce the quiet of the street. I swear I felt the feedback in the floor as if the game had all sensory feedback installed. This was happening too fast, faster than my brain could process.

Then my guy turned to Martinez. It wasn't so much fear than sheer dread on his face, I could make out above the odd shaking his whole body was doing.

"Dude, dude, be cool now, be cool, please—I never meant..." Martinez's blubbering was interrupted.

My avatar raised his machete up to point straight at the trembling quarterback and for the first time we heard my game character speak, "Go long, asshole."

With that, Martinez instinctively turned and did his own Carl Lewis impression down the street as my guy swung the machete back, like a Red Sox pitcher, and launched the machete in the direction of Martinez. The machete spun through the air and struck him between his shoulder blades with an audible crunch and the feedback in the console controller seemed to vibrate at the moment the blade went in. It was as though all the lights in Martinez went out mid-sprint—like a marble statue falling from a truck at high speed. He fell forward and hit the ground, but was already dead.

"Oh my god! Oh, my fucking god!" I stumbled around to the back of the machine, unable to make the washroom to throw up. Marcus was dry heaving too. The screen read *3-0* in dripping red text and then shut down. Marcus and I just stood frozen for what felt like hours with our mouths open to try to understand what had just happened.

"Okay, okay what was that, man? Did your wildest dreams just play out in 3D, or did the game just read your mind?" Marcus said, only just finding the words now.

"Bro, I got no idea, but I'm fairly sure I know what it's like to cut hands off people now. The god damn feedback is wild. It felt surreal," I said.

"It looked pretty fucking real to me," Marcus said.

He was right. Whatever corporation had made this game, they were years ahead of anything else on the market. The detail was incredible, the sound design was perfect, and the graphics... Christ, the graphics were like nothing I'd ever seen. The game seemed to have intelligence, to actually hunt, to learn your patterns and adapt to your strategy, which in this case was my pissed-off mood. Most arcade games, you could figure out the patterns after a few plays, learn to exploit the programming.

But *Slaughter House Five* felt different. It felt like you were playing against something that was actually thinking—learning.

"Let me try again," Marcus said. I'd been to the actual washroom and cleaned up behind the machine. I was surprised he wanted to go back in after what just happened.

Marcus selected the Hunted option. This was generally

the harder route in gaming terms as you were mostly outgunned at every turn, and you needed a higher skill level, as your level of gameplay was what got you through.

This time, his character appeared in what looked like his own house—the big colonial where he lived with his mom and stepdad, complete with the stupid lawn gnomes his stepdad collected. But something was different. The house felt wrong somehow, like someone had taken all the familiar details and twisted them just slightly out of tune.

His character made it almost to the end of the level, hiding in the basement while the killer stalked through the rooms above. We could hear the footsteps through the speakers, slow and deliberate, accompanied by that breathing sound that seemed to come from everywhere at once.

Then the lights went out—in the game and in the arcade.

"What the hell?" Jimmy's voice came from behind the counter, followed by the sound of him fumbling around for a flashlight. The emergency lighting kicked in a few seconds later, casting everything in that sickly yellow glow that makes everyone look like they're dying of jaundice. Or long term exposure to a short-term solution—arcade gaming.

"Probably just a blown fuse," Jimmy called out. "Give me a minute, I'll get you up and running."

But the game was still running. Even with the power out, *Slaughter House Five* was still humming along, its screen the only bright spot in the darkened arcade. Marcus' character was still hiding in that basement, and we could still hear those footsteps moving around upstairs.

I remember asking Marcus the obvious question, like a herd of God damn elephants in the dim-lit arcade room— "how is this still running, maybe interdimensional forces…" but Marcus cut me off with a motion of his hand. I didn't mind because my question was rhetorical.

On screen, his character was moving toward the basement stairs. Not because Marcus was controlling him— Marcus' hands weren't even on the controls. The character was moving on his own, climbing those stairs like he was being drawn by something we couldn't see.

The killer was waiting at the top.

Marcus' character died just as the lights came back on, and the scream that came from the speakers was loud enough to make everyone in the arcade turn and look. But it wasn't just coming from the speakers. For just a second, just a split second, it sounded like it was coming from everywhere at once.

"You kids okay over there?" Jimmy called.

"Fine," I called back, but I wasn't fine. Neither was Marcus. We were both staring at the screen, where the *Game Over* message was flashing in those dripping red letters. We were kind of a big deal in Neon Dreams, and the other kids just looked from a distance, mostly at Marcus' accomplishments on the various game cabinets.

"I think we should go," Marcus said quietly in a way I'd never seen him use before, especially at Neon Dreams, where he ruled supreme. If I'm honest, I crushed on Marcus' persona—I mean, he only played the coolest games and in the coolest ways.

I nodded, but I couldn't take my eyes off the screen. Because just before the attract mode started up again, just for a frame or two, I could have sworn I saw something else. Someone standing in the background of that suburban house, watching from a window.

It was cinematic, so completely and utterly surreal that either Tobe Hooper or John Carpenter would have been proud. Then I checked myself, which under the circumstances wasn't easy, because what I saw or thought I saw was a figure that looked an awful lot like the killer from the game.

High Score.

We didn't talk about the game for the rest of the day. We hung out at the mall, caught a movie, did all the normal summer stuff that teenagers do when they're trying to pretend everything is normal. But I could tell Marcus was thinking about it, the same way I was thinking about it. It was like having a song stuck in your head, except instead of a melody, it was the image of that killer stalking through my virtual house, hunting a pixel version of myself.

That night, I had the dream for the first time.

I was in my house—my real house, not the game version—but everything was wrong. The furniture was in the right places, the family photos were on the right walls, but the colors were all slightly off, like someone had adjusted the contrast on a TV. And there was a sound, a low humming that seemed to come from the walls themselves.

I was trying to get to my bedroom, but the hallway

kept stretching out in front of me, getting longer with each step. Behind me, I could hear footsteps, slow and deliberate, accompanied by that breathing sound from the game. I didn't want to turn around, didn't want to see what was following me, but in dreams you don't always get a choice.

The killer was there, or I was there. It was hard to say under the circumstances if I was the hunter or hunted. But the dreamscape was exactly like in the game. Coveralls, a welded mask, and in his hands... in his hands was a weapon I'd never seen before. It looked like someone had taken a circular saw and made it get a shotgun pregnant, creating something that belonged in a horror movie from hell.

I woke up screaming.

My mom was at my door in seconds, asking if I was okay, if I'd had a nightmare. I told her I was fine, just a bad dream, nothing to worry about. But I couldn't get back to sleep. Every time I closed my eyes, I could see that killer standing in my hallway, could hear that breathing sound echoing in my ears.

The next morning, Marcus called me at eight AM, which was weird because Marcus never got up before noon during the summer.

"Did you dream about it?" he asked without preamble.

"Yeah," I said. "You too?"

"All night. Different weapons each time, but always the same house. Always the same…" He trailed off. "No wait," He yelled, but not out of anger, out of excitement that he remembered something urgent. "Dude, I totally saw Martinez's letterman jacket over a coffin in a room I went into. The room was packed with people in black and crying." He fell quiet.

"Say what?" I asked.

"Same feeling. Like he was really there, you know? Like it wasn't just a dream." Marcus said.

"Marcus, what aren't you telling me?" I knew exactly what he meant, but I didn't want to admit it. Because admitting it would mean acknowledging that something was seriously wrong, and I wasn't ready for that. Not yet.

"We should go back," Marcus said. "I mean, we should set our intentions before playing."

"Say what now, bro?"

"Stay with me, dude. It's a thing my mom does when she does her witchy stuff. You gotta set your intentions." Marcus paused. "Look, when you played hunter mode yesterday, you said it yourself, you were pissed before you demolished the better part of the football team, right?" He asked.

"Yep, I'm with you so far."

"Okay, well, before going to sleep, I wrote in my diary about the machete stuff and if the thing was real. Now you know, yeah I keep a diary man—no jokes, dude, okay" Marcus asked.

"So that's something else we got in common, bro, no jokes here." There was no time to do some extra bonding over an intimate detail like that; we had more pressing matters. We were, after all, sensitive arcade types.

"But seriously, Marcus? To the arcade? Are you insane? Besides, how do we set our intentions?" I asked.

"It's fairly easy, and I think the best way to get the best out the game, or at least not be freaking weirded out by it. You were angry yesterday and chopped those guys to pieces and I was worried about you before going to sleep and I stumbled into one of their funerals. Think about it, Danny. That game, it's not normal. The graphics, the AI, the way it knew what our houses looked like... And now we're both having dreams about it? That's not a coincidence."

"So what are you saying? That it's haunted? That we're cursed or something?"

"I'm saying we need to figure out what the hell is going

on. And the only way to do that is to play it again."

I wanted to say no. Every rational part of my brain was screaming at me to stay away from Neon Dreams, to never go near that game again. But you do recall the part about me being a 17-year-old boy, right? If dumb shit's going to get done, I'm going to do it.

Marcus was right about one thing—what had happened wasn't normal. And if we didn't figure out what was going on, who knew what might happen next?

"Fine," I said. "But if I die in some horrible way, I'm haunting your ass for eternity."

"Deal," Marcus said, and I could hear the relief in his voice. "Meet me there at noon."

The arcade was busier when we got there, filled with the usual crowd of summer kids and a few adults who should have been at work but were apparently more interested in perfecting their Galaga skills. Jimmy was behind the counter, reading a magazine and looking like he'd rather be anywhere else.

Slaughter House Five was in the back corner where we'd left it, but there was already someone playing. A girl, maybe our age, with short black hair and a Misfits t-shirt. She was good—better than either Marcus or I had been. Her character, which looked disturbingly like her, was actually managing to evade the killer, hiding in closets and slipping past him when he wasn't looking.

"Holy shit," Marcus whispered. "She's actually surviving in Hunted Mode."

We watched, mesmerized, as the girl's character made it further into the game than either of us had managed. The house she was navigating looked like it might be hers—I could see family photos on the walls, familiar furniture arrangements. But something was wrong with the killer's behaviour. Instead of hunting efficiently like he had when we played, he seemed confused, stumbling around like he couldn't quite lock onto his target.

The girl's character made it to what looked like a garage, where there was a car waiting. She climbed in, started the engine, and crashed through the garage door into the night. The screen flashed *LEVEL COMPLETE* in those same bloody letters, but this time they looked almost... disappointed.

"Whoa," the girl said, stepping back from the machine. "That was intense."

"You beat it," Marcus said, approaching her. "You actually beat the first level."

She turned to look at us, and I got my first good look at her face. She was pretty in that punk rock way, with dark eyes and pale skin and a silver ring through her lower lip. But there was something else, something that made me take a step back.

She looked scared. Not the good kind of scared you get from a horror movie or a roller coaster, but genuinely, deeply terrified.

"Yeah," she said. "But I don't think I should have."

"What do you mean?" I asked.

She glanced around the arcade, then moved closer to us, lowering her voice. "I had the dreams last night. Same as you two, I'm betting. The killer, hunting through my house, using weapons that don't exist. He went into my folks' room, but they aren't here this week, and I saw him look in my mother's drawer where a red book was. I literally nearly puked this morning when I found it too. There's no way on earth I could have dreamt that."

"How did you know we..." Marcus started.

"Because you both look like you haven't slept in a week, and you're standing here staring at this game like it killed your dog." She held out her hand. "I'm Zoë, by the way. Zoë Chavez."

"Danny," I said, shaking her hand. "This is Marcus."

"So what do you think?" Marcus asked her. "About the game, I mean. What's your theory?"

Zoë glanced at the *Slaughter House Five* cabinet, which had returned to its attract mode. The killer was stalking through another house now, this one unfamiliar to any of us. "I think," she said slowly, "that we're dealing with something that isn't just a game. Something that's using the game as a... I don't know. A doorway, maybe?"

"A doorway to what?" I asked, though I was pretty sure I didn't want to hear the answer.

"To us," she said. "To our world. And I think every time someone plays it, every time someone feeds it quarters and attention, it gets a little bit stronger."

As if responding to her words, the attract mode changed. Instead of showing the killer hunting through that unfamiliar house, it was now showing three houses. Mine, Marcus', and what I assumed was Zoë's—a small ranch with a distinctive red front door.

The killer was moving between them, checking each one like he was planning something.

"Okay," I said, my voice coming out higher than I'd intended. "That's officially creepy enough for me. We should get out of here."

But even as I said it, I knew we wouldn't. So I relied on Marcus' idea about setting intentions. I wasn't angry or upset about anything beyond a generalized anxiety about playing this out of this world game.

We lasted for fifteen minutes each as we wrote our intentions down on a piece of paper each and put them into Zoë's Steelers Hoodie pocket. We either got chopped up or did the chopping.

Our planned "whole day" event fell apart after the last of us died, and the other two opened the intention of the level. Marcus wrote happy for his intention as his level ended in the corners of his mouth being cut open with a letter opener to each ear—like the Joker from *Batman*. Mine was absent-minded as my brain stem was pulled out from my newly opened skull and hung on the coat rack.

Zoë raged at us to not open her paper after the murderous avatar ate her fingers and thumbs from a sandwich he made after murdering her. We'd reached the end of our respective tethers. My nerves were shredded, just like Zoë and Marcus.

We lasted for a fraction of the time we planned on because the game had us now, had hooked us with its impossible graphics and its invasive knowledge and its promise of a mystery we couldn't quite solve. It had us, and it wasn't going to let us go.

Not until it was finished with us.

Game Over.

The dreams got worse.

Over the next three nights, they came every time I closed my eyes. The killer was getting closer, more persistent. His weapons were getting more elaborate— things that looked like they'd been designed by someone with intimate knowledge of human anatomy and a deep appreciation for causing maximum pain. Chainsaw-flamethrower hybrids. Nail guns that shot railroad spikes. Something that looked like an industrial blender crossed with a medieval mace.

But the worst part wasn't the weapons. The worst part was that the killer was learning. Each night, he remembered more about my house, found hiding spots I'd used in previous dreams, cut off escape routes before I could even think to use them. It was like playing a video game against an opponent who had access to all your previous attempts, who could study your patterns and adapt accordingly.

There was no way to outsmart him, no canny workaround that had us coming out on top.

Marcus and Zoë were having the same experiences. We met at the arcade every day, drawn back to *Slaughter House Five* like addicts to their drug of choice. We told ourselves we were trying to figure out what was happening, that we were gathering information. But really, we were just feeding the thing, giving it more data to work with.

"This is getting out of hand," Zoë said on Friday afternoon. We were sitting in a booth at the diner across from the arcade, picking at fries and trying to pretend we hadn't just spent three hours pumping quarters into a game that was slowly driving us insane.

"Tell me about it," Marcus said. He looked terrible— dark circles under his eyes, hands shaking slightly from too much caffeine and not enough sleep. "Sarah Chen called me last night, crying. She said the killer in her dream knew about her diary, about things she'd never told anyone."

I thought about my own dreams, about how the killer

seemed to know which floorboards creaked, which windows stuck, which door had the lock that didn't quite catch. He knew because the game knew, and the game knew because we'd told it. Every time we played, every time we navigated our characters through those virtual houses, we were giving it a blueprint of our lives.

"We have to stop," I said. "All of us. We have to stop playing, and we have to convince everyone else to stop too."

"You think that'll work?" Zoë asked.

"I don't know. But it's worth a try."

But it wasn't going to be that simple. Because that night, while I was lying in bed trying to convince myself that I didn't need to go back to the arcade, that I could resist the pull of *Slaughter House Five*, something happened that changed everything.

The killer didn't wait for me to fall asleep.

I was lying there, staring at the ceiling and listening to the sounds of my house settling around me, when I heard it. Footsteps on the front porch, slow and deliberate. The sound of the doorknob turning.

My mom was at her book club. I was alone in the house.

I held my breath, telling myself it was just my

imagination, just my brain playing tricks on me after days of horror game-induced nightmares. But then I heard the front door close, heard those same footsteps moving across the hardwood floor of our entryway.

I grabbed my phone and called Marcus.

"Danny?" His voice was groggy, confused. "What time is it?"

"He's in my house," I whispered. "The killer from the game. He's actually in my house."

"What? Danny, you're dreaming. You have to be…"

"I'm not dreaming!" I hissed. "I'm awake, I'm completely awake, and there's someone downstairs moving around."

The footsteps had stopped. The house was quiet again, but it was the wrong kind of quiet, the kind that makes your skin crawl because you know something is watching you.

"Okay," Marcus said, and I could hear him sitting up, becoming alert. "Okay, I'm coming over. Can you get out? Can you get to your car?"

I thought about it. My bedroom was on the second floor, but there was a tree outside my window, the same one I'd climbed down a hundred times when I was sneaking out. If I could get to the window without making noise…

"Maybe," I said. "I'm going to try."

I ended the call and slipped out of bed, moving as quietly as I could toward my bedroom door. I pressed my ear against it, listening for any sound from downstairs. Nothing. But that didn't mean anything. In the game, the killer was patient. He would wait.

I felt like every single pretty girl who opened the door to the house with a dirty roof, or opened a book that looked like it was written by Dracula. I turned the doorknob slowly, wincing at the tiny click it made. The hallway was dark, lit only by the streetlight coming through the window at the far end. I could see the stairs leading down to the first floor, could see the shadows at the bottom that might be hiding anything.

That's when I heard the breathing, the God-awful, bass-filled breathing.

It was coming from downstairs, that same rhythmic sound from the game. But this wasn't coming through speakers. This was real, echoing off the walls of my actual house.

I backed away from the door, my heart hammering so hard I was sure it was loud enough to give away my position. This couldn't be happening. This was impossible.

But I could hear him moving again, those slow, deliberate footsteps. And they were coming up the stairs.

I ran to my window, fumbling with the latch. My hands were shaking so badly I could barely grip it, but finally it came free. I pushed the window open and looked down at the tree, at the branches I'd used as a ladder so many times before.

The footsteps had reached the top of the stairs.

I swung my leg over the windowsill just as my bedroom door opened. I didn't look back–I couldn't. If I looked back and saw him standing there, saw that welded mask and those coveralls and whatever weapon he'd chosen for tonight, I knew I would freeze. I would fall out of the tree and break my neck, and that would be the end of it.

Instead, I focused on climbing down, branch by branch, trying not to think about the sound of my bedroom window sliding shut behind me.

Marcus was waiting for me in his car when I reached the street, engine running, passenger door open.

"Go," I said as I threw myself into the seat. "Just go."

"What happened? Did you see him?"

"I heard him. In my house, breathing, moving around. Marcus, this isn't a game anymore. It's real."

Marcus pulled out his phone as he drove, dialling with one hand while steering with the other.

"Zoë? Yeah, I know it's late. Listen, we have a problem. A big problem."

Final Boss Fight.

We met at the twenty-four-hour diner on the edge of town, the one that truckers used and that always smelled like bacon grease and desperation. It was three in the morning, and we were the only customers except for a guy in a baseball cap who was methodically working his way through a stack of pancakes and what looked like his third pot of coffee.

"So let me get this straight," Zoë said after I'd told her what happened. "You think the killer from the game actually showed up at your house. Like, physically manifested."

"I know how it sounds," I said. "But I heard him. I was awake, I'm sure of it."

"Okay, let's say you're right," Marcus said. "Let's say this thing is somehow able to cross over from the game into the real world. What do we do about it?"

Zoë was quiet for a long time, stirring her coffee and thinking. Finally, she looked up at us. "We have to destroy it," she said. "The game, I mean. We have to find a way to destroy the cabinet."

"Just smash it up?" I asked.

"I don't think it'll be that easy. This thing, whatever it is, it's not just software. It's something else, something that's using the game as an anchor to our world. If we're going to get rid of it, we have to do it right."

"Meaning what?"

"Meaning we have to beat it first. We have to play the game through to the end, all the way to whatever final boss or conclusion it has. And then, when it's vulnerable, when it's put everything it has into that final confrontation, we destroy the cabinet."

It was a crazy plan. It was the kind of plan that only made sense at three in the morning in a diner that smelled like other people's bad decisions. But it was the only plan we had.

"There's just one problem," Marcus said. "None of

us have been able to get past the first level. How are we supposed to beat something we can't even survive?"

"Together," Zoë said. "The game has single-player and two-player modes, right? Maybe even three-player. We play together, watch each other's backs, pool our knowledge."

"And if that doesn't work?"

She shrugged. "Then we're probably screwed. But at least we'll go out fighting."

We spent the rest of the night planning, going over everything we knew about the game, trying to figure out patterns and weaknesses. By the time the sun came up, we had something that almost resembled a strategy.

The arcade didn't open until ten, but Jimmy let us in early when we told him we were thinking about organizing a tournament. He seemed excited about the idea, started talking about how it might bring in more customers, maybe get some attention from the local newspaper.

If only he knew.

Slaughter House Five was waiting for us in the back corner, its attract mode cycling through images of houses we recognized. Mine, Marcus', Zoë's, and at least a dozen others belonging to kids who'd played the game over the past week. The killer moved between them like he was making rounds, checking on his territory.

"You sure about this?" I asked as Zoë fed the first quarter into the machine.

"No," she said. "But I'm tired of being afraid to sleep in my own house."

The game began differently this time. Instead of starting us in our individual houses, we were all together in what looked like the arcade itself. Our three characters–pixel-perfect versions of ourselves–were standing in front of the *Slaughter House Five* cabinet.

"Meta," Marcus muttered.

The killer appeared at the front entrance of the virtual arcade, that same welded mask glinting in the fluorescent lighting. But he wasn't carrying any of the weapons we'd seen before. Instead, he had what looked like a remote control, covered in buttons and switches.

He pressed one of the buttons, and every other game in the virtual arcade came to life. Pac-Man ghosts poured out of their cabinet, followed by Space Invaders, Galaga ships, and things from games I didn't recognize. They filled the virtual arcade, an army of 8-bit nightmares under the killer's control.

"Well," Zoë said, her fingers dancing across the

controls, "this is new."

We fought our way through waves of video game enemies, our characters working together in ways that felt natural despite the fact that we'd never played cooperatively before. Marcus was good with strategy, calling out patterns and weak points. Zoë was aggressive, taking risks that paid off more often than they should have. And I... I was just trying not to die.

But we were making progress. Slowly, painfully, we fought our way through the virtual arcade toward the killer. With each enemy we destroyed, with each obstacle we overcame, I could feel something changing. The game was responding to us, adapting, but it was also becoming more desperate, more erratic.

We reached the killer just as our virtual selves reached the Slaughter House Five cabinet. The final boss battle began, and it was unlike anything I'd ever experienced in a video game. The killer didn't just attack us–he attacked the game itself, causing glitches and distortions that made the screen flicker and warp.

"He's trying to crash the system," Zoë said. "He knows we're close to beating him." She said, turning to Marcus and I, which was a huge mistake as the killer launched a dagger right at her. I grabbed Zoë just in the nick of time for her to avoid being skewered, but not quick enough for me to avoid it. The sideways step I made pulling Zoë out of harm's way left my back open to the flying dagger.

It didn't hurt at first due to the adrenaline and sharpness of the blade. I didn't even notice it at first.

"Fuck me, bro, your back, your back." Marcus yelled. "Deep breath, bro, keep on pressing, we're almost there," Marcus yelled.

I thought it was sweat running down my back, and I was too amped to stop playing. The stakes were too high for us all.

But we kept fighting, kept pushing forward even as the game world around us began to fall apart. And finally, after what felt like hours but was probably only minutes, we managed to corner the killer in front of his own cabinet.

Marcus' character used a move I'd seen Marcus perform time after time, his signature move. It was a feint down to the left and like a boxer stalking his prey, distracting his prey while he brought his right hand over the top, making a *thump* sound as his dagger drove into the killer's left temple. The blade came out of the right side just a little due to the weight Marcus had put on his thrust. The perfectly timed attack sent the killer stumbling backward into the virtual *Slaughter House Five* machine. There was a flash of light, a sound like breaking glass, and then...

Silence.

The screen went black. The cabinet stopped humming. And for the first time since we'd started playing, the arcade felt normal again.

"Is it over?" I asked.

"I think so," Zoë said. But she was already reaching for a crowbar that Jimmy kept behind the counter, the one he used for opening crates. "But let's make sure."

"No wait, look," I said as the screen decals bubbled up, melting. "Look—it's catching fire," I said as the screen went blank, off-grey to be replaced by a growing fire. Jimmy came rushing over with a fire extinguisher.

"Stand clear you kids, the sprinklers don't reach all the way down here. This'll take a minute." Jimmy said emptying the extinguisher's contents onto the very melted arcade cabinet. We hung around to watch, to make sure it was over. Jimmy stood back after the fire was out while we smashed the rest of the melted unit down to splinters and glass. "Sheesh, you guys really do not like that game, huh?" He said as we disposed of the fragments into the dumpster out back.

"Good riddance," he said, watching as we threw the last of the circuit boards into the trash. "Thing was giving me the creeps anyway. Showed up one morning with no delivery receipt, no installation instructions. Should have known it was trouble."

The adrenaline crash hit me hard on the walk to Marcus' car. That's when the pain in my back really started, and I realized the wetness I'd felt wasn't sweat at all. By the time we got to the hospital, my shirt was soaked through with blood.

However, that night, for the first time in a week, I slept without dreaming. No killers, no weapons, no breathing sounds in the darkness. Just peaceful, empty sleep.

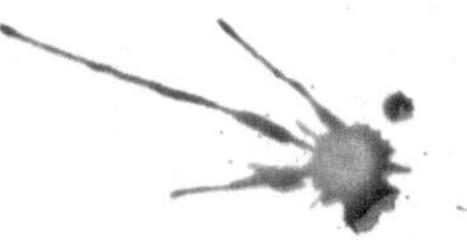

New Game.

I had 135 stitches in my back and had to answer some very uncomfortable questions from the doctor at the hospital. It didn't hurt that night, but did every day for the next six weeks. That was three months ago. Marcus, Zoë, and I are still friends, though we don't talk about what happened at the arcade very often. It's the kind of experience that bonds you together but also makes normal conversation feel weird. How do you go back to complaining about homework and weekend plans when you've literally fought a digital demon for your life?

The dreams stopped for everyone who'd played the game. The nightmares, the break-ins, the feeling of being watched–all of it just stopped when we destroyed that cabinet. Life went back to normal, or as normal as it gets when you know that sometimes, the monsters in video games aren't just pixels and code.

I still go to arcades sometimes. Marcus does too, though he's pickier about which games he'll play. Zoë started a blog about weird gaming experiences, and it's gotten pretty popular with the horror gaming community. She never writes about *Slaughter House Five* specifically, but she drops hints sometimes, warnings about games that seem too advanced for their hardware, too personal in their content.

Jimmy bought new games for the arcade, safe ones like *Pac-Man, Street Fighter,* and *Galaga.* Normal games that don't know where you live or what you're afraid of. The corner where *Slaughter House Five* used to stand is empty now, just a bare patch of carpet that's slightly cleaner than the rest.

But sometimes, late at night when I'm lying in bed, I wonder about the game. I wonder if destroying the cabinet really destroyed whatever was inside it, or if we just freed it, sent it back to wherever it came from to wait for another opportunity. I wonder if somewhere out there, in some other arcade in some other town, a new cabinet is appearing overnight with no delivery receipt and no installation instructions.

I wonder if some other group of kids is finding it, feeding it quarters, giving it access to their homes and their fears and their dreams.

And I wonder if they'll be smart enough to stop playing before it's too late. But hey, that's just how the game goes. And the game never really stops.

It just waits for the next player.

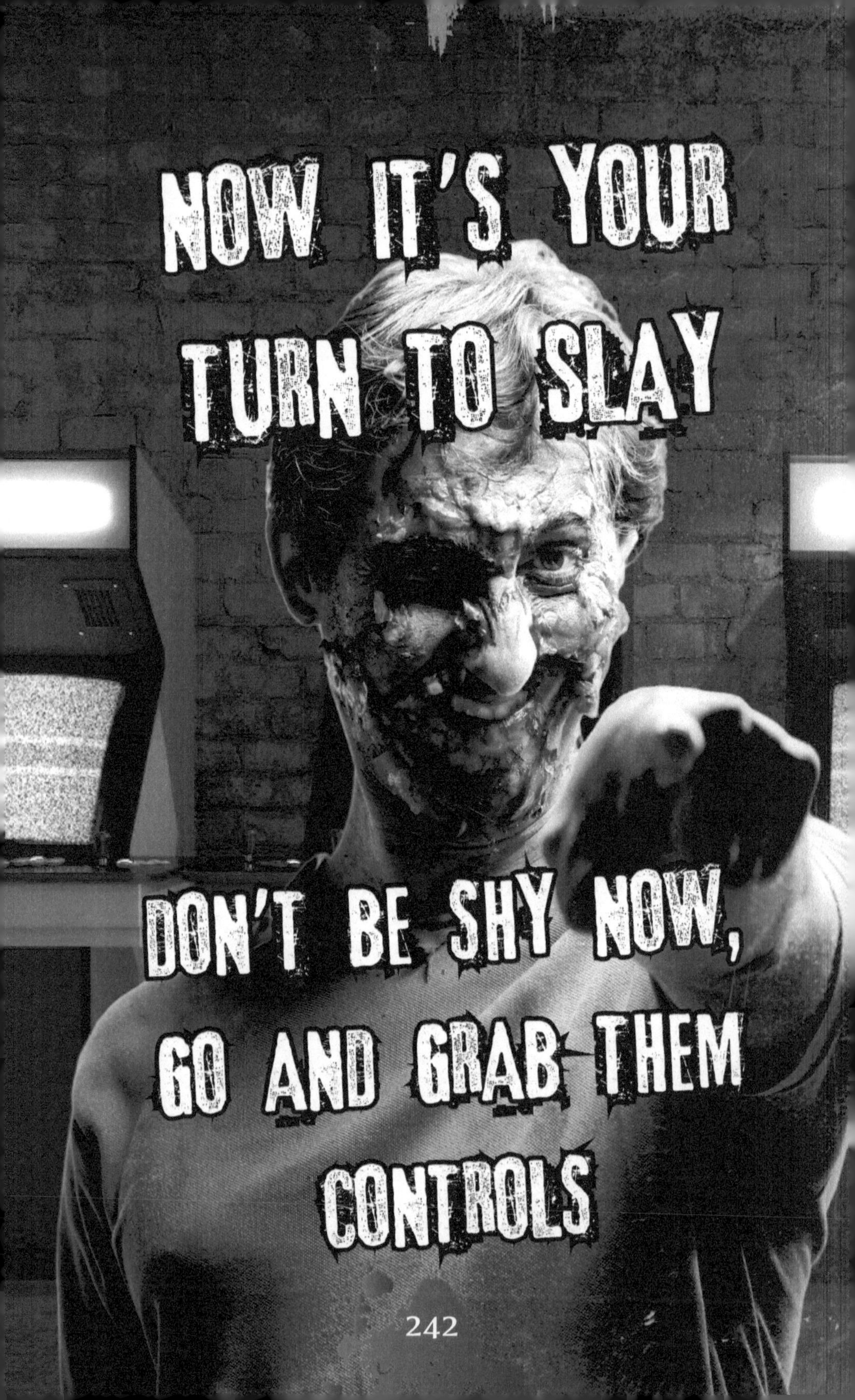

NOW IT'S YOUR
TURN TO SLAY
DON'T BE SHY NOW,
GO AND GRAB THEM
CONTROLS

WOULD YOU LIKE TO
PLUG INTO THE NEFARIOUS
NARRATOR TO BLAME FOR
THIS NEON NIGHTMARE?

THERE'S NOTHING QUITE LIKE
KILLING TIME AROUND A
GOOD OLD CAMP FIRE

CAMP
BLOOD
BY STEPHEN HERCZEG

CAMP BLOOD

BY STEPHEN HERCZEG

"What character are you playing?" Susie asked, stuffing another chip into her mouth and munching away.

Julie looked up from the letter in her hand. Dripping red lettering announced the name of their intended destination for the weekend.

Camp Blood.

She read again, a frown growing on her face, before answering. "I think I'm just a random camper. The instructions have me hovering around the main building and then traipsing all over the place."

"It doesn't say you get killed?" Susie's face lit up. "You're the final girl. Cool."

"What do you mean?"

"It's like one of those cheesy horror movies. Everyone

gets killed, but there's always that one girl who survives and kills the killer or runs away at the end."

"Yeah," said Peter, his face obscured behind Susie's blonde head. "You're the lucky one who gets to live. Though you'll probably get killed off in the sequel." He reached around Susie with one muscle-bound arm and grabbed his half-finished burger.

"Oh, yeah," said Stephen from across the table. "Remember *Friday the 13th*? The chick that survived the first movie is Jason's first victim in part two. Ice pick to the head." He stepped behind Angela, throwing an arm around her neck and mimicking the death scene while making squealing noises.

Angela screamed in horror, standing up as she pushed him away. "Idiot," she said before turning and running off behind the café.

"Well, I think someone just stuffed up their chances for the weekend," said Peter, laughing at the now remorseful Stephen.

"Damn. It was just a bit of fun."

"Dude, we warned you that she was a little fragile. Won't you ever learn?" said Mark, sitting with his arm around Julie and reading along with her.

Staring after her friend, Julie added, "God, I hope she doesn't want to go home. Nice work, bozo." She dropped the letter on the table and chased after Angela.

Shrugging, Stephen dropped back onto his seat and grabbed a handful of fries. "Thought it was funny, that's all. If that's how she's gonna be all weekend, I'll stick to myself."

"That won't be a stretch," laughed Peter.

"Fuck off!"

The sudden appearance of a craggy old face next to Stephen made them all jump. Stephen bumped the table, knocking over several cans of soda.

"Jesus," cried Susie, jumping off Peter's lap and staring at the dribbling liquid, then at the old man.

A toothless mouth grinned back at them. "You're all doomed. Mogo Mack's gonna get ya." The man was dressed in dark clothes, covered in a layer of dust, and made from homespun fabric that looked almost as old as he was.

Peter rose, a huge fist balling, ready to finish off the interloper. "What the hell do you think you're doing, man?" He stepped forward. The old man only grinned wider and hopped from foot to foot.

"Mack's gonna get ya. He's back and ready to kill. I tells ya."

As Peter stepped forward, his lips curling up into a sneer, a voice yelled from behind him.

"Get out of here, Carl, go on, shoo. Leave these folks alone." The matronly-looking waitress stepped between Peter and the old man. "If you come around here again with those crazy tales, then I'll have the cops onto you."

The dusty interloper shuffled off with a final, "You're all in danger," before mounting his bicycle and riding unsteadily off down the road.

"Damn fool," said the waitress. Turning to the group of young customers, she said, "I'm so sorry, can I replace those drinks and get you anything else? All on the house."

Peter and Mark were quick to add new orders for food on top of their drinks.

As Julie stepped around the corner of the café, she found Angela standing outside a phone booth searching through her purse.

"Hey," she said, sidling up to her friend, and trying to make light of the stupidity that Angela had run away from.

"Hey," was the answer.

"What you doing?"

"Trying to find some coins so I can ring and find out if there are any buses due through here today. I'll grab one and head home."

"Aw, no. Don't leave. Stephen's just an idiot. We'll make sure he doesn't try anything again."

"No. It's not just that. I'm not up to stuff like this yet. I just want to be on my own. Find some peace and quiet."

Julie stepped in front of Angela and placed a comforting hand on her shoulder. "Hey, I know how things are. It's been almost a year. I don't know how I'd feel about losing my boyfriend like that, but I know I'd want to rejoin the living. Maybe go out and have some stupid fun. If only to forget about things for a while."

Angela looked into her friend's eyes. "But this? This is too stupid for words."

"Yeah. Yeah, it is. But dumb, stupid shit like this can sometimes be fun." Julie shrugged. "Hey, who wouldn't want to play act in a ridiculous 80's horror movie, with a dopey masked killer chasing after them?"

Shaking her head, Angela pursed her lips and said, "You do know that the stupid movie was based on a real killer. He lived near here about fifteen years ago."

A look of shock drew across Julie's face. "Really? But it's just a movie. I kept telling myself that." Angela almost bought it before Julie broke out into a wide smile. "He's long dead. If not, then the only stalking he'd be doing is with a Zimmer frame."

"I suppose."

"Besides, it's all you can eat and drink tonight." Julie grabbed Angela's hand and started to pull her back to the others. "So, if you don't want to do the murder mystery, you can get stupidly drunk, and who knows, there might be other guys there."

"Seriously, you are a nutcase."

"Look, you better start turning over a profit on this place pretty darn quickly, or we'll be in here to close this flea-bitten excuse of a money sink before you can say Jack Robinson," the suited man stood with his hands on his hips and stared down at the immaculately dressed man sitting behind the large, dark wooden desk.

Phillip Heyward stared up at his financier and smacked his lips. "Now, Mr Johnstone, please calm down. This is only the fourth weekend since we opened. You've got to expect a slightly slow uptake at first. We will start showing a profit once we get settled and make a name for ourselves."

"You've already got a name for yourselves. You said that you could sponge off the infamy of this Mogo Mack movie and people would just roll on in."

"And that's correct. Mack originally stalked around this area. The film was shot near here. People still remember the legend of Mogo Mack, and they remember the movie, even if it was over five years ago. We've even petitioned the TV stations to play it, and they have. Bookings have started to roll in. We are fully booked tonight, and next week we already have full bookings for both Friday and Saturday nights."

"That's great, but that still leaves the rest of the week with this place doing nothing."

"Just consider us like a nightclub. The real nights are Friday and Saturday; the rest of the week they make a complete loss, and most don't stay open."

Johnstone mulled this over for a moment before pointing at the seated man and adding, "I'll accept that for now, but if this thing hasn't shown an upturn in the next month, then we're closing you down."

"Don't worry. I've got a couple of ideas that will give this place a real name for itself."

Johnstone replied with an angry harrumph. "We'll see." He turned and headed for the door.

"Have a pleasant trip back," said Heyward, waving and hiding his disdain in case the man overseeing the camp's financials looked back. When the door finally closed, he dropped his well-groomed head into his hands and mumbled to himself. "Christ, I hope we get some more bookings soon."

The constant rumble of tyres on the rutted, baked-mud road drowned out the static blaring from the radio as Johnstone drove. He leaned forward over the steering wheel and stared at the seemingly endless dirt track before moving back and slamming the wheel.

"Dammit, why'd I have to come to this fucking place? Christ. Next time they want me to come down here, I'll tell them to stick it up their ass."

Taking a deep breath in an attempt to quell his anger, he leaned back into the squeaky vinyl seat and drove on with one wrist balanced on the top of the wheel, while the other fiddled with the radio.

"Godforsaken country. No fucking radio. No fucking hope."

A plume of dust rose ahead. Two cars appeared around a bend in the road. Johnstone jumped, grabbed the wheel, and veered across to the left to allow the others to pass by. His car was showered with dirt and dust as the other vehicles screamed past.

"Shit."

A loud bang followed, and the car swerved as the tyres lost traction. Johnstone let out a stream of obscenities aimed at the other drivers, Heyward, God, and anyone else that came to mind as he fought for control. Finally, he brought the car to a standstill and burst out, grabbing at his chest to calm his heart down.

"Fuck, fuck, fuck, fuck..."

As he dragged air back into his lungs and coughed and spluttered on the dry, lingering dust, Johnstone caught sight of the flat tyre on the rear of his car. His fear turned to anger.

"Goddamn it. I'll never get out of here."

He turned and looked at the boot of the car with a strained sneer on his face. There was no way he was going to flag down any help. He had to remember how to change a wheel and then limp into the nearest town to get the flat fixed. His only hope now was that the spare had air in it.

After almost half an hour, Johnstone had the car up on a jack, the new tyre on and had almost replaced the wheel nuts. Tools littered the ground near the open boot. He'd tossed his suit jacket onto the lip. The heat was playing havoc with him; his underarms were pools of sweat, and the stench of his own body odour was making him gag. Lowering the car, he tightened each nut in turn before removing the jack and breathing a sigh of relief that he could finally be on his way.

The crunch of gravel echoed out from behind him. Snapping his head around, he noticed a pair of dusty leather boots.

"All finished, thanks mate. Would've been great if you'd turned up about half an hour ago." Grabbing the jack, he stood up to face the stranger. The sight made his face drop in confusion. "Who the fuck are you?"

The stranger's arm moved blindingly fast.

Johnstone gasped. The jack dropped from his hand and clattered to the ground. He clutched at his stomach, his hands wrapping around the handle of the screwdriver buried deep, and staggered back several steps, his face pleading with the newcomer. A silent "Why?" formed on his lips as he dropped to his knees before falling face-first into the dry dust and lying still.

"Good evening, ladies and gentlemen." Heyward's voice cut through and quelled the incessant chatter from the assembled guests. He stopped for a moment, scanning the faces and taking in the mood of his audience. They were a ragtag group of early twenty-somethings. Only here to be titillated by the prospect of some horror-related activities, or something else, during their private moments. The last thought bloomed when his eyes rested on the over-muscled jock and his bimbo-like girlfriend. They were almost caricatures out of the same style of movie that the night's activities would replicate.

With an inward sigh of resignation that none of this lot would care any for his theatrical experience or abilities, he repressed himself into the stoic role of master of ceremonies for the evening.

"Fifteen years ago, Death walked the highways and byways of the South Coast of New South Wales. They called him Mogo Mack, and over a two-year period, he was blamed for the deaths of at least 34 people. On his final blood-soaked night. Mack killed a family of four, just after their evening meal."

He looked at every face, pausing for effect before continuing.

"Tonight, you are all invited back to Heathburn to recreate that fateful night and hopefully shed some light as to the true identity of Mogo Mack."

A slight hint of oohing and aahing went through the group. Mostly the women, especially the twins, Ali and Christine. They appeared to be keen on the terror, bloodshed, and violence of the night. The other six were a tight-knit group, with a requisite nerdy hanger-on, the dour-faced loner girl, the jock couple, and Heyward's chosen final girl and her boyfriend. "I am Mr Heyward, your master of ceremonies, narrator, and guide for the evening."

Holding up a copy of the standard instruction letter, he continued. "Each of you have been sent a set of instructions for the night, and a story about your part. I hope you will stay well within the character you have been assigned and follow your instructions to the letter. Tonight's events have been specifically tailored to revolve around that script, and I would hate for anything to spoil the surprises and shocks." His eyes roved around the room, stopping on each face in turn, searching for any hint of deviation from secrecy.

"Now," he motioned towards the double doors leading into the dining room, "Please partake of a wonderful meal prepared by our chef, and at the requisite time, move off to the locations outlined in your instructions. If you have any questions or difficulties, then don't hesitate to find me or one of the other staff members." With a bow and a flourish, he couldn't help himself on occasions such as these, he added, "Enjoy your evening. For now, I bid you adieu."

"Food and beer," yelled the jock, as he dragged his girlfriend through the doors.

Heyward sighed once more as the rest sauntered after them. "I left the Sydney Theatre Company for this?"

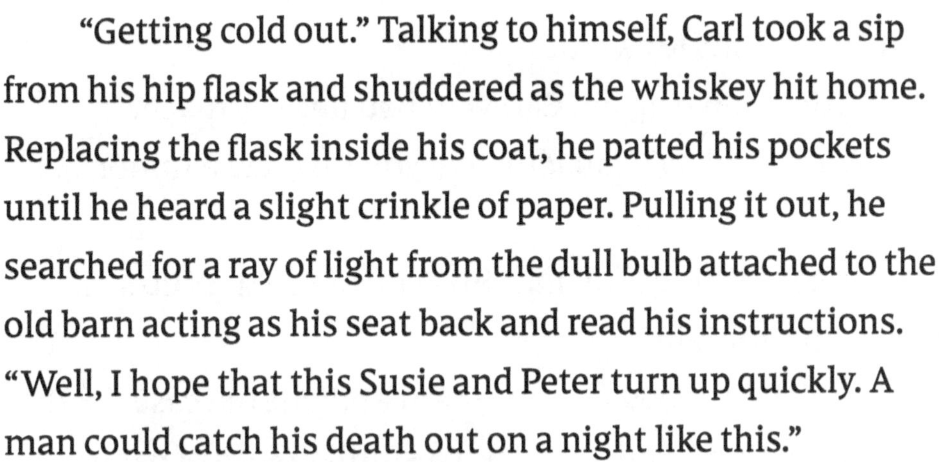

"Getting cold out." Talking to himself, Carl took a sip from his hip flask and shuddered as the whiskey hit home. Replacing the flask inside his coat, he patted his pockets until he heard a slight crinkle of paper. Pulling it out, he searched for a ray of light from the dull bulb attached to the old barn acting as his seat back and read his instructions. "Well, I hope that this Susie and Peter turn up quickly. A man could catch his death out on a night like this."

A rumble of thunder echoed from far off in the distance. Carl's face dropped as he stared towards the source. Dark clouds were beginning to grow on the horizon, blotting out the stars and threatening to bring a wild storm towards the camp. "Damn. If that's coming, I hope it waits until I'm inside."

A voice from the gloom grabbed his attention.

"You talking to yourself again, Carl?"

A pretty, young woman with a mop of curly blonde hair stepped into the yellow light. She struggled against the weight of a large case. Carl stood and nodded towards her burden. "You need a hand with that, Patricia?"

"I'm fine," the makeup artist said. Grunting slightly as she took several steps towards the barn. "I brought the big case for the weekend. Wanted to make an impression on the customers, and Heyward."

Sitting down again, Carl watched her approach.

"Are you okay? You look like you just had a minor stroke."

"Nah, nothing like that. Just getting cold. Who's on your menu tonight?"

Patricia stopped for a moment and put the case down. "Good question." She fished out a similar piece of paper to Carl's and struggled to read it. "Peter, some big jock, and his blonde girlfriend, Susan."

"Same as me. I'll scare 'em good for you. Then you can kill 'em."

The makeup artist chuckled. "Well, as much as I'd like to, I'll restrain myself to making them look dead. Okay?"

"If you must."

As he watched her walk past, a filthy thought floated into his mind.

Carl, if only you were twenty years younger.

He smiled at the idea before the follow-up thought

erased his smirk quickly.

You'd still be old enough to be her dad, you damn fool.

Grumbling at himself as Patricia disappeared into the barn, Carl pulled out his flask and took another swig, leaning his head back to drain the very last drop. As he drank, he heard heavy footsteps approach. Dropping his head down once more, he saw a familiar sight standing before him.

"You're early," he said to the large figure wearing a heavy waterproof coat and an Akubra hat. Spying the large-bladed knife in the figure's hand, he added as a gentle quip, followed by a chuckle. "And be careful with that thing, you don't want to be cutting anybody."

The figure remained silent, simply staring at Carl.

"What? You cut your own tongue out or something?" Waving his hand at the figure, Carl added, "Go on, get. You're supposed to be stalking the guests or something, ain't ya? Not bothering us working folk." Under his breath, he dismissed the silent figure, "Bloody amateurs, give 'em a small part, and they think they're professional actors."

Instead of leaving, the dark shape took one step forward and brought the knife up quickly. The last thing Carl saw was a golden flash of the shiny knife catching the yellow light as it slammed deep into his skull.

Knock, knock.

"Hello? Miss Nichols? Mr Batchelor?" Patricia waited until she was sure there was nobody inside.

Good. Haven't come early. Still time to set up.

Pushing the door open with one foot, she struggled in with the heavy makeup case and moved through the barn into the small space she had prepared for herself. The area had been built in the far corner, away from where the action would take place later.

It suited her purposes. There was a table to hold her makeup, brushes, applicators, and other sundry items, complete with a mirror surrounded by bright fluorescent lights. Two stools sat before each other, one for her, one for the victim. Nearby, Heyward's company had installed a bathroom, complete with toilet and sink, to give her and the victims an area for cleaning up afterwards. To ensure that the other guests were oblivious, Patricia had arranged a wall of hay bales to shield the area from view.

Hefting the case up onto a bale, she moved around the area to ensure it remained undisturbed since the last event and was set up correctly for tonight's performance.

Good, no one's been here.

Moving across to a small intercom on the wall, she pressed the button and waited for someone to answer.

"Patricia?"

"Yes, Mr Heyward. Just checking in. I'm setting up in the barn. No guests have arrived yet."

"They are still in the dining room. You've got about thirty minutes or so."

"Are you sure that Mr Feakes can undertake his own makeup? I left enough supplies in the bathroom, but I would have time to do him as well."

"He said he looked forward to it. So, relax and concentrate more on your next victims. You're doing brilliantly, keep up the good work."

"Alright. Patricia out."

The intercom went dead. A small wan grin came to Patricia's face at the thought of Heyward's shallow compliment. She shrugged and continued to unpack.

When she was happy that all her wares were laid out in an orderly fashion, she stepped back into the main area of the barn and scanned the spot where the victim would eventually lie down, ready for discovery. She shook her head at what was about to transpire. The whole gig was as lame as they come. Her role was to make up several of the guests to look like they had been brutally murdered by some lame-ass masked killer. The guests would be positioned around the camp, ready for discovery, while the other guests got to work out where the killer would strike next and whether the killer was one of them.

It wasn't. It was all a ruse.

A thought triggered in her mind. She hadn't seen Ivan, the actor hired to play the killer. He was a tall, lumbering fellow, very short on words, but big on presence. Shrugging, she took another look at the barn floor, happy that it was covered in fresh straw.

Everything's in order; now we wait.

As Patricia moved back to her area and took a seat, a single drop of fresh blood fell silently from the loft and splattered in the hay. The source of the blood lay on the floor above. No more would Ivan play the silent and brooding killer.

Several minutes passed as Patricia sat waiting for her clients. She looked around, moved the makeup around, straightened brushes, but was generally bored.

Would have preferred to make up Mr Feakes. Bored. Should have brought a magazine.

A sudden thump from above grabbed her attention.

What the hell was that?

Patricia stared at the ceiling, waiting for the noise to repeat itself. The hairs on the back of her neck rose as fear grew in her.

Stop it, you idiot. There's nothing. It's this stupid murder mystery thing; it's got you all worked up.

A scraping sound filtered from above. Her head snapped up as her eyes bored into the wooden ceiling and tried in vain to see the cause.

Goddamn it. Probably a guest playing around.

Standing, she moved across to the ladder leading to the hayloft. "Right. Whoever's up there, you can't be here. It's against the rules and not safe. Now, stop it. I'm coming up." Steeling herself, she gripped the ladder and climbed.

The hayloft had been set up to resemble an American-style loft. "Why?" Patricia had asked the question and been shushed by Heyward early on. "Atmosphere," had been the answer. "Bullshit," she'd said under her breath, eliciting chuckles from the cooking staff nearby.

Scanning the area, she only saw bales of hay stacked up four high. To her right, she noticed that two had fallen over, possibly the cause of the thump. *But what had caused the scraping noise?* Stepping towards the tumbled hay bales, she noticed a dark shape lying on the floor. The figure was wearing a brown waterproof coat. *Ivan?* Rushing to the prone body, she dropped down and shook him.

"Ivan? What are you doing here?"

The actor rolled over, revealing a deep gash across his neck.

"Why are you made up? You don't get killed; that's your job." Confused and annoyed, she poked the body in the chest. "Get up, buster. You've got a job to do. So do I, for that matter." She checked her watch. "Those guests will be here soon."

Another hay bale fell forward, thudding to the floor. Patricia's eyes snapped in that direction before widening in shock. Behind the wall of hay, another tall figure dressed identically to Ivan stood holding a pitchfork.

She jumped to her feet and stepped away from her co-worker.

"Who are you?"

The figure stepped around the hay bales and moved

forward, the pitchfork extended and aimed at Patricia.

"Hey, put that down, it's dangerous. Mr Heyward will be mad if he finds you here."

The silent shape closed on Patricia, taunting her with the farm implement by thrusting it forward.

The makeup artist stepped back, moving away from the deadly tines. "Come on, this is silly, you could really hurt someone."

The pitchfork wielder took another step, stabbing forward. Patricia stepped back, once, twice... Suddenly, her foot found only air. With her arms flailing and grasping at nothing, she fell backwards.

Air burst from her lungs as she slammed into the dirt floor. Blades of stray hay blew up around her, casting straw dust all around.

Groaning in pain, Patricia sucked air back into her lungs and groggily got to her feet. Glancing up at the hayloft, she saw her attacker staring down. He moved to the ladder and began to descend.

Get help!

She stumbled around the hay bale wall and staggered to the intercom. Pressing the button, only static rang out of the little speaker box.

"Help! It's Patricia. There's someone in the barn. They attacked me."

Releasing the button, she heard only static again.

"No. Please." She pressed it several times. "Help! The barn. There's someone here."

Static again.

A scream erupted from the makeup artist as a machete slammed down onto her wrist, severing her hand and spraying blood across the wall. She grabbed at the stump, incredulous at the fountain of crimson spurting from her arm and turned to face her attacker.

The figure stood tall. Clothed in a simple brown weatherproof coat and a large Akubra hat. His face cast in shadow and featureless. Even through the pain and confusion, Patricia thought that whoever it was had created a perfect likeness of Mogo Mack for this performance.

The killer prized the machete from the wooden wall and raised it high in the air.

Patricia's eyes were drawn to the bloodied tool as it hovered above her. It was the last thing she saw.

"Dinner sucked. I'm still hungry."

Peter and Susie walked hand in hand through the darkness behind the main hotel building.

"And I only had two beers. I don't even feel any buzz. How the hell am I gonna last for the rest of this stupid play-acting thing?"

"Oh, don't be like that, it'll be fun," said Susie, grasping Peter's arm with both hands and looking up into his face. When he finally peered down at her, she smiled with a wicked grin and added, "Besides, I'm sure we can find a quiet place for dessert."

"What are you thinking?"

"Well, I don't need to be with the makeup artist for at least another quarter of an hour. I'm sure we can find something to occupy us for that time. It's a nice night." A sudden rumble of thunder off in the distance drew her suddenly confused gaze. "It is for now, anyway. I'm feeling a little chilly and could use a pair of nice warm hands all over me."

Peter stared down at her and smiled. Susie had chosen a tight-fitting t-shirt and matching shorts; even in the dull light, he could tell that there was nothing else under the shirt. He reached for her butt and drew her towards him, kissing her long and deeply. "Do these hands work for you?"

"Oh, yeah, I think they'll do fine."

Breaking away, she took him by the hand and led him off the path between two bushes. There sat a small lawned clearing, surrounded by bushes and trees. A tiny, but secluded place that invited the very acts that they wished to undertake.

"I think this will do even better," Susie said, spinning around and stripping off her t-shirt in one movement.

Peter was never one to need a second invitation. He moved in quickly, removed his own t-shirt, and wrapped both arms around his girlfriend, crushing her naked body against his own.

As the two collapsed into a writhing mass of limbs, shrouded in grunts and groans, neither saw the dark shape standing alone in the shadows, watching them intently.

"Hey, you should probably get back to the drawing room."

Julie looked at her boyfriend and chuckled.

"What?"

She found it hard to imagine that her handsome, young lover was the same person sitting beside the mirror before her. Mark had revealed a hidden talent she'd never seen before. He had aged himself to be in his late forties and added horrific gashes and a deep slash across his neck. Plus, a set of dowdy old farm clothes had been provided. He looked like he'd been on the land all his life.

"Yeah, you're right," she said. "I'll be back here soon, anyway. You should probably get into position."

Mark took one last look at himself, admiring his work. "I'm good. I'll tell you what. Wait until next Halloween, I'm going to go over the top this year."

"You could go professional."

He smiled, careful not to break any of the latex and adhesives keeping the wounds intact. "We'll see, from what I've heard, it really doesn't pay much?"

"Get on the bed."

Mark crawled onto the bed carefully and lay on his back. Julie moved across and leaned over him.

"I'll see you soon, lover." She playfully grabbed his crotch, eliciting howls of both anger and pleasure from Mark.

"Tease," he said as she left him alone. "Now I wait, I suppose."

Grunts and groans shattered the still night as Peter and Susie engaged in their favourite activity.

A sudden crack of thunder broke over the camp, stopping them mid-stride.

"What the hell was that?" cried Susie.

Annoyed at the break in rhythm, Peter grumbled, "Nothing. Thunder. Who cares?" He tried to regain his cadence, kissing Susie on the neck, but a sudden flurry of cold rain pelted across their prone forms.

"Shit," Peter cried.

Throwing him off, Susie rose and grabbed her discarded clothing. A fork of lightning pierced the sky and lit up the barn a mere fifty metres away. "The barn. Come on." She raced off, regardless of her nakedness. Peter stumbled to his feet, picked up his own clothes and followed.

As they raced into the barn, dressed only in their soggy socks, they stopped for a moment, regarding each other's drenched naked form, and then the fake authenticity of a mid-west American barn, before bursting into laughter.

"What the hell is this place?" asked Peter.

"Dunno. The brochure mentioned something about a barn. I think the dudes that created all this didn't want a standard Australian cowshed, so went for an American look instead."

"Should we look for Jeb and Billy-May in here somewhere?"

"Maybe." Unfazed by her state of dress, Susie moved across to one of the many hay bales and laid her t-shirt and shorts across it. "Hope they'll dry quickly. Starting to get cold."

Suddenly, she felt the warmth of Peter's body press against her. "I'll keep you warm."

As she felt his manhood press into her, she added, "That's not all you'll do, it seems." She turned and looked past him. "I was meant to be here about 9:30, to get made up. It's almost that now. Where's the makeup artist?"

"Should we look, or continue on then?"

A licentious smile grew on Susie's face. "Mmm. Perhaps, at least it will give our clothes time to dry. Well, I hope so anyway. Think you can keep going for that long?"

"Oh, you're cheeky." He tossed his t-shirt and jeans onto the hay bale and grabbed Susie, picking her up and carrying her around the little bale wall and into the make-up area. "I'll prove it to you here."

Lying Susie gently on the hay-strewn floor, he began to kiss the nape of her neck before moving down to her breasts and belly. Before long, Susie began to moan with pleasure, and the barn echoed to the sounds of their lovemaking.

Suddenly, Peter arched his back and cried out.

"What? That's it?" asked Susie with a tinge of disappointment.

"No. Something cold dripped on my back. The roof must be leaking."

Smiling, Susie reached her arms towards Peter and said, "Don't worry about it. Come back." Her smile was quickly replaced by a disgusted gasp, as a cold drop hit her chest.

Peter took one look at the small red puddle and knelt back. He tentatively reached for the drip and touched it, bringing his fingers back to study the liquid. "I think this is blood."

"What?" Susie's face broke out in confusion, then horror as she spied movement above them. "Move," she shouted, pushing Peter and rolling to the side, just as something crashed to the ground.

Standing, the pair looked down at the horror before them. A body, with blonde hair matted with thick, red blood, one hand was missing, and a deep gash running down her forehead.

Peter began to laugh out loud, eliciting a shocked look from Susie. "What the hell are you laughing at?"

"It's part of the whole show. It's fake. Just a dummy."

"But it looks so real."

"Cool, huh!"

Susie stepped towards the body and bent down. She reached a tentative hand out towards the fake corpse, reeling back as her fingers touched real skin. "She's real."

"Can't be. Come on. They've spent all this money on this stupid barn; they won't be stingy on the props." Still chuckling, Peter stooped down and patted the dead girl's cheek. "See fake." His smile faded as the reality of what he felt dawned on him. Hunkering down, he felt the girl's skin once more. His eyes widened in horror. "She is real. You can't fake that feel." He stood and backed away; a tremor came to his voice as an alien feeling of fear entered his mind. "What the hell is going on here?"

"Aaahh," Susie screamed and pointed.

A tall figure wearing a heavy coat with a face-obscuring hat stood on the other side of the small hay-bale wall. It stepped forward and raised the deadly-looking machete.

Instinctively, Peter stepped in front of Susie, his fear giving way to false bravado. "What the fuck you want?"

Mogo Mack lashed out with the weapon, leaving a thin red line across Peter's chest. He cried in pain, his hands going to his chest and smearing the weeping blood. "Run," he yelled at Susie, "run."

She darted to one side and sprinted towards the doors. Slipping slightly on the loose straw, she ducked through the opening and raced into the rain. Peter circled around, keeping a wide distance from the killer. He spied a shovel next to a pitchfork and seized it. As Mack waved the machete towards him, Peter swung the shovel, knocking the machete from the killer's hand. He used the distraction to his advantage and threw the shovel, spear-like, at his adversary. It knocked Mogo Mack backwards. Peter took his chance and ducked through the open doors.

With her heart thumping in her chest, Susie waited for Peter to emerge from the barn. The rain had stopped, bringing a slight breeze that chilled her naked body, and a strange quiet to the area.

She didn't know whether to just flee or go back to help. Cries and metallic clangs rang from inside the barn, followed by the creaking of the doors as they opened further. Only two people could emerge from the barn. A lump grew in her throat, but relief flooded her being as Peter stepped out.

He waved at her. "Go. Don't wait."

She turned and ducked between two dark bushes, racing to the other side of a small lawned area before stopping and looking back for Peter. He rushed through the gap, catching several loose branches and crying out as they tore into his skin. A lone rock proved his undoing, snagging his ankle and toppling him forward. A loud crack echoed across to Susie, followed by a howl of pain from Peter.

He struggled back to his knees, attempted to put weight on his right foot and screamed. Susie saw the foot bend awkwardly and shivered as she realised the bones were shattered.

Running to her boyfriend, she helped him back to his knees. "Christ, Susie, it hurts. I can't walk. Go get help."

Another scream erupted from him, followed by a choking gurgle from deep in his throat. Blood spewed from his mouth, spattering Susie's naked chest.

Peter gagged and dropped his head. Susie followed his gaze. Several metal prongs jutted from his stomach. His hands grasped the tines of the pitchfork sticking out of him. Turning to Susie, he gasped for breath, trying to speak, before raising one hand to her, leaving a smear of blood across her face as he fell forward.

Susie noticed the tall, dark presence still holding the end of the pitchfork. Mogo Mack dropped the implement and reached for her.

Self-preservation became her only emotion. She ducked back out of his range, turned and fled across the lawn.

Bursting through another set of bushes, Susie found herself completely lost. She stopped, searching for any lights, but only finding the deep, dark foliage around her. She could see neither the hotel nor the barn. Her heart sank.

She was alone. Naked and afraid. Scanning the area, she chose a direction and ran. Branches tore at her skin. Blood flowed down her body as the scratches multiplied, but deep inside, she knew she had to find help.

After what seemed like hours, she stopped to catch her breath. The night was silent. The rain had gone. The breeze had died. Even the animals had gone silent. Relieved, she let out a long sigh and tried to think of her next actions.

Snap.

Her heart jumped into her mouth. Its pounding blotted out any other noise. Something was close. Something had made that noise.

Peering around her, she took several tentative steps backwards, hoping to find another path to follow back to the hotel. Behind her, bushes and trees stopped any progress. Grasping at the foliage, she felt the sharp spikes of tiny twigs and the smooth, wet bark of the tall eucalypts they had seen on the way to the hotel.

Then something different. It felt like smooth, wet leather.

She turned and looked straight up into the darkened face of Peter's killer.

There was nothing in earshot to hear her final, brief squeal.

Knock, knock.

Julie turned the doorknob. She looked back at Stephen and the twins. Staying as much in character as she can, she added, "It's unlocked. Should we go in?"

The two young women simply stared at her with dull expressions. "No. We should just stay here all night. It can't get much more boring than it has already," said Christine.

"Hey, it's early," said Stephen, defending his friend and trying to stay in the mood for the murder party. "Obviously, everybody else is off getting made up or into character. So, yeah, it's been slow to begin with, but this is the first room we've had to investigate. It should get more fun from here on."

"Fine," said Ali, pushing past Julie and entering the room. A slight squeal echoed back, forcing the other three inside.

"What's wrong?" asked Christine, staring at her sister as she stood with terror written large on her face. Ali simply pointed at the bed.

There, Mark lay in a pool of blood, with gruesome wounds covering his face and neck. Julie almost yelped when she saw Mark.

Wow, the makeup artists must have returned. She did a great job. He looks much worse than before.

"Oh, that's cool," said Stephen, moving across to the bed and leaning in close to get a better look. "Wow, you can even see into his throat. That is really good."

Christine turned to her sister, "Nice scream, too."

"Hey, just getting into character," returned Ali. She regarded the scene once more, "though it is pretty gruesome."

Julie scanned the bedroom for clues. Stepping to the other side of the bed, she pointed at the floor. "Hey, there's straw scattered across the floor here. I reckon we should check out the barn." Looking back at the other three, who had gotten over their initial reactions to the fake dead body and returned to one of disinterest, she received three shrugs.

"I suppose, if that's what the script says," said Ali.

Julie shrugged. "The script said come into this bedroom. That's where it ends. The rest is up to us."

"Fine. The barn it is." Ali moved towards the doorway,

followed by the other two.

Sighing, Julie shook her head. She had hoped for a bit more fun, but being stuck with this lot was dragging her down.

Once the others had left, she leaned towards Mark and said, "Hey. You can stop the act now." He remained still. "Okay, have it your own way. I'll see you in the room later. Hope I can force these idiots to spot the clues and solve this thing quickly. It's getting cold, and I'd like someone to warm me up. You better get cleaned up beforehand."

Mark remained unmoving, eliciting another smile from Julie.

I didn't think he'd take this that seriously.

She moved to the door, taking one last glance at the supine figure, before shrugging and leaving the bedroom.

Throom!

A massive peal of thunder broke across the camp, loud enough to shake the hotel and rattle the plates and items in the various display cabinets.

Heyward stood in his office and stared out at the sheeting rain that thrashed the windows and drowned out any noises from within the house.

"Damn," he said to himself. "I can't have the guests out in this. How will they ever get to the barn?"

Moving to the large table in the corner of his office, he scanned the intricate map and diagrams that showed the anticipated and planned movements of the participants during the night's entertainment.

"Hmm. We have two actors to be discovered in the barn and woodshed. Ivan makes his first appearance, forcing them back to the hotel." He traced one of the highlighted lines. "One of the twins, Christine, will be stopped on the way." Shaking his head. "I need to address this and quickly."

He moved back to his desk and pressed the intercom button for the barn. "Patricia, can you please find Mr Schaeffer and Miss Nichols for me?" Nothing but static responded. "Annoying." Pressing the button again several times, he waited, then repeated his request. When only silence and hissing replied, he cursed under his breath, took one look through the window again and braced himself.

Opening the door to the rear of the hotel, Julie was thrown back a step by the gusting wind and driving rain. She slammed the door shut and stared through the internal windows at the storm outside.

"Well, that's going to make it hard to get to the barn."

Turning, she realised she was alone.

"Where did they go?" Her shoulders slumped. "God dammit, this is turning into a shit night."

"Oh, this is turning into the best night ever."

Stephen lay on the bed, naked, his wrists and ankles tied to the four posts of the oversized bed. His state of happiness clear for all to see. The twin objects driving that delight danced naked before him, stopping every now and then to kiss or fondle each other and tease groans of gratitude from their captured audience.

Got to keep it together. Got to keep it together.

Never had he found himself in such a situation. Even the rare single encounters he'd found himself had ended in embarrassment and disappointment for his partners. Stephen took deep breaths to control himself, flicking his eyes away from the raunchy dancing of the twins and picturing the disapproving face of his mother or grandmother in an attempt to dampen his enthusiasm.

Then the girls moved to the bed. All memories of his family dissipated; it was time to live in the now.

Without a word, Christine climbed on the bed, kissed him deep on the lips, before straddling and mounting him. She set a slow but steady tempo before being joined by her sister, who sat behind and cupped her breasts, matching the rhythm at play. Stephen took deep, steady breaths and concentrated hard on anything else.

As the pleasure intensified, eliciting moans and groans from all participants, no one noticed the door to the bedroom quietly open.

The rhythmic movements quickened, reaching towards the inevitable crescendo. Just as Stephen closed his eyes, arched his back and let out a howl of pleasure, the two girls cried in unison.

A hot gush of liquid across his chest delighted Stephen; he assumed it was some strange sex-play from the girls. His smile was a delirious testament to his pleasure, and he slowly opened his eyes, expecting the same from the girls.

The dull look on Christine's face confused him. The steel spike protruding between her breasts confused him even more. He looked down at his chest. The dark red pool of liquid matched that leaking from the wound in Christine's chest.

He tried to move, but the weight of the girls stopped him.

A figure stepped from behind the dead woman. They carried something long and shiny. Stephen tried to cry out in terror, but the blade was quicker.

"Ah, Miss Moore, I'm so glad that I found you." Heyward stood in the doorway of the common room. Rather than brace the weather outside, Julie had retreated to the room until the rain abated or other instructions had been issued.

She sat on a couch, a fresh glass of white wine in one hand, with the Camp Blood letter in the other. Glancing up at the master of ceremonies, she chuckled to herself. Heyward had donned a heavy rainproof coat.

"I know I'm meant to be going out to the barn with Stephen and those two bimbos, but they disappeared when the rain hit. So, thought I'd come here until it dies down."

"And an admirable idea too. The intercom to the barn isn't working. I was going to go out there and bring everybody back into the house. We can restage the events in the warmth and comfort of the hotel's environs."

"Should you just cancel the rest of the mystery, and we can come back another night? This rain has already screwed things up. With Stephen and the others gone, the narrative will be destroyed."

Stepping into the room, Heyward put on his best front in an attempt to rescue the situation. Johnstone's voice echoed through his head. The last thing they needed was a group of peed-off guests clamouring for their money back. "It should all be fine. I'll let you in on some secrets, which we will reset and carry on with. Upon finding Mr Feakes in the upstairs bedroom, you found the straw, which should lead you to the barn, where you find Mr Schaeffer and

Miss Nichols. There are clues there to lead you towards the woodshed, where Miss Stroop should be."

"Ah, I wondered where Angela got to."

"Yes. The clues there lead you back here. On the way, one of the twins, Miss Christine, I believe, would be disposed of by our resident Mogo Mack." Heyward stopped for a moment and thought out loud. "Hmm. Ivan? I haven't heard from him all afternoon."

"Who's Ivan?

Recovering, Heyward simply waved the question away. "Oh, just one of our actors. You don't need to know their names. They should just become part of the furniture." Holding up a single finger, he added, "Now, you just stay there. I shall have everything sorted momentarily." As he moved towards the other doorway, he stopped. "Speaking of the others, just now, do you happen to know where the rest of your little group went?"

"Probably one of the bedrooms. Those two girls were all over Stephen. God knows why." She took another sip of wine.

Heyward nodded, made a little bow, then stepped towards the exit.

Julie, quite bored with the proceedings, placed her

instructions down and looked around for something else to pass the time. Heyward's voice came back into the room from the outside corridor.

"Ivan? What are you doing here?"

Intrigued, Julie looked towards the exit.

"Wait, you're not Ivan. You're far too short. Has that stupid agency sent a replacement? This will not do."

A short, sharp cry followed.

Intrigued that this was another part of the show, Julie placed her glass down and stood up, craning to see through the opposite doorway.

The sudden appearance of the MC jolted even Julie's tired and bored mind. He held his throat with one hand and gestured with the other. Nothing but choked gagging noises emanated from the normally garrulous man. His eyes pleaded with her as he dropped to his knees. His hand released his throat and showed Julie the reason for his silence.

A deep gash ran across his neck. Blood poured from the wound.

A momentary smile broke on Julie's face.

"How did you do that? That looks amazing."

Heyward's choking gurgle continued as his eyes rolled

back into his head and his protestations lessened. With one last pleading look, he fell forward, thumping to the ground.

A glimmer of doubt ran through Julie's mind. The fact that the man who was running the entire show had been eliminated in this display of death didn't make any sense. He wasn't meant to be part of the show itself, merely the narrator and orchestrator of events.

Stepping over to the man, she knelt and jostled his shoulder. "Mr Heyward. What's all this about? I thought you were going to bring everybody back into the hotel?"

Heavy boots thudded into the common room.

Julie looked up to see a figure standing several metres away. They wore a heavy rainproof coat, with an Akubra hat pulled down to hide their face. A slight chuckle came to her throat as she stood.

"Ivan? Mogo Mack? Who the fuck are you?"

The figure held up the large butcher's knife, still replete with fresh blood, and pointed it at Julie.

Stepping back to the couch, Julie picked up the instructions. "I'm not meant to die. I'm the final girl. It's all in here?" She waved the sheet of paper before pointing down at the prone body of Heyward. "Hang on, is this the change to the script that he mentioned? Do I have to escape or something?"

The silent figure took one step forward. A husky voice filtered out from beneath the brim of the Akubra. "You idiot." With his free hand, Mogo Mack pulled the hat off, revealing his identity.

"Angela? What are you doing? Heyward said you were going to be killed in the woodshed or something. Why are you dressed like Mogo Mack?"

Tossing the hat aside, Angela took one look at Heyward before a salacious grin crossed her face. "Why? Why take over from a serial killer? So that I can take my revenge without any trouble from the victims."

"What victims? What revenge?"

"Stephen, Mark. You. Then I'll finish off with Peter and Susie."

"What do you mean? What did we do?"

"You killed Tom."

"What? We were his friends. We didn't do anything. He died in a car accident."

"Is that what you believe?" She spat the words out, defining the rage that boiled inside her. "He was drunk, yes. Thank your boyfriend for that. Have you never wondered why he was first on the scene?"

"It was just coincidence."

"Idiot. They were racing. They'd done it before. Tom, Mark, Stephen, Peter, had all been drinking beforehand. Peter urged Tom on. He shouldn't have been driving, let alone dragging in that piece of shit car of his. If you were all friends, you would never have done that. Friends would never let one of their own drive drunk."

"I ...I don't ... It doesn't make sense. Mark said ..." Julie thought for a moment. "What have you done? To the others?"

"Dead." That grin turned into a wide smile, with matching wide-open eyes above.

"Mark? Stephen?"

As Julie rattled off each name, Angela simply nodded. "Oh, yes. And then I'll kill that Susie bitch. But Peter. Oh, I'll make Peter suffer. He was driving the other car."

Fear and confusion came to Julie's face. She still wasn't sure if this was real or just part of the script for the night. As she tried to clear the confusion from her thoughts, Angela rushed forward, raising the knife and slashing down. The blade nicked Julie's arm and buried itself in the couch.

Crying out in pain, Julie darted backwards, grabbing at the wound. Glancing at Angela in confusion, she turned and bolted through the nearby doorway. A shout of annoyance followed her.

Racing down the narrow corridor, Julie found the stairs and climbed to the bedrooms.

Ducking in through the first door, she turned to find the corpses of Stephen and the twins strewn across the large four-poster bed. Stifling a scream, she ducked back out and scanned the hallway. Mark was in the last room on the right. She ran towards it. Stopping only when she heard heavy footsteps on the stairs and Angela's voice calling out to her.

Shit!

Grasping the doorknob, it slipped through her bloodied hand. Wiping her hand, she turned it again and slowly pushed the door open, hoping to dull any squeaks and conceal her hiding place.

Inside, Mark lay sprawled on the bed. A chill ran up Julie's back. Staring at her boyfriend, she prayed to any gods that would listen that his chest would rise and show him breathing.

Nothing.

Tentatively, she stepped across to the bed and reached for his neck. His skin was cold, and his pulse was still. She swallowed a small gulp of sorrow and took a deep breath.

It was all too real. It was all too frightening. A true serial killer was loose. The night of fakery had turned into a night of terror.

A shiver ran through her at the realisation. She had a decision to make. Survive or succumb. Taking a deep breath, she took one final glance at her dead boyfriend and chose the former.

Stepping towards the door, her foot struck something lying beneath the bed. Retrieving the heavy object, she felt the blade of the axe. It was probably a prop, but it wasn't fake, and even though it wasn't sharp, it could still bludgeon somebody pretty well.

Listening through the door, all seemed quiet.

Julie turned the knob again slowly, annoyed as the latch clicked with supersonic noise in that soundless space. As Julie pulled the door ajar, it burst open, followed by the slashing blade as Angela tried to bury the knife in her. Clumsily, Julie brought up the axe and swatted the knife away. It dislodged from Angela's grasp and clattered across the floor.

Angela took one look at Julie's tear-filled face, smiled and leapt for the knife, leaving Julie a wide-open exit.

"Come back, you little shit," Angela yelled at Julie's

retreating back.

Hoping to find the front foyer and exit from the hotel, Julie stepped back into the common room and stopped. Her shoulders slumped at the realisation. She traced her memories for the map of the hotel. The other exit led straight to the foyer and freedom.

Moving forward, she stopped when Angela appeared mere metres away, the blade held high, ready to strike. A leering grin on her face.

"Isn't this convenient?" she said.

Julie stared at Angela standing in the exit, turned fully around and bolted for the other doorway. A sharp cry burst from her mouth as a virtual doppelganger of Angela materialised before her.

This Mogo Mack was taller. Water dripped from the Akubra that hid his face. Instead of a simple kitchen knife, this version held a long, wicked-looking machete in a hand that wore a torn and dirty leather glove. The blade was stained dark. Holding onto the belief that all this was fake, a single, strange, hopeful thought floated through Julie's mind.

Probably paint, not blood.

In that situation. With all that had happened. The

silent spectre seemed even more frightening than it should. Julie backed away, keeping distance between her, Angela, and the newcomer. The towering presence simply moved slowly into the room.

"Who the fuck are you?" asked Angela.

"Ivan?" asked Julie.

"Who the fuck is Ivan?"

"The actor playing Mogo Mack."

"Nope, got nothing. I assumed they just pretended there was someone doing the killing."

The silent giant turned his head from one to the other.

"Ah, who cares, you're a witness," said Angela, weighing the blade in her hand. She took one step forward and threw the huge knife across the room at the new Mogo Mack. The knife hit him flat in the chest with a dull thud, dropping to the ground with a soft clatter.

All three stood still for a moment. The tall Mack slowly looked down at the chef's knife, then back up at Angela. With surprising speed, he crossed the distance between them in a flash, grasping the woman around the neck and lifting her with ease.

Slamming Angela into the wall opposite, he changed his grip on the machete and drew it high into the air before driving it point-first through her chest and deep into the wall behind. Letting go of both the woman and the knife, Mack stepped back. Angela thrashed around in agony for a moment before all life left her, and she hung limp, impaled to the wall.

Julie cried out, drawing unwanted attention from the new threat.

The other Mack turned towards her.

Survive.

The word blared through her mind. She gripped the axe in both hands and launched herself at the killer. The blade struck him fully on the shoulder, knocking him sideways, where he crashed through a small side table bearing glasses and a decanter. Julie considered hitting him again before glancing towards the doorway and running for her life.

As she reached for the exit door handle, she noticed the flashing blue lights outside.

"It wasn't real. It can't be. This was all just play-acting. Everybody should be fine." Julie spoke her mantra out loud to herself.

Sitting alone in the police car, the crunching of gravel drew her attention. She turned to see an old police officer crouch down and look into the car.

"Did you find anyone?" Julie shivered despite the thick blanket wrapped around her. The area was awash with blue and red strobing lights, giving her and the nearby officers a sickly hue.

The policeman shook his head. "Sorry, Miss. They were all dead."

"But Angela said she was going to kill Peter and Susie next. They were supposed to be in the barn. They are okay, aren't they?"

Shaking his head again, the policeman added, "No. I'm afraid not. We found five bodies in the barn. Two of them match this Peter and Susie. I'm so sorry, miss."

"But it couldn't have been Angela. Why would she say that?"

Julie stopped and thought for a moment. Her eyes went wide.

"It was the other one. The man that killed Angela. He was dressed like Mogo Mack."

"We found another body. Sounds like this fellow. Heavy

raincoat. Akubra hat. Big fellow. Probably the same guy. You must have been mistaken."

"No. That's Ivan. The actor. Must be."

The policeman shrugged. He looked around, hoping to find a free paramedic or female police officer. He hated babysitting survivors; they didn't think straight. Their stories were always wrong and changed every time they told them.

Suddenly, Julie grasped the policeman's shirt and stared straight into his eyes. The effect was startling and made the hairs on his neck stand up.

"He's out there. The other one. He's still out there. Waiting."

She turned to stare into the darkness beyond the wash of police lights.

"Mogo Mack. He'll come back again. One day."

WELL DOESN'T THAT SOUND
LIKE A FUN LITTLE GETAWAY
SPOT?

PERHAPS YOU SHOULD LOOK UP THE BLACK-HEARTED BOOKWORM BEHIND THIS BLOW OUT AND SEE IF YOU CAN MAKE A BOOKING

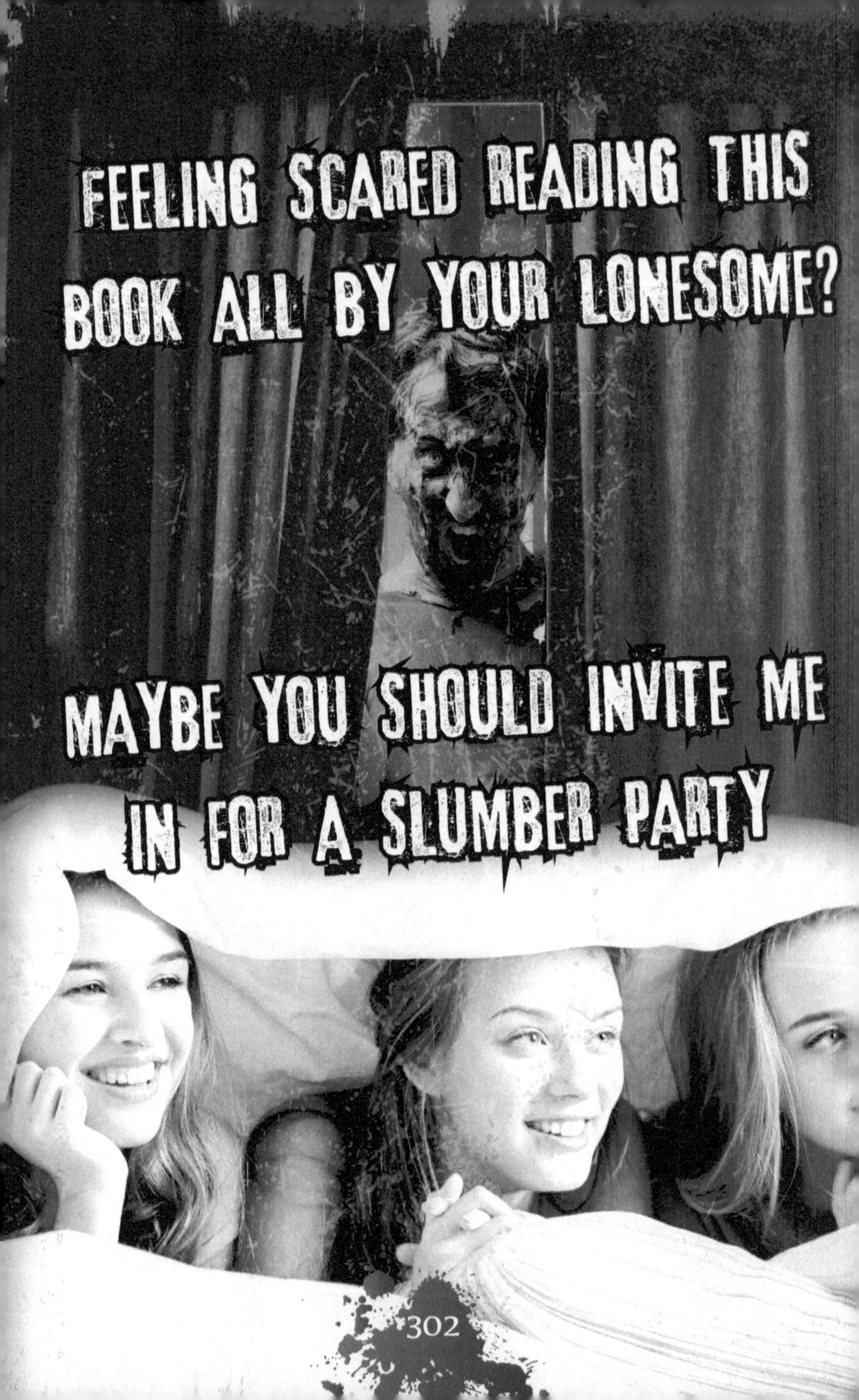

FEELING SCARED READING THIS BOOK ALL BY YOUR LONESOME?

MAYBE YOU SHOULD INVITE ME IN FOR A SLUMBER PARTY

Surprise GUEST

BY GABI EVANS

SURPRISE GUEST

BY GABI EVANS

The sun was just beginning to dip in the sky when 17-year-old Melody Kent's parents finally pulled the car out of the driveway, her father honking the horn and waving at her in his usual dorky way as they drove off. Melody waved back and remained standing in the driveway until the station wagon was out of sight. She had been feverishly planning this night for weeks. Her parents were headed to the lake for the weekend, a getaway they'd taken every spring without fail. Mel had promised that she wouldn't throw a rager. Just a few close friends, girls only.

"It's just us," Mel has assured her mother as she packed the car. "Sandy, Deena, and Crystal. No boys, no big party, no drinking."

Her mother's face was a mixture of concern and relief. It was the first time in so long that Mel was taking a further step towards returning to life as normal, rather than just going through the motions. With that in mind, she relented.

"Lock the doors. Don't open for any weirdos. Don't forget the emergency numbers on the fridge. And if I find out that there's been any alcohol…"

"Definitely not!" Mel smiled and hugged her. "We'll be fine."

She was actually feeling good about that night. Finally, something to look forward to since everything that happened the year before. Hosting a sleepover felt like some kind of declaration: I'm okay now. We're okay.

After Eric's death, Mel had completely withdrawn under a suffocating blanket of grief and guilt. It was an accident. A horrible, horrible accident that she had relived every day and every night without fail. It had all happened so fast. She closed her eyes and took in a deep breath of warm spring air, trying to push those thoughts out of her mind. Just for one night, at least.

That evening, the living room was awash in warm

lamplight and the flicker of a VHS tape playing *The Lost Boys*. Pillows, sleeping bags and magazines were scattered across the floor, and a half-empty popcorn bowl balanced precariously on the arm of the couch. Cans of Tab and Cherry Coke and nail polish bottles clinked on every surface, while cicadas buzzed outside in the warm night.

"Okay, but tell me—honestly—who do you think is hotter, Kiefer Sutherland or Corey Haim?" Deena asked, twirling her raspberry Twizzler like a baton.

"That's easy. Kiefer," Sandy said without looking up, as she applied neat strokes of electric blue polish to her long, talon-like nails. "Bad boys are always hotter."

Mel rolled her eyes. "You only think that because he's got that vampire swagger. If he worked at the gas station, you'd run the other way."

"If he came flying through the window right now, tell me you wouldn't let him bite your neck," Sandy said, pausing to blow on her nails.

"I'd stake him before he even got through," Deena chimed in, brandishing a Twizzler like a weapon.

Crystal laughed softly, seated cross-legged near the fireplace. While Mel, Sandy and Deena had been close friends since middle school, Crystal was the newest to the group. She had only moved to town about a month ago, having transferred to their high school from somewhere up north. She had an air of shyness to her—soft-spoken and polite. She wore her dark hair tied back with a scrunchie, her bangs sitting just above her ever-observant brown eyes. She always seemed cold, even if the weather was stifling outside.

"I think Corey's cuter," she offered. Her voice was quiet, but it cut through the chatter.

Sandy smirked. "You would!"

Mel was glad things were going smoothly. After everything that happened last year, she and the others had fought hard to feel normal again.

The girls were sprawled across the floor later, halfway through their second movie, *April Fools' Day*, when Deena's voice broke through the lull.

"Do you guys ever think about Eric?"

The energy of the room instantly shifted. Mel's throat tightened. She hadn't expected his name tonight. They didn't talk about him much anymore. Not at school, not with friends. They all tried to move on. Or pretended to. Sandy began nervously twisting locks of her long, blonde, crimped hair and sighed.

"I still can't believe it. I thought he was going to pull

through.”

Mel stared down at the string of Twizzlers in her hands, pulling them apart, one by one. Her knuckles were white.

“He shouldn’t have gotten in the car,” Deena said softly. “None of you should’ve been driving.”

Mel’s voice came out small. “I know.”

An awkward silence followed. The kind that thickens in the air, becoming hard to breathe through. Crystal looked between them all, chewing her lip.

“I didn’t know him,” she said after a moment. “But I’ve heard things.”

“What kind of things?” Deena asked.

Crystal shrugged. “That he didn’t want to be in that car in the first place. That he was the one who suggested a taxi.”

Mel flinched. “That’s not true! I mean, we had all been drinking, but he was happy enough to get in the car with us.”

Crystal tilted her head. “You were the one driving, right?”

Sandy closed her eyes and exhaled deeply. “Okay guys, I don’t think tonight is the night for this. Let’s just change the subject, please.”

Mel stood abruptly. “I’m getting another Coke.”

She stormed into the kitchen, her vision blurring with unshed tears. Even now, a year later, that night still haunted her—the screech of tyres, the deafening bang, the flashing lights of the paramedics. The twisted wreckage of the car and Eric's blood on her. She'd only had a few beers at that party. They'd all been drinking, but she had shrugged off any doubt about driving. It wasn't as if they had far to go, and it just seemed simpler than calling someone up for a ride.

And then, he was gone.

Back in the living room, the girls resumed talking about lighter things. School, Mrs Fernwood's insane tests, Dylan's new haircut. When Mel returned, Crystal offered her a sympathetic smile and a quiet, "Sorry."

Mel nodded, blinking furiously.

At midnight, the phone rang. Sandy, nearest to it, picked it up.

"Hello?"

A low raspy voice answered: "Pretty girls shouldn't be staying up so late."

Sandy blinked, then grinned. "Dylan, I swear to God, if you're trying to scare us..."

But the line went dead.

She turned to the others, laughing. "That boy tries too

hard."

"Dylan?" Mel asked, grateful for the shift in mood.

"Has to be. Total horror nerd. Bet he's been waiting all night to do that creepy voice."

Deena shivered. "Don't even joke like that."

"Did he even know that you guys were coming over tonight?" Mel asked doubtfully.

"Maybe someone mentioned it to him at school yesterday," Sandy shrugged. "Besides, doesn't he live on your street? He probably saw us all arriving."

The phone rang again. Crystal answered it this time. Her face paled.

"What is it?" Deena asked, her voice wavering.

Crystal slowly set the receiver down. "They just breathed heavily. They didn't say anything."

"You should have just told him to fuck off," Sandy said. She leaned over and picked up the phone receiver. "Or better yet, leave the receiver off the hook."

The girls soon lost themselves in the movie again, forgetting all about the phone calls, until they were interrupted by banging at the window. Deena got up and parted the curtains, cupping her hands around her face to see out the window.

"I can't see anything," she said.

Sandy jumped up, heading towards the front door. "I'm gonna catch Dylan in the act."

She yanked the front door open and stepped onto the porch. The night outside was black and quiet, apart from crickets chirping and trees rustling in the breeze.

She turned back. "No one's there."

As she stepped back in, the porch light flickered and went out. So did every other light in the house until darkness swallowed them whole.

Deena screamed. "Okay, that's not funny anymore!" She cried. "Turn the lights back on!"

"They're not coming back on," Mel said, after flipping the light switch a few times. She felt her way in the dark toward the kitchen and began fumbling in the drawer for a torch.

A loud bang echoed from outside. Then another.

"Is someone outside?" Sandy asked, her voice now trembling.

Mel turned on the torch, its narrow beam slicing through the dark. The light hit the faces of her friends, shining on their widened eyes.

Another bang came, closer this time.

Crystal screamed and pointed toward the back window.

"I think I saw someone!"

"Lock all the doors," Mel called out as she ran to the back, sweeping the torch beam across the yard. Nothing.

Then, another scream. Sandy.

The girls spun to see her back-pedalling from the hallway.

"He was in the hall!" She gasped. "Tall, in a hoodie, holding something—a knife or a pipe, I don't know! He saw me!"

"Call the cops!" Deena hissed.

They rushed over to the phone, and Mel grabbed the receiver and held it to her ear. There was no dial tone. She frantically pressed the hook switch numerous times.

"The line's dead," she whispered.

"We have to hide," Deena said shakily. "He's already in."

"What if it's just Dylan?" Crystal whispered hopefully.

"No way," Sandy replied. "That wasn't Dylan. That guy was big."

They all froze as another crash was heard from upstairs.

The house was no longer theirs. Mel turned to the others, voice calm but shaking.

"Split up. Find a place to hide. We'll meet back here if

and when it's safe."

"No!" Deena protested. "We stay together!"

But already Crystal was vanishing into the dark. Sandy followed. Mel took Deena's hand and pulled her towards the downstairs coat closet. They squeezed in together, their breaths shallow, trying not to make a sound.

Then came the screams.

First one.

Then two.

Then silence.

Mel held Deena's hand so tightly that her fingers had gone numb. The closet was pitch black, the only sounds their panicked breathing and occasional groans of the house. The silence following the screams was worse than the sounds themselves; hollow, final. Then the heavy footsteps started up again.

"Do you think they're okay?" Deena whispered, her voice cracking.

"I don't know."

A floorboard creaked just outside the door. Slowly. Deliberately.

Deena gasped, clamping a hand over her mouth. The creaking continued, approaching the closet. Mel squeezed her eyes shut and waited.

The doorknob began to twist.

Deena whimpered, and Mel reached out, pressing her hand against the knob to keep the door closed. It stopped.

Then came three deliberate knocks.

Knock. Knock. Knock.

Mel's heart hammered inside her chest. She didn't dare move. Whoever was outside...they knew.

A pause.

Then footsteps retreating. Slow and taunting.

Why didn't he open the door? Mel's best guess was that he was playing a game with them. He wanted to toy with them, the way a cat tortures and plays with its prey before going in for the final attack.

They stayed in the closet for what felt like an eternity. Maybe it was only five minutes, maybe it was an hour. Time no longer moved normally. It stretched and warped in the dark.

"We have to find the others," Mel finally whispered.

She slowly opened the closet door as quietly as she could and peeked out. The hallway was dark, but empty. No sign of him.

They crept into the living room, and Mel switched her

torch back on.

The room was in complete disarray. The curtains were ripped down, and the couch was overturned. But more chillingly, drops of blood were spattered all along the carpet.

Mel's knees nearly buckled.

"Oh my God…"

Deena turned, retching into the corner.

Behind them, they heard a floorboard creak. Mel tightened her grip around her torch, prepared to use it as a weapon as they spun around.

Crystal stood in the kitchen doorway, her face pale, spattered in blood.

Mel rushed to her. "Are you hurt?"

Crystal shook her head. "The blood's not mine. It's…it's Sandy's."

"No," Deena whispered.

"He caught her near the stairs. She tried to fight him off, but he—he was too strong."

"Is she still there?" Mel asked, panic rising.

"I don't know… once he started attacking her, I just ran and hid."

Mel turned towards the stairs. "We have to look. What if she's potentially still alive? I mean, she'd be barely hanging on if she is, but…"

Deena hesitated. "But what if he's still there? And what can we do? We can't even call an ambulance!"

"Then we run," Mel said. "But I'm not leaving her."

Together, the three crept over to the stairs. The light of the torch rested on something that made the bile rise in Mel's throat. Sandy lay at their base, limp as a rag doll and soaked in blood, her eyes wide open in terror, her mouth frozen in a wide scream. Multiple stab wounds covered her chest. Deena raised her hands to her mouth and sobbed.

"Giiiiirrrrlllsssss…" came a deep, sing-song voice from somewhere in the house.

"Go! Just go! Now!" Mel whispered and pushed Deena and Crystal towards the stairs. They all bolted up the steps as fast as their trembling legs would allow them and rushed into Mel's parents' bedroom. Deena crawled under the bed, and Mel and Crystal hid in their closet, pulling the door shut behind them. There was just enough room for both girls to sit side by side, pressed together in the dark. Mel still clutched her torch, but she didn't dare turn it back on.

Silence.

Then—

Whump. Whump. Whump.

Heavy footsteps entered the bedroom.

Mel held her breath.

"Come on, girls," came the man's voice again, followed by a chuckle. "Come out, come out, wherever you are..."

Mel and Crystal watched through the slats of the closet door. Moonlight poured in through the window, and she could make out the figure of a man reaching down to check under the bed.

Oh no...no, no, no.

"Well, look who we have here!"

Mel heard the sound of Deena being dragged across the carpet, followed by her scream.

"No!" Deena cried amidst terrified sobs. "Please! Why? Why are you doing this?"

She continued to plead with him as he forced her up and pinned her against his chest with his arm. Then in one swift movement, Deena's pleas dissolved into wet gurgles as he sliced her throat. He released Deena, letting her collapse to the floor in a heap. Mel sat rigid with fear as she listened to the sputters, chokes, and gurgles coming from where Deena lay. The man knelt over her and began plunging the knife in and out of her body. Mel felt her nausea surge as she heard the wet, slicing sounds of the knife. Once the sounds from Deena grew silent, he called out,

"I'll leave the other one for you." Then he turned and left the room.

"What?" Mel whispered once his footsteps had faded. "Was there someone else with him?"

"Don't worry," Crystal said. "It's almost over."

Mel turned to her, confused. Crystal was staring straight ahead, not blinking.

"What do you mean?" Mel asked.

Crystal didn't answer straight away. When she did, her voice was eerily calm.

"It's kind of poetic, don't you think?"

Mel shifted uncomfortably. "What are you talking about?"

Crystal turned slowly to face Mel and smiled, her face visible in the moonlight filtering through the closet slats. "I used to think justice didn't exist, that the world just let people get away with anything. But then he and I got talking. And planning."

Mel's stomach dropped. "What are you saying?"

Crystal reached into her denim jacket and pulled out a knife.

Mel recoiled, hitting the back wall of the closet. "You..."

she whispered. "You helped him?"

Crystal's eyes gleamed. "You didn't recognise him at all? That was Eric's brother. Kyle. I'm their cousin."

Mel couldn't breathe. Crystal leaned in, pressing the cold blade against Mel's throat.

"Do you know what it felt like to get that phone call? To hear that he was gone, and it was because of you? Because you got behind the wheel drunk and thought nothing bad could happen?"

"It was an accident," Mel whispered, shaking uncontrollably.

"You killed him," Crystal hissed. "And your pathetic little friends covered for you. Laughed. Moved on. You cried your fake tears and played the victim."

Tears streamed down Mel's cheeks. "It wasn't like that! I—I never stopped thinking about him! I never forgave myself! Please..."

Crystal's voice softened. "Don't worry. You won't have to think about him for much longer."

She raised the knife. Before she could bring it down, a loud crash sounded from downstairs.

"Police!" A voice shouted.

Crystal paused, and Mel used the moment. She shoved

Crystal sideways, slamming the closet door open. The knife just missed her as she pushed past and ran. Behind her, Crystal screamed in fury.

Mel bolted down the stairs and almost made it to the landing before she tripped and fell. A searing, agonising pain arose in Mel's head from where she hit it as she landed. Crystal leapt from the top step and landed on top of her. She raised the knife again when Mel heard approaching footsteps and the cocking of a pistol.

"Police! Drop your weapon!"

Everything began to swim before Mel's eyes, just before the darkness came.

Mel lay groggily in her hospital bed, moving back and forth between sleep and alertness, but sleep was winning the battle. It was not as though there was much to look at while awake: bland white walls and fluorescent lights topped off with a pungent scent of disinfectant.

She glanced down at the cast now adorning her right arm. The impact from when Crystal landed on her had left her with a broken arm, as well as a concussed head. She closed her eyes again, trying to process everything that had happened the night before. She kept hoping that she was going to wake up soon from a very sick nightmare and that she would find herself back in her own bed. Her friends would still be alive, and her life would still be somewhat intact...but it hadn't happened yet.

She had been interviewed in length by the police that morning; her concerned neighbour had called them after hearing the screams coming from her house. She had told them as much as she could. The officer who took her statement was very gentle and patient with her as she tried to form sentences from the jumbled, terrified mess that her mind had been reduced to. Her parents had also been contacted and raced back as fast as they could.

Mel could not imagine how she would ever face setting foot in that house again. She didn't even know Eric had a brother—she didn't remember him ever being mentioned. But it turned out that Kyle was already known to police and had been in and out of institutions for the past few years. He and Crystal had orchestrated everything after Mel had invited her for the movie night– from the cutting of the power and the phone line to the attack itself.

A gentle knock on the door made her reopen her eyes. They widened in surprise and alarm to discover Eric and Kyle's mother gingerly standing in the doorway. Mel had felt so uncomfortable and guilty around Mrs Manning since the accident. She had apologised profusely, of course, cried with her, and offered limitless condolences. But couldn't look her in the eye ever since without feeling that heavy, twisting feeling at the pit of her stomach.

Mrs Manning's eyes were red-rimmed with dark circles underneath, her unkempt hair coming apart from where she had braided it down her back.

"I might be the last person in the world you want to see right now. You can tell me to leave if you want. But this won't take long," she said. "I just...I'm in complete shock. I don't know what to say..."

Her voice began to waver, and she paused to take some steadying breaths before continuing.

"I'm just...I'm so, so very sorry. I can't believe it. Kyle had a lot of problems, but I never in my wildest dreams imagined this...." Her words broke off into a sob. "I'm so sorry. That obviously won't fix anything, but..."

Mel nodded. "I know."

Mrs Manning hesitated, then placed a package on the

bedside table. As she did so, the package knocked off the nurse call bell that had been resting there.

"Whoops," she picked up the corded button, and still holding it in her hand, she continued, "I know this isn't much...quite pathetic really. But I know you always liked these, and well, I just had to...do something, at least see that you were okay."

"Thank you," Mel said weakly and tried to smile.

"Anyway, I don't want to keep you. I'll let you get some rest, but I'll be thinking of you." She replaced the call bell in its holster above the head of the bed, gave an awkward smile and began to leave the room.

"Oh, wait," Mel began, "sorry, could you please put it back on the table? I just can't reach back there..."

She had already gone. Mel took the box with her good arm and pried the lid open. Slices of homemade chocolate cake. Mel had almost forgotten what an amazing cook Eric's mother was. She took a slice and had a bite. Beautiful. She never could get enough of Mrs Manning's baking.

After devouring another slice, she lay back and shut her eyes again. She noticed her mouth beginning to tingle. Curiously, she ran her tongue along the inside of her mouth. The tingling remained. If anything, it was growing worse.

Sharp pains began to shoot through her muscles.

"Argh!" She cried as her back arched uncontrollably backwards. She tried to take a deep breath, but it was a struggle. Each breath she tried to take required more and more effort. Her arms and legs grew stiff, and frantically she tried to look for the nurse call bell, then remembered that Mrs Manning had placed it out of reach.

"H-help," she rasped, but breathing was so laborious now that she couldn't speak properly, let alone shout. Her back arched further, her limbs so stiff and painful that she could barely move. Suffocating in her own body, she began to grow lightheaded. The last thing she saw as she glanced at the window to her room was Mrs Manning. She stared at Mel from behind the window, a triumphant smirk spreading across her face.

DID YOU WANT TO JOIN THE WRITER OF THIS ROTTEN REVENGE TALE FOR A SCRUMPTIOUS SLICE?

THEY SAY THAT SURVIVING HIGHSCHOOL CAN BE MURDER

BUT THEY SHOULD TRY CLEANING UP AFTER THE LITTLE BASTARDS

MALIBU
Prom Night
GOREFEST

BY MARK OXBROW

MALIBU PROM NIGHT GOREFEST

BY MARK OXBROW

"Stupid feck'n a-holes." The Janitor, Eugene, hated the students. He hated the teachers, too, the Deputy and the Principal Hoag, but he especially loathed the students.

They blocked the toilets, stuck gum under the desks, stubbed out cigarettes on the walls and scribbled profanities on the restroom doors. They deserved to die. All of them. Slow, painful and unusual.

Tonight was the worst. Prom Night.

He had to work late. Confetti, balloons, streamers,

stupid hand-painted banners. Eugene hated confetti. He'd be stuck, after midnight, sweeping up confetti and cleaning up vomit.

He stabbed a Pepsi can with the trash spike and stuck it into a garbage bag, limping across the carpark, dragging his bad leg.

There was that punk girl and the French exchange student. He never bothered to learn their names. They were smoking Gauloises cigarettes and whispering. Always whispering something.

Eugene hobbled into the school, shoving balloons and streamers out of the way.

He ignored Miss Huggins, the school librarian, wishing him a good evening.

Noxious red punch pooled on the floor. Students hanging around lockers, giggling.

There was Mitsy, the cheerleader, blonde hair and lavender mohair sweater, flirting with some jock basketball player. Chad or whatever his name was.

Her ex-boyfriend, Trent, was staring daggers from down the hall. Ex-boyfriend, ex-quarterback, ex-somebody. Recent nobody. Trent had been a bully since Elementary School. Toxic. He swore, smacking Kody's head into a locker as he grumped by.

Kody with a K. Loser, class clown, court jester to Queen Bee Mitsy and her stupid clique of deadbeats. A-hole. Like all the others. Better off dead.

Eugene jangled the school keys. Unlocked the door to the boiler room. He slammed the door behind him, shambling down the stairs into the dark. A single lightbulb sparked as he flipped the switch. Boxes of toilet rolls and plastic bottles of bleach. Workbench. Toolboxes. Shears to hack at the hedges, a hefty shovel, garden fork, leaf rake, hatchet, double headed axe.

Eugene snatched a half-bottle of Kentucky bourbon out from under the rags in a metal bucket. He took a swig.

He sat near the boiler, downing the whiskey. A smile cut across his face. Eugene clawed a broken brick out of the way and dragged a wooden cigar box out of its secret hiding hole. He swirled the last of the bourbon and opened the box.

Two dozen human fingers.

He'd severed them all. Cut a finger off each victim. He'd started in Fairfield, Maine. Tortured and murdered his way west across America.

Eugene picked up a putrefying finger. San Antonio, Texas. Hot pink nail polish. A diamond and ruby engagement ring. He never bothered to learn her name either.

Always heading west. But then he hit California. Found himself in Malibu, staring out at the Pacific Ocean. Nothing but waves and blue sky.

Eugene hated Malibu. Hippies and surfers, bohemian Tinseltown types and Los Angeles money buying up the beachfront.

He got himself a dead-end job. School janitor. Saving enough cash for a second-hand van. He'd be back on the road by September. Killing again. He'd got an empty cigar box and new pruning shears. He was thinking about his happy place.

"Hush."

"What?" Eugene jumped up.

The whiskey bottle fell to the concrete floor, splintering into a thousand razor-sharp shards.

"Hush."

Eugene stared, eyes wide, as the skull-masked slasher stuck nine inches of carving knife into his left lung. He gurgled, drowning in his own blood, spluttering for breath. The knife slid out, slashing across his throat. It cut Eugene's carotid artery, slicing his windpipe down to the spine.

The janitor slumped to his knees, the cigar box falling from his hand, severed fingers rolling out across the basement floor.

Indigo sniffed. "You think we should go back in?"

She wore a red tartan prom dress with studded leather belts and Doc Martin boots. It wasn't easy being punk in Zuma Beach High School.

"Bordel de merde!' Eloise rolled her eyes. "I think I would rather eat my feet."

Eloise helped Indigo survive.

She'd appeared out of nowhere a year and a half ago. A French exchange student from Paris. She drank inky black coffee, smoked Gauloises cigarettes and could get the best weed this side of the canyons. Eloise was wearing a little black Chanel dress she'd stolen from her mother's walk-in closet. Indigo was pretty sure that her father was a cocaine smuggler.

"Come on," Indigo reached out. "Let's stick tequila in the punch."

"Ok." Eloise smiled, taking Indigo's hand and hauling herself up off the steps.

Kody with a K hadn't expected to die in High School. He always thought he'd die rich in some Hollywood mansion, ancient, with facelifts, a TV-star wife and a Lamborghini. He was wrong. He was going to die on Prom Night, dressed as the school football mascot. Vik the California Vole.

Go Voles!

The axe hacked into his jawbone, slashing flesh and shattering teeth.

"Hush."

This should have been his big night. The greatest prank of the year. He had a sheep shut in the library, dressed in Trent's varsity jacket. Ready to run, bleating, into the auditorium when they announced Prom Queen and Prom King.

The Vole mascot costume was itchy. The axe slashed through fake fur and split Kody's skull. He dropped like a stone, blood and brains spilling out on the art room floor.

The slasher's black leather gloves gripped the axe hilt, swinging the axe, decapitating Kody. Dismembering the furry corpse.

"We can do this."

Indigo held Eloise's hand tightly as they neared the doors to the auditorium.

'Footloose' by Kenny Loggins echoed down the hall. They heard a thud as the DJ fumbled the next record. INXS, 'Need You Tonight'.

Eloise pushed the door. It was far worse than she could have imagined.

Disco lights were swirling. The smoke machine was belching out wisps of smoke. A luminous sign screamed *PARTY!* in green neon. Half the High School Seniors were dancing, the other half were lurking in the shadows, drinking, gossiping, trying to vanish, or furtively staring around the room.

Trent stumbled past, smacking into Indigo's shoulder, growling as he stormed out.

"Ow! Jesus," Indigo rubbed her shoulder, glaring at the back of Trent's head. "Jock dumbass."

Trent didn't hear. He raged down the hall, fingers curling into fists. He'd find Mitsy and smash that loser Chad's face in. He kicked open the door to the cafeteria. They had to be around somewhere.

Meanwhile, Eloise kept an eye out as Indigo poured a quarter bottle of Jose Cuervo tequila into the punch. She snatched two paper cups.

"Hey, arriba, honey!' Indigo handed a cup of punch to Eloise.

The DJ dropped the needle. It bounced, scratching, playing Prince's 'Let's Go Crazy'.

Trent swore and kicked a refrigerator. The kitchen was quiet. Maybe they were someplace else.

"Hush."

"Huh?" Trent spun about.

He saw a dark red costume, scarlet cloak, crimson waistcoat. White skull mask. He barely saw the hammer as it flew at his face, cracking his skull two inches above his left eye.

Trent crumpled like a hog in a slaughterhouse, eyes twitching, legs and arms flailing.

"Hush."

The slasher hit him again, harder, denting the side of his head.

Trent flinched, drooling as the slasher dragged him across the kitchen. He wanted to scream as his face was carved thinly in the meat slicer, but his jaw broke in the fall. The slasher disembowelled Trent with a kitchen knife, feeding his kidneys and intestines into the meat grinder, slowly turning the handle.

"Where's Mitsy?" Indigo frowned. "She should be here. Can't crown her Prom Queen if she's a no-show."

"Maybe," Eloise said. "She finally grew a brain and split?"

Indigo nodded, "I like that thinking."

Mitsy tousled Chad's hair.

"Tell me you want me."

She breathed in his ear.

"Yeah, you know I do, baby."

"Tell me you'd do anything for me," Mitsy whispered. "Say it."

"Uh," Chad fumbled with the zip on Mitsy's prom dress.

"Hush."

Chad's right eye jutted out, impaled on the trash spike. Blood gushed out of his empty eye socket. He stared blankly, body spasming.

Mitsy barely had time to scream. The trash spike pierced her left eye, skewering it back into her brain. The sharp spike stabbed a hole in the back of her skull.

Indigo and Eloise knocked back the dregs of their

punch. Billy Idol's 'White Wedding' was playing.

"Let's go." Indigo took Eloise's hand and led her out the auditorium doors.

The hall was quiet. Rows of lockers. Prom Night banners. A lurid trail of blood on the floor.

"Uh," Eloise squeezed Indigo's hand. "Do you see that?"

"See what?" Indigo was oblivious.

"Blood," Eloise edged closer. "There's blood. A lot of blood."

"Oh."

Indigo blinked, staring down at the blood trail.

"Something's wrong," Eloise said. "Like *Friday the 13th* wrong. *Silent Night, Deadly Night* wrong."

"*Chopping Mall* wrong?" Indigo squeaked.

"Yeah," Eloise nodded. "*Halloween* and *Terror Train* wrong."

"Oh.

"Indigo," Eloise said. "Hit the fire alarm."

Indigo didn't hesitate. She ran to the wall, broke the glass and pulled the fire alarm. Eloise wrapped her sweater around her fist and punched through the glass covering the hose and the fire axe. She snatched the fire axe with both hands.

"Oh my goodness," Miss Huggins whimpered. "Oh my goodness."

Eloise spun around, raising the axe.

"Help me!" Miss Huggins, the school librarian, stood quivering in the hall, her pink cardigan splattered with blood. "They're all dead!"

Principal Hoag shoved the auditorium doors open, teachers and senior students at his back. He saw the librarian, hands raised, dripping blood and the French exchange student wielding an axe.

"What the prickly Hell...?" He started to shout.

"No!' Indigo yelled, waving her hands about. "It's not like that!'

Miss Huggins shook her head. "No, it wasn't the girls. You have to see."

The blood trail led down the stairs, into the boiler room. Blood dripped from the lightbulb.

"Dear God!" Principal Hoag shuddered.

Kody's decapitated head was jammed in a woodworking vice. Pieces of furry Vole mascot hung from hooks. Mitsy and Chad lay in a pool of blood, their faces speared together. Stainless steel bowls full of Trent sat on the bench. Entrails and organs, eyeballs, peeled skin and his perfectly trimmed hair.

"Look," Miss Huggins said. "It was him. He killed them all."

A body sat, slumped, by the incinerator. Dressed in a dark red costume with a scarlet cloak and a bloodstained white skull mask. A kitchen carving knife jutting out of its heart.

"Edgar Allen Poe's *The Masque of the Red Death,*" Miss Huggins tore off the mask. "It was Eugene, the Janitor."

"What?" Principal Hoag gasped. "Eugene?"

"See there? He had a cigar box, full of fingers!' Miss Huggins pointed at the severed fingers on the boiler room floor.

Indigo was frowning.

"What is it?" Eloise said.

"But it doesn't make any sense." Indigo's brain was whirling. "In the library, you gave me a book. A book about serial killers. Ted Bundy, Gacy, Berkowitz."

"What does this have to do with anything? Principal Hoag snapped.

"Shut your face," Eloise snarled, raising the fire axe.

"Serial killers. They kill one victim at a time," Indigo said. "They keep trophies, like the fingers, and they don't change their M.O."

"Which means?" Eloise said.

"Which means that if Eugene was the serial killer that took all these fingers, then he wasn't the spree killer that murdered everyone tonight."

"So," Principal Hoag squinted, brain struggling to keep up. "Who's the killer?"

"Isn't it obvious?" said Indigo.

"You're pretty clever, bookworm." Miss Huggins raised a carving knife, pointing it at Indigo and Eloise. "You see what a little book learning can do?"

"What?" spluttered Principal Hoag. "Why?"

"Why? Why?!' Miss Huggins spat. "Do you know what a school librarian earns? And I had to deal with these ungrateful, spoiled children day after day. Blockheads like Trent, who never finished a book. Just watched the movie instead. Mitzy, who folded over the corners of the pages, like she'd never heard of a bookmark. Chad and his overdue library books. Two years. Two years I've waited for Chad to bring back *The Scarlet Letter*."

"And Kody?" Indigo said. "Why did you kill Kody?"

"Really?" Miss Huggins snapped. "Kody with a K? Didn't you all want to kill him? Kody with his stupid pranks and mindless tricks. Always thinking he was so bloody funny. And there is a sheep, wearing a varsity jacket, in my library."

"The cat's out of the bag, Miss Huggins," Indigo said. "What are you going to do?"

"Me?" Miss Huggins smiled sweetly. "What am I going to do?"

She lunged at Principal Hoag, plunging the carving knife into his belly. With a delighted shriek, she gutted him, ripping the knife up to his ribcage, severing his intestines.

"Hush."

Miss Huggins whispered, a finger to her lips, as the senior students screamed.

Eloise swung the fire axe. It flew from her hands, spiralling. The axe blade buried itself deep in Miss Huggins's face, splitting skin, muscle and skull, slicing her tongue in two.

Eloise took Indigo's hand. "I think I cracked her spine."

Indigo stared at her.

"Her spine," Eloise grinned. "You get it?"

Indigo swore under her breath.

PERHAPS YOU SHOULD SEE WHAT THIS WORRISOME WORDSMITH DOES TO THOSE WHO DEFILE HELPLESS BOOKS

KEEP YOUR PRETTY LITTLE
EYES FIXED ON THAT
REARVIEW MIRROR NOW
CAUSE OBJECTS MAY BE
CLOSER THAN THEY APPEAR

A COLLECTION
OF MADNESS
BY ROBERT VELD

A RECOLLECTION OF MADNESS

BY ROBERT VELD

Sometime in October 1985
About 2:00am

In the black of night, the 1974 Holden Kingswood stabbed its way through the dark at speed with Split Enz's 'Six Months in a Leaky Boat' playing courtesy of a cassette player that had seen better days. With only its weathered, yellowing headlights offering any kind of illumination in the darkness, it wrestled with the well-travelled dirt track on its way to its destination. The car swerved and turned without hesitation. Its driver knew the way, even all the way out here in the middle of nowhere.

The driver, a guy named Rick, gripped the steering wheel with determination as he was thrown about in the driver's seat. At 38-years-old, he looked 58; even in the dark.

With thinning hair that was already grey and a hardened, leather-like layer of skin adorning his face, the last stump of a cigarette hung precariously from the far-right corner of his mouth. His appearance was one that only a lifetime of chain-smoking cigarettes and substituting a well-balanced diet for a daily carton of beer could achieve. And, the less said about his dental hygiene, the better.

After tearing over hills and swerving into dips, the Kingswood slowed abruptly to a stop. The car's headlights shone into the side of a large, part-brick, part-timber wall that was also adorned with irregular sheets of corrugated iron. It was part of a large building, one in which a great deal of recent effort had been put into keeping the walls upright and plugging the many holes. In its prime, probably close to a century ago, it had once been a large horse stable. Unfortunately, in 1985, it served a far darker, more sinister purpose.

Turning off the ignition and pushing his door open, Rick got out and stood up. There was almost perfect silence, except for an irregular and inconsistent muffled thumping coming from the back of the car.

He dropped the last, miserable dregs of his cigarette onto the ground and smeared it into the dirt with what remained of the rubber tread on his well-worn, steel cap boot. However, he wasn't in a rush. He turned back around and dove back into the car, searching for another cigarette. He emerged a moment later, deeply satisfied. Having found another one of the damned things, he lit it with nervous excitement. His body filled with the sudden calmness that came with satisfying its constant nicotine craving.

After taking two long drags of the cigarette, he placed it into the corner of his mouth and made his way around to the car's boot. He planted the key with precision into the lock and turned it, despite the lack of any light, and placed his fingers under the edge of the boot, lifting it open. It was then that the boot's light turned on and shone across its contents.

"Hello, my little darlings," Rick said in a sly voice. "You pair were certainly making a lot of noise back here. I don't like it when people don't listen to what I tell them. I told you both to stay still. Well, it doesn't really matter anymore, does it? Go ahead, you can try screaming your fucking heads off now. We're miles from anywhere. No one's going to hear you."

Wrapped in grey duct tape, with their hands held tightly behind their backs, the women stopped struggling against their restraints at the sound of Rick's voice. They couldn't see him or scream, even if they wanted to. The torn lengths of cloth, despite only being the crudest of blindfolds and mouth gags, did their jobs well enough.

A second, much larger figure appeared beside Rick. At over six feet in height, even in the darkness, he seemed to throw a shadow. He was holding a large sea sponge in his right hand.

"So, Rick," he said in a heavy, deep voice, "where did you find this pair?"

"One was out wandering through the park along the river, that was the blonde. She said her name was Stacey. She was easy, Full of grog that one. Took my offer of a ride home real easy. The brunette, on the other hand... shit."

"Put up a bit of a fight, did she?"

"Bloody oath. I thought that I might have had to use the crowbar on her. She'd had a few drinks, but she still had her wits about her. She was out walking along the road out behind the racecourse. She told me to piss off when I drove up beside her. She'd just broken up with her boyfriend, or some shit like that. She scratched the shit out of my arm. She begged for me to let her go. Didn't you, Amanda?" Rick said, laughing as he looked down into the boot.

"While you were out collecting our specimens, did you remember the extra fuel for the generator, Rick?"

"Bloody oath I did."

"Good. Tomorrow night we get to have some more fun."

The mountain of a human being stepped forward and pushed Rick aside. He bent down and rammed the sponge into the faces of the two helpless victims, one after the other. There was a brief moment of strained movement and a muffled wheeze from each of them before they went limp. The chloroform did its job quickly enough. A short moment later, both men pulled the unconscious bodies from the boot of the car and carried them into the building.

Huddled on a concrete floor in only her underwear, a loud rumbling sound brought Amanda out of her forced sedation. It was a sound that her mind could not yet make sense of.

Her head thumped relentlessly with the excruciating pain of an intense headache. Realising that there was no longer a blindfold covering her eyes, she tried hard to open them.

Initially, all Amanda could see was a blur of intense light that emitted from a number of fluorescent lights suspended from the roof. However, as her eyes regained their ability to focus, her headache suddenly disappeared and was replaced by instant dread.

A large cement mixer sat rumbling with a full bowl of wet cement off to her left, but it only drew her attention for a second. In front of her, four lifeless bodies, bloodied and butchered, were strung up over near the opposite wall. Each one was buried up to their knees in a block of concrete. Chains running down from eye-bolts in a large overhead timber cross beam held their wrists up over their heads, heads that were covered in blood and disfigured beyond recognition. Their torsos were mutilated and riddled with wounds; one had even been skinned completely.

Blood covered large parts of the floor and severed limbs; legs, arms and heads were strung from the roof like ornaments. The stench was putrid, but the smell wasn't exactly what preoccupied Amanda's attention. All of her senses were overrun by what she was seeing. She was trapped inside a human slaughterhouse.

She tried to scream, but the mouth gag meant that

she only produced a muffled howl. She then attempted to get to her feet and run, but it was at this point that she realised that she was also chained at the wrists. She pulled hard at the chain, but it was fixed to an eye bolt set into the concrete.

She continued to scream and pull at the chain, but it was useless. A rush of tears ran down her face as a feeling of total helplessness took over. She didn't even notice the blood that now ran from her wrists.

It was then that she heard the rattle and scraping of a chain and a similar muffled howling coming from her right. Looking across, through tear-filled eyes, she saw a young twenty-something-year-old blonde chained to the floor several metres away, also stripped down to her underwear. It was the same woman who had been thrown into the car boot with her. For now, at least, they were alone. Rick, the bastard who had kidnapped them and the other tall mountain of shit were both outside having a smoke. However, they wouldn't be out there all night.

The large timber door pulled open. Both women shuffled their bodies hard up against the wall and went silent. They shook with fear.

The two men walked in and slid a large slide bolt across

to lock the door. Both were wearing dark blue overalls. Rick, the kidnapping bastard, looked even more unhealthy under the bright lights. He really did look like a miserable piece of shit. The second man was a far more imposing figure. He was built like a man mountain. Rick was almost six feet tall, but next to this guy, he looked short.

With dark brown hair and an expressionless face covered in at least three or four days of stubble growth, he looked like something carved into the side of a mountain. His name was Frank, though Rick called him Franko. He looked incapable of anything other than smashing rocks.

"Blonde or brunette first Franko?"

"The blonde. I always have more fun with blondes," he replied in a deep monotone voice with a grin.

"Ok then, blonde it is. You grab her, and I'll undo the padlock."

The blonde woman began frantically pulling against her chain and screaming uncontrollably as the skin around her wrists became smeared with blood. However, her efforts to pull the chain free were in vain.

Rick bent down and grabbed the chain to unlock the padlock while Franko started to pull the woman up by her wrists. He then wrapped his other massive hand around her throat. Any attempt at trying to scream now was pointless. She couldn't drag in enough air to breathe properly, let alone make noise.

He dragged her over to a free-hanging chain and released her throat. With his free hand, he grabbed the chain.

"Bloody hell, Rick. This one's bloody short."

"Do you want to still use the concrete on this one Franko? Or do you just want to have some free-swinging fun?"

"The brunette's taller. We'll give her the concrete boots instead. Just keep the mixer on so that the mix doesn't start going off. Grab the tape and tape her ankles together. Once we hang this one up, we don't want her kicking like a bitch."

With the blonde woman's ankles taped, she was hung by her wrists from the chain. Yet despite her predicament, the look of anguish on her face wasn't because of the excruciating pain shooting down her arms. She knew that she was going to die, and it was going to be agonising. All Amanda could do was watch, knowing that she was going to be next.

Frank walked over to a large timber bench off in the left corner of the building and flicked a switch on a radio which crackled to life. As if by some cruel joke, Duran Duran's 'A View to a Kill' filled the air. It would have been funny if someone wasn't about to die.

He shuffled some stuff that littered the bench, mostly loose hand tools and some short lengths of cut chain. He then grabbed an electric drill fitted with a long timber auger drill bit and walked back over towards the woman who was now squirming wildly on the end of the chain in a futile attempt to break free.

"Hey, Rick. Plug this bastard in for me."

"No worries, Franko, but I'm going to have to use the extension lead that the cement mixer is plugged into. Unless you want me to unplug the radio?"

"No, no, no. You know that I love my music while I'm watching them bleed."

"Ok, Franko. You're the boss. You should be right to go now."

Frank held the drill up near the face of his intended victim so that she could see the drill bit and pressed the drill's trigger. It whirred into life, and he started to laugh. All the poor woman could do was make a number of muffled sounds as the tears continued to stream from her face. She was actually begging for her life, but the mouth gag made it all inaudible. Unfortunately, the bastard didn't care.

"Listen here, my dear," Frank said, mere inches from her face. "I want to see if I can put a hole in you and see if I can see all the way through…"

In an instant, the blonde kicked out wildly with her legs and collected Frank in the groin with great force. Despite the fact that he was a big man, he dropped the drill, snarled in pain and collapsed to his knees, clutching at his balls.

"Grab the bitch, Rick! Grab the bitch!" Frank screamed, gasping for air.

Rick rushed over and grabbed hold of the woman as she continued to kick and shake at the end of the chain. He pulled down hard with all of his weight to try to bring her under control. It was at that moment that there was the cracking sound of bone as the woman's wrist bones broke, and the eye-bolt in the overhead timber cross beam holding the chain tore out. Rick fell back onto the concrete floor, still holding the woman in his arms. The large steel eye-bolt hit the floor only inches from his head.

Despite the chain still being fastened around her now broken wrists, the woman scrambled like a caterpillar off Rick and began to make her way across the floor.

Unfortunately, it was all to no avail. Frank regained his feet and yanked the chain back, pulling the woman back a few feet. She was now on her back, and all she could see was the great hulking mass of Frank, kneeling over her as he raised the power drill with the long timber auger bit in the chuck over his head.

He plunged it repeatedly into her chest and her stomach, over and over again. With each stab, blood sprayed from the woman's body like a water fountain, but the drill started to get heavy, even for a man like Frank. He got up, went back over to the bench and grabbed a large hunting knife. The sick bastard, who by now was covered from his head to his knees in blood, returned to the woman's body and continued stabbing it with the knife.

By the time he was finished, there wasn't much left resembling a human body. He stood up, knife in hand, and held out his arms. He looked up and let out an almighty yell before looking back down at his handiwork and throwing the knife across the building towards the bench.

Even though he was some four metres away from the massacre, Rick was splattered with blood too. All the skinny bastard did was to stand there with a sickening look of excitement on his face, like a kid about to be picked for his first sports team.

"Shit. She was a fighter, Rick. My balls still hurt."

"I saw you get right into it, Franko. Shit, you really got into that one. Not much left of her."

"No," Frank said quietly before raising his voice sharply, "but I'm still on a high man! Let's grab the brunette and keep the action going! I'm on a bloody high! Let's just go for it!"

Amanda was madly yanking at the chain as Frank and Rick walked toward her. Frank grabbed hold of both of her arms as Rick opened the lock that held the chain around her wrists. She had no chance of breaking free of his giant hands, but she put up a fight regardless as she was being dragged upright across the floor.

"For crying out loud, Rick. Get back over here! Grab her bloody legs. She's kicking like a fucking horse! Forget about plugging the damn cement mixer back in."

"I thought that you wanted the concrete for the brunette!" Rick called back over the rumble of the cement mixer that was now running again.

"Stuff it! Just get the hell back over here and help me with this bitch!"

As Rick made a clumsy attempt at trying to grab at

least one of Amanda's legs, she lashed out with a vicious kick that landed across the side of his jaw. Rick fell sideways and hit the floor. He was momentarily stunned and spat some blood-coloured saliva onto the floor along with a loosened tooth.

Frank lowered Amanda so that she was no longer quite so vertical. Instead, she was now being restrained in a position in which she was no longer able to kick so freely.

"Get up, Rick." Franko called, "Rick, get up!"

In an instant, Amanda bent her knees enough to plant her feet firmly on the concrete floor. She gave a sudden, sharp kick-off with all of the strength that she could muster, and launched a headbutt into Frank's groin.

"Oh shiiiit! Oh shit! Oh Shit! Oh Shit!" he screamed as he dropped to his knees for the second time tonight.

Suddenly, Amanda was free. She dropped to the floor but instantly scrambled to her feet. She knew she wouldn't get far if she tried to escape now. She ran over to the timber bench and fumbled through just about everything on it. Her right hand finally took a firm grip on a length of chain that was about two metres long. She liked it. Her left hand found a screwdriver.

She ran towards a still hunched-over Frank and swung

the length of chain at his head like a whip. A spray of his blood hit the floor as the chain cut a gash across the left side of his head and partway down his face. He let out a deep scream as he grabbed at the stinging pain and hit the floor.

Not stopping to admire her handiwork, she turned to run towards Rick, but was struck with a solid right-hand punch. The chain-smoking moron had already gotten to his feet. Amanda hit the floor hard and dropped the chain in the process. Rick stood over her. The fall hurt, and her forehead was now bleeding, but her will to survive held firm.

Without a second thought, she drove the screwdriver in her left hand upward and straight into Rick's groin. The blood flowed fast and dark. Rick let out an agonising howl that would have put a dingo to shame, and he collapsed into a heap on the floor.

With the sting of blood and sweat in her eyes, Amanda ran to the door and dropped the screwdriver. With her hands trembling, she fumbled frantically at the large slide bolt on the door. Adrenaline overrode the pulsing pain that was coursing through her body. The desperation to escape was her only priority.

The slide bolt surrendered its hold and slid free of the catch. Amanda slammed her body into the door, and it jolted open. She ran through the opening and out into the night.

"Get back here, you bitch! Get back here!" Rick screamed out, still clutching at his groin and wincing in pain.

Amanda ran frantically, but she stopped after making some distance from the building. She had no idea where she was, with the only light and sound coming from the slaughterhouse that she had just escaped from. She couldn't see anything as she spun herself around in a circle. She then had a thought and turned and ran back toward the direction of the building.

She ran to Rick's car and yanked at the driver's side door handle, which she was praying would be unlocked. The door opened, but the key wasn't in the ignition. Picking up a large rock, she ran back into the building.

Rick was still squirming on the floor in pain, just as Amanda had left him. Without hesitation, she raised the rock and smacked him in the head with it. He fell unconscious. She frantically searched the pockets of his overalls and managed to find the keys before running back out towards the car. She didn't look back.

The car started without a problem, and Amanda flicked

the headlights on. Starship's 'We Built This City' screamed from the car's speakers, courtesy of the cassette player.

Oh, fuck off! Amanda thought as she smashed the knob to turn the damn thing off. She put the car into gear, and the car started to roll forward as she pressed down on the accelerator with her foot.

A length of chain came smashing through the driver's side window and threw pieces of glass throughout the inside of the car. Amanda was dazed. Initially, she had no idea what had just happened, and the car came to a stop. However, she regained her senses as the car door was pulled open. It was Frank.

Amanda slammed her foot down hard, and the car took off. Frank held on to the door briefly, but stumbled and lost his grip. She drove off and managed to shut the door as she went, but after travelling about fifty metres, she stopped. Thoughts of what she had seen tonight played over in her mind. She turned the car back around and could still see Frank in the headlights several metres in front of her. Amanda made a decision. *This shit ends tonight!*

The car kicked as Amanda planted her foot, and it accelerated quickly. Frank looked like a stunned deer in the headlights. He had nowhere to go.

The Holden Kingswood threw him several metres backwards as it hit him at speed. She reversed the car back some way and noticed that he was struggling to his feet. She accelerated again, but he jumped out of the way.

Amanda looked around frantically before throwing the car in reverse and accelerating again. Unfortunately, the car veered off to one side and hit a tree. The engine was still running, and the car was still drivable, but the rear windscreen was shattered, and the boot had sprung open. The hit stunned her, but she recovered and put the car back into gear and rolled it forward to make sure that she could get free of the tree.

The passenger side door was suddenly slung open, and Frank lunged partway into the car. He pulled Amanda out of the car and threw her to the ground. She scrambled to her feet before Frank could grab her again. He had lost some of his speed. The hit with the Kingswood had managed to hurt him after all, but he was still dangerous.

Amanda had a thought. She ran towards the back of the car, but Frank managed to give her a partial backhand as she went. She hit the left-hand rear panel of the car before bouncing off it and hitting the ground again. A stream of blood began running from her nose.

"I'm going to enjoy killing you bitch!" Frank screamed at her.

"Fuck you!" Amanda yelled back as she threw a handful of dirt towards his head.

Frank stumbled backwards in the darkness, wincing in pain and clutching at his eyes. The dirt hit its mark. The bastard couldn't see.

Amanda got back to her feet and felt around madly in the boot of the car, just as Frank appeared behind her, and grabbed her shoulder. She spun around with speed and drove the straight claw end of a crowbar up into the underside of his jaw. His arms flew around wildly as she pulled the crowbar left and right. She then jolted it upward, beyond the roof of his mouth.

Frank's body went limp and got really heavy, really quickly. It fell against the back of the car and partially folded. The majority of his torso collapsed into the open boot space. Amanda let go of the crowbar and then, with all of her strength, she heaved the rest of him in and pulled down the boot as best as she could. The bastard was finally dead. It was time for her to go.

Sunday 2 November, 2025
8:30pm Channel 9

On tonight's episode of Australia's Greatest Unsolved Mysteries, we take a special in-depth look at one of Australia's greatest serial killers on this, the fortieth anniversary of the discovery of his bush shack of horrors in the highlands of New South Wales. In 1985, he was given the name Highland Killer. He was a killer whose murderous deeds could very well have remained a secret, except for an anonymous note that was found pushed under the door of a police station in country New South Wales. As we take a look back at the discovery of the scene of his horrendous crimes and we talk to the family members and friends of his victims, we will also ask some key questions: Who was the Highland Killer, and could he still be alive and living somewhere amongst us forty years later?...

Monday 3 November, 2025
10:35am

Walking into the church, the elderly woman moved slowly. Her advancing years and the disease that afflicted her body dictated the extent of her movements. She didn't stop to seat herself at any of the pews as she progressed, but from time to time she reached out seeking their support as she made her way further up the aisle. She was headed for the confessional.

Seating herself inside the small timber stall and closing the door, a small timber panel to her right slid across to reveal a small panel of lattice-like mesh. The woman raised her head, but her gaze remained straight ahead.

"In the name of the Father, and of the Son, and of the Holy Spirit. Amen," the voice said through the mesh. "May almighty God help you to know your sins, and trust in his mercy."

"Forgive me, Father. I have never confessed to my sins

before," came the woman's reply. "I have carried something with me for most of my life, and I now feel that I must unburden myself of it."

"It is never too late to confess one's sins, my child."

"Where does someone normally start with something like this, Father?"

"From wherever you like. However, I do find that the beginning is a good place to start."

The woman clenched her aged hands together before taking a deep breath. She glanced at the small rectangular opening and exhaled. *Well,* she thought, *I don't know you, and you don't know me. At least not yet...*

"I am going to murder someone tomorrow, and I am also going to ask God to forgive me for it. First though, I need to tell you my story. I need to do this before I die..."

Tuesday 4 November, 2025
11:10am

The elderly woman walked into the palliative care

wing of the Benjamin Paget Aged Care Centre without an issue. Despite the fact that her body was riddled with cancer and in great pain, she moved with a surprising amount of ease. Her mind was focused on something else today, and no one challenged her. For all the staff knew, she was likely a resident of the centre on her way to seeing a friend in palliative care. She headed down towards room fifteen and walked straight in.

In front of her was the frail frame of an elderly man lying on a bed. He looked dead, but he was still alive. Though there could be little doubt that it was only the oxygen tube running into his nose that was keeping him alive at this point. Time certainly wasn't on his side.

As she approached the bed, the old woman looked up at the name above the bed head and smiled before looking down at the face of the old man. The only things that moved were his eyes. The rest of him was all but immobile.

"Hello, Rick." She said, "I like the fact that you changed your name. I did the same thing. After all of the bullshit you put me through, I just wanted to disappear. You obviously wanted to do the same, but I've got to you in the end. How the hell did a piece of dog shit like you manage to live this fucking long? When I last saw you, blood was pissing out of you like a tap. Is that old scar on your head one that I gave you? Did you ever manage to use your dick again after I stabbed you?"

The old man's eyes bulged with fear.

"Oh, don't worry, Rick. Cancer won't kill you. I'm going to do that. This little syringe is full of shit that is really going to hurt you like hell. It's a shame that you won't be able to scream."

Friday 7 November, 2025
4:22pm

Responding to a concern for a welfare check, two police officers kicked in the door to the small, scantily furnished apartment. It didn't take them long to find the body lying lifeless on the bed, or the two empty sleeping pill bottles and the empty drinking glass that sat on the small bedside table beside a plain manila folder.

Leaning across the bed, the senior constable felt for a pulse. There was none. He turned and looked back towards the young female officer, only a couple of weeks out of her probation.

"I still do it, you know. Even though I know that there won't be one," he said to her.

"Do what, sir?" she asked.

"Check for a pulse. She has been dead three or four days by the looks of it. Suicide, I'd say by the look of those empty pill bottles. Stay here with the body, I'll radio this in." He said in reply as he wandered back towards the front door.

Looking down at the manila folder on the bedside table, the young constable picked it up and opened it. An old cassette slid out and onto the floor. She bent down and picked it up. Inside the folder was a set of old rego papers and about fifty typed A4 pages that she quickly flicked through with her thumb, before returning to the first page...

To whomever finds this,

For forty years, this miserable bastard of a world has known me as Michelle Timmins, but my real name is Amanda Brody. I grew up an orphan, a product of the system. By the time I was a teenager, I had already been through five different foster homes. I was a real problem child. The world was never going to miss me.

Officially, I am listed as a missing person, presumed to be a victim of the Highland Killer. This assumption isn't too far from the truth. I almost was.

With the events of that night burned into my memory, I have re-lived them every day of my life. I have suffered like hell for my survival. There have even been times when I have wondered if I would have been better off dying that night all those years ago.

But I have been very much alive until now. Cancer has managed to do what that bastard couldn't, I just decided to finish the job myself. I couldn't take the pain anymore. A good long sleep is what I very much look forward to.

A lot of information that you need to fill in many of the holes in the story of this killer is in the pages that follow. I can assure you that he is very, very dead, and he has been for forty years. I know this because I was the one who killed him.

However, there is more to the whole case of the Highland Killer. He had help and didn't act alone. I can assure you though, that you don't have to worry about his accomplice. He's dead now too.

This is my story...

I REALLY DO ENJOY
THEM STORIES WITH
A HAPPY ENDING

DID Y'ALL WANT TO MEET THE SINISTER SCRIBE BEHIND THIS TOTALLY TWISTED TALE?

TIME TO DIE
IF YOU THINK THESE STORIES ARE SCARY
YOU SHOULD TRY
WORKING IN RETAIL

31/86
FALL OF ALL
SAINTS
BY MATTHEW R. DAVIS

31/86 (FALL OF ALL SAINTS)

BY MATTHEW R. DAVIS

Friday October 31, 1986
All Saints' Eve

Aisling has just changed out of her regulation blue X-Mart polo shirt, hanging it in her locker and slipping into a Christian Death tee, and is heading out into the hall to punch her time card when Barclay appears in the doorway of his office and calls her name. He's got that don't-fuck-with-me tone, and she knows full well what this is about, has been dreading this reckoning for hours, but she holds her head up proud as she strides down the store's rear corridor. Callie, the manager's secretary, sends her a sympathetic look as she heads through the receptionist's antechamber into the boss's office beyond.

Barclay's already sitting behind his desk, leaning

his balding bulk back in that lavish chair like an ageing king lolling on his throne, one finger stroking his thick moustache. Declan Holly, the young Assistant Manager, is standing to one side, a big Halloween badge pinned to his polo, looking like he's about to witness an execution.

Aisling decides to get in first. "Before you start, boss, you know how that guy treats our staff—"

"You're fired," Barclay says, and she stammers to a halt. "Ash, I know damn well how rude that bloke is, but he's still a customer. And here at X-Mart, we do not throw coffee in a customer's face."

"It was stone cold!"

"I don't care if it was holy water and you were baptising him in the name of Jesus Christ!" Barclay barks. "Look, I like you, Ash. But rules are rules, and even after five years, you just won't listen. Enough's enough. Clear out your locker, kid."

Aisling glances between him and the sheepish Declan, who, despite being twenty-five like her, is shifting on the spot like a nervous schoolboy. "Wait. You don't even want me on the night shift tonight?"

Declan clears his throat. "Boss, you could at least keep her on for the changeover. We're going to need all the bodies we can get."

"No," Barclay declares, straightening his tie as if firming his resolve. "From now on, you may partake in the excellent goods and customer service provided by X-Mart and its employees *as* a customer. Maybe that will give you some crucial perspective."

"But I *need* that shift!" Aisling cries. "I'm counting on it!"

"And I was counting on you. But you let me down. Goodbye, Ash."

Barclay grabs a sheet of paper and starts scribbling a rough draft of her termination notice for Callie to type up. Aisling throws an incredulous, beseeching look at Declan, who winces and shrugs. With a croak of dismay, she spins on her heel and storms out. She brushes by Barclay's coat rack on the way, disturbing the costume hanging on it—a Father Christmas outfit, an empty red sack of Santa. Perhaps he's wearing this to a Halloween party tonight. In any case, it seems this jolly old bastard has put her on the naughty list two months early.

Well, Merry Christmas to you too, you self-righteous arsehole.

Aisling firms her face into a proud mask as she passes

through reception and returns to the hallway, refusing to cry. She feels both more and less like letting the tears flow when she sees JJ and Jackie waiting outside the lunchroom, their expressions knowing and kind. Still, she has a reputation to uphold. Aisling O'Hanlon is tough as leather, a pit bull in a tight skirt—the product of an Anglo-Irish father and Nigerian mother who both died young and left her to fend for herself, born and raised in a country that's awash with the blood of its proudly colonial past and often acts like the White Australia Policy is still in effect, she's always had to be harder than everyone else. Fate lurks in the shadows like a masked slasher, ruthless and unstoppable, and the moment she shows weakness, she's just another victim. And she's sworn that this is one black girl who will make it all the way to the end, who'll be left holding the machete when the sun comes up and the credits roll.

"You okay, sweetie?" JJ clasps her arm, a liberty he alone amongst her male co-workers is allowed—a gay man and her best friend, he can be trusted to touch without unwanted intent. "How did it go?"

"I've been 86ed," she says. "I'm an ex-X-Martian."

"Oh, Shandy." From anyone else, that nickname— derived from the drink, brown beer mixed with white lemonade—would be derogatory and wildly inappropriate, but the scandalous JJ somehow makes it charming. "This is an injustice. We'll start a petition. We'll hold a rally. We'll go on strike! We'll march until Aisling O'Hanlon is returned to her rightful position as head checkout bitch."

Aisling can barely muster a snort at this. "Don't bother. Barclay's made up his mind. I'm even off the changeover shift tonight. I'm so broke, this month's bills will kill me."

JJ steps back, folding his arms. Tall, slender and unrepentantly swish, he always looks too good for his surroundings. Aisling knows how much shit he deals with in this town, how often he's been harassed and terrorised, and regards his refusal to hide who he is as one of her biggest inspirations.

"Oh, dear. Looks like it's the docks for you then, honey."

"At least we'll still be working together," she snaps back, and JJ hoots in amused approval.

"This sucks, dude. It won't be the same without you," says denim-clad Jackie, his long, blonde Vince Neil hair held back from his face with the usual bandanna to expose a genuine sadness. Aisling suspects this sweet rock kid has a crush on her, but she's too kind to squash it underfoot. "We still got Halloween, though, right?"

"Bloody oath!" JJ agrees, slashing left and right with an imaginary machete. "Midnight murder and mayhem at the Crimson Curtains! And now you don't have to do this stupid evening shift, you can hang out in the parking lot and get shitfaced with us before the film. A blessing in disguise, Shandy!"

Aisling quirks one side of her mouth in a vague smile. She's been looking forward to the midnight screening of *Friday the 13th Part VI* across the road from the X-Mart, planning to go straight from the changeover shift to the parking lot for some quick beers and then into the cinema, but the thrill of flagrant slaughter is diminished when an uncertain future looms on the other side.

"See you tonight, guys!" Jackie calls into the lunchroom. Zipporah and Barry sit at the table there, looking up to send him waves and grins in return. Blonde waif Zipporah is halfway through one of her gaudy horror paperbacks, chomping an apple like a gluttonous Snow White, whilst bearish Barry's mouth is dripping with reheated spaghetti and sauce the colour of his beard. Both are working the night shift, and Aisling feels a minor tug of loss that she's no longer their colleague.

JJ and Jackie flank her down the central aisle of the

X-Mart, almost like prison bulls escorting her out of comfortable confinement after time served. Aisling eyes the endcaps of the shelves that line the walkway, dressed up with plastic pumpkins and wispy webs and other cheery Halloween tat. This is the reason for the night shift; Barclay has decided that all this Samhain stuff is to come down on the very night it's celebrating, to be replaced with Christmas decorations fresh for Saturday morning's patrons. Yuletide promotions beginning on All Saints Day? Looped Christmas jingles rotting brain cells for two whole months? Aisling finds this commercialism not just crassly premature but gross and tacky to boot.

No longer your concern, babe. At least you won't have to endure fucking 'Jingle Bell Rock' ten times a day.

Outside in the parking lot, a group of X-Martians has gathered around Mike's yellow Sandman panel van. Beefy blonde Mike himself, of course, wearing his traditional Hawthorn football guernsey as faithfully as a Shia Muslim wears a turban; Priscilla and Tilly the party girls, one blonde and one brunette and always colour-coding to complement each other's stylishly sexy outfits; Tupu the skinny Samoan nerd, who's writing a book about the horror films he never sees himself represented in; Eugene the white nebbish rap fanatic in his spectacles, Adidas tracksuit, and gold chains; Carl and Simone and Big Paula and Metal Fred. Some are working the night shift, and all are catching the new *Friday* afterwards. Aisling looks across the street and sees the cinema's neon signage is already lit, or at least half so; the first word is dark, leaving only *CURTAINS* to burn red through the afternoon air. She finds that bitterly appropriate.

Mike throws Jackie a tinny of West End Draught, which is cracked and guzzled with relish.

"Better not let Declan see you drinking," Priscilla notes, a vision in a fawn sweater and ivory mini skirt. "Goody Two-Shoes will dob you in."

"Let Barclay fire me, I don't care. Me and Ash, we'll start our own business. Party Incorporated!"

Jackie batters an invisible drum kit, cries "Go!", and segues into an air-guitar solo off the new Metallica record. Brunette Priscilla rolls her eyes at blonde Tilly, whose sweater and skirt are an ebony reflection of her own, as they light their Escort Blues off the same flame.

"What's the new *Friday* going to be like, my man?" Eugene asks Tupu, consulting the expert. "Is it the real Jason this time?"

"Absolutely," the studious Samoan replies. He spends his breaks reading the latest *Fangoria* imports, though they're always a month behind. "I've seen set pictures. Tommy Jarvis is back, but so is the real Voorhees. Machete, mask, and everything."

"Long as there's boobs and blood and beer, I'm good," Mike notes.

"All the classics," JJ agrees, holding out his hand for some skin, which Mike gives with gusto.

"Since when do *you* care about boobs?" Tilly asks him, incredulous.

"I can enjoy looking at things without wanting to root them, you know! Mike's shaggin' wagon here, a precious flower—even lady boobs. I just love slashers, and sadly, they aren't filled with naked men being menaced in the shower."

"Well, there was that scene in *The Final Chapter*," Tupu points out.

"Ah, Doug! Gone so soon. And *you* were into girls, you traitor."

"All those dudes are!" Eugene points out. "No queers at Crystal Lake, apparently."

"Yeah, *right*. You notice how every *Friday* has some nice hunky boy in a knitted sweater who hangs around the heroine but never does anything with her?" JJ sings the Bay City Rollers chant with a twist. "G-A-Y, G-A-Y, G-A-Y as A-M I!"

Eugene splutters on his beer, tickled pink. "You should be on a stage somewhere, man."

"Aw, I'm touched. And no, don't even think about it."

"Relax, MC Euge is only into black chicks," Mike quips, and like clockwork, everyone turns to look at Aisling.

"Fuck you all and see you tonight," she declares, not keen to discuss her dismissal—it's too fresh, raw as a new wound. Her friends wave her off to her beat-up Datsun 180B, the best thing she can afford right now... and for the immediate future, given her new state of unemployment. She cranks the little engine over, and her tape deck bursts to life where it left off, halfway through Samhain's *Halloween II*. Her special cassette, cut together just for tonight and now somewhat lacking in celebratory lustre. Aisling lights a cigarette and gets rolling, eager to be away from the site of her shame. As she pulls into the side street that separates the parking lot from the cinema opposite, she throws her arm out the window and flips her old job a defiant middle finger.

Rack off, Barclay. You'll never see me again.

As eight o'clock approaches, Aisling is in the bathroom of her cheap unit, doing her makeup in preparation for Halloween. Her tape deck booms from the lounge, spinning her Samhain mix: 'Monster Mash', 'Goo Goo Muck', 'Mummy, Can I Go Out and Kill Tonight?', 'Bela Lugosi's Dead', and—of course—'He's Back (The Man Behind the Mask)', the new single from tonight's movie soundtrack. She feels a sting in her soul every time she remembers she was supposed to be at work tonight—*needed* to be there, as demanded by her red-stamped bills—and every time, she takes another swig of beer and snarls defiantly into her mirror. The woman who sneers back wears the same black bra, the same upper arm tattoos—a triskelion for her Irish father on one side, the goddess Oya for her Nigerian mother on the other—and Aisling feels the stronger for her reflection's support. She's going to need that strength in the coming weeks.

The screen door rattles beneath the impact of knuckles. Her flatmate Kelly is out with her boyfriend Tran, planning to meet the X-Martians at the parking lot later, so the treats are on her. Aisling sighs and puts down her eyeliner pencil, drags on her shirt and slinks out through their threadbare lounge to answer the call.

The front door opens to reveal the tiny walled-in patio they've garnished with potted plants from the X-Mart's garden centre, its shadows lengthening as the daylight-savings sun makes its belated exit. Three junior monsters await her: a white-sheeted miniature ghost, an amateur Frankenstein's monster, a pale vampire with crimson lips. She praises their efforts, grabs a fistful of sweets from an old Pyrex bowl filled with discounted treats, and dishes them out. Then the children are off to the next unit, and Aisling is back in her bathroom, lighting a smoke as she peruses herself in the mirror. *Good enough?* Her long matte-black hair is down, her eyes thickly lined, her lips sticked to match. She's wearing her favourite Alice Cooper tee, a studded leather jacket, tight black skirt with fishnets; her ebony pumps wait by the front door. And that's not all, apparently, as now the screen rattles beneath the force of further knocks.

"All right, all right, keep your skin on!"

Leaving her smoke burning on the edge of the sink,

Aisling pads out to the door again, grabs a handful of lollies, opens the portal to reveal... no one.

But not nothing.

On her doormat, a severed head—

Wait, that's a jack o' lantern... isn't it?

It's not a pumpkin, it's smaller and paler than that, misshapen—but still carved into a gruesome grimace. She recalls that ancient pagans used turnips for this purpose and wonders who else remembers such obscure facts. A candle burns inside her visitor's empty cranium, smoke wisping up from its slitted eyes and ghastly grin.

"Top marks for effort," she calls out to her unseen visitor as she squats to get a closer look at the turnip. The smoke curls up around her face, a pungent and spicy scent she doesn't recognise, and when she recoils and stands, her head spins like a woozy top.

"Whoa, *shit*."

Aisling drops the sweets and plants her black-nailed hands against the door jamb to keep herself upright, trying to blink away the shadows that run into her head from the dimming patio. Something steps out of that darkness, already blurred by her fading vision, and she's not entirely sure it's real—its shape is all wrong, and antlers spread out from the crown of its head like spidery fingers.

Terror spikes through her, but it can't punch through the fog. She slides down to her knees, takes a defiant swing at the treacherous turnip, and then falls back into the darkness as the grotesque shape reaches down for her. She's gone with a muttered curse before she can catch a glimpse of its face.

Consciousness returns in a surge like a wave of vomit, bucking Aisling up from her slumped position. Her nostrils are thick with the echo of some acrid oddity, and her body instinctively recognises that she's not at home. The narrow walls close in around her, and she braces herself against them to hold them back, struggling to make sense of things as she stares at the blue curtain drawn across before her.

Wait...

She doesn't know how or why, but she knows exactly *where* she is: in one of the six cubicle-sized changerooms at the back corner of the X-Mart.

What the FUCK!

Aisling rises from the bench seat, realising that she's not wearing shoes; bar the fishnets, her soles are bare against the floor's cool tiling. Her jacket is gone and—what the *hell*—someone has replaced her Alice Cooper top with a blue X-Mart polo... *hers*, the one she left behind in her locker today, *Hi! I'm ASH* embroidered over one breast because her full name confused people. A quick self-exam reveals that nothing else has been fiddled with, her bra safely in place with tonight's movie ticket tucked into one cup for good luck, but still she shudders. Her clutch has been left behind—not that she needs money or tampons or lipstick right now, but her startled nerves are craving a cigarette. Her wristwatch remains frozen at 7:59, broken at the time of her capture.

The cubicle wall draws her eye—it's been freshly graffitied in black marker. A crude, leering pumpkin, two words above it and three below.

RUN... HIDE...

TONIGHT YOU DIE.

"Whoever's out there, you better have a *really* fucking good explanation for this!"

Unwilling to wait for revelation, Aisling rips the curtain back and lunges out of the cubicle. No one in sight, though the shop lights are on; she hears no sounds other than the low hum of the fluorescents. She's come to in the end changeroom, and before her is a door leading into the back hallway and staff area. She tries the handle: locked from the other side.

If this is a Halloween prank, it's a real doozy. She might even forgive whoever pulled it off.

JJ, right? Only he would have the bloody nerve. But he couldn't have done it alone... how many of my friends are in on this? And did they really think it would still be funny after I got fired?

Aisling slinks past the changerooms and the X-Mart opens out around her—a cream-coloured commercial hangar, high ceiling and distant walls. Directly ahead, the Womenswear, Menswear, and Kidswear shelves are ranked in parallel rows; fashionably attired mannequins stand at the ends like sentries and on podiums in the closed display windows with their faces turned away like punished children, hidden from the main street by closed rugose shutters. *Nighttime, then—but how late?* If the lights are on, she should be able to hear the late shift doing the changeover.

Why's it so QUIET in here?

Aisling walks the aisle beside the Womenswear shelves, infected by a sense of wrongness from being here when she shouldn't. She can't help but feel the pale mannequins are watching her with their empty eyes, stepping off their podiums to follow her into Manchester; the idea of being stalked by things in summer suits and tropical shirts and gaudy sweaters should be ridiculous, but somehow the innocuous fashions only add to their menace, and she keeps looking over her shoulder to assure herself that the natural order of things remains uncorrupted.

She passes the frilly bedding section, and when the public toilets come up on her right-hand side, she cuts through Automotive, Camping & Outdoor, and Sports to get to the central service desk. She half-expects to find someone here—this position is never unoccupied during opening hours—but the squared-off desk is devoid of life. She ducks under the counter hatch and stands at the heart of the entire store, feeling more lost than ever.

It's strange to be here instead of her usual post at the checkouts up front. As JJ had alluded, she'd felt like her five years' standing and natural authority awarded her seniority, made that team hers to command. No wonder Priscilla and Tilly had been a little surly at times. The way she bristled when Declan gave her an order must be just how the other checkout chicks felt when she threw her own weight around, fully expecting to be treated as their superior.

Weird that it took me getting fired and then shanghaied back into the store after hours to realise that.

From this point, she has the best possible view of the X-Mart. Directly ahead, she can see down the centre aisle all the way to the front entrance, which is shuttered as comprehensively as the windows to either side of it. The endcaps are still stocked with Halloween paraphernalia, but there are signs that the changeover has at least begun: near the front door, a high-sided pallet has been rolled out on a two-pronged jack to be filled with takedown stock. No one is near it, though, and when she runs her gaze around the store in a slow three-sixty, she spots no movement or other signs of progress, except for some dropped boxes between her and the storeroom in the back left corner of the building.

The silence gnaws at her nerves. This store once felt as chafing yet comfortable to her as an annoying sibling, but tonight it's an eerily empty set waiting to be walked by horrors. Aisling reaches for the PA mic, thinking to broadcast across the store and ask what the hell is going on, then pauses. The LCD display beside the cash till reads 11:11.

I've been unconscious for three hours!

Worse: the brown handset of the service phone has been trimmed of its beige curly cord and sits in its cradle free of an umbilicus.

Someone has sabotaged the outside line.

Aisling's unease blossoms into true fear. Weirdness is afoot here, but she has to *do* something. Her eyes fall on the cartons that have been dropped on the way to the storeroom, spilling rubber spiders and orange and black streamers on the floor, and she slips out from behind the desk, follows that trail around the edge of Homewares to the swinging *STAFF ONLY* double doors. To her left, the garden centre looms behind its green mesh walls, and she can hear its sprinkler system quietly going about its work. The sound of trickling water centres her, and Aisling pushes through the storeroom doors.

The wide, grey cement space catches echoes of her entrance in its high corners, where they dance across the upper reaches of the pallet racking that holds tonnes of store stock. To her left, the roller door that admits entry to the loading dock is pulled down and secured—not just with its usual chain, but also with a shiny new padlock from Hardware. To her right, a regular door leads into the

Staff area where she'd been summarily dismissed that very afternoon. Ahead of her, a pallet has been left in the middle of the room, divested of shrink wrap to display a stack of white boxes marked *XMAS*, some of them opened to reveal loops of glittering tinsel, inflatable candy canes, Yuletide baubles; another stands beside it, still on a wheeled jack, piles of plastic skulls peering at her from poorly packed cartons. Another sign that the Halloween-to-Christmas changeover began but hit some inexplicable pause.

Aisling passes the pallets and does a double-take. On the bare cement floor behind them is a large plastic washing tub filled almost to the brim with water. Red apples float on the still surface, undisturbed by the girl who kneels before it like a demented penitent, her head shoved into the tub. Her arms lie flat beside her, and her damp, dark hair splays out across the water like tendrils of black algae.

"Priscilla...?"

Aisling's heart races at this surreal sight. Why would her colleague be bobbing for apples here and *now*? Why is her face still underwater ten seconds after Aisling entered the storeroom?

You've seen enough horror movies to know why.

Chilled by this fatalistic thought, Aisling grabs her

workmate by the shoulder of her fawn sweater and pulls her head free of the water. Then she yelps and lets go, shuddering convulsively as limp Priscilla slumps to one side of the tub. Water dribbles from still cyanotic lips, marble eyes stare blindly at nothing.

All the signs are shockingly clear: *dead.*

Oh my GOD!

Before she knows it, Aisling has pushed back through the double doors and is running, running, back around Homewares to the service desk and then straight on toward the front doors, her shocked mind defaulting to the main exit. Shelf endcaps flash by, orange and black and green, still shilling Halloween and not Christmas. The pale tiled floor is hard and cold beneath her bare feet, her passage muted by the lack of shoes, but her panting breath sounds loud enough to echo throughout the entire X-Mart.

Aisling dashes by the half-full pallet and the denuded shelving behind it, staggers to a halt at the front entrance. The shutters are down here, too—and to her horror, they're also affixed with a brand-new padlock, its tiny, tight mouth mocking her.

How do I get OUT of here?

Her eyes fall to the bottom of the shutter. Whoever

closed them left a gap of perhaps three inches between the bottom edge and the floor. If she can wedge the pallet jack's prongs beneath that and crank them up, maybe she can bust off the padlock and get to the doors beyond. Mind whirling with hope, she dashes back to the high-sided pallet and grabs the jack's handle.

And then she sees what lies inside.

It's Mike, awkwardly sprawled atop smashed and sodden boxes of Halloween stock. His Hawthorn guernsey has been ripped open, and seven savage wounds are punched deep into his bare torso, one below each nipple, the other five forming a rough semi-circle across his belly. The copious blood that ran from each mortal blow, still glistening wet, does nothing to disguise the intent—the stab wounds form a crude picture. A grinning face.

Mike is now a human jack o' lantern.

Aisling slaps a hand over her mouth, too late to catch the cry that bursts free from it like some triumphant bird making a bid for the open skies. She cannot, *must* not make a sound. She's been kidnapped and trapped here, and whatever the reason, she is not intended to leave alive.

And now, from somewhere within the X-Mart, a strange cry rings out in answer to her own. It's like nothing she has ever heard before, primal and carnal, but it puts her in mind of a hunting horn.

Someone hears her distress. And they are on her trail.

As quietly as she can, Aisling ducks around the pallet and slips down the aisle between perfumed Beauty on her left and austere Office on her right, staying low. Once past the former, she sees the shuttered display windows that face out onto the parking lot, and at once she remembers—her *friends*! JJ and the other X-Martians are out there right now, drinking beer and smoking weed and *holy shit,* they have no idea that just behind these walls, their friends are dead and Aisling O'Hanlon is running for her life. If she could somehow make them hear her... but no, even if she were to batter on the shutters, they'd never catch that clatter over the blare of the Sandman's stereo. And the killer would be onto her like a flash.

Keep running!

In the front corner of the store, the in-house cafeteria lies dormant, its tables swabbed empty and its grill grown cold. Aisling veers to her right and her eyes hook left, caught by the shelves between her and the side wall. This is her favourite section—Books, Music, Video, Hi-Fi, Computing—and she's spent so much of her wages here. She helped Tupu to curate these endcaps, a labour of love.

King and Koontz rule the bookshelves, backed by Barker, Saul, Rice. 'Master of Puppets', 'Somewhere in Time', and 'The Ultimate Sin' have pushed 'Graceland', 'Invisible Touch', and 'Dancing on the Ceiling' aside for the spooky season, joining the still-charting 'Thriller' in a display of festeringly festive cassettes, their covers blown larger for the new CD format and more so for the few LPs still in stock. Horror VHS tapes are ranked together in chronological order, *Friday the 13th*, *Halloween* and *Poltergeist* collections joining a selection of Universal monster classics. Even Computing has a display of grisly games for Amstrad, Amiga, and Commodore 64: *Cauldron, Castle of Terror, Zombi*.

She even helped to garland the aisle that passes by this section with reams of dangling blood-red streamers, something she regrets now as she ducks under the low-hanging crepe paper.

Why did I ever think this was a good idea? Now I can't see if anyone's closing in on me!

Right on cue, something slaps against her face, wet and warm, and Aisling slams to a halt, blindly lashing out. Nothing but a crimson curtain of streamers, trailing down around her head... and a pair of feet swinging slowly before her, one still shod in a black pump that had inspired her purchase of the pair back at home. Gripped by a grim knowledge, she looks up.

And meets the blank, petechial gaze of Tilly, hanging by her neck from the crosspiece that Aisling herself had tied the streamers to, her face choked deep red. And oh, *fuck*, some of those drooping things aren't crimson crepe at all, they are slopping out of Tilly's slashed-open belly to dangle and drip—

Aisling bites off a scream, nipping her lip hard enough to draw blood that mixes with her black lipstick to create a unique, waxy, coppery taste. *Maybe I've just invented a new Halloween candy flavour,* she thinks, trying not to laugh in disgusted shock. Frantically wiping her face where Tilly's innards touched it, she runs on. Her only thought: a way out. And she's picturing the fire exit door in the rear corridor.

She dashes past the garden centre again—is something burning in there? No time to stop and investigate—and hits the double doors into the storeroom. She worries that by retracing her steps, she'll make herself more vulnerable to attack, but no one leaps out of the pallet racking to accost her as she crosses the chamber and hits the internal door.

Now she's in the rear hallway, hustling past the staff toilets and changerooms and lunchroom, and she's standing before the fire exit.

It's been padlocked shut, of course. Her eyes cut to the glass case on one side of the door, thinking she can maybe hack through this barrier, but it's been broken open, and the fire axe has been removed.

Fuck! No way out!

Aisling turns away, and light catches her eye, spilling through the half-open door of Callie's reception area. This is always left closed, so why? She pads closer, cautiously pushes the door wider, and sees that Barclay's office is lit up and open, too.

Is he here tonight?

She creeps across reception and peeps into the domain of her former boss. His grandiose desk is unoccupied, the room silent and still, but something about this sets her teeth on edge—*wrong, wrong, wrong*—as if she can sense him hiding in here, watching her. There's nowhere he could conceal his considerable bulk, but as she turns, she notices that the coat rack inside the door is now as nude as a winter tree. Barclay's festive costume is gone. Somehow, this makes everything worse.

Pensive and suspicious, Aisling slips back out to the hallway, and she's musing about all the things she's seen and how they might fit together when the lunchroom door swings open. She's already halfway through an involuntary spasm of shock when she recognises Jackie, flinching just as hard.

"Ash! Holy *shit*, dude! What are you doing here?"

"I don't know! Right now, trying not to get killed!" She's so relieved to see someone else that she slips into defensive anger like a comfortable coat. "What are *you* doing?"

Jackie gestures with one hand, which holds a cold meatball sub he's just filched from the staff fridge. "I didn't know what else to do. That psycho's running around attacking people, and there's no way out!"

"You've *seen* them?"

"I saw him go into the changerooms, so I found the keys and locked the bastard in."

Jackie uses his free hand to throw up the horns in shaky triumph. Aisling sees what she should have on the way by: the master keys, usually kept in reception, dangle from the changeroom doorknob.

"Good work! We need to get out of here, call the cops!"

"How? The phones are down, and the doors are

padlocked!"

Water runs inside Aisling's head, and she's not sure why—thirst from exertion and being drugged? Remembering poor Priscilla?—and then she clicks her fingers in excitement.

"The garden centre! There's another way out through there!"

Jackie's eyes widen. "Ash, you're totally bitchin'. Let's go!"

Aisling watches him turn away, a wave of sudden suspicion washing over her. Why should she trust *anyone* right now?

Maybe HE's the killer... chilling with a bite to eat now he's bumped off the whole night shift team...

A few details reassure her: he would hardly turn his back so easily if he hoped to get the drop on her, and he hasn't got a single splash of blood on him, and hell, he's *Jackie*—sweet, goofy, friend-but-never-more Jackie, safe and familiar in his battered denim jacket and homemade CLIFF LIVES shirt. She lets herself relax and starts to follow him.

As they pass the changeroom door, something slams into it from the other side. They reel back, turning to see what it is, and an axeblade crashes through the wood. From behind it, from its unseen wielder, a wordless cry of anger and frustration.

"He's coming through!" Jackie helpfully points out.

"Here's Johnny, all right! Who's in there?"

"Who do you think? Come on!"

Followed by the sound of the door rapidly splintering, they hurry down the hall and push through into the storeroom where poor Priscilla lies still as a landed fish, oblivious to their passage. Jackie hisses a hurt curse under his breath, and then they're shoving open the double doors. To their right, the shade cloth walls of the garden centre, and on the other side of that, a blessed exit.

Assuming the killer hasn't chained that one shut, too. And he seems to know his way around, so yeah, he probably has.

He's one of us, isn't he?

The list of suspects is mighty short. She thinks of what she saw—and didn't see—in the office, what she saw smashing through the changeroom door, and it reminds her of a crappy festive slasher she's watched... but then she remembers the turnip, the antlers.

Why won't anything make sense?

Aisling follows Jackie into the fragrant surrounds of the darkened garden centre: blooming flowers, fresh soil, rich oxygen. She's always loved the atmosphere in here: the quiet, calm aura of the plants, everything green and lush and verdant, a tiny rainforest in the centre of the city. Ferns and fronds reach out from the walls, water drips from hanging pots, and everywhere she looks, the big room is full of life.

And tonight, death.

As they walk toward the middle of the space, which has been dimmed down to murk and cleared of shelving in favour of some odd installation, Aisling notices three more familiar corpses on the cement floor. Her gorge rises as she recognises Eugene, Barry, and poor Zipporah. A mystic circle has been drawn around them in blood, unfamiliar symbols traced inside its rim. Within, their slaughtered forms are arranged into an oddly familiar pattern, their feet together in the centre, their torsos and arms bent into matching unnatural curves; Aisling thinks of the triskelion tattoo on her arm, recreated in twisted limb and broken bone.

Jackie howls in shock and sorrow. Grinning faces watch his torment from around the room: pumpkins and, yes, more turnips—a dozen carved jack o' lanterns with candles burning inside, placed to bear witness to whatever insanity is being played out here tonight. And insanity is the word, might just be the world as far as Aisling's mind is concerned right now, because beyond those brutally reshaped corpses, someone has arranged a strange kind of doorway. They've stood a wire garden arch in the centre of the room and draped it with vines and creepers, surrounded it with drooping ferns and grasping palms until it looks like the entrance to some kind of forest barrow... and through it, Aisling sees something impossible to credit. She noted firelight in here before when she passed by, and it turns out that flickering isn't coming from the jack o' lanterns. Beyond the archway, deep inside and further away than the X-Mart wall, a bonfire is burning.

"Am I going bonkers?" Aisling grips her skull between both hands to keep her throbbing brain subdued. "What the hell *is* this?"

"This is the *true* All Hallows Eve," someone says, and they spin around to see that they've been followed into the garden centre. "This is Samhain, once and ever, exalted and bloody."

"Oh, crumbs," Jackie whimpers, dropping his meatball sub.

The figure blocking the doorway stands as tall as

he, but it seems much more imposing. This is because an animal skull is mounted on its head, antlers affixed on either side and strings of bone trinkets hanging down around its face, which is half-covered by a dirty rag mask that seems stiffened with blood; it's because a fur cape is draped around its otherwise unimposing shoulders, fringed with more sharpened bones; it's because the pale body beneath is naked except for paganistic whorls and swirls of blue woad, that and less symmetrical splashes of drying blood from the slashed corpses of their friends. Not to mention the crimson knife that is clutched in one sure hand, its six inches slaked but ever thirsty.

"Mankind has forgotten the true meaning of Halloween. Instead, we venerate the birth of a feckless idol with chintzy cheer and chestnuts and candy canes! But tonight, all will be blood and fire and sex and meat. Behold the gate, open and ready to welcome wilderness into our world!"

Aisling gapes, not least at the immodesty of this incredible outfit.

"*Declan...?*" She can't help but laugh, a cracked and dismaying sound. "Shit, man. I knew you were really into Halloween, but this is... *You crazy son of a bitch! You killed our friends!*"

Declan shrugs at her outburst, his eyes glowing over his dirty half-mask, and points his bloody blade at the corpses on the floor. "What are friends for, in the end? They've helped me to fulfil my destiny. As you will, Ash. I tried to stop Barclay from firing you—you were to be the final sacrifice! So I brought you here to make it right."

"You're a murderer! You're *sick!*"

"Ash, come on!" Jackie blurts, and he turns and runs across the room toward the outside exit. Aisling can see that door from here, can see no forbidding padlock on it, but she is slow to follow. For one thing, she's reluctant to take her eyes off Declan for more than a moment. For another, she's spotted a spread of foliage placed on the shadowed floor before the exit, and she doesn't like its sly insinuation of careful forethought.

"Look out!" she cries, but this only distracts Jackie, causing him to look over his shoulder as his tennis shoes plough into the greenery piled up on the floor. He turns back just in time for his face to meet what his feet have sent rocketing up: the wooden pole of a rake. He grunts and freezes like a cartoon character, missing only a cymbal accent on the soundtrack, and Aisling boggles at the sight—

after everything else, has Declan really booby-trapped the exit with mere garden tools? But then Jackie staggers back, and though his grasping hands are empty, he brings the rake with him. It's pinned to his forehead by a long, wicked nail hammered through the shaft.

"Jackie!"

He's reeling like a drunk now, shaking his impaled head as if confused, stumbling around in circles. Declan laughs in delight as if watching a slapstick comedy—*Ernest Goes to Camp Blood*, perhaps—and Aisling hates him with a queasy, despairing intensity almost as strong as her fear of him.

"Cool, I was hoping that would work." He turns to her, blade gesturing in her direction. "Now... I've saved the best for last. And I want my new friends to watch you suffer."

A metallic taste swamps her mouth—*I'm going to die, this is real, I AM GOING TO DIE AND DIE HARD*—but she forces it down. She remembers who and what she is, grasps it with a mortal fervency. Aisling O'Hanlon clamps her lips into a grim grin of defiance.

"All right, then." She throws up both middle fingers. "Come and get me, you poxy prick!"

Declan twitches into motion, legs bowed and arms outstretched, his eyes alight with the thrill of the hunt.

Aisling turns her back and flees, counting her options: one, run for the door and hope it's not locked—certain death; two, use one of those rakes as a weapon against a crazed killer—certain death; three, bolt headlong into the unknown and hope for the best.

Well, fuck it.

Aisling hopscotches through the twisted, ceremonially arranged bodies of her workmates and plunges into the lush archway. Declan's laughter follows her through, not just pleased but triumphant, and then it's whipped away by the wind... as is the topsoil of her strained sanity.

The night sky opens wide and full above her. She's outdoors now, but not in the alley alongside the X-Mart. Somehow, she's come out onto a hilltop, its grassy slopes running smoothly down and away into the shadows to meet other rising knolls in the distance, and the evening air is crisp enough to nip at her through her shirt and skirt. Directly ahead of her, the bonfire she'd seen through the portal is blazing, ten feet high and wild as nature itself. A thousand ancient stars stare down at her, neutral and cold.

And all around her, the people look on.

There must be thirty of them, all arrayed in furs and leathers and woad, their hair clotted with mud and dye.

They hold pear-headed spears and leaf-bladed swords and curved handaxes, carry stretched-skin bodhráns and metal torcs and flaming torches. They stand around the hilltop in a wide ring that closes off the bonfire from the rest of the world, both the portal and Aisling herself inside it. Their eyes widen in surprise, their yellowed teeth bared in challenge. Some of them cry out in a language she doesn't understand, though her Irish roots run deep enough that she recognises it's something like Gaelic.

Aisling staggers to a halt, her mind stuck like a gear jammed by some completely unexpected object. If her senses can be believed, she's now in another place and another time, surrounded by pagan Celts so foreign to her they may as well be aliens—and yet, perhaps her distant ancestors. She can't stop an incredulous laugh, as if she's sustained a serious head injury and all this is some wild hallucination.

"Well, I'll be fucked."

Stern mouths snarl at her incomprehensible words. Weapons are raised to keep this dark apparition at bay. The air is thick with the pungency of unwashed bodies.

"Welcome to Samhain as it was and always should be."

Declan's voice, right behind her. Aisling realises she's

still frozen in shock after lunging through the archway, an easy target—she can almost feel his knife driving into her back. She twitches into desperate motion, and just in time. As she darts forward, his blade rips through her sleeve and nips at her skin. Had she not moved, it would have torn right across her shoulder and into her throat.

Aisling cries out as she turns to face her enemy and staggers backwards, the bonfire growing closer and hotter behind her. Declan wiggles to a nearby drumbeat like some grotesque parody of a stripper, shaking his bones as he delights in the hunt, and he seems to fit right in with the ancient pagans around them. They might not agree, however, they glance at each other in a way that's familiar even across millennia—*is this guy for real?* None of them are wearing skulls on their heads, let alone antlers, and none of them have their tackle out, swinging insouciantly in the breeze.

Dude's nothing but a dorky Assistant Manager dressed up like some D&D nerd's idea of a Celtic druid. He isn't even cool enough to be an X-Martian—the girls titter at him behind his back, the guys flout his authority every chance they get. I'm going to be murdered and gutted and laughed at by a fucking JOKE.

Suddenly, Aisling is *furious*. Bad enough that crappy

men get all the damn breaks and tap-dance their way to success on the skulls of women ten times greater than they'll ever be—going out as this silly prick's victim is just taking the piss.

"Declan Holly!" she cries, holding her ground as he snakes closer. "Everyone thinks you're a suck-up, a loser. You're a sad little wanker, and it doesn't matter how many people you kill, you always will be!"

He hisses in displeasure, probably making a mental note to cut out her tongue, but she's on a roll now.

"And something else you should've thought of, dickhead: you brought me into this because you wanted one last girl to kill. But if you ever paid attention to your slashers, you'd know that the last girl always wins. Well, here I am, motherfucker! And I am going to kick! Your! *Arse!*"

Aisling grabs the torn sleeve of her polo and rips it free, but the tear races across to the neck and ruins the shirt, so she pulls the whole thing off in a fit of pique and waves it at Declan like a toreador taunting a bull with a blue rag. Then she tosses the hated X-Mart uniform over her shoulder toward the bonfire and assumes a battle stance. She hasn't been in a proper scrap for years, her reputation dissuading most who might try stepping to her, but she's ready to fight tooth and nail tonight. She will punch and kick and gouge and scratch and bite. She will make this bastard regret the day he slopped out of the womb.

A murmur goes through the crowd to her left. A few of the Celts have edged forward, their eyes fixed on her. Are they titillated by her near nudity, confused by her modern bra? No, they've seen the tattoo on her bicep: the black triskelion she'd had inked in on her twenty-first birthday as a tribute to one half of her heritage. Four years on, it stands out proud against her brown skin, a nod to her past... and, perhaps, a tenuous link to her future.

The pagans know this symbol. Maybe they think it marks her as one of them, despite her apparent exoticism. One young Celt seems to think so, for she edges forward, hefting a blazing brand in one hand, and makes sure Aisling sees it before tossing it gently in her direction.

She knows better than to try to catch the torch, but as soon as it lands on the grass, she's onto it, scooping it up with a grateful nod to the girl and guttural cry of satisfaction. Declan slows his approach, his eyes narrowing at this unexpected turn, and Aisling gives him no time to recalibrate his expectations. Since paying tribute to her father has worked in her favour, she cries out in honour of her mother—"*Oya!*"—and springs at her foe, shoving the flames toward his half-exposed face.

Declan swears and ducks to one side, bone trinkets clinking, free hand rising to stop the antlers from falling off his head. Aisling laughs—how did he ever make it through all those doorways back at the X-Mart? How had he fit into a car to come and kidnap her from her own home?—and touches the torch to the unguarded edge of his fur cape. The flames lick the material and blacken it, and now Declan is dancing backwards as he attempts to flap the cape out while also fending off Aisling's attacks. The brand darts at his head, igniting the stiff flap of material hanging over his face, and he shrieks as he prances away, plucking the burning matter free and throwing it to the grass.

Too easy! Finish him!

Aisling realises that she's forced Declan a quarter of the way around the circle of surrounding Celts. The portal back to the X-Mart stands unguarded, and there's no way he can stop her from reaching it. At once, the gamble of this fight seems less important than the certainty of home. She turns and takes in the locals, their fierce gazes, their dirty faces, and though she knows they won't understand, she cries out to them.

"He is not one of you! I am!" She displays her triskelion tattoo again, proud and bellicose. "He should never leave this place!"

And with that, she throws the torch at Declan's face. He tries to bat it away, but she's already turning, pelting toward the archway that brought her here. Some of the Celts raise a ragged cheer of what she hopes is farewell—what if she's stuck here now, forever?—and then she's fixing her eyes on the dim interior of the garden centre, plunging through the arch.

Please...!

A sense of incredible relief douses her like ice water as the familiar surrounds of the X-Mart coalesce around her. She's back to her own place, her own time.

Then her momentary jubilation blinks out as her foot catches in Eugene's gory armpit and she hurtles over the twisted bodies, crashing to the cement floor. Gasping at this fresh set of pains, she hears heavy feet thumping her way. Aisling looks up, realising that she's not alone, and sees—

A fantasy figure striding out of the gloom toward her, a childhood myth writ large and seething, an axe held at port-arms in its furious grip. A white beard foams around its grimacing mouth, and its felt hide is the colour of blood.

Boots and belt buckle gleam in the dim light.

She's been bad, and now Santa Claus is coming for her.

Oh, for goodness' sake—

Delirious, Aisling raises one arm in self-defence, in hopeless negation. She's escaped a Halloween-obsessed lunatic only to be carved up by Kris Kringle. This night is just too much.

Santa stops, stares down at her. What an insane last sight to have! But the axe doesn't fall.

"Consider yourself unfired, Ash," Santa growls, but it's Barclay's voice. And it's his face, bruised and bloodied behind the fake beard. "Now, get out of the way."

She almost laughs as she rolls to one side and comes up on her haunches, ready to run if she's misjudged the situation. But no: Barclay stands on this side of the portal, bringing the axe around like a baseball bat, and roars as Declan leaps through from the distant past to continue his reign of terror.

"Knock *me* out, will you?" her boss yells. "Make a mess of *my* store?"

The Assistant Manager sneers at his festive costume. "Your time is over, old man! Yule is for fools! Submit to Samhain!"

"Declan... *you're axed!*"

And then Santa Claus steps in, swinging the blade at the neo-pagan's head, Christmas clashing with Halloween right before Aisling's eyes.

The two of them feint and swing and circle, the fight moving away from the arch.

"I always hated you, *boss*," Declan emphasises the word with a stray stab. "Almost as much as the foul, commercial stench of Christmas!"

"Halloween's about as scary as a wet fart." Barclay laughs, unhinged. "And now... I'm going to deck the halls with bowels of Holly!"

As they battle, Aisling sees Jackie, still stumbling about with the rake nailed to his face like a drunk with no destination. He's probably beyond help, so she's moving to assist Barclay when her eyes fall on the portal. Celts have gathered around the archway to peer through, one of them waving her blue polo over their head like a shamanic totem. How long before the first of them gets brave enough to follow her and Declan into the twentieth century? How long before all of them do?

Despite Declan's dramatic proclamation, they don't pose much of a threat—even if they were evil, thirty Iron Age pagans would stand little chance in a trigger-happy world living under the threat of nuclear Armageddon—but the idea of the past leaking into the present strikes her as deeply wrong. What if Declan rewrites history by luring some important Celts out of their own epoch, effecting massive changes as a result? What if a cult grows around the cryptic symbol of the X-Mart logo and the mysterious message *Hi! I'm ASH*, if an archaeologist is uncovering a two-thousand-year-old machine-woven polo shirt in this very moment and changing the way humanity considers itself? Declan's insane ploy might damage time itself, and she's watched enough *Doctor Who* on the ABC to know how bad that is.

Aisling reluctantly sets her hands on the bodies of her dead friends. Grimacing at the grisly sight, at the slick and heavy and mortal feel of them, she drags them apart, uses their weight to smear the blood-circle Declan drew around them. When she glances up again, the ancient tor is gone—nothing on the far side of the archway other than a door leading to the side alley and the loading dock.

Day saved, easy as.

Not yet...

Aisling checks the progress of the battle royal. Barclay is bigger and stronger, but his axe is unwieldy; though he's managed to smash the skull and antlers off his opponent's head, Declan is leaner, faster, meaner. The side of the axeblade thumps against Declan's left arm, but before Barclay can recover, the knife is flashing in. It punches through the chest of his Father Christmas costume once, twice. Barclay roars in pain and outrage, hefting the axe, but then Declan leaps onto him and rides him down to the cement floor. The impact knocks the wind from Barclay, and before he can recover, his former employee is stabbing him in the throat, the face, the eyes. His fake beard provides no protection, the manager gurgling horribly as freshets of blood gout from fatal wounds like hot cranberry sauce. Declan brutally strikes him until he lies still, then pants and slowly stands, favouring his good arm.

"Now, Ash," he rasps, "where were we?"

He steps forward, intent on his prey, and that's when Jackie comes wheeling in from the other side, completely oblivious to the fray. The rake tangles between Declan's bare legs, and he crashes forward onto the ground; Jackie is spent, spiralling in the other direction, losing his feet and collapsing face-first. The cement drives the nail deeper into his brain, and he stills, at peace at last.

Aisling has to make this advantage count. She reaches

for one of the pumpkins Declan had set about the place as mute witnesses to his triumph and charges in. As Declan gets one foot beneath himself and starts to rise, she slams the jack o' lantern down over his denuded skull. The pumpkin envelops his head, blinding him, burning him with its candle. He cries out and drops his knife, grabbing for the offending vegetable with both hands, trying to wrest it off like a Halloween mask that got stuck. Aisling thinks of all her dead friends as she steps in, eyes on her former colleague's dangling tackle, and delivers her hardest kick directly to his soft balls. Declan howls and collapses, hands instinctively flying to his groin, helpless.

And Aisling spots the axe lying beside Barclay's still hand. Her words, her actions are instinctive now, directed by a dozen slasher endings.

"Merry Christmas, fuckhead."

It's just like chopping firewood, really, only wetter, and Declan's throat and spine are much softer than a tree trunk. It only takes her five swings to completely sever his pumpkin-clad head from his twitching body, and by then, she's soaked in gore. It's well-earned, warm. Feels kind of nice.

And then, finally—the ordeal over, the threat defeated—

Aisling drops the axe and lets the darkness smother her in comforting cotton for a while.

The garden centre door proves to be unlocked, after all. The night air is less crisp than it had been on the Celtic tor some two thousand years before, and she barely feels it drying the blood to a crust on her skin as she staggers down the side of the X-Mart. Then she's in the parking lot, stumbling on through the haze. She expects to be accosted by familiar voices at any moment, but that doesn't happen. She does pass a yellow panel van as she approaches the edge of the lot, but there's no one around. Empty beer cans litter the bitumen in place of the people who drained them.

One word draws her on, blazing red neon through the night ahead: *CURTAINS*.

Tyres screech and horns beep as she lurches across the road. "Stupid Yank bullshit!" one driver yells, not a fan of Halloween; maybe Barclay would've agreed. But she doesn't care, and now she's on the footpath, ignoring wolf-whistles from passersby. A tiny fire drifts near, and she reaches out, plucks a cigarette from strange fingers. "All yours, babe," someone says. She drags deep, flicks the butt away at the door.

Into the foyer. She knows this place well, doesn't even have to think. A rash of hockey masks has spread amongst the people lined up at the bar, turning to take her in. Voices mutter, in English, not Gaelic, and fingers point, but they are not knives. She doesn't care. It's over. Time for her reward.

The ticket guy mumbles something complimentary about her costume as she fumbles in her bloodstained bra and produces her paper ticket. She barely hears him recite the aisle and seat, but she doesn't need that. She can already see JJ's head above a cushion halfway into the auditorium.

"You made it!" he says as she slumps into her seat between him and Tupu. Further along, gaping at her: Kelly and Tran, Carl, Simone, Big Paula and Metal Fred. "Damn, Shandy, that's a bold costume choice. Blood and boobs, the classic horror combo. Where the hell have you *been*, anyway?"

She wrestles the bucket of popcorn from his grip, and JJ laughs it off.

"Weirdo. Hey, have you seen the others from the night shift? Barclay must be keeping them back late, huh. What a bastard."

The lights dim as the feature begins. She chomps popcorn on autopilot as a grave is dug up, as a stray lightning bolt revives a remorseless killer, as a machete swings again and again. The red blood flows, such a poor facsimile of the real thing, and the more bodies that fall, the more she understands just how little anyone knows of anything anymore. The past has taught people nothing; thousands of years of accumulated wisdom wasted. The living have never been further removed from death, even though it breathes down their necks each and every day, and these fools will never understand—not like she does now. It's so fucked that it's hilarious.

The red blood flows, and Aisling laughs, and laughs, and laughs.

DID YOU WANT TO DO A LITTLE OVERTIME WITH THE CREEPY CREATOR OF THESE HARROWING HOLIDAY HIJINKS?

HAVING FUN YET?

PERHAPS WE SHOULD TAKE A LITTLE TRIP TO SEE ALL THEM FANCY SIGHTS OF THE BIG CITY

NEON Nights
BY ANTHONY FERGUSON
427

NEON NIGHTS

BY ANTHONY FERGUSON

Brodie Burns turned his collar up and pushed on through the damp evening wind. A fine mist of drizzle sprayed across his face, making him curse. He swore at the weather, swore at the local council for putting the only free car parking spaces so far away from the arcade, he swore at the work colleagues who mocked him every day, especially the women.

I'll get them all back, one day.

His mood brightened as he spied the LED lights of the Castle Arcade looming up ahead. He wrapped the coat around him and scurried across the busy road, cursing the incessant traffic. How dare they impede his progress!

Brodie shuffled through the wide-open double doors and felt himself immediately enfolded in the warmth and welcoming arms of the colourful interior, with its crackling static and the glow of row upon row of retro 1980s video arcade games. They were all there, all the ones he remembered and loved from his teenage years, even a row of old pinball machines along the back wall.

This arcade in Vic Park was one of three in the franchise dotted around the city, and Burns almost kicked himself that he hadn't thought of the idea himself and got in on the action. They even had a bar and kitchen, serving up huge New York-style pizzas, dripping with greasy goodness. The place was buzzing, even on a Wednesday night, and he could imagine how much money they must be raking in. Still, he knew he was kidding himself. He didn't have an entrepreneurial bone in his flabby, middle-aged body. He would always remain what he was now, a low-ranking public sector nonentity, living alone in a one-bedroom flat he could barely afford.

In his all too rare moments of clarity, he would acknowledge his failure in almost every aspect of life and curse his late parents for not making him work harder at school. There was always someone to blame. Someone who was holding him back from his rightful place atop the social pecking order.

That's what he loved about the arcade: it allowed him

to drift back to his youth in the good old eighties, when life was full of promise, even for Brodie Burns. It was the era of big hair and MTV, heavy metal and new romantics, *Rock 'n' Wrestling,* iconic anti-hero serial killers, and the mainstreaming of the porn industry via VHS tape. Brodie remembered how his dad would sneak off to the video store and order the illegal sex tapes from under the counter, the ones he would watch in secret after wagging school and letting himself into the house.

Great days.

At least that was how he preferred to remember it. Suppressing the memories of getting bullied and ostracized at school, of being mocked and rejected by all the girls he wanted so badly.

Brodie sidled up to the bar and ordered his first drink of the evening and a family-size pepperoni, as well as topping up his user card. The card system had replaced the old coin slots, on account of nobody using actual money anymore, another change in the modern world which irked him, for a reason he couldn't quite put his finger on.

It was convenient anyway. You just swiped your card in the place where the coin slot used to be, the only alterations to the old-school machines, and you were away. Sometimes, he would even find credits left on the games, from patrons who had grown bored and wandered off to play something else.

Brodie steered clear of the more innocent games like *Pac-Man* and *Frogger*. His range was the more violent shoot 'em up style machines, like *Big Game Hunter*, *Galaga* and *1942*. He had almost completed the latter, but there was one machine that had captured his imagination more than any other.

Grabbing his drink, he swung as he always did toward his favourite game and bristled at the guy who had beaten him to it. The flashing lights and familiar jangling theme tormented him.

Neon Nights encapsulated everything Brodie romanticized about the eighties. Huge flashing neon-lit signs, thronging streets, bars and loud music. Even better, it was set in Times Square, a place he fantasized about and, although he had never been there, had even researched the place in-depth online.

Not the current day sanitized version of Times Square, but the dirty, seedy place that existed in the eighties, before the do-gooders cleaned it up. Streets full of thrills and danger, with pimps and street hookers, drug dealers and gang bangers. Where sleazy porno cinemas and live sex dens flashed their wares along the neon-lit strip, and danger lurked in every dim-lit alleyway.

The Square even had its own real-life serial killer. Brodie was endlessly drawn to documentaries focused on the adventures of Richard Cottingham, a man not unlike himself. Middle-aged, stuck in a dreary government job. In his spare time, Cottingham prowled the sin-laden streets, drinking it all in. Brodie was dimly aware that the Square back then must have been a breeding ground for psychopaths, and Cottingham fit the bill to a tee. Picking up hookers on street corners, taking them to flea-bitten hotels, and having his way with them with his knife. Brodie thrilled at the story of Cottingham casually strolling through the lobby with the head of one of his victims in a carry bag, as the police officers called to the scene on account of the smoke coming from his rented room rushed past him. The psycho had set fire to the body after dismembering the head and hands to avoid easy identification. The mere thought of it gave Brodie an erection.

This was the lost paradise Brodie Burns prowled in his dreams. *Neon Nights* was the closest he could get to it in the real world.

The game followed the trajectory of two antagonists—the mysterious, cloaked Slasher, a demonic serial killer bathed in darkness who stalked the quiet streets around the main strip, and his would-be victim, Mysty Rose, a streetwalker with a heart of gold. A good girl fallen on hard times. The perfect dichotomy betwixt angel and whore. Your role was that of a street vigilante, straight-backed and heroic. Your task to get to Mysty before the slasher did. The play pattern of the game depended upon the decisions you made on the mean streets of the Square. In conjunction with the number of credits you poured into the machine.

Brodie had spent countless hours poring over the many set trajectories of the game, trying to master every street and alleyway. As well as committing them to memory, he had, in his own time, created a grid map of this fictional Times Square, and would study it intently whenever he could.

His fingers twitched with the anticipation of getting back into the game. He ran through various scenarios in his head. Ideas and formulations garnered from past experience and previous attempts to rescue Mysty and get her alone. He glared at the back of the head of the young idiot who was keeping him away from his girl, fantasizing about pulling him back by the hair and slashing his throat.

A buzz in his pocket alerted him that his pizza was ready, and he sat at one of the tables across the room watching the gamer, cramming thin, crispy slices of tangy cheese and salty pepperoni into his mouth.

"That's disgusting," a female patron said as she walked past his table. "At least close your mouth when you chew." She looked back at him over her shoulder.

Brodie bristled with indignation. "Fuck you!" He muttered quietly, aware of the company he was in, then a shock of vague recognition suffused his rage. The girl was gorgeous and looked slightly familiar, and was that the hint of a lingering smile she gave him as her words tailed off?

His thoughts were interrupted as he saw the annoying youth abandoning his game. Shoving the remnants of his dinner aside, Brodie bolted toward the machine before anyone else could get there.

Salivating almost as much as he had over the family pepperoni, Brodie swiped his card and marvelled as the gaudy neon-lit skyline of 1980s Times Square unfurled before his carnivorous gaze. Slipping into the first-person persona of the hardened street vigilante, he took his time walking the beat down a street of porno theatres, gazing lasciviously at the suggestive movie titles. He wished he could maneuver his character inside the door, past the huge, gaudily dressed barker, hawking the wares in the doorway. In his mind's eye, he imagined taking a seat near the front row, drinking in the action on screen, until a scantily clad porn groupie sidled up to him on her knees in the semi-darkness. He would press an eager hand down on her head as he enjoyed the visceral double shot of pleasure on the screen and between his thighs.

Frustrated at his persona's obstinate attention to duty, he moved instead to a side street where the hookers plied their trade. Ostensibly for the avatar to ask them questions to further the plot, but in reality just so he could ogle the scantily clad whores, with their high heels, fishnet stockings, bulging breasts spilling over low-cut tops, and tight hot pants or mini-skirts barely covering their plump behinds.

The ensuing discussion played itself out on teletext along the bottom of the screen, and Brodie perked up when he saw the name Mysty Rose appear. She was not only the object of the game, but Mysty had become his favourite object of desire. Brodie didn't know what it was about her, the alluring way her body filled out the many outfits she modelled on screen, the curve of her hips, the swell of her breasts, the coquettish look she presented as she gazed out from the screen, the blonde bob haircut with the purple tips.

Brodie had never been in love before. He had lusted after many girls, for sure, but after pursuing Mysty for so long, with such ardour, he had convinced himself that what he felt for her was love. The way his voice caught when he called out her name, at home, in front of the mirror, or lying in bed at night, pleasuring himself. If only he could have a 3D version of Mysty. He had perused the websites of several companies selling the newest robotic sex dolls, and he was aware that you could purchase one to resemble anyone you desired. There were plenty of Manga dolls available, for example, so he need not be cowed by asking for a doll based on a figure from an arcade game. However, it was the pricing he found prohibitive. It would cost him several months' rent to own one. If only he had gotten one of the promotions he had sought, but as usual, those jobs went to the more proactive staff, usually younger women.

Brodie yanked on the stick and mashed the buttons furiously, as he tracked the nefarious Slasher to his lair. He had reached this stage a few times before, and once again he caught a glimpse of Mysty, cowering on her haunches in the corner of the screen, mascara smudged by her tears. He felt a surge of anger and more than a tinge of desire as he turned his attention to the knife-wielding, hockey-masked Slasher.

He knew the foe was hard to kill. It was what made the pursuit worthwhile. There were certain key points to unlock. Hidden crevices containing weapons and extra energy. Trawling his memory, he unlocked a knife to match the Slasher's. The adversaries circled each other in the grim, ill-lit warehouse. Brodie lunged, and the killer parried his blow. A flash of blade and he saw crimson appear along the arm of his avatar, accompanied by a scream of fear from Mysty.

Enraged and energized, he struck the Slasher a glancing blow to the face, which dislodged the killer's mask. Brodie recoiled, having never achieved this goal before, as a hideous, deformed visage appeared. Mysty screamed again, and Brodie moved in for the kill. But, like so many times before, he was a second too slow, his greasy fingers slipped on the button at the climactic moment, and the Slasher buried his knife in Brodie's gut with a cruel sneer.

The room shuddered in the vigilante's vision as he stumbled backwards. The image began to fade as Mysty stood, a look of despair on her face as she reached a hand out toward him. The last thing Brodie heard was the familiar, cruel laugh of the triumphant Slasher as the screen faded to black, and the familiar words which seemed to summarize his life appeared on screen.

GAME OVER.

Exhausted by his efforts and feeling somewhat dispirited, Brodie ordered another drink and sulked in the corner. Later, as the last customers of the night drifted away in groups and couples, he left alone and walked the quiet streets toward his car. A fine drizzle set in, further dampening his spirits.

His thoughts drifted back over the events of the past few weeks at work. The look on his colleagues' faces when he turned up at the pub for team drinks on Friday night. Did he just imagine the hint of disdain and quiet mockery? His attempts to chat up the office girls were dismal. He felt he had not really achieved anything interesting in his entire life. He had no passions outside of gaming and thus had not much in common to discuss with anyone, let alone a woman. He had no game, no banter. Talking one-on-one with women made him perspire.

He shuddered at the memory of the day, just a month or so ago, when he plucked up the nerve to ask one of the office girls out via email. Sure, she was a decade or more younger than him, but she always spoke politely to him and seemed sympathetic. The response was a terse *t*hanks, but I think we should just stay friends.

Friends!

What a cop out. We're not even bloody friends. She hadn't spoken to him since, and he slunk away whenever he spied her around the office. Still, that was better than the response he got to an attempted conversation with Bree, the office bitch, who told him he was a creep and that he smelled funny.

It had been a long time between drinks, so to speak, but it wasn't as if he were a total virgin. He'd had a couple of girlfriends in his time, but both had eventually got shot of him, and found someone better. There was always the local red light district, of course, and he had indulged occasionally, but those girls didn't really count, did they? The thought reminded him that there was a massage parlour not a few blocks from the main street right here, and checking his wallet, he turned and headed in that direction, his breath coming out in short steamy bursts in the cold night air.

The change of course took him up a slight rise and

past a three-storey apartment block he recognized. He recalled he had once shared an apartment on the top level with a former friend back in the late eighties, when the rents in town were more affordable. It was around the time he scored his first public sector job. He remembered how happy and productive he was for the six-month period of his probation. It was only after achieving his permanency that reality finally kicked him in the guts, slapping him with a multitude of failed promotion attempts and abortive relationships. No wonder he had retreated deeper and deeper into the gaming world. It was the only place he felt welcome.

In passing, Brodie's gaze swung upwards to the row of apartments along the top level, and to his surprise, he saw a figure clearly bathed in light through a window. A young woman no less, in the process of disrobing. It seemed she had forgotten to draw the blinds. In less than a minute, the girl was completely naked, and Brodie could clearly see the outline of her buxom figure and the curve of her hips.

He froze to the spot, gazing in wonder, then on instinct he dove forward into a convenient row of bushes, bathed in shadow. Peering through the foliage afforded him a great view of the girl, and he felt a surge of power flow through him, as she was unaware of his presence. Even the onset of a patter of rain failed to disturb his viewing pleasure.

As he shifted his weight to get more comfortable, Brodie recoiled as the girl approached the window and appeared to look straight at him, meeting his gaze. He blushed and lowered his head. To his amazement, she reached out toward him and beckoned him with a finger, a wide smile breaking out across her face.

He felt his heart pound in his chest. She curled her finger again and pushed her fulsome breasts up against the window.

Mesmerized, he rose and stepped forward out of the cover of the foliage. She pointed toward the stairs, familiar in his memory from his younger days. He turned and moved toward them, blood coursing through his veins. *Oh my God. Was she really calling him upstairs? Did she really want to invite him inside?*

He walked along the balcony on the third level, and suddenly remembered this was his old flat, a weird coincidence. Like a part of life that had turned full circle. He knocked on the door, half expecting her not to answer. The whole thing being just a cruel prank to torment him.

Those thoughts evaporated as the door opened and the

mystery woman greeted him with a smile. She had taken the time to pull on a negligee, which barely hid her fine figure.

"There he is. Come in, you'll catch your death out there." Her voice soft and mellifluous. She unlocked the screen door and pushed it open.

Brodie walked in. He stood before her, arms by his side, unsure of what to do or say.

"Come on, I've got the fire on inside. Let's get you warmed up."

He followed her into the main room, remembering the layout. Except the fluffy white carpet had gone, replaced by smart bare floorboards. His ridiculously big stereo no longer occupied an entire wall and had been replaced by a smart cabinet and flat screen television. The screen frozen on a visage of a cityscape at night. Bright lights and signage. Out the window toward the balcony, the city, his own city, glittered beyond the river.

She sat on a black leather couch and beckoned him to sit beside her. He saw in the clear light that she was stunning, and familiar. She was the girl who had commented on his eating habits in the arcade earlier. He hesitated, then sat. As he did so, she rose, and he feared he had done something to offend her. He was afraid that the whole thing was a setup now, a ruse to mock him.

"I'm sorry, how rude of me. Would you like a drink... what is your name?"

"Brodie," he blurted quickly, folding his hands in his lap.

"I'm Holly," she said, "but friends call me Mysty."

"What?"

She laughed, a trill, delicate sound. "You know, Mysty Rose, from the arcade game, *Neon Nights*. I've seen you playing it."

He blushed anew. "You have?"

"Sure. I love the arcade. Anyway, what can I get you, a beer?"

"I don't drink beer."

"You do drink, though?"

"Yes," he said a little too defensively. I like..."

"Wine?" she finished for him.

"Not really. Tastes like paint stripper. Bourbon?"

"Yes, of course. I have bourbon. Regular pisshead, this girl."

She laughed, and her use of rough language sent a tingle through his loins. "With cola?"

"Sorry?"

"You want cola with your bourbon, or do you take it straight?"

"Oh, cola, please."

He listened to her rustling in the small kitchen just off the loungeroom and turned his attention to the big screen. Like the flat and the girl, the night cityscape itself also seemed vaguely familiar.

"Here we go."

She returned with the drinks, bourbon for him, a beer for herself. She sat beside him and turned toward him, folding her legs beneath her on the couch.

"So, Brodie, what do you do?"

"Well..."

"Do you mind if I smoke?" Without waiting for a reply, she reached across to an expensive-looking handbag on the coffee table and withdrew a pack of cigarettes and a lighter. She lit up and inhaled deeply. "Bad habit, I know, but I'm a creature of habit and a slave to my addictions."

She put emphasis on the last two words, sending another surge of pleasure through him.

"Go on, you were telling me what you do for a living."

He picked up his glass and smelled the rich aroma of

Kentucky bourbon. Ice swirled and clinked as he took a gulp, fighting back the urge to belch.

"Well, I'm just a public servant, I'm afraid."

She reached out and touched his arm, making him shudder. "Oh, honey. There's nothing wrong with that. A noble profession."

She picked up her beer and took a swig. Another drag of the cigarette. Brodie watched her, images of stereotypical bad girls, drinking and smoking, flooded his brain.

"What do you do?" He blurted out.

She gave a lascivious smile and ashed her smoke. "Well, since you ask... do you know that brothel around the block from here?"

He sat mouth open. "Cassandra's?"

"Ah, you do know it."

He blushed again. "You work there?" He racked his brain, trying to recall if he had ever seen her on his occasional visits.

"Nah, just messing with you," she laughed, reaching out and squeezing his knee. "Let's just say I'm a lady of leisure."

"What does that mean?" He swallowed.

"I have a presence online, and men subscribe to look

at me and talk to me, and they send me gifts, or give me money."

"You mean OnlyFans?" Brodie had heard of that, but had never indulged, being too timid.

"God no. There's no sex, nothing like that," she smoked and extinguished the butt. "I just point to things I might like to have, like an expensive pair of shoes, or a handbag like this one. One guy even bought me a new car. The technical term for it is rinsing."

"Really?"

"Yeah. Men are pretty pathetic, really. No offence. I just offer them the possibility of meeting or romance, but I never follow through."

"Isn't it dangerous?"

She shook her head and supped her beer. "They don't know where I live. Some of them are overseas. Besides, what's life without a little danger? Drink up."

She clinked her can against his glass.

Brodie glanced at the screen. "What are you watching?"

"Ah, now this is interesting. It's a documentary on Times Square back in the 1980s, when it was really gritty and interesting."

"What the..." Something clicked in his mind, but he

found his head spinning, like he was under a spell.

"Yeah, a real coincidence, wouldn't you say?"

She put her hand on his knee, and he noticed for the first time how long her nails were, and how sharp.

"Who are you?"

She laughed quietly. "I told you. I'm Mysty Rose."

Brodie fell back against the couch. "What's going on?"

She rose and walked toward the screen, unfreezing it with a wave of her hand.

"Come on, let's have some fun."

Brodie blinked as the girl stepped into the giant television. She disappeared in a blink of static, then reappeared on screen on the street.

"Come join me." She reached out a hand and beckoned him with a curled finger, just like she had done at the window earlier.

Brodie rose in a daze and stumbled toward the flatscreen. He turned in time to see his unconscious body slumped on the couch, just as he tripped, or was pulled into the television screen.

He landed in a heap on hard bitumen and let out a yelp.

"You alright there, buddy?" A hand reached down to where he lay sprawled in the gutter and yanked him to his

feet.

"What the... where am I?"

"You concussed, motherfucker? You want me to call you a bus?"

"Huh?"

"An ambulance, sucker, you know, medics."

"No... no." Brodie shook his head and looked around as he got his bearings. All about him, huge garish neon signs flashed their messaging at him. Brands familiar to him, and some long gone and forgotten. Others he'd never heard of.

"Is this Times Square?" he asked the garishly dressed figure in the orange suit who stood before him.

"No, motherfucker. This is Disneyland, and I'm Mickey Mouse."

"Okay. But what year is it?"

"Jesus H Christ, boy. You high? Hey, you want some coke? I got the goods here, man."

Brodie shook his head. He took in the sights around him. In every doorway, on every corner, scantily clad women prowled, some looking his way. Yellow cabs buzzed and hummed by, and big sedans crawled along. The sound of revelry emanated from dozens of bars and clubs.

The man in the orange suit smiled. "Now he's with us.

You want some pussy, brother? Got the finest pieces of ass in the Square right here."

Brodie looked from girl to girl. Every shape and size and ethnicity imaginable, and there, on a far corner, Mysty Rose waved at him.

Somewhere in the distance, a countdown began, and a clock struck twelve times, followed by the bellow of an enormous crowd.

The garish pimp punched him on the arm. "Happy New Year, sucker. Welcome to 1985!"

Brodie stared, open-mouthed. "Fuck!"

A neon sign appeared floating in the air in front and just above him. It shimmered like smoke.

CHOOSE YOUR PLAYER

A hooker in a low-cut leopard skin halter top yanked the arm of the pimp. "Forget it. This creep is cooked."

Brodie ignored them as two images, obviously visible only to him, appeared above him. One was a straight-laced, chisel-chinned vigilante in a long overcoat, the other, the hockey-masked slasher, brandishing a blood-soaked knife. Beside each of them, a button marked *Player 1* and *Player 2*.

The pimp and hookers dispersed and gave him a wide berth, ignoring him and hailing the curb-crawling cars. All except Mysty, who waited at the edge of his vision at the lip of an alleyway. She looked from Brodie to the avatars wavering in the air above him, awaiting his choice.

He nodded, and a surge of adrenaline shot through his veins.

Brodie mashed button 2 and picked the Slasher.

He felt his body shimmer and change, felt himself grow taller and more muscular. A large knife appeared in his hand. The nearest street walkers screamed. The pimp turned to him.

"Yo, mother-fucker. What the hell you..."

"Shuddup!" Brodie said as he stuck the pimp in the guts. A pool of blood spread out from his blade in a circle across the orange waistcoat. The pimp looked at him wide-eyed and let out a gasp.

"Realistic blood, too," Brodie smiled. "I like this game." He jerked the blade in a horizontal line across the pimp's midriff and yanked it free. The man wheeled around, trying and failing to hold his spilling intestines in.

Hookers screamed and fled in all directions. Their high heels clacking on the cracked pavement.

"Yeah, you better run, bitches," Brodie yelled, warming to the role. "The Slasher is here, in the flesh, baby!"

A shot rang out, and Brodie felt something strike him like a rock. He swung around to where a hooker stood brandishing a pistol.

"Eat this, scum sucker!"

Before he could react, the girl shot him point-blank in the chest. Brodie recoiled, then looked down. He felt no pain. A blood spot appeared on his shirt, then started to fold back in on itself and disappear. He roared with laughter.

"Yes! I'm invincible, fucking A!"

The girl stood quaking in fear. The gun dropped from her hands. She held her arms up in supplication. "Oh God... I'm sorry. I didn't..."

He slashed her across the throat and shut her yap. A spurt of blood fountained as she toppled over, quivering.

His gaze shot across to where Mysty stood, as if frozen to the spot. Her coquettish confidence had fled at the turn of events.

Brodie moved in her direction, pointing the weapon at her.

"And you! I fucking loved you, Mysty, but you turned out like all the other girls. Teasing me, leading me on. You give it to all the other guys, but not to me! Well, now it's my turn." He waved the knife in the air, circling the garish signs of a multitude of strip clubs and porn theatres.

Sirens wailed in the distance, but Brodie ignored them.

"You dragged me here, to wherever the hell this place is, but I'm a God now, this is my game, and you are my prey."

Mysty turned heel and fled. Brodie started to run after her.

He bounded down the alleyway, following the sound of Mysty's heels clicking on the dirty cobblestones. He was mildly annoyed to find the alleyway branching off in several directions, like a labyrinth. A prostrate bum, lying propped up against a grimy wall between some trash cans, hailed him as he slowed.

"Hey, buddy, you got a dime?"

Brodie paused, reached into his pockets, and sure enough, found a handful of change, which he tossed to the hobo.

"Sure, pal. Which way did the girl go?"

"That way." The bum pointed. "Thanks, man, you're a pal."

Brodie smiled and stuck his blade in the hobo's throat under the chin. "Anytime, pal, and get a shower. You stink."

The sound of running feet caught his attention, and he loped off in pursuit, a cruel smile breaking out over his face beneath the mask. He was really starting to enjoy this.

The further he descended into the darkness, the less Brodie felt the Times Square vibe. He sensed more of a Dickensian London feel. It reminded him of the documentaries he had watched on Jack the Ripper and the tours they held in London. He chuckled, feeling another surge of power.

"I'm the Ripper now," he said to the walls.

He paused at a juncture, sniffing the air, wondering how far his new powers extended. Would some preternatural sense lead him straight to her?

At the far lip of two adjacent passages, he spied Mysty, peeking around the corner at him.

"There you are, bitch!" He yelled and set off at a run.

Exiting the passageway, he found himself somehow back on the main drag. Before him, a row of X-rated porno houses. Suggestive titles bore down on him in neon. Hulking figures guarded doorways. He saw Mysty slip inside a theatre, and stalked across the street after her.

"Hey," the barker on the door stepped in front of him. "You can't come in here like that..."

A flash of the blade opened the big guy up across the middle, and he grunted and fell in the gutter. Brodie flexed in anticipation, but none of the other denizens on the street seemed to take any notice, so he shrugged and pushed his way through into the foyer.

The spotty teenagers at the candy bar swore and ducked behind their counter. The ticket seller in his tiny booth cowered. Brodie pushed his way through the dark curtain into the cinema.

Sounds of sleazy sex assaulted his ears, and on the huge screen in glorious technicolour, a peroxide blonde with pneumatic breasts took turns fellating a circle of men. He turned his attention to the sparsely populated arena. To his right, a middle-aged man sat masturbating, his pants around his ankles. Sensing he was being watched, the voyeur turned his head to look at Brodie, but continued pleasuring himself, even when he saw the knife.

"Oh man. This shit just gets better and better," the guy said, mid-stroke.

Brodie shook his head. "Disgusting." With a sweep of his blade, he sliced the pervert's erection clean off, eliciting a scream at last.

Alerted, the other patrons rose and fled the scene. Looking around, he saw Mysty in the semi-darkness up on stage. Behind her, the blonde was now on her hands and knees, being penetrated from behind while still servicing three other men in turn.

"Christ, I love the eighties," Brodie said, as he encroached on Mysty, pulling off the hockey mask and tossing it aside. She was now backed up against the screen, barely masking the obscenities.

The image beyond her flickered and paused, right on a money shot from one of the actors. The groans of artificial pleasure abated into silence. He heard the projectionist swear and the sound of feet pounding down a set of stairs and away. The two antagonists stood alone in the empty theatre, bathed in artificial light.

Mysty cowered and blustered. "Brodie, we can talk about this, work it out."

"No, darling, I'm all done talking." He placed one hand against the screen beside her head. "I'm done listening to false promises. Now I'm taking what I want."

He heard the sound of his own heavy breathing as he grabbed her by the hair and yanked her face toward him. Mysty's eyes grew wide.

Brodie laughed, low and cruel, and slid the blade beneath her low-cut top, popping the buttons, one by one. Her full, firm breasts swung out into view, and he groaned with desire. "Mmm, bigger than they were off-screen. This game is amazing."

He rubbed the blunt edge of the knife gently against one nipple, making her gasp. His gaze moved slowly upward from her breasts to her face, and he was taken aback to find her smiling.

"What's so funny?" he asked. "There's no vigilante to save you now, Mysty."

"Yeah, you made your choice, Brodie. I gave you the option."

"You gave me fuck all," he said, a hint of hesitation creeping into his voice.

She reached down and grabbed his erection through his pants. "That's where you're wrong, loser."

The theatre and the world around it dissolved in a flash of neon. Brodie found himself in what appeared to be a garage, strung upside down and hanging from the ceiling. He looked up to a large chain shackled to his legs and wrapped around a steel girder, running across the top of the ceiling.

"What the fuck? Where am I?"

He looked around the brightly lit garage, empty apart from the neatly arranged metal shelves dotting the sides of the space. Shelves filled with a variety of sharpened tools. He saw an upside-down version of Mysty Rose, clad in the same negligee she was wearing earlier in the evening.

"You're in my basement garage. You've been here a while, actually. While I let that fantasy play out in your head."

Brodie squirmed and shook. "What's going on. Who are you?"

"What am I would be a better question," she mused. "My kind have been around a long time. We've become somewhat mythologized. Sometimes as vampires, sometimes werewolves. I prefer the term 'shape shifter'."

"Ah, this is bullshit. Let me down, you crazy bitch."

"Can't do that, I'm afraid." She turned aside and picked up a pair of hedge clippers. Clacked the blades together. Shook her head and put them back. "You're not a big reader, are you? You see, your authors got some of the story right. I do need one thing to survive. Blood." She gave him a toothy smile, and saliva dripped over her chin.

He swallowed. "I have money. I'll give you all my money."

She shrugged. "I have plenty of that. Tends to build up when you've been alive for centuries."

Brodie thrashed as Mysty's flesh warped and changed before his inverted vision, from a young woman to a deformed, leather-skinned monstrosity with glowing red eyes, and back to Mysty Rose again. He began to whimper.

"I may be a monster, Brodie, but I'm an honest one. I gave you a choice to make, and you chose poorly."

The words came out in a slur, as the teeth in her mouth grew long and razor sharp. Her slender fingers curled into cruel talons.

"Oh God, please no!"

"I'd love chat, I really would, but gaming makes me awfully hungry."

"I love you, Mysty..." His words gave way to screams as the first sweep of her claws opened his belly.

"Game over, Brodie."

WANNA HIT THE TOWN
WITH THE REVILED
REPROBATE RESPONSIBLE
THIS RAUNCHY RECOUNT?

DOES A THOUGHT OF A TRIP TO THE MALL GIVE YOU THE HEEBIE JEEBIES?

THE TALL MAN
WITH THE
SNAIL FACE
BY SHAKEEL ROA

THE TALL MAN WITH THE SMALL FACE

BY SHAKEEL ROA

They're going to die here, hiding in this dark, abandoned mall, cowering and hyperventilating behind the counter of a café.

One of the girls begged for their lives. "Please God… Please, God, I've been kind. I've followed your teachings—"

"Shut it," whispers the other, "You're gonna get us caught."

"Why did you make us do this… I didn't wanna do this!"

A hand wraps around the girl's mouth. "Shut it. Now I'm gonna look for my boyfriend and get the hell out of here."

The panicked one begins to cry, shaking her head.

"Follow, or don't. I don't care."

Taking her hand off the other girl's mouth, the braver of the two looks over the counter. The mall is still pitch black;

you can only just barely see the reflection of the moon on the polished floors. But all in all, it looks clear. They haven't seen that thing since it dragged one of them out of the arcade. She just needs to go find Jason, and then they can get the hell out of this place and find some cops to deal with all this.

"Alright, the coast is clear. Good luck."

The panicked girl lunges forward, grabbing her leg. In looking back, she sees tears in the other girl's eyes, snot running down her face.

"Wait... p-p-please."

"Let go."

"Don't leave me here!"

"Keep quiet! Let go!"

The panicked girl hugs her leg tighter, clutching it for dear life.

"Bitch I said let go!"

With a hard stomp from her other foot, the braver one is free to make her escape. She runs out from the café, making a mad dash across the open centre of the mall. She can make it. She's a part of the track team after all. They just won regionals.

Still sobbing behind the café, the remaining girl tries

to stand, pulling herself up from the dust-covered floor. She needs to go with her.

Already halfway across the mall's open centre, the brave one catches sight of the large front doors. She thinks she sees a silhouette; thinks she sees a familiar jacket.

He waited for her.

As she reaches the figure at the doors, the panicked girl lifts herself out from the counter and yells out, pleading for her companion to wait.

That was a mistake.

It heard.

As the brave one brings her hand to Jason's shoulder, as the pleas from across the room echo out into the mall, every single light turns on all at once.

The sudden flash of light blinds them both, and the brave one sees that Jason didn't wait for her at all. Instead, the shoulder she is clutching belongs to his corpse, bloodied and chained to the door.

It was a trap, and as she jumps back, slipping on the blood that has pooled around him, she sees it.

It isn't far, just off by the stairs to the second floor. It's a man. Or at least what looks to be a man. He's tall, freakishly tall, wearing an ill-fitting tight suit. It's covered in black feathers, all except his face. It's small. Again, freakishly so. It looks as if it's the head of a doll, white and porcelain.

She gets up and runs; it's hot on her tail.

There is nowhere else to go but back the way she came, towards the café, towards the girl who got her caught. She doesn't even make it halfway.

Now in the light, still hiding behind the café counter, the panicked girl sobs as quietly as she can. She can hear the other girl dying, being gutted. The screams and wails... she can't take it. She prays to God again, prays that it all stops. But the sobs are too loud, God doesn't hear her, and the sound of wet, ripped intestines leaking onto the floor threatens to leave her dry heaving.

Eventually, the noises do stop, however, in a bubbling groan. The human body can only be punctured so many times, and so she is finally left alone.

Or so she thinks.

Suddenly, something heavy slams down onto the café counter. She doesn't dare look, but slowly, blood begins dripping down onto her. It hits her scalp, sliding down across her forehead and getting in her eyes.

She wipes it, wipes it again and again, not daring to look up. She can hear his breath. Heavy breathing, almost asthmatic.

It whistles a tune above her, and tears mixed with blood fall across her cheeks as she finally raises her head.

She sees the small porcelain face and lets out a final plea.

Engrossed in a marathon of beloved eighties slashers, Owen scoffs down popcorn as Johnny Depp is pulled into his bed, his chewed up remains being regurgitated up into the ceiling.

"Holy shit!"

"I know, right? Definitely a contender for slasher death hall of fame—" Owen winces as a hard jab to the shoulder cuts him off.

"Not the movie, man. Why do you have to be such a geek?"

Rubbing his shoulder, listening to the screams coming from the TV, Owen flips him off. "You're as much of a loser as me, Roy."

"Nuh uh, guess who just got invited to tonight's

Halloween party?"

"What party? There's a million going on tonight, and no one wants us at any of them."

"Well, we're going to the most important one. Team captain himself, Jason-motherfucking-Meyers, just dropped me the invite."

"You sure he isn't just trying to lure you somewhere to kick your ass again?"

Roy waves the possibility off. "What? Dude, I told you those were just team bonding rituals."

"Bonding rituals between their fists and your face?"

Roy knocks the bowl of popcorn out of Owen's hands. "Get your ass up, we got a party to go to."

Picking up the mess Roy's hurt feelings caused, Owen shakes his head. They can't be doing this. "You know what he has your name down as in his phone, right?"

Roy yells out from the front door. "I'm an important part of the team!"

"It's supposed to be Ironic! You're not even on the team!"

"Then why do I have a jacket!"

Texting a number named *best on the team*, long gloved fingers toss the phone into a dark corner.

The next victim is on his way. The trap needs to be reset.

First, however, the newest addition to his collection must be put with the rest. And so, untying the now dead team captain from his position on the door, the tall man with the small face strips Jason of his team jacket. It's still pristine, little to no blood having dripped onto it.

Perfect.

Walking across the mall to take his position, the tall man turns off the lights, once again engulfing it in darkness.

Both boys arrive at the party's location.

"You're sure it's happening here?"

Roy checks his phone again and hums in confusion.

There's no service out here for some reason.

"This place hasn't been used since... what? The eighties?"

"Maybe that's why it's a good place to party? It's empty, big, no one around to make a noise complaint..."

Owen looks around the parking lot. There is one other car here; Roy might be right for once. Or they're gonna get their asses kicked.

Arriving at the entrance of the old, abandoned mall, Owen can't help but notice how well preserved it is. Even looking through the glass doors, one wouldn't be blamed for thinking they somehow stumbled back in time.

Roy tries to get in, yanking at the handles. It doesn't budge, but he keeps trying, only stopping when a bright flashing light shines onto them.

"What the hell are you two doing?!"

Turning around, frightened by an old gravelly voice behind them, both boys instinctively raise their hands, as if they were being arrested.

Luckily, shining a torch directly into their eyes, only stands a security guard. He looks down on them, being rather tall, even with how he seems to be perpetually hunched over.

"You wanna answer me?!"

"S-S-Sorry… we were just looking around."

The guard eyes up Roy's team jacket. "High schoolers… You play?"

Owen shakes his head, but before he can get a word out of his mouth, Roy cuts in.

"Damn right," he says confidently, acting as if he wasn't on the verge of pissing himself moments earlier. "Best player you'll ever see."

The guard seems to be set off by that, a fire igniting in his eyes. "The best players were the ones in the old days, from before you two even cried for the first time."

Roy scoffs, about to make another retort, when the guard takes a step forward, getting right up in his face. Both boys fear he'll take a swing. The way he's scrunching his free hand into a fist isn't helping.

"Get outta here. I see either of you two again, I'm calling the cops."

Owen nods, and as the guard walks away, Roy aims to insult the man behind his back, flipping him off and saluting.

A smack over the head from Owen knocks some sense into him.

"Stop that dumbass."

"You see how he got up in my face? I'll kick his grumpy old ass."

Owen shakes his head, leading the way as they walk away from the mall entrance. After a few seconds of silence, Roy interrupts it by kicking at rocks in the parking lot. It's starting to get on his nerves.

"Well... wanna stop for more popcorn on the way back to mine? Watching all those death scenes made me hungry—"

"We're finding a way in there."

"Huh?!"

Roy pulls Owen back towards the mall. "Come on, Jason probably left us a way in around back."

He was right, as, in rounding the corner, they found a large emergency exit door propped open. Upon further inspection, a large slab of wood keeps the door ajar, with a welcome mat inviting them in. This mall must be the team's recurring party spot. It also makes one wonder how the security guard has never found this entrance.

Once inside, with their eyes struggling to see anything in the darkness, neither Roy nor Owen can find any remnant of Jason and the team. The mall looks pristine, as if the staff had only left a few hours ago, instead of decades. Even the decorations and store signs, while having gathered a slight layer of dust, somehow hadn't rotted or developed any mould.

Did someone still come by and clean?

Making their way to the centre of the mall's ground floor, Roy attempts to call out to Jason and the team. Of course, no one answers.

Owen stays back, finding a café on the edge of the food court to sit at. It's small and open, with a single counter and a few seats. "I really don't think they're here. They're messing with you."

"Can you stop with that, dude?"

He gives up and stays silent, tapping his foot as Roy looks around. Something gives him pause. His foot, although tapping on the tiled floor, sounds as if it's going in and out of a small puddle.

Looking down, he sees a small pool of liquid. It looks dark, thicker than water, and it sticks to the bottom of his shoe. He stands, notices a trail of it leading into the café area. Like a trail from a snail, it spills across the floor, leading up and over the counter.

In the dark and silent mall, he leans over the counter.

Something in the stale air keeps him on his guard.

He thinks he sees something and becomes aware of a faint smell.

Suddenly, the lights overhead turn on, and below him, the source of the trail and odour is revealed.

Lying bloodied and twisted, curled up and hidden, are the bodies of two girls he recognises.

All the popcorn and candy he's eaten in the last few hours come back up, burning his throat. He tries to keep it in, but fails as the chunks mix with the blood on the floor.

He tries to call out to Roy, but coughs through it. They need to get out of here. Get that security guard, get the police.

Before Owen can make a move, however, a tune echoes throughout the mall. He can't tell where it's coming from; every direction is equally as likely as the last.

"Roy...?"

Looking around, there's no trace of his friend. He contemplates just leaving him, but then he thinks he recognises the tune. It's just whistling, forced and imperfect, but he recognises the song it attempts to emulate. It's the team chant, a song that Roy mumbles to himself often. It makes him let his guard down.

That's when it sounds louder, closer. In fact, it could be coming from right behind him.

The tune stops when he spots it. Just down at the other end of the café. A small, porcelain doll's face almost lowered to the floor. It looks up at him.

"Roy…"

In an instant, the small face rises almost a foot taller than him, revealing the tall, thin figure attached to it. It takes a step, and Owen bolts in the other direction. It's fast, its own feet threatening to step on the backs of his shoes, but luckily, he reaches some stairs that lead to the second floor. The thing behind him struggles to make the sharp turn, buying Owen time to make it up.

That's when he spots Roy, inside an arcade, waving him over.

"Get the hell over here!"

Roy reaches up, slamming the security roller door closed once he's inside. Owen takes a second, hands on his knees as he gasps for air. "We need to get outta here."

"I know, I fuckin' saw that guy, man. What the hell is going on?"

Owen's hands are trembling, his adrenaline starting to wear off. "I-I don't know… I found two bodies. You remember

Jason's girlfriend, a-and that girl she always bullied?"

"You see em? The teams here?"

"I found them dead. Cut up."

"Jesus Chris—"

Roy's words are cut off as something slams against the door of the arcade. They know what it is.

Roy pulls him away from the door, leads him past row upon row of old arcade machines.

They think they see a back door, a way out, but the security door rolls back open behind them.

The boys look at each other, and Roy mouths one word, *Hide.*

Owen, already at the back wall of the arcade, decides to squeeze himself behind a row of arcade machines. He has to lie sideways, back to the wall, chest to the machines. It's a tight fit, but as long as he doesn't breathe too hard, he'll be fine.

Suddenly, behind him, at the very end of the row he's hiding behind, a machine slams into the wall.

Hard.

So hard that the machine crushes in on itself.

Owen keeps quiet, but then another machine does the same, glass and shards of laminated timber falling to the floor. They land on his shoes, and as a third machine begins to move, he barely pulls his feet out of the way.

He needs to move.

Unable to crawl because of the tight fit, Owen has to rely on his upper body strength to pull himself along the tight gap. But he isn't fast enough. Machine after machine slams into the wall, and eventually one crushes one of his feet between itself and the wall. He hears the ankle snap, feels each toe fold over the other. He isn't even sure if it's still attached.

He holds back the most violent of screams, but it doesn't matter. It knows where he is now.

As the machine is slowly, agonisingly pulled away from his foot, the skin of which feels as though it's being pulled off along with it, the whistling starts again. Right above him. He thinks he feels fingertips at his hair before—

"Hey, asshole!"

Owen, eyes shut so tight it hurts, hears all manner of things smashing and being thrown, until two sets of footsteps run out of the store. Roy's profanities get quieter and quieter as they run, before eventually, Owen can't hear anything.

Waiting until it's clear, he crawls out from behind

the machines. He does it slowly, fearing that any quick movement will make his foot come clean off. Only when he's finally out does he look, examining his mangled and limp appendage. Blood slowly pools out from where bone had broken through skin, and every second the pain gets worse.

But he has to get out. Roy bought him time. But will it be enough?

Almost passing out as he looks around the now destroyed arcade, Owen spots a bucket and mop. They won't get his blood out of the carpeted floor, but he could use the mop as a crutch. And use it he does, as he slowly but surely makes his way out of the arcade, only to run into his next obstacle. The stairs.

He takes it slow, each step a painful one. The only sound in the quiet silence of the abandoned mall is the tapping of his makeshift cane, each signifying another step cleared.

Tap.

Tap.

Tap.

He's almost at the bottom when suddenly, the lights turn off.

Every muscle in his body tightens and freezes him in place, but he can't just leave himself stuck on the stairs. Even if he can't see, Owen uses the end of the mop to feel out the next steps.

Tap.

Tap.

Tap.

He's almost there. His eyes have started to adjust, and he thinks he can see the ground floor.

Tap.

Tap.

He miscalculates, and the end of the mop slides off the edge of the next step. It sends him tumbling down the rest of the way, the movement bringing his pain to a crescendo. Everything gets fuzzy. He sees stars.

The fall must have knocked him out, just for a few seconds, because when Owen opens his eyes again, he sees a clothing store with its lights on.

It lures him in like a moth to a flame. The tap, tap, tapping signalling his every move.

As he gets closer, cautiously looking for the tall man with the small face, Owen discovers something odd about the clothing store. It's the only place in the mall that's been changed, altered from the state it was in when the mall first closed down.

It's been converted into a trophy room.

Each aisle, each clothing rack and coat hanger holds a team jacket.

Owen enters further into the store, reading jacket after jacket, taking note of the years on each. They start at 1990.

But Owen disregards that, because out of all the jackets, Roy's isn't among them.

What he does find, however, on the cashier's counter, is a security uniform.

He checks the pants' pockets and finds an ID. It's long expired, looking as if it was issued when the mall was still open. If one imagines the person in the photo much older, much angrier, it would be the spitting image of the security guard he and Roy met just outside. But did the tall man kill him or...

The team anthem starts again, this time whistled slowly, as if congratulating him. Or mocking him.

When Owen looks up, he's there, standing in the door frame, holding Roy's jacket in one hand and a bloodied knife in the other.

Both of them just stand there, looking at one another, a

duel. Owen lets the tall man sing his song, knows that once it's up, that knife he's holding is headed right for him. He isn't making it out of here. Roy bought him time, sure, but all it did was give him time to figure out why their lives were being cut short.

"So, what... peaked in high school?"

He gestures at the jackets around them, at the mall around them.

"Stuck in your fantasy of being some eighties' star athlete?"

The small porcelain face just stares at him, continuing on with his whistling.

"Let me guess... You gave everything to the team... You thought they cherished you?"

The knife rises, shining in the overhead lights.

"You probably never even played. Probably stepped foot on the field as much as Roy there." He points at his now deceased best friend's jacket, tears rolling down his face. He can barely stand, but God help him if he's going down curled up and cradling his foot.

The song is nearing its end. Owen can tell that what he's saying is angering the tall man with the small face, can see the shaking in the man's hands. The pure fury.

"Well, come on then, asshole!

The whistling ends, and the tall man moves inhumanly fast.

He should have just stayed home and watched those movies.

NOW DOESN'T THAT JUST FILL YOUR HEART WITH GOOD OLD FASHIONED TEAM SPIRIT?

WANT TO MEET THE
TORTURED TEAM MASCOT
WHO CRAFTED THIS
FEEL GOOD FABLE?

HEY THERE GOOD LOOKING
PERHAPS YOU SHOULD LET YOUR UNCLE HENLEY TAKE YOUR MIND OFF OF THEM TROUBLES

HAIRSTERICAL
BY PERSIMMON GWYNNE

HAIRSTERICAL

BY PERSIMMON GWYNNE

Hair No Evil

The bell rang for final drinks, patrons sculled their last beers and scattered into the sweltering night. A brand-new Volvo 240 hooned around the corner, looking evermore like a coffin on wheels. Jeers from the teenage occupants were drowned by Bon Jovi blaring from the cassette deck. Two girls in hyper-colour crop-tops flashed their tits. The cars were moving too fast to see.

Sweat rolled from human pores as exhausted bodies were exposed to the stale night air. The crowd thinned as the suburban blocks rolled on. Only a few isolated drunks staggered the last streets towards a comfy bed.

"Hey, love. Why walking by yourself tonight?" Their shadows had almost overlapped when he started speaking.

She already knew he was there. It was a female sense. It started three blocks back. When she turned left, he turned left. She quickened her pace across the car park; so too did he.

She never looked back, never turned her head. Making eye contact would invite a greeting. That is not what she wanted. Ignoring him would not make the man go away. But it may keep him at a distance.

Her mind moved through the techniques taught to young girls. Keys in hand, ready to punch. Legs primed to kick. Eyes scanning for police. Ears alert for help.

The woman did none of these things. She maintained her pace, turning down a quiet alley towards stout rows of townhouses interspaced with empty blocks of dried grass. A fresh 80's design, newly installed to clean up the inner-city suburb.

The lights were dimmer here, but she felt better. The change of lighting dragged her shadow along the cement path to embrace the approaching man. A gust of breeze fluttered through her long black hair. It swirled with a mind of its own.

"Oi, darling. I'm talking to you." He had quickened his speed at the alley entrance. He thrust a hairy hand to grab her arm.

The man twisted her firmly. She did not resist.

Emerald green eyes pierced the man's gaze without blinking. His breath reeked without relief. She did not flinch. His drunkenness did not allow him to back down. A streetlight twinkled in and out of existence as the aging bulb failed. The daily strain of pulsing electricity through its circuits had taken its toll.

"How's about a quickie?"

She blinked her green eyes.

"Do you... find me beautiful?" she cooed with a thick Cornish accent.

Of course he did. Sleek red stain fell off her body as a waterfall, hiding enough temptation to heighten the aura. Long black hair, smooth and flowing like gentle ripples across a pristine pond. This was a modern woman, strong and proud, with the material wealth to back it up.

She blinked. Long black lashes dripping seductively over her eyes.

"Shit yeah," he drawled the last words of his life.

She blinked a third time. Her eyes opened—pitch black as if the darkest corner of the universe had entered her soul. The angelic face melted into a ragged hag; two centuries of punishing age etched into its wrinkled face. Torment of convict life blistered to the surface. Across her back, chest, shoulders: a scar for each whip of the cat-o-nine-tails. Dozens of wide strands of baked blood trails traversing the sun-baked body.

Glaze washed from the dazed man as he staggered back in terror. She let him go. Let him think that he was dreaming, that it was alcohol playing tricks with his mind. Let him think he was escaping.

Strands of ethereal black hair clustered into twine and raised into whips, cracking the air around her. The man fell backwards; his *Ghostbusters* T-shirt covered in brown grass clippings. Swamped with fear, he tried to roll and stand.

Nine braids of knotted hair shot out, snaring him in a crushing embrace. Firm cords held the man tighter than steel, suspended above the ground, trapped like a fish in a net. Another tendril slowly caressed his face with the tenderness of tears. A caress the creature had never known when alive.

The caress deepened, darkened, and blood oozed as the snaking hair transformed into a jet-black butcher's hook. Thoughts of hanging by the ankles like a pig carcass flushed the last vestige of alcohol from the man's bowels.

His scream sliced through the night. Strands of long dark hair clutched around his torso. Two more swung into action around his skull. Together, they rotated the head and body in opposite directions. The snap echoed down the suburban alley.

Smoothly, the woman retracted into her youthful form and drifted away from the scene. In moments, the darkness of night had swallowed her.

Did I Dye?

Evan had been standing alone in the elevator for seven floors. This morning's journey to the office seemed to take longer than normal. Three times, he had adjusted the grey silk suit out of boredom. Jazz muzak played quietly over the speakers. It was much better than the ghetto blasters the kids had spurting rock music through the parks. He mused that he would have to purchase a Walkman. Another great Japanese invention to keep the world at arm's length.

When the elevator doors opened on the wrong floor,

he decided his luck had changed. A hungry stare took full note of the long, toned legs wrapped delicately in red cloth. Evan's eyes lingered, appreciating the way the loose ruby outfit gripped two firm breasts and draped provocatively around a graceful neck.

"That is a very sexy dress for the office," he growled.

The nymph did not respond. Evan finally looked above the shoulders. The girl's face was pristine. No sign of age wrinkled the skin. Two pure emerald eyes drew the man's gaze deeper.

"You are very beautiful," he growled as a lion circling its prey.

The girl gave a small giggle, perhaps revealing a trace of accent, but did not reply with words.

Evan's eyes drifted down her body again, following the endless cascade of picturesque black hair. Smooth, untouched, enchanting. Black as only seen at the end of the universe. The hair seemed to glow with a life of its own. His mouth glistened with moisture.

As the elevator doors slid quietly together, Evan's eyes reached the end of their journey. The hair tailored to a point. In this case, five points. Five braids of blackened fingers knotted as a cat-of-nine-tails. Evan's jaw fell limp as the hair twirled and tangled into a human hand. The braided fist slowly raised itself beside the pert young girl. Evan's eyes followed, captivated in horror.

"My eyes are up here," the innocent voice purred, the Cornish accent dancing like angels in heaven.

The knot of hair reached level with two piercing green eyes. Evan's eyes joined them and fixated in the deep pools as they hued into a pitch black matched only by the girl's hair.

Horror engulfed him, a fear known only by the man facing the noose on the gallows. The time for escape had passed.

The girl's youthful face shattered and burst as a cracked vessel. Unblemished skin exploded into deep crevices, hardened by fourteen years of erosion in the harsh Australian sun. Exposed night and day to the elements, worn to the bone by Red Coats and colonial masters, tormented by the cries of a thousand natives. Skin dried and taut across the thin body.

Terror grew into action. Evan opened his mouth to scream. Black hair jetted forward, clasping itself tightly upon the man's jaw, trapping sound in the bloodied cavern.

Behind the monster, mirrored walls drew Evan to

witness his widening eyes. Another reflection revealed a whip of hair rise beside him. Struggling was futile. Bound in braids as strong as steel chains, Evan could do nothing but watch as the hair evolved into a long butcher's hook. With a taunting graze, it slipped smoothly across Evan's neck. A single drop seemed to take eternity to drip from fear-encrusted skin onto a freshly pressed white collar. Evan's pupils dilated. His last thought was of the urine running down the inside of his silk trousers.

The hook swung violently as a broken mast in a hurricane. The return journey ceased as it was buried deep in the pulsing jugular vein. A moment lapsed before the black, hairy blade passed out the other side of the neck.

Death was not instant. It was inevitable. The hook retracted. Evan's body collapsed to the elevator floor.

His last image was of the monster reverting into a petite maiden. More blood outside his body. He never heard the giggle.

Split Ends

Another night brought little relief from the heat. The city felt as if an oven door had been left open. Suburban homeowners forced straining air-conditioners to overload. Streets warped with heat, and pubs churned a profit. Each cold ale was a dream of escape.

Bar stools were draped with dark suit jackets: grey, black, the odd brown shade. Dignified men during daylight hours now paraded unbuttoned shirts and rolled long white sleeves to exposed sweating skin. The beer provided liquid sustenance, the alcohol making people forget the heat.

Bill nursed his drink, elbow soaking in bar juices. The beer in his hand had stopped being useful. For all intents and purposes, it was warm piss, yet Bill would not let go.

"You know something, mate," drawled Bill, rolling himself in a half circle to face the crowded tables. "The weather brings out the breast in women."

Rodney did not join Bill in the joke. "That is the third time you have said that tonight. It may have been funny the first time. Now it is just crass."

"Mate, there's nothing wrong with enjoying the view."

Rodney looked around the room. Bill was right. Female skin was everywhere. Tight business skirts creeping over the knee. Power-suit jackets over chairs and silk shirts rolled like the men, with buttons undone to reveal glimpses of skimpy underwear. Non-businesswomen were draped in loose cotton shirts hanging carelessly off one shoulder. Classes mingled when the heat dictated. It was an unwritten law in the Australian summer.

"Enjoy without ogling, mate. Women need to escape the heat as much as you and I do. If they want to wear that sort of clothing... let them. With this bloody temperature, they don't need us drooling over them as well."

Beer spectacles covered Bill's eyes, and his ogling continued.

"Excuse me," a bob-haired girl with jet black hair tried to squeeze past Bill. It was not her European accent that drew Bill's attention. A blood-red satin shirt clung to her petite frame, tugging and threatening to burst with each breath.

"Yes, love. What can I do for you?" asked Bill, continuing to block her path.

"I need to get past."

"Sorry, am I in your way. I didn't notice," Bill's voice was filled with sarcasm, his breath filled with putrid aromas. "Why don't you join us? I'll get your next beer."

"No thanks," she inched forward.

"Well, that isn't polite of you. Are you an arrogant bitch?" Bill's tone was light but increased in strength. "Or are you just a little slut?"

"Bill!" Rodney stepped against his friend, leaning him out of the way so the girl could move through. "Sorry."

Silently, the girl passed, but Rodney could sense the words she wanted to say.

"She wasn't my type anyway," said Bill. "Bugger me, those hooters were standing to attention like…"

"Bill, it's time to go home. You've had enough." Rodney commanded.

Rodney grabbed his mate's arm and led the way to the door. Divorced from the support of the bar, Bill offered little resistance. With a shove, the door opened into a heat like that from the outskirts of hell.

A petite woman in a flowing red dress turned down a side street ahead of them. Her long black hair seemed to hang in the air, beckoning the men to follow. They obliged.

Ten minutes later, Bill fell towards a suitable gumtree: fumbling for his zipper, dropping his pants and urinating on the bare bark. "Check that out." Bill slurred.

In a nearby playground, a solitary figure was sitting

complacently by herself. The glow from family homes cast random patches of light across the woman. Enough was revealed to see her shining face and curvaceous red dress.

"G'day, love," drawled Bill.

"Don't start, Bill," Rodney sighed. "She doesn't need your shit. Ma'am, are you OK?"

"Shove off, Rodney."

Startled, Rodney froze at the aggressiveness. Bill took a step closer. The woman did not move. "Hey, honey. What are you doing out here by yourself?"

The words seemed harmless, but there was a deeper intimidation in the tone. The woman said nothing.

"Were you hoping that a strapping young bloke like me would come along and whisk you away to heaven?"

"Bill, stop."

The woman stood slowly. Red cloth hung seductively down her shapely body. Long, silky black hair caressed her slender neck.

Bill turned to Rodney and smiled. "She is from heaven."

"Maybe we should phone the police to come and help her."

"Do you think I am beautiful?"

The angelic voice sliced across the night. Both men

paused and looked at her. Even Rodney was captivated by wispy Cornish tones.

"Yes, ma'am. You are beautiful," he admitted. "But you shouldn't be out here by yourself. Can we call you a taxi or something?"

"Good idea, mate," said Bill. "You run off and get a taxi. I'll stay here and look after this sexy little thing."

"No way, Bill. I do not trust you to find your own home, let alone keep your hands off an innocent girl. We can both help her to safety."

"Thank you, young man," the woman smiled knowingly at Rodney. "I appreciate your chivalry."

The delicate moment vanished as swiftly as the beautiful creature before him. Rodney staggered backwards, tripping over his own feet and falling on the dry grass.

The smooth face melted away to be replaced by bursting crags and ripples of raging canyons traversing the face. Rodney's face shifted into terror as he tried to claw away from the monster.

Bill laughed. In his drunken state, he had only seen his friend fall over. It wasn't the first time that one of them ended up on the ground after a night of drinking. The gloss over his eyes blinded Bill to the enchanting rhythm of the woman's dancing hair. Rising from her shoulders, the hair swayed like snakes charming their victim into submission.

In the dim light, the long, silky black hair continued, climbing into the sky and forming into a platoon of evil plaits behind the woman. Each strand of hair calmly moulded itself into a three-pronged harpoon. Any single barb would hold a small dugong. Together, they would torment a pod of whales. Here, in a lonely suburban park, they were poised in front of a single drunken man. A man who was not aware of the last seconds of his life.

He burped, loud and deep as only an alcoholic can achieve. The woman's black hair responded.

Shooting forward in sequence, the harpoons pierced Bill's skin. The neck, the chest, the arms, and the legs. Each barb pierced and retreated, rising up again in preparation for the next strike. Bill felt no pain. By the time the first barb reached out for its second exploration of the human body, Bill was already dead. His empty body hung in the air through the strength of each blade of black hair as they paused before the next intrusion. With a final flurry, two barbs buried themselves through Bill's eyes, retreated and allowed the corpse to drop against brown grass.

The creature slipped back into her human form; her

pristine face again peeked through in the glimmering suburban darkness. Black hair smoothed itself into place as if it had recently been brushed. The slight figure in a loose red dress standing in a playground showed no emotion about the violence it had just delivered.

Rodney was emotionally pinned to the ground. He was sweating, but not from the summer heat. The woman held out her hand to the terrified man.

At a loss, Rodney could do nothing but stare with a ghostly white face. Even immersed in the beauty in front of him, Rodney still saw the horror that lay beneath. The woman clicked the fingers of her outstretched hand, inducing him to take it.

Rodney rapidly responded to the click. Fear of what this woman was, what she could do, drove him more than any coherent brain function. Reaching a hand to the air, he found it embraced by delicate, gentle fingers before he was hoisted effortlessly into a standing position.

She tenderly brushed dirt and dead grass from Rodney's shirt and straightened his clothes. He was completely sober, but there was a hollowness in his eyes.

"Do you think you can get yourself home?" asked the smooth female voice.

"What? Yes." Rodney muttered routinely, not really comprehending the question.

"Good. Then I leave you here," she faded into the darkness and paused. "Do you want me to call you a taxi?"

"What? No. Thank you, ma'am," Rodney said.

"Ma'am. I like that."

She faded into the night. Drowning in shock, Rodney sat on the swing and stared at the mutilated body of his friend.

Some hours later, the sun rose.

It was in this position that the residents found the forlorn figure. After much coaxing, they extracted a single word from him: "Eliza."

I DON'T KNOW ABOUT Y'ALL
BUT THAT MADE MY HAIR STAND ON END

MAYBE YOU SHOULD SHOW
A LITTLE COURTESY TO THE
SINISTER STORYTELLER WHO
PENNED THIS FRIGHT FILLED
TALE OF FIENDISH FOLLICLES

YOU KNOW WHAT I LOVE MOST ABOUT 80s SLASHERS?

EVEN WHEN THE KILLER MEETS A GRISLY END...

THEY STILL KEEP
BRINGING THEM
RIGHT BACK
HERE LIES
HENLEY
HACKEN LASH

KNIVES
NIGHTMARES
& NEON II
BACK
FROM
THE
GRAVE
SEE Y'ALL IN
THE SEQUEL KIDS

UNCLE HENLEY WILL RETURN